THE HEAT OF DESIRE

"I tried to stay away."

Her words were whispered. Sorrowful. They raised an ache in his heart. He understood. He, too, had tried to put her from his mind. "You will never be sorry." He kissed the backs of her hands, first the right, then the left.

Slowly, she turned hers, covering his in turn and traced the scar across his fingers. She visited the pads of calluses on his palms from years of wielding a sword. He lifted her hands and placed them on the edges of his robe. He felt the heat of her fingertips as she discovered the intricate stitches that edged the silk. His heart pounded like a war-horse racing to battle. He drew the edges open wider, bared his chest, placed her hands on his skin. When her fingers moved to explore the shape of him just as she had traced the embroidery, the pleasure of simple arousal gave way to a fiery need.

Lord of The Keep

Ann Lawrence

LOVE SPELL BOOKS NEW YORK CITY

I dedicate this book to my perfect hero.

LOVE SPELL®

December 1999

Published by

Dorchester Publishing Co., Inc.
276 Fifth Avenue
New York, NY 10001

ISBN 0-505-52351-5

Printed in the United States of America.

ACKNOWLEDGMENTS

I'd like to acknowledge a few special people who helped *Lord of the Keep* become a reality. Many thanks to Alicia Condon, Jennifer Bonnell and Carolyn Grayson who mentored and guided me through the process. I'm indebted to my critique partners, Judy Di Canio, Edna Frankel, Nan Jacobs and June Kovelowski for insightful suggestions. I'd also like to extend a special thanks to Lisa Hollis McCulley, Lena Pinto and Sally Stotter for last minute reads and rereads. Lastly, I'd like to thank Terri Brisbin for "inspiration" and her expertise in searching out anachronistic phrases and objects. Those remaining are deliberate and at my behest.

Lord of The Keep

Cast me not off in the time of old age;
forsake me not when my strength faileth.
—Psalm 71:9

Prologue

Hawkwatch Castle, England, 1190

"I have never seen such a collection of rabble and complainers." Gilles d'Argent turned from his closest friend, Roland d'Vare, and stared about the hall of Hawkwatch Castle. A line of petitioners and petty criminals stretched across the great stone chamber and wound itself about the perimeter. "Did these people feel so unjustly served that they waited upon my father's death to make their petitions? Some of these complaints are months old."

"You have no need to trouble yourself with this chore. Be gone." Roland, a tall, spare man with streaks of silver running through his hair, pared an apple, discarding the skins to the rushes beneath the table. "Your father, God rest his soul, felt much the same when King Henry granted him the barony. He made a point to be away for these events."

13

"And I find no pleasure in being sent to take his place." Gilles frowned as a cat leapt and danced after the curling strips of apple peel.

"Whilst you may dislike your task, King Richard values your lands and would be loath to see them fall to Prince John's scheming."

"Aye, it did not take Richard long to rue granting John control of five shires."

"Now men like you must offer restraint." Roland grinned as another cat pounced past Gilles's boots to join the first tumbling feline.

"I served the old king from the age of nine. After three decades of duty, I scarcely warrant such a sentence. Guard duty! Saving one brother from another—pitiful. And must you entertain my mousers whilst old Garth is sleeping?" Gilles growled as yet another cat skidded among the rushes and apple skins and tumbled over the mongrel hound that stretched, oblivious, at his feet.

"I believe you are delaying the matter at hand, my lord," whispered Thomas, the cleric who had been frantically scratching out Lord Gilles's judgments all day. He repeatedly wiped an impatient hand over his tonsured pate.

Roland ignored the man and grinned. "You have bailiffs, reeves, me, your newly appointed steward, to handle this. Why try your patience to such an extreme?"

Gilles grinned back. "You know the answer."

"Oh, aye. You must put your long nose in every matter, sniff about like a hound." He lowered his voice to a barely audible whisper. "You would make a better sheriff than lord."

"I shall not be given the choice. But I feel I must take the measure of these men." With a sweep of his hand, he indicated the cleric and the village worthies who sat in

14

anxious awe of his assessment. He made no effort to lower his voice, a subtle warning to them. "I believe they have wrung more silver for their own pockets from these miscreants, than for my father's coffers—" He paused in midsentence and lifted his head.

"What is it?" Roland straightened and followed Gilles's gaze to the stout oak doors of the hall.

"I don't know. I feel . . . " He didn't finish the sentence. A woman and an old man had entered the hall, drawing his eyes. Mayhap it had been but the chill air that accompanied them that raised the gooseflesh on his arms. He watched the couple advance toward him. Unbidden, as if approached by ones of higher consequence, he rose from his chair.

"You must await your turn," Thomas said to the couple, pointing with a long, bony finger in the direction whence they'd come.

"I shall hear them next," Gilles said.

"But, my lord!" Thomas began, then sputtered and coughed at Gilles's raised eyebrow. "Of course, my lord. Forgive me. State your name, sir."

A flood of words spilled from the old man before them.

Gilles d'Argent held a hand up. "Hold. I can scarcely follow your words."

The old man petitioning him was dressed in filthy attire, his odor offensive even from ten feet away. His ocher skin indicated disease, his lank hair, personal neglect.

In contrast to him, the young woman at his side stood tall and lithe and, better yet, clean. Her mantle could challenge the gentians for glory. It hung well from her shoulders, clasped with a simple knotting of the cloth.

Her dignity before the manorial court impressed

Gilles. She somehow seemed aloof from the proceedings, untouched by the torrent of words flowing in an obscene stream from the old man. She did not gawk at the crowd on the benches about the hall who had gathered to be heard and to be entertained by the telling, but kept her eyes dutifully lowered.

Gilles returned to his seat on the dais. He did not wish to appear unduly interested in the young woman. Her hair, the color of summer honey, fell loose about her shoulders. Her pale cheeks seemed almost colorless, as if she had been ill. He willed her to look up, to allow him to assess her beauty.

"State your name again for Lord Gilles," his cleric said, whilst trying to fend off a feline determined to climb his woolen cassock.

Gilles contemplated the young woman. He wondered if she found him forbidding. Did she fear his decisions? He arranged his face in what he hoped was a less forbidding aspect.

The old man rasped out his name once more, this time slowly and distinctly. "I am Simon of Lynn and my brother's been dead these past few years. I've the wardship of his only daughter—and a sore trial it be. He had only this female, and before he died, promised her to a worthy Yorkshireman, Jacob Baker by name. 'Twas a bargain that would have greatly benefited me. Now 'tis all for naught. She's soiled herself and my good name. Demand she name the cunning knave who stole her maidenhead. Make him take her to wed and end the shame that will surely fall upon me and mine."

The old man's malicious voice rose like a wind foretelling a coming storm. Quick as a viper, he turned and struck the young woman on the face, forcing her head up

16

as she stumbled and fell to her knees. The crack of his hand reverberated around the vaulted hall.

"Hold," Gilles thundered, leaping to his feet again. The attack had caught him by surprise, for the man was skinny and small. The young woman struggled back to her feet, unaided, and again stood composed and mute before him. The ugly red mark of the old man's fist stood out starkly against her pale complexion. She never raised her eyes from the floor.

"She's made a whore of herself and shamed my family. Make her name the man and wed him, my lord. Why should I be providing for her and her bastard? Make the man pay the price." The old man spat onto the stones at his feet.

Gilles subsided into his seat, though he felt the strong throb of his pulse in his throat and temple, and considered the two diverse individuals. "Your name, mistress?" Gilles asked. He tempered his tone to the one he used with his youngest squire when he wanted to sound stern yet reasonable.

The young woman raised her head and her eyes, mirroring the mantle's vibrant gentian color, and looked steadily at him. Although pleasing, he realized she was not beautiful. It was her compelling eyes, so large in her face, and her dignity that made one notice her. Once noticed, Gilles mused, never forgotten.

She watched him for a moment, then with a soft voice spoke into the quiet. "Emma, my lord," she said, then bowed her head and considered her toes again.

"What have you to say, Emma? Three others have been before me today with the same complaint—love satisfied, but not sanctified." Gilles stroked his closely cropped black beard. This woman had not the demeanor of the other young women, and he wanted to hear from her, not the uncle.

"My Lord Gilles, the fact remains—" her uncle began.

"Silence, old man." Gilles's voice cut through the man's words.

The young woman knotted her hands before her, her only sign of agitation. "Lord Gilles, I have no complaints to bring before you. I am content with my lot and just wish to return to my weaving."

Her words surprised him. She spoke as one from a station of life far above her companion.

The old man flew into a paroxysm of vituperative adjectives describing the young woman, her mother, and her mother's mother. When Gilles raised his hand, the old man stamped and swore.

"Again, old man, do not speak until I direct you." Gilles leaned forward and rested his elbows on the arms of the ancient oak chair in which he sat. He reached down and scratched Garth's ear for a moment, although he did not take his eyes from the young woman. She stood as still as a statue, as composed as if naught concerned her, stately and calm.

"Emma, your uncle seems to think he has a complaint. As you are his ward, he has complete control of you, your thoughts even. If he has a complaint concerning you, it is your complaint, too."

This time her chin jerked up and her deep blue eyes flashed defiantly for a moment. Then her head bowed quickly as if she'd gained control and remembered her place, her anger suppressed as she answered. "I cannot help what my uncle thinks, or others, my lord."

"Are you a maiden?" Gilles watched intently as the question brought a red flush up from the mantle's braided edge to stain the rest of her face the color of the angry mark on her cheek.

"Nay."

The one word prompted another round of angry invectives from the old man and a cuff to Emma's shoulder.

"William." Gilles snapped his fingers at William Belfour, a young knight of his company who, along with others, had been avidly watching the proceedings. "Take this old man out until I have finished questioning his ward." The knight, tall, blond as a Viking, and thick with a warrior's muscles, unceremoniously dragged Simon from the hall. The old man looked like a small child dangling from the knight's large hand.

"Now, Emma, mayhap we may proceed without interruption. Your uncle is—not unreasonably—upset that you have lost your maidenhead. What is so entertaining?" Gilles spoke sharply. The small smile that had appeared on the young woman's face disappeared at his tone.

"Forgive me, Lord Gilles. It is just that I find the idea of a 'lost' maidenhead amusing."

"How so?" he asked, puzzled by her attitude, for most often such boldness in a serf resulted in, at the least, a few lashes. Of course, she was a free woman. Her speech and demeanor indicated gentle birth. His curiosity was piqued.

"Lost implies one may find the object in question and so have the benefit of its use again, and we know that is not the case here, my lord."

Though her posture had stiffened at his rebuke, Gilles noted that she no longer avoided his eyes now that her uncle had left the hall. Gilles smiled despite his inclination to sternness. He kept the smile in place to reassure her. He had brought a sharp discipline to Hawkwatch

19

Keep, a discipline resented by many who had grown lazy under his father's haphazard regime. His manner, coupled with his sun-darkened skin, hard features, and black hair, had many thinking him the spawn of Satan.

Gilles let his spine relax against the chair back and stretched out his long legs. He had no wish to rush this judgment. He had no wish to rush such a lovely creature from his presence. In truth, he considered that if she were indeed no longer a maiden, if she had been well bedded, he might wish to have her himself. She had more than a compelling face and pleasing figure. She had some indefinable aura that drew him, sent his blood rushing as if he were a boy in his first flush of manhood.

"The loss of a maiden's virtue, Emma, is not a matter of amusement," he lectured, trying to maintain a serious demeanor and shake off the attraction.

"Aye, my lord," Emma returned.

"How does your uncle know of . . . this happenstance?"

"Why, I told him so."

Gilles sat bolt upright and stared at her, dumbfounded. The cats scattered in a rush. Garth lifted his head and yelped. "You? You told your uncle? Surely you could have foreseen the consequences of such an action?"

She looked away from him, and he watched her stare down the long stone hall with its high ceiling and brightly woven tapestries. She seemed to consider each person who loitered or sat at ease before deigning to answer him.

"Nay, I did not foresee *these* circumstances, my lord. I meant only to end the connection my uncle had arranged for me. I do not believe my father intended any such alliance as this for me."

"Why? 'Twas surely an honor." Gilles's sympathy rose; he empathized with the difficulty of answering his questions in a public venue. The dais upon which he sat stood a goodly distance from the folk in the hall. Still, her uncle's commotion had ensured that many took an interest.

"When my uncle came to me with the marriage plans, I felt duty bound to tell him that I loved another. I believe his words were that a woman's wishes meant naught. Master Jacob and he had marked their names to the documents. My uncle said the contract was met. And so I told him 'twas more than a woman's wishes. 'Twas a deed done." Her voice broke on the words.

"Do you not wish to name the man who took your innocence so you may wed him?"

"Nay." Her answer came swiftly. There was a silent entreaty in her eyes.

"Hmm." Gilles tented his fingers beneath his chin, then steepled his index fingers and stroked his mustache.

"Did you give yourself of your own free wish? Has someone abused you?" Gilles asked, quietly and gently.

She shook her head, sending her hair flying out in a golden bell. "Nay, my lord, nay."

"Would naming the man cause him distress?"

"The distress would be mine, my lord." Her hair subsided, along with her agitation.

He is pledged to another woman, he thought, *or already wed.*

Emma studied Lord Gilles as he considered her. Outwardly calm, inwardly a sea of screaming emotions, Emma remained determined to give away nothing of her inner turmoil or the sickness in her belly at being so publicly examined. She thought Lord Gilles too intelligent to accept the denials she had practiced on her way to the judging.

As she and her uncle had stood outside the hall, Emma had paid sharp attention to the gossip about Lord Gilles's

21

attendance at the judging. It was generally accepted among the satisfied that he cut swiftly through to the core of a matter. He dealt judiciously with petty squabbles and in some cases was just as likely to think of an unusual settlement as dismiss the complaints as a waste of his time. He listened fairly, but suffered fools not at all. Of course, the dissatisfied thought him cruel, a blight on their future. Emma had decided that she would say nothing and offer no denials, for 'twas obvious Lord Gilles accepted none.

Now her heart beat in panic and fear; the panic and fear of a decision made that might bode ill for the future.

He had looked right through her.

She had sworn to keep secret her lover's name. When the time was ripe, they'd acknowledge the vows they'd spoken together. She had never doubted it for a moment—until now. She had thought she had his most sacred vow, could withstand any beating she received.

Until today, this hour, her heart knew her lover would take her away when his obligations were fulfilled. Although she had known him but a few weeks—he was a member of an advance guard of Lord Gilles d'Argent's— Emma had fallen in love with a stunning swiftness that defied sense. She had accepted her lover's promises for the future and sealed those promises with the joyful giving of herself.

Emma looked about the crowd and her gaze rested on her lover. His interest in the proceedings seemed to have waned. Indeed, he stood in haughty disregard of the proceedings and her presence. Feigned, she hoped. He no longer looked in her direction.

Suddenly, he seemed a shadow of a man compared with the power and force of Gilles d'Argent. In vain, Emma tried to shrug away her thoughts, telling herself she merely sensed the difference found in a man of but a single score of years and that of a man of two score years or possibly more.

Surely, one would note the strength of a warrior tested and honed in battle and one not yet tried, not yet called to prove himself. From the moment she'd entered the hall, she'd been struck with Lord Gilles's power. It radiated to her from across the long chamber, like tendrils of creeper extending along a garden wall, drew her forward as if someone had taken her by the hand.

Did everyone feel it, that power, as she did? 'Twas obvious from the gossip some feared him, whilst others felt grateful to rest their cares with him. Why did no one remark on this intangible pull? His physical presence drew her, too. His fierce expression did not frighten her; it beguiled her. She felt somehow mesmerized by the lord's every word.

Nay, I must not let my fears entice me to these doubts, she thought. She had made sacred promises, sealed them with more than a kiss. All would come right if she but kept her silence, as she had promised her lover. Surely, God would help her, answer her frantic prayers.

"Emma?" Gilles's voice jolted her to the present. "Do you not think that whatever difficulties may arise for your lover, you will bear greater ones if you do not name him?"

"Nay, my lord. I see no difficulties for myself."

"Have you lived in a cloister to not know what becomes of unmarried females without male protection? Surely, this whim of yours to protect your lover will bring you to grief. Should your uncle scorn you, you may find yourself earning your living at the whim of less patient men. Your uncle may cast you out to earn your own way if you bring shame on his household."

"He brings his own shame by dragging me here and stating his ugly accusations for all to hear, my lord." Her anger flared anew. "I believe he thinks less of my predicament and more of the weight of Jacob Baker's coin."

"Aye. 'Tis most likely true. No one would know of your predicament for a while, but only for a while. Surely you know that you cannot hide a child beneath your skirts for long."

"Who said I am to have a child, my lord? If all such . . . encounters caused birth, this keep would be overrun with babes. I see few in the village and fewer here." She allowed an amusement she did not feel to enter her voice as she swept out her hands to indicate a room with many people but few children.

"True. But, as I have seen to the disposition of three such cases today, I can be sure that such encounters often result in birthdays. So, your uncle comes early to see to your honor—and his. May I ask, Emma, how you wish this resolved?"

"My lord, if I were to be a farmer's wife, the farmer would not see this as some shameful circumstance. Indeed, he might even demand I prove my fertility before he would wed me—"

"You are no farmer's wife!" Gilles retorted. "You were to have been wed to a baker, a man of worth."

"I do not hold Jacob Baker in great esteem, my lord."

"Nay? And are maids picking their suitors these days?"

"Would that they could, my lord." Emma met his amusement with serious intent.

Gilles lost his grin before her frown. "I believe I have been chastised! And by a simple maid!"

Emma swallowed. Deep lines radiated from his obsid-

24

ian eyes. Eyes narrowed now in displeasure. She clamped her teeth on her tongue to stay the torrent of words bubbling up inside her.

"Again, Emma. How do you wish this resolved?"

"Allow me to return home, my lord. I wish to return to my weaving. If I should prove wrong and . . . a child results, I shall pay my sixpence fine."

"You will find even sixpence a fortune without your uncle's protection." When she did not answer, Gilles signaled to William Belfour, who stood at an arched stone entrance to the hall. William hustled Emma's uncle back into Gilles's presence.

"It seems, old man, that you come early to seek a wedding. Emma says she is not with child. I am reluctant to dictate solutions to events that have not some tangible consequence."

Simon spluttered his indignation. "My Lord Gilles, she is ruined. She has no dowry. How am I to make a marriage for her when she has given away her only possession worth anything? Who would have her now that she has spread her thighs for some nameless man? All know she is no longer a virgin. You asked her before this company, and she has admitted her shame. She is worthless. 'Twill cost me dear to keep her bastard, too."

"Well, old man, you certainly made sure every man, woman, and child was aware of her loss of virtue by presenting this case. If you had held your tongue, no one would have been the wiser."

Every one of their words cut Emma deeply. Pain flared and blossomed, swelled and grew to ugly proportions. Soon the pain would be there for all to see, for surely in another moment she would weep.

Wait for the proper moment, her lover had said. Surely, this was that moment? Tears in her eyes burned to be

25

released as she fought the urge to turn to her lover and demand he speak for her.

Her breath began to labor; she breathed deeply to still the faintness encroaching on her.

She offered up a silent prayer for the judging to end. She wanted nothing more than to escape to the forest, to silence and peace.

"Demand his name, my lord. I demand compensation."

The old man cowered as Gilles rose on the dais. His crimson mantle flared about him, angry in its own inanimate way. His black eyes flashed a warning. Emma silently prayed her uncle would heed it, else they might find themselves in the lord's prison. Simon scuttled back as Lord Gilles stepped from his place to stand before them.

"So, we come to the crux of the matter. Compensation. I have asked you to hold your tongue. I am at the end of my patience. Speak again and it will be you I punish, you who will pay compensation."

Gilles moved to stand before Emma with arms crossed on his chest. A single shaft of afternoon sun pierced an arrow slit high above, causing a sparkling flame to radiate from the blood-red ruby on his left hand.

"I will not force you to name your lover. Yet I know few men of quality who will have you without your virtue intact."

He spoke intimately to her, so only she could hear his words, spoke softly as if to spare her further torment and yet, torment her his words did. She bled inside.

"Emma, did you not realize the consequences when you took a lover? What manner of man would leave you to face a judgment such as this?" He swept out his hand to the company before crossing his arms again. "Why did you give away your most precious possession?"

Emma found herself unable to speak. This close to him, she could not hide from his intent scrutiny. She could not hide from the terrible twist of realization his words forced upon her. *What manner of man would leave her to face this humiliation?* Her lover could have come forward. He could have saved her this humiliation—claimed her before the company, admitted the vows they'd spoken. He could have stayed Simon's fist. She must lie to Lord Gilles and to any other who chanced to ask the same questions as he.

"Speak. Why did you give away your most precious possession?"

She slowly shook her head.

"Answer me, Emma." His voice gentled, but there was a power in his words that made her unable to refuse him.

She swallowed the lump in her throat and met his eyes. "You have answered your own question, Lord Gilles. You see—I had nothing else to give." So saying, she bowed her head.

They stood in silence for a few moments. "Pray God your lover holds your gift in high esteem." His voice was harsh.

He resumed his seat, once more at that impossible distance, ready to pronounce her fate. As he moved away, she felt the loss, as if his power had included her, had given her the strength to explain, to stand here before this company, exposed. With distance, she felt frail and alone. Her stomach churned, her knees threatened to fail her.

"Old man, take your ward home. Mistreat her and you face my wrath. If a child results, see me at the next manorial court. You have wasted my time."

Simon grew red beneath his yellow complexion and in anger wheeled away, swearing as he scurried up the aisle of the hall.

27

Emma vowed to hide her pain, hold it inside. She looked once more on Lord Gilles. She wished to steep herself in the power that shimmered about him, as if that inner power of his might sustain her in the days to come, for suddenly, her future seemed tenuous and frightening. She locked eyes with him for a moment, boldly drinking him in from his ebony hair to the hard lines of his warrior-trained body, knowing instinctively he'd not punish her for meeting his eyes. She nodded once and, head held high, she followed her uncle.

The cold air that greeted them as they left the hall did naught to cool her feverish brow and sweaty hands. For one brief moment, she whirled and reached out for the iron latch of the door to his hall. She grasped the curved metal that held the double doors to Lord Gilles's life closed to her—held his world closed to her. And, she now realized, that of her lover, too.

Despite the humiliation and pain of the judging, Lord Gilles had treated her kindly, more kindly than she had expected. She was beset with confusion.

"Come, you worthless bitch," Simon called from the bottom of the steps that led up to the hall doors.

"Worthless bitch," Emma murmured, her hand falling from the latch. She raised the hood of her mantle to conceal her face and turned away, following her uncle into the roiling mass of humanity that moved about the bailey.

Chapter One

The forest near Hawkwatch Castle, 1192

Despite the vociferous protests of his squire that a lord should not indulge in such behavior, Gilles knelt at the edge of a rushing stream and began to skin a rabbit. Deftly sliding the knife between the skin and the flesh, he worked it off in one smooth, practiced motion. He offered the hare to the hovering young man and then cleaned his knife, thrusting it into his belt. Dipping his hands into the icy water, he used sand from the streambank and the water to cleanse the blood from his skin and nails. The squire handed him a linen cloth.

As Gilles dried his hands, he looked about the assembled company of men who sprawled at ease at the edge of the ancient pine forest. In the distance stretched the wetlands giving onto Hawkwatch Bay. He propped himself against a tree and waved off the offer of a tankard of ale.

The marshy scents mingled with the sharp odor of burning pine.

Gilles frowned. He had been playing lord of the keep for nearly two years. Running a wealthy manor was tedious, if time-consuming. Even Prince John's forays into brotherly insurrection caused little more than a ripple on the tides of Gilles's life. He straightened and stretched.

There was little reason to hurry the roasting of the meat, for the sooner they ate, the sooner they would return to Hawkwatch Castle. Hunting offered a short respite from the checking of accounts, the judging of complaints, and the endless training of the younger men.

"Have you need of anything?" Roland d'Vare asked, coming to Gilles's side.

"Need of anything? Aye. Relief." Gilles smiled at his friend.

"Yon bush should be adequate to your needs." Roland grinned in return and tossed Gilles his mantle.

"You know what I mean." Gilles waved away his squire and pulled on his black woolen mantle. Hubert dearly loved the niceties of ceremony whilst Gilles detested the fussing. "You would think I was not capable of securing a simple pin," he muttered at the young man's downcast face. "By relief I meant that beyond a hunt such as this, the training of the men is the only diversion here."

"Diversion? You mean hard work, do you not? I had never seen such poorly trained men 'til we came here. No technique, no tactics. 'Twas shameful." Roland raked his fingers through his silvery hair as if the men's incompetence yet tried his patience.

"Aye. I wonder to what my father devoted his attentions whilst his men slacked at their work. At least now they are fit fighting men. Yet . . . the hours I spend at arms practice do not make up for the grinding boredom of my other responsibilities. What I would have given to have been with Richard, testing myself against this Saladin at Acre. Instead, I train men who will do naught but chase an occasional brigand."

" 'Tis younger men who follow Richard—not those loyal to Henry. Our day is past."

"Mayhap I should invite Prince John for a gallop across the estuary—as the tide is coming in."

"He'd be swallowed by the quicksand. He cannot travel without the weight of his own importance." Then Roland grinned. "Ah, I see, 'tis just what you are hoping for. With John out of Richard's hair, you might be called to more active duty."

Gilles shrugged off the suggestion, but he could not prevent a rueful smile from touching his lips.

He turned his back to the trees and looked off to the distant thread of white that indicated the bay and, farther, the North Sea, his mind on other times and other places.

Roland followed the direction of his gaze. "I, too, occasionally feel what you do."

Gilles turned to his friend in puzzlement. "What is it I feel? Even I do not know."

Roland hesitated.

The forest behind them was dark and silent. The voices of the men sounded loud and intrusive. Gilles lowered his voice to keep their words between just them. "Do not fear to offend me, my friend. I know you ofttimes find it hard to forget the distance betwixt lord and vassal, but I prefer you speak plainly as you did when we were equals, before my father saw fit to expire and put this damnable iron weight of responsibility about my neck."

"Then speak plainly I will. You believe time has passed you by. I feel the passage of time less than you. I have Sarah. I find I am content these days to sit by a fire with her and"—Roland's grin split his face wide—"bask in her warmth at night. You need a leman."

Gilles snorted in derision and tossed the edges of his mantle off his shoulders. "I need no woman. When I feel the urge, there are wenches aplenty. The lord of the keep has but to raise a brow and his needs are met—well met. A leman would be about, constantly, like a wife, God forbid. I need no companion to harp at me for jewels and ribbons, nor bore me with gossip."

"A woman need not be so shallow. Sarah neither connives, nor prattles at me, although I imagine she is privy to all the intrigues. I never seem to know who is warming a man's bed, more's the pity." Roland laughed, then sobered. "A woman is more than gossip and soft thighs, Gilles."

"Little more." Gilles turned and strode away to join his men. He sank to the ground by the fire so Hubert could serve him with a trencher of meat. The gangling boy was hopeless with bow and arrow, but at least he cooked plainly. Frowning, Gilles contemplated the bird before him. But today's fare had not been cooked well enough to placate him in his present ill temper.

While Gilles thoughtfully chewed the meat, charred in spots, raw in others, William Belfour sank down beside him. "You have something to say, William?" Gilles asked, watching the knight from beneath his glowering black brows.

"I thought you might like to hear of a new wench awaiting me on our return. She has the softest of blond curls between her thighs—"

"Are you, perchance, offering her to me?" Gilles interrupted, stripping some meat from the bone and casting it

32

into the fire. The scent of sizzling meat joined that of the burning wood to fill the air.

William, as usual, missed the underlying hint of sarcasm in Gilles's tone. "Oh, you may use her if you wish. 'Twould be a shame to take her before I've finished training her, however. She has incredible passions." William looked about to see who eavesdropped before lowering his voice and leaning toward Gilles. Gilles rolled his eyes, knew he would have to hear of the young man's escapades. "I took her behind the mill four times the other night, and she bit like a vixen. The moans and screams—I thought the miller would be out with a pitchfork!"

Gilles's mood plummeted and he cast aside the bones of his offensive meal. Mayhap he should have waited upon the hare he'd skinned. "I think you need to spend more time at arms practice to use up some of that energy. If you have the potency to take a woman four times in one bout, you are slacking at your training."

He unfolded his long frame and walked to where Roland tended his horse. Gilles patted the mare's neck and spoke softly to her, praising her dappled gray coat and ancestors. Irritation would have been how he described his feelings for William. William drew the eye of every wench and lady of the manor with his tall, blond good looks. The women flocked to his side. He boasted of his conquests. That most of his stories were exaggerated did little to lessen Gilles's irritation.

Gilles knew Roland had struck at the heart of his discontent. He spoke as much to the horse as to Roland. "You have it aright. Age sits hard upon me. I hanker to be on horseback, riding with King Richard wherever his adventures might take him. I feel useless here, holding property against John's possible treachery. Would that I could be content to sit with a wench by the fire."

Roland lifted his horse's hoof and used his knife to pick out the clots of earth packed from hard riding. "Mayhap you have just not met the right wench." The mare snorted and tossed her head as if in agreement.

"It chafes at me, this idleness," Gilles continued as he soothed the mare. A long silence stood between the men.

"Defy Richard's wishes and join him." Roland released the hoof and straightened.

Gilles looked over Roland's shoulder to William Belfour, now the center of the other men's attention. Gilles could imagine the story William told by his expansive and graphic gestures.

As if alone, Gilles spoke aloud, his eyes locked on William Belfour. "My sword elbow aches on bitterly cold days. The cook's rich sauces unsettle my belly. A simple run up the castle steps feels as if an arrow were embedded in my right knee. Look at this hand." A stark white line ran across all four of Gilles's fingers where a sword had slashed him, opening his hand to the bone. "Hubert, who stitched this gash, remarked that I must be slowing up. Slowing up. Aye, I am slowing up. I teach technique these days to the men in training. I do not test them myself, nay, I leave that to younger men."

"It troubles me that you are so discontented," Roland answered sharply. "What need have you to compete? All know of your abilities. There is scarcely a man alive who could best you."

Gilles raised a black brow at his friend's swift defense.

"Oh, I could best most of them." He thrust his chin in the direction of William and the other men. "But only because they do not think or plan; it is thinking and planning upon which I must depend. I can no longer trust the speed of my reflexes or the sureness of my foot against a youth of William's age and prowess."

Turning at the laughter coming from the fireside, Roland grimaced at William. "Belfour." Roland spat in the dirt.

"Few of them will see our age," Gilles continued. "Few of our companions remain."

"Your father lived to three score years and five. You are not yet two score," Roland rebutted.

"At the next Epiphany, I will be that age, the age of men who sit at the fire, hands on their fat bellies, dozing." Gilles ran his hand down the mare's neck and ignored Roland's sudden laugh.

"Pardon me if I find that image amusing. Your father never had a fat belly and was too busy wenching to doze. I believe he died in the act, by God. You've not a white hair on your head, I might add." Roland smoothed a hand over his own thinning hair, silvery gray for many years. "I have five years on you. You insult me with your complaints."

The words were lightly spoken but Gilles sensed he had truly offended his friend. He clapped Roland on the shoulder. "Forgive me. I am grown maudlin from inactivity. Forget I spoke."

As Gilles watched the group by the fire, William Belfour rose and lifted his tunic and relieved himself into the fire amid shouted crass remarks relating to his masculinity and sexual prowess. Gilles turned abruptly to Roland. "A godlike display!"

"Aye, a sword to put all of theirs and ours to shame. He plies it with carelessness. 'Twill bring him down one day."

"Would that I should be so endowed."

"Gilles, you surely are not jealous of William?" Roland threw his knife into a nearby tree.

"Jealous?" Gilles drew his dagger and, with a flick of his wrist, it joined Roland's in the trunk, quivering against the other's haft. The two men grinned at each other as they retrieved their knives. Gilles sheathed his and said, "See, we behave like children. But, aye, I find I am jealous of William's youth and vigor. What woman of worth would not prefer a man such as that one—" He broke off and turned from the men at the fire, turned to face the woods at their backs.

"What?" Roland froze, peering into the thick trees whose heavy branches turned afternoon sunlight to night-time shadow.

"Do you hear it? The baying of dogs?" A shiver coursed down Gilles's spine. The hair on his nape stirred.

"Nay." Roland found himself talking to air as Gilles plunged into the trees.

Something called to Gilles in the distant wood, some sensation of danger. He could no more ignore the summons than deny his lungs breath.

He paid no heed to the noise he made. He drew his knife from the sheath at his side and held a hand before him to fend off the low-hanging branches. The ground beneath his feet was thick with cushioning pine needles; the scent of damp earth and fecund growth filled the air about him.

Gilles had been saved many a time by an extraordinary sense that warned him a heartbeat before death or danger appeared. He heeded that sense now as it called to him.

He held up one hand to halt Roland, who crept through the trees in his wake. Something caught Gilles's eye—a glimmer of motion, a swirl of blue between the thick branches of the conifer trees. The color tantalized his memory. He hastened to it. A shaft of pain swept down his leg, inexplicably, for he had received no injury. The baying grew louder. "Wild dogs. They hold some hapless creature at bay," he said as Roland gained his side.

"Let us leave them to it." Roland paused. The undergrowth, thick and matted, would necessitate bending nearly double to work their way beneath the low-hanging branches.

Gilles plunged ahead, almost running, crouched low, branches snatching at the ebony mantle aswirl behind him. He burst forth into a wide sunny glade, lit from above like a natural cathedral. He leapt into a pack of circling dogs, slashing with his knife.

Their guttural growls rose as blood poured from one dog's throat. He snatched the stick from the young woman who swung it wide to hold the dogs at bay.

Nine in all, the dogs were thin and menacing. Long streamers of saliva hung from their mouths as their heads swung back and forth, following the stick and awaiting their moment. Teeth bared as the stick hit home. Low growls and yips seemed to be secret words passed back and forth as they planned their strategy and crept near.

Gilles clouted the closest. With an ugly crunch, the stick embedded itself into bone. The dog fell dead. Gilles jerked the stick back and drove it into the leaping hounds who turned to savage their fallen comrade. Another fell. The remaining hounds howled and cowered into the undergrowth, slinking away, bellies low as Gilles charged them.

"Are you injured?" Gilles asked the woman, the stick held in one hand, his bloody knife in the other.

In answer, she crumpled in a heap at his feet, her head striking a ring of stones surrounding a banked fire.

"Jesu!" He bent over the woman. A strange, hiccuping sound made him draw back her mantle's edge, which had concealed her face and form.

Roland dropped at his side.

"Jesu," Gilles repeated, for a tiny head, covered in a nimbus of flaxen curls, poked out of the folds of cloth. The child opened its mouth, issuing forth a protest loud enough to bring King Richard's army from the Holy Land.

Chapter Two

Gilles glanced up at Roland, who backed away in consternation, hands palm up. "Look not to me, Gilles, I know little of babes!"

"Then you will learn." He picked up the wailing infant. Its tiny legs churned and beat the air. A female. Too young to be off the breast. Despite Roland's sputtered protests, Gilles handed him the child.

Going down on one knee, he placed a hand to the swollen breast of the fallen woman. "Emma . . . the weaver," he said softly to himself, his memories of the manorial court where he had met her as sharp in his mind as if it had been yesterday and not two years before. He nodded once as he felt her heart's beat, strong and well beneath his palm.

"You know the wench?" Roland held the screaming babe at arm's length.

"Aye." Gently, Gilles grasped Emma's chin in his hand

and turned her head. "Blood." It ran down her neck and stained the earth beneath her. "Go back to camp and summon aid."

"The child?" Roland danced from one foot to the other.

"Put her down, for surely she will land there one way or the other."

"Aye, my lord!" Roland placed the child on the ground as gingerly as he might a venomous snake. The two men watched the tot scramble in the dust to hide by her mother's body. Gilles lifted the edge of the woman's mantle and covered the two females.

As he waited for the return of help, Gilles watched anxiously over Emma. He lifted her pack, a simple leather satchel, and looked for some cloth to cushion her head. He found only plants and seeds and barks. If they had medicinal purposes, he did not know them. Lacking a more suitable cushion, he closed the pack and slipped it under her head. Roland returned with alacrity, bringing Hubert to see to the woman.

"Her head injury is grave, my lord. These bites need stitching," the squire said, drawing up Emma's gown to display her wound and at the same time a slim leg clad in a worn and bloody woolen stocking.

"Do it whilst she is unaware. Then we will take her to Hawkwatch." Gilles stripped the bloody hose from Emma's leg, then hovered like an anxious mother hen.

Hubert used wine to douse a long tear along Emma's ankle where the bone showed white against her skin. He carefully stitched the wound closed.

Gilles recognized the blue mantle. He remembered the woman, remembered her name and face. After her humiliation at the manorial court, he had not quite forgotten her. For several weeks he had expected her obnoxious

uncle to drag her before him, declaring her with child.
When the pair did not appear, Gilles assumed that the
young woman had been lucky. He saw now that she had
not. Her child appeared to be the right age for conception
at the time of his first manorial court.

Ignoring propriety and flinging up Emma's mantle
and threadbare gown, Gilles inspected the slash of teeth
marks down the young woman's leg. He turned back to
the child, who continued to scream her head off and paw
at her mother. He felt for the child, felt her anguish in an
unusually tangible way.

Gently, he examined the raw edges of Emma's wound,
now neatly stitched. He knew a hound's teeth could leave
suppurating sores. He slipped his hand along the inside of
her leg to her knee, turned it, and checked that what he
could see was her only wounding. Satisfied, he tucked
her gown and mantle close about her ankles.

The babe burrowed in the curve of her mother's body.
Gilles touched his hand lightly to the child's towhead.
Her hair tumbled in a mass of short curls like silk and he
let his hand linger in appreciation of her tiny beauty. He
offered her what he hoped was a reassuring smile and
was rewarded by a sudden cessation of noise. Her cries
subsided to hiccups. Her eyes grew wide. A thumb, no
bigger than the first joint on Gilles's smallest finger, crept
into her mouth.

Roland knelt at Gilles's side. " 'Tis good the wench
fainted. Stitching is painful work."

Gilles nodded. They watched Hubert clean a wound
on the back of Emma's head. The babe oversaw the pro-
cedure as she suckled her fingers. She crept from her
mother's side to lean curiously on Gilles's thigh to watch
the youth work.

" 'Tis done. But I think it should receive a poultice or

some such," Hubert said. "See here where her head is bleeding? She is not in a simple faint, my lord."

"We will take her to Hawkwatch and see to it there." Gilles leaned forward and checked the bandages, careful not to disturb the curious child, loath to bring on another bout of wailing. His hand smoothed over Emma's hair to her hood. His fingers lingered for a moment on the unusual weaving of her blue mantle. It reminded him of how a field of bluebells might look when the wind blows from first one direction and then another. He imagined he could catch the scent of those flowers.

Shaking himself from his reverie, he scooped up the babe and, grinning, handed her to Roland, who shot him an evil look. She clung to Roland's shoulder and stared back at Gilles as he bent and swept Emma up into his arms. He carried her like a piece of rare window glass, for somehow the child's scrutiny made him more aware of the precious nature of his burden.

Rich scarlet linen formed a canopy above Emma's head. Gathered yards of the cloth, tied with braided cord of golden threads, were held against bedposts carved with leaves and fruit. Emma twisted her head about to see beyond the bed and saw a man seated by the fire. She shut her eyes as quickly as one would a lid on a coffer of snakes.

Slowly, she opened one, just enough to peek between her lashes. 'Twas Lord Gilles d'Argent who reclined in the roomy chair of solid English oak.

Cradling Angelique in his arms.

Emma watched her daughter kick her little bare feet and push them against Lord Gilles's lap. Her mouth worked busily on her thumb. He tried to pull it from her mouth. Emma knew the strength of that grip. She fully understood why he gave up and left Angelique to her pleasure.

Emma lay motionless except for occasional restless movements of her injured limb. It ached and throbbed from her foot to her knee. Only the pain in her head rivaled it. She held her breath as Angelique reached out for Lord Gilles's beard, stroked her fingers along it, then giggled when he laughed.

The masculine laughter drew Emma from her feigned sleep, her heart beating rapidly. She could not pretend to sleep any longer. She rose on her elbows, moaned as pain sliced through her head. It took only one more moment for her to realize she was nearly naked, clad in naught but a loose linen shift. Not her own. Her milk-filled breasts ached and begged to be emptied. Drawing the blanket to her chin, Emma sat up.

Gilles stood and then turned to Emma.

"Your babe seems hungry." He stepped into the gloom that surrounded the bed and gently laid Angelique in her mother's arms. Angelique immediately clutched at Emma, who became intensely aware of Lord Gilles standing at the bed's edge. He stood so close she could smell the leather of his garments.

She felt the blood rise to color her cheeks as Angelique rooted about at her breast.

"I will send you food and drink," Lord Gilles said. He reached out and lifted her chin, ignoring the child. With great solicitude, he inspected a bruise on her temple, then wordlessly removed his hand and turned away.

Like a frightened rabbit in a burrow, Emma snuggled into the blankets, her breath short until the door closed behind him. 'Twas her injury, she told herself, that made her blood pound in her head, increasing the pain and leaving her confused. She slipped the loose shift down and fed her hungry babe.

She didn't know how to proceed. Should she arise? Should she search about for her clothing? Was she to eat at the long linen-draped table she saw on the far side of the bedchamber? With great indecision, Emma remained buried in the huge bed, her nose the only thing visible above the covers, a sated Angelique tucked tightly at her side.

A stout serving woman with red cheeks and frizzled gray locks appeared at the door laden with a tray. She plunked it on the long draped table with a grunt of relief and beamed at them.

"My name be Meara, Mistress. May I help ye rise?"

"Aye." Emma shoved back the coverlet, her hand lingering on the linen sheet that separated her from the woolen blankets and soft furs. She savored the fine weave, smooth and lustrous. "Thank you," Emma said to Meara when the woman helped her to the oaken chair in which Lord Gilles had sat. Perched atop it was a carved hawk in flight, a snake clutched in its talons. It loomed over her shoulder as if to make sure she did not steal from the tray.

"Ye'll be cold." Meara rummaged in a nearby iron-strapped coffer and then wrapped Emma's shoulders in a spare blanket. Emma pressed her nose into the cloth, for it held the scent of man, the scent of leather and weapons laid up after being well-oiled. She knew the scent from her father. For a moment, she missed her cheerful father as if his death had been but yesterday and not five long years before. His death had meant the difference between living in a stone house with a fire and plenty of food and living in Simon's hovel with only scraps for the table.

Meara whipped off the napkin that covered the dishes, releasing the scents of rich gravy and freshly baked bread.

"Is all of this for us?" Emma gaped at the tray. The food arrayed before her represented enough food to feed a family of four. The delicious aroma made her head swim. Intangible memories of another time brought tears to her eyes.

"Aye. 'Is lordship ordered it so. 'Tis just for ye—and the babe. Have ye need of anything else, Mistress? 'Is lordship said yer to have whatever ye need." Meara stood before Emma awaiting her wishes just as if Emma were a fine lady.

"I-I can think of nothing. We are most grateful to you for your service."

Meara nodded, patted Angelique's head, and silently left the room. Emma turned back to the feast before her. The trencher, a slab of day-old bread, held a rich meat dish thick with onions and gravy. Its aroma tantalized and set her mouth watering as she tore off tiny slivers of the trencher, sopped them well in gravy, and fed them to Angelique. She would soon need to wean Angelique. A hungry mother did not produce much of a milk supply for a developing child. On the other hand, she also knew a child weaned too soon had less chance of living past three summers.

Emma forced herself to eat slowly and savor the fare. A polished pewter salver held fruit. When she tentatively tasted of the dish, she realized it was pears poached in a delicate wine and honey syrup. *Ambrosia, fit for the gods*, she thought.

Warm goat's milk, also sweetened with honey, completed the repast. Emma held the cup to her daughter's lips and stroked her warm, silky tresses, urging her to try the new drink. Her own mother had much loved a cup of honey-sweetened milk.

When their bellies were full, Emma resisted the urge to lick the pewter plate clean. She set it aside with great care, then hefted Angelique to her shoulder and paced before the fire. Each step sent shooting pains through her leg, but she knew she must move it or it would seize up and cripple her. 'Twas a long, steep hill from the castle to her humble village.

Her curiosity got the better of her. She examined every inch of the chamber. A spigot yielding water into a stone basin made her jump and squeal aloud with delight. Beeswax candles made her breathe deeply and remember her mother at the task of making just such candles during her childhood. Now she was grateful if there was suffi-cient oil in which to float a wick. His coffer beckoned, but she was not brave enough to lift its lid and touch his belongings.

Meara appeared at the doorway. "Yer clothing be clean now. If ye'd consent, 'is lordship ordered ye a bath." Meara hefted the tray onto her sturdy shoulder.

"Sweet blessed heaven, Angelique! A bath." She limped forward, then stepped back as a hulking man delivered a wooden tub to the room. He said nothing, but his interest was acute and Emma felt a flame of heat cross her cheeks.

When an army of serving boys departed, a deep wooden tub of steaming hot water stood behind a wooden screen. The tub, painted about the sides with flowers and vines, was small, intended for a feminine form and most certainly not one that would be used by a man of such a size as Lord Gilles. Emma wistfully stroked her hands over the art that graced the tub.

Meara helped Emma climb into the bath, careful that her leg remained propped on a soft pad of cloth on the rim, and then handed Angelique over. Angelique played a slapping game with the bubbles formed as Meara washed them. The child's delighted squeals brought tears to Emma's eyes. Joy supplanted fear. What luxury, Emma thought, to have someone scrub their hair and rinse them clean.

Sighing with contentment, Emma leaned back and steeped in the lavender cloud that enveloped them, and allowed the serving woman to wrap her hair in a length of warmed linen. Meara lifted Angelique from her arms, wrapped her up, and dried each tiny toe. Emma smiled at her babe, so warm and clean, in Meara's arms.

Lord Gilles had saved their lives.

How might she ever repay him? Would she even see him again or be close enough to him to offer her thanks? What a gift from providence that a man such as he was in the woods when she most needed aid.

Was it her imagination that painted concern in his dark eyes and more than gentleness in the touch of his fingers? Mayhap 'twas just a fancy born of loneliness. Unbidden, her hand moved to where he had touched her.

Meara roused Emma from her languor. "Ye'll catch a chill if ye linger much longer, Mistress." Meara extended a linen drying cloth. "Lord Gilles directed me to put ye in his wife's chamber."

Chapter Three

A cold hard knot formed in Emma's throat. Her heart lurched. For a brief moment the room spun and a pain flooded in, new and ripe. *Of course he would be wed.* "His w-w-wife?"

Meara nodded. "O' course, Lady Margaret's been dead these many years. Saw less o' 'er than we ever did o' Lord Gilles in the years 'is father were alive. 'Ated it 'ere, she did. She loved court, the gowns, the fine folk there," Meara continued. "Bein' ye might know some o' them fine folk yerself, Mistress."

"Me?" Emma whipped around to stare at the serving woman.

"Oh, aye. Ye can't hide quality. Ye might 'ave 'oles in yer shift, beggin' yer pardon, but ye've a certain way about ye."

Emma forced herself to smile. Whatever she might

49

have been when her father and mother had lived, she had fallen far since. "I'm no better than you, Meara."

"As ye wish, Mistress." Meara shrugged and then prattled on about Lady Margaret and her silk gowns and miniver-lined mantles.

Emma did not comment, for she'd been taught by her mother that gossiping was not ladylike. *But I may no longer call myself a lady. I am of Meara's station now. A free woman mayhap, but of the lowest station nonetheless, my stature lost through untimely death and ill luck.* The thought further squeezed her throat. She had not yet accepted the fact that despite her parents' best efforts, she, their beloved daughter, lived from hand to mouth.

"Once 'is lordship's son Nicholas went to foster in King 'Enry's court, she wouldn't stay 'ere when Lord Gilles were off wiv the old king. 'Ated the old lord, she did. Couldna abide this place and bein' alone wiv his lordship's father." Meara lowered her voice and grinned slyly. " 'Twas said she 'ad a lover at court." She sniffed. "Only deigned to grace us wiv 'er presence when Lord Gilles demanded she do 'er duty. Cried at nothing, she did, if I do say so. Quick wiv a pinch, too, deserved or not." Meara bustled about gathering up wet cloths and the precious block of soap, which she put into a wooden box. "I keeps 'er chambers clean, ye understand, God rest 'er soul, but empty rooms be musty—no matter ye sweep 'em daily. Yer to lie yerself down 'ere 'til the beddin's changed."

Emma did not wish to picture the ghostly Lady Margaret. As she gingerly sat on the edge of Lord Gilles's bed, she turned the conversation. "You say his lordship has a son?"

"Oh, aye. Just the one. A bonny lad. Married 'e did this past spring. 'E holds one o' 'is lordship's keeps down the coast. Seaswept, by name." Meara shivered. "Now there's a bitter place to be in winter!"

At the thought of winter, Emma shivered too, then snuggled into Lord Gilles's mattress, surely stuffed with goosedown and not common straw. She made a place for herself and rubbed her cheek on the edge of his bed linens. *His linens. His scent.* A tiny shiver coursed through her.

Emma rolled abruptly to her side to banish her thoughts. She drew Angelique close, curling herself into a tiny ball, the child at the center. She would not allow her mind to dwell on such a man as Lord Gilles, a man with a married son, a wealthy baron with at least two estates. He lived in a world now as far beyond her reach as the dust motes Angelique tried to catch.

'Twas a falsehood that her gentle father, a knight of Baron Ramsey's household, had wished her to wed Jacob Baker. Still fate had taken that gentle knight before he'd penned his wishes. She'd been destined by her uncle's wardship to no higher than the baker, a man with one cheating hand on the scale and the other wandering where it shouldn't.

Tears gathered. She fought them. But as she lay in Lord Gilles's bed of luxury, each fiber touched her skin and teased her senses with the reality of her situation in life. She sank into misery. Lord Gilles's own words, spoken two years before, had ofttimes haunted her in the lonely night, and now came back to haunt her anew.

. . . *few men of quality will have you without your virtue intact* . . .

In truth, *no* man of quality would have her now. Nor, if she desired another, could she have him. She'd said her vows, plighted her troth. 'Twas done, acknowledged or not.

51

Emma's head ached, her leg throbbed. She no longer felt the sensual surfaces, she felt only shame and regret for how she'd allowed her life to go awry.

She said her nightly prayers, first one of thanksgiving for Angelique and second a prayer to ask forgiveness for not using her wisdom to hold herself innocent for some man who would honor her gift. Last, she offered a lengthy prayer that Angelique and she might survive the coming winter. She closed her eyes a moment, then whispered a quick word to God on Lord Gilles's behalf for saving their lives.

What seemed moments later, but was actually more than an hour, Meara roused Emma from a deep sleep.

"I dreamt I lay upon a cloud." Emma yawned and stretched, letting her hand stroke over the bed furs for a final time before rising.

" 'Tis surely the closest to a cloud in this keep, although Lord Gilles would be just as content below wiv 'is men." Meara smiled.

Emma scooped up Angelique and, wrapping her mantle about them, she followed Meara to a smaller but equally luxurious chamber, just two turns up the stone stair from Lord Gilles's. They moved slowly, Meara's hand under Emma's elbow as she limped along.

The bed hangings in Lady Margaret's chamber were the color of a summer sky. The linens were embroidered with lilies and butterflies. The chamber chilled her, as did the bedclothes, so she curled her toes and tucked her feet into the hem of the borrowed shift. The glowing brazier had not yet dispelled the dampness of a chamber long closed.

"No one lives here, Angelique," Emma whispered, sensing no ghosts, no remnant of the lady who had once sat at the small table across the chamber and used the ivory comb that still lay on a silver tray. "Lady Margaret

52

has been gone for a long time." Emma tucked Angelique into the crook of her arm and, despite the throb in her head and leg, she fell into a deep sleep.

Gilles stripped naked and slipped into his bed. He settled into a hollow of particular warmth where a feminine form had slept. He became aroused by the warmth of the space. The sweet scent of lavender soap entwined him in a seductive web. His mind conjured Emma in his bed, fresh from her bath. He remembered the press of her full breasts against her thin shift and the dusky hint of a nipple barely suggested. Gilles fought his arousal because he denied his attraction to Emma, denied that bringing her to his chamber meant anything other than Christian charity.

He reminded himself that Emma was wounded and that the most likely place for her to rest would be in the warmest place in the keep. He tried to convince himself that his arousal meant naught, 'twas just a coincidence.

Gilles lost the battle with his logic, closed his eyes, and let his imagination roam. He stretched her out in a field of intoxicating lavender. His imagination cupped her lush breasts, learned their shape, traced the sweep of her hips, and stroked the smooth length of her thighs. With a bewitching clarity, he thought he could scent her arousal. He took a shuddering breath.

"Sweet heaven," he whispered to the night. His chest tightened, his whole body shivered. Turning over on his stomach, he forced himself to think of something bland and martial. He contemplated fighting techniques until he ruefully admitted that his contemplations were lasciviously filled with swords being sheathed and lances being couched. At least it brought his humor back, and his humor brought peace.

At last, he slept.

* * *

Long before creepers of light slipped beneath his shutters, Gilles arose. He dressed hurriedly, pulling on what lay at hand, black wool and black linen. With a haste to his stride that betrayed his eagerness, he flew down the steep stone steps and into the hall. Ignoring the yawning servants who were set to the task of assembling the many tables needed for the daily meals, Gilles spread out a large roll of vellum on an oak table and looked over the plans to his stable addition.

He did not make his way to the bailey when the ring of metal on metal told him a dawn workout was progressing as scheduled. Instead, he remained standing over his plans.

Gilles knew immediately when Emma made her appearance. He sensed her first. A flush of warmth swept through him. With a forced nonchalance, he lifted his eyes. She hesitated on the lowest step of the stone stairs that led to the tower chambers before coming toward him. He waited on the raised flagstone hearth before the mammoth fireplace in which could be roasted a full boar. With hands braced on the table, anchoring the plans, he watched her come. Her limp made her progress slow, giving him ample time to drink in her appearance: her compelling eyes and her honey-colored hair, now tamed in braids that fell on her breasts. The child still slumbered at peace on her mother's shoulder.

A pink blush stained Emma's cheeks. Gilles thought of roses, full-blown summer roses, petals spread, offering their fragrance to the warm air.

He sensed no fear as she approached him. The lack of apprehension made a tightness in his chest uncoil. So many shied from him, gave him respect tinged with a healthy dose of fear for his position and his power over their lives. A sudden desire to grin swept through him and he gave in to it.

Emma came eagerly now, smiling back, not watching the floor as servants were wont to do. She met his eyes with a vibrant joy as if they had some secret between them.

"Good day, my lord," she greeted him, shifting Angelique to her uninjured side and dropping into a lop-sided curtsy.

"Mistress Emma." He savored the feel of her name on his tongue.

"Lord Gilles, I wish to thank you for saving our lives."

" 'Twas nothing." Could she hear the seduction in his tone? He prayed his voice did not betray him, for it sounded hoarse to him, plagued with lust for her sweetness, an elusive scent on his mind. How ridiculous he felt—beguiled by the scent of a woman lingering on his bedding.

Their eyes met. "You are mistaken, my lord. 'Twas everything."

"What do you call your babe?" He moved to her and because 'twould be unseemly to touch her, he placed his hand a moment on the child's head. Aware that even that small gesture betrayed him, he turned and resumed his place of power on the dais.

"I have named her Angelique, my lord."

"Why does your husband allow you to wander unprotected?" Gilles could not prevent his voice from growing cold and abrupt. Her face registered the change in his tone. Her smile died, her marvelous eyes dropped, and her hands plucked at the child's woolen wrap.

"I have no husband who acknowledges me, my lord."

Her choice of words puzzled him. "Explain yourself."

She took a breath and drew the child closer to her. "The man with whom I exchanged vows chooses to deny them—and us."

"It does not trouble you to tell me this?"

She lifted her head, her chin rose. "I have learned that to shrink from truth is to face it later in a more difficult guise."

"I see. . . . Then who looks to your care?" A sudden heat rose on his cheeks.

"I look to my own care, my lord," Emma said softly. "Should you check your ledgers, you will see that I paid my sixpence fine."

"I have no memory of your coming before me."

"You were in York then, my lord. Your steward saw to the matter."

A thrill of excitement clutched at him.

She was, for all intents and purposes, unprotected.

He could not speak. Her seductive presence left him speechless like Hubert in the presence of Beatrice, a buxom serving wench with saucy blond curls and a wide smile. With difficulty, Gilles cleared his throat. "I had thought you smitten with love after your last appearance before me."

He waited. Her eyes did not avoid his, but a sweetness fled them as the sun flees before a black storm cloud. "I no longer believe in love, my lord."

"I see." *Abandoned.* He stroked his hand over his close-cropped black beard. A curious sympathy made him gentle with her. Love was a jongleur's game. He'd never felt its snare, nor believed in its lure. Yet he felt a curious sadness that this lovely young woman should feel as he did, he who was a generation older in wisdom and hard living. "I am sorry for it."

She did not respond. She shifted her child and he

watched the soft tint of color on her cheeks become large blotches of unbecoming red. "If I may go, my lord? I have need to return to my weaving. I've a piece promised that needs finishing."

Nothing could have prepared him for the hammer of his blood in his veins. He wanted to reach out and seize her, hold her, keep her—slake his lust in her. Her tall stance, her brave look, her lithe figure drew him. He wanted to hold her before him, drink her in, trace the shape of her face with his fingertips, know again the warmth of her breast beneath his hand. 'Twas a madness. He'd gone too long without a woman, 'twas all.

Emma still wore her gentian mantle although the color had faded and the hem was worn. Gilles thought the color perfect on her. It had lodged in his mind, never to be forgotten. He thought her hair like gold spun from a magic distaff. Unbound, he imagined it would fall over her shoulders and down to her waist in ripples of silk; he yearned to bury his hands in it. His blood boiled to possess her. He searched for some way to hold her before him.

"You speak well for a weaver." Jesu. He sounded like a mewling page, and condescending to boot.

A curious smile, at once rueful and self-mocking, touched her mouth. "My father did not realize my mother's lessons would one day be needed to stave off starvation."

"Your father was . . . ?" he asked. He cared not a whit who had sired her.

"Sir Edmund Aethelwin, my lord."

"An old name. A knight, you say?"

She nodded. "First of Baron Ramsey's house, then a free lance when Baron Ramsey died. Unfortunately for my mother and me, as Papa grew older he did not do well on the road." She recounted her story with no emotion in her voice. "As his fortunes fell, we had need to leave our home. My father settled us with his brother Simon until he might recoup his losses. He fell in a tourney in France ere he could return to us."

"Your mother taught you to weave?" Gilles scrambled about in his brain for something to hold her before him.

"Aye, I learned at my mother's knee, my lord. She had a canny hand for spinning as well, but disappeared when—"

Sorrow tinged her voice, and she busied herself tucking a small blanket about her daughter's shoulders.

Gilles resisted a powerful need to offer her comfort. Somehow her grief reached him. "When?" he prompted gently.

She met his gaze as a knight's fine lady would. "When my father's brother tried to force her into wedlock with him. Simon said she walked into the sea one night. I believe he killed her when she scorned his suit and so put about the other story to spare himself the hangman's noose. He had beaten her many times, and oft lost control of himself."

It was not pity she wanted from him. He read it in her stalwart stance and direct gaze. "Did anyone question your mother's fate?" he asked. "Why was this matter not brought to my attention?"

" 'Twas before your time here, my lord."

"Then surely my father—" he began.

"I brought the matter to his cleric's attention. A penniless weaver's fate is not of much note. A man's word is gold to the base metal of a woman's voice."

And so lay the gap betwixt lord and vassal and men and women. Gilles knew his father would have thought little of a woman's accusations in comparison to a man's protestations of innocence. He had ofttimes seen his father beat his own mother for little more than a meal ill-

58

prepared by the servants. The sight had nourished a hatred for his father, and as a consequence, he'd never raised a hand against a woman in his life.

"What of your uncle, this Simon?"

"He died of a seizure not long after he sent me to . . . seek my own way."

Cast out—as he had predicted. The thought sat ill with him.

She broke into his thoughts. "May I go, my lord?"

"You may go." He choked it out. The results were devastating. Emma made a curtsy and turned away. With halting steps, she crossed the great expanse of rush-strewn flagstone between him and the iron-strapped doors that led to the bailey.

With the closing of the door, Gilles realized he might never see her again. He had not asked her where she dwelt. One step was all he took from the raised hearth before sense asserted itself and he returned to his plans.

A youth would run after a maid. Knighted barons did not run after weavers. The lord of the keep had more reserve, more dignity than that. He clutched the table's edge to hold himself in place. At last his hands relaxed and he straightened, smoothing the vellum before him and forcing his attention to his stables.

She did not dwell in his world.

Chapter Four

Emma picked her way through the crowds of men and women who were going about their daily chores in the inner bailey of Hawkwatch Castle. Children dashed before her limping steps as she finally passed through the lower bailey to the gate. She called a greeting to the gatekeeper as she crossed the drawbridge that allowed access to a beaten path down a steep hill.

The castle was built upon a high promontory overlooking Hawkwatch Bay, soaring up as if thrust from the very earth. Thick outer stone walls surrounded the castle. 'Twas King Richard's father, old King Henry himself, who'd ordered the fortifications that had made Hawkwatch a vast fortress, to protect the royal interests from marauders who might come from across the North Sea.

Clustered about the sheer walls of local stone were other huts and hovels like Emma's. It took her twice as long as usual to make her limping way through the village to her hut. Pain shot up her leg with every step. Angelique seemed to weigh as much as a child twice her size. With a sigh of something akin to sadness, Emma stepped over her threshold. In the broad light of day, 'twas much shabbier and ruder than she cared to admit. With just pallet and stool, Emma had almost no room for the simple upright loom propped against the rear stone wall. Many small pots and bowls held plants and barks for dyeing. Their myriad scents filled the air and soothed Emma's troubled mind.

She gently placed Angelique on her pallet and offered her a stuffed woolen ball. Taking out her eating dagger, she dug about in the dirt in one corner until she unearthed a leather pouch. With shaky fingers she counted out what remained of her meager store of silver pennies. Also in the pouch lay her father's gold spurs and her mother's cross. Sighing with relief, she replaced the dirt and stamped it flat with her good foot. Her father's gold spurs were all she had of him, and no amount of need would make her part with them. Likewise, she'd retained possession of the delicate silver cross from her mother's family. She'd sold the chain the previous month for food. Both were possessions that reminded her that once she'd had a beamed roof overhead and a hearth to warm her in winter.

Her head rang with pain. Her stitched wounds burned. Where in heaven had all the noise come from? Outside, geese hissed, carts rumbled over ruts in the paths, children shrieked, a smith rang his hammer on the anvil. She groaned and forced herself to sit down at Angelique's side and sip slowly from a stone bottle of ale. The ale was rank in comparison to Lord Gilles's honeyed milk.

She bent her head and kissed Angelique's small head. "What, my sweet, is this effect Lord Gilles has upon my senses? Is it just that he holds the ultimate authority here? Or is it that he is the antithesis of *him*? No, these feelings are unique. They come only from his lordship." Her arms tightened about her daughter. "We owe Lord Gilles our lives. I could not have held the dogs off much longer. I prayed God would let us die quickly. I prayed God would not let you suffer," she whispered against the silky tresses. "We have been given another chance."

"Talking to yer little angel again, are ye?"

"Widow Cooper!" Emma cried joyfully to the figure standing in her doorway. Angelique strained to be clasped in the widow's arms.

"Come, my angel," crooned the older woman, her gray hair hidden beneath her snowy-white headcovering, her wide girth swinging to and fro to amuse the youngster. "Who gave ye a chance, my friend?"

"Why you, of course!" Emma smiled at her friend, putting one hand to her throbbing head. "Who bribed young Bert to build me a loom? Helped me birth Angelique?" Her smile fled. "Who defends me at the well?"

Widow Cooper blew into Angelique's small palm and set the child to giggling and kicking her feet. "Humpf. The women are just jealous. They've not the backbone to take their men to task for sniffing about yer skirts, and so must place the blame elsewhere. A woman alone be prey in this place. Brainless, the lot o' them."

"The women or the men?" Emma quipped.

They shared a laugh; then the widow spied Emma's bandaged ankle. "Sweet heaven, child. What is this?" She settled Angelique on Emma's straw pallet and lifted the hem of Emma's skirt.

"I was gathering in the woods and was set upon by dogs."

63

"How many times must I tell ye not to go about such business alone?" the widow scolded.

"I am alone. You have your son and his five children to help, and cannot be rushing off each time I need to gather a few berries, or barter some cloth, or . . . or draw water!" Emma knew life was hard enough for the widow, whose daughter-by-marriage had perished birthing her last babe. Secretly, Emma suspected the widow was grooming her for her son's next wife. In her weaker moments, she considered it herself.

"Well, I'm glad yer not torn to pieces." She tutted over the bruise on Emma's head.

"Don't fuss, please."

The widow withdrew her hand. "Have ye finished the last of the trim for the Abbot?"

"Almost." Emma reached up into the thatching of her hut. She drew down a narrow wooden box. Inside lay a long strip of trimming that she'd labored hard upon. She desperately needed the pennies she'd earn for it. Usually, her weavings earned naught but bartered food.

The widow stroked the intricate design. " 'Tis very fine. The Abbot will be well pleased."

"Angelique needs warm winter wrappings for her feet and hands." Emma hoped the trimming would allow her to purchase the necessary wool to weave something that would earn her more than food. She was loath to part with her few pennies. "I was grateful for the work. We've been blessed with mild weather, but 'twill soon be winter."

The two women watched Angelique tumble about from pallet to loom to pallet. Neither voiced their common fear that Angelique would not survive without food and warmth. Emma knew that she might look more kindly on becoming the mother of five young children if it meant Angelique did not starve. The thought of the conjugal privileges she must then give Widow Cooper's son made her shiver. Her one time with a man had made her sure she did not wish to repeat the effort. She had fended off the widow's hints with reminders that although her husband did not acknowledge her, she had made vows and considered herself wed. How she wished she'd made those vows on the church steps instead of in private.

"Ye've a melancholy look. Are ye in pain?" Widow Cooper touched Emma on the knee.

"Nay. Oh, aye. The stitching hurts. Pray 'twill not fester! But nay, 'tis not my wounds that ail me." She whirled to her friend. "How could I have been so blind? Why did I not see him for what he was?" Her voice broke; tears flowed down her cheeks. "How could I have offered myself to the first man with smooth cheeks and a sunny smile that paid me attention?" The tears spotted her woolen gown, her only gown. "I acted the fool for a man's honeyed words. Snared by poetry! Fool. Fool."

"Now, now." The widow rose and wrapped an arm about Emma's waist. " 'Tis not like ye to feel sorry for yerself like this. Yer not the first to be taken in by a fine figure and pleasin' face. I think ye were lonely, in need of love. Yer uncle were a vile man to have the care of a young maid. 'Tis not the end of the world."

"Isn't it? Look about you. I barely keep us fed."

The widow grasped Emma by the shoulders and shook her. "Now, none o' that! What has happened to ye? Where's the strong maid who took her knife to Ivo when he come sniffin' in the night to bed her?"

Emma managed a small wan smile. The village had been all atwitter with the story of Ivo's comeuppance, less from the paltry wound on his arm than from the beating his wife had given him when he'd slunk home. Her smile died. The village women had held her responsible,

65

Ivo's wife telling her at the village well, that Emma was to keep her hands off Ivo from then on, as if she'd issued the knave an invitation. "You champion me. 'Tis the only reason we survive."

"Nonsense. Now, I'll 'ear no more o' this. I'll send a pottage by way of the baker's lad and a poultice for yer wound. Ye'll never go hungry as long as I'm about."

Emma thanked her friend, grateful there was no mention of marriage to her son. They decided on a time for Emma to hand over the trimming so Widow Cooper could deliver it to the abbey when she and her son went to the nearby port of Lynn. They parted company with promises to meet in a few days.

Emma stared after the widow. Widow Cooper's son had a cast in his eye and was missing the fingers on his left hand. She did not really hold his infirmities against him. 'Twas the whispers that he'd beaten his first wife at the slightest offense that made her cringe. With sadness, Emma hoped the widow never learned what was whispered about her son.

Angelique had curled into a ball on the pallet and her soft puffs of breath filled the lonely silence. Gently, Emma stroked her daughter's back, watched the small thumb disappear into the rose-petal lips. "Believe in no man, Angelique. Expect lies and you will never be played the fool. Believe only in the power of God's love and in the power of nature."

She felt a need to give instruction to her sleeping child, more to reassure herself than to impart wisdom. "Revere the plants that yield the glorious color for dyes. Respect the gift of the wool given by the sheep. Honor nature's gifts. They give us life."

She looked at the rough stone wall that formed the back of her hut, the castle's outer wall. *His wall.* "There are mysteries and forces greater than I can understand, my angel. Lord Gilles, he is one of the mysteries. He appears mortal man, yet mayhap if we were to meet again—

"Forget this foolish musing! Wild dogs will not beset us again just to assure his lordship's attention! I am surely mad to think such a man might notice us, crouched here at the base of his walls." In truth, she was not sure she wished any man to notice her ever again.

Emma's stool sat before an upright loom, but it was to the hand loom she looked. Made from a flexible branch crotch cut from a tree, 'twas the loom on which she had made the trimming sold to the Abbot. It was in the weaving of trimming and beltwork that her mother had excelled and 'twas her legacy to Emma.

She plucked up the hand loom and stroked her fingers along the smooth wood that had seen years of work from both her and her mother. A glimmer of an idea ran over and over in her head. " 'Twould be audacious. Presumptuous even, Angelique, to weave Lord Gilles a gift. But what else have I to give in thanks for our lives?"

She moved back to her daughter's side, leaning down and kissing the dainty cheek. "I'll need alder bark, winter berries, bedstraw to make the dyes," she whispered to her daughter. "We shall borrow a kettle from Widow Cooper. The stink will be terrible, but worth it."

The scent of lavender soap lingered in Angelique's hair. Stroking her fingers through the curly mop, Emma tried to draw into her nostrils the scent that would forever remind her of that luxurious bath in *his* chambers.

Her thoughts were interrupted when a shadow crossed the beaten floor of her hut. Emma could barely restrain herself from squeezing Angelique. William Belfour crossed her hut in a single stride and dropped to one knee. He scowled down at Angelique.

"What do you want?" Emma cried, clutching at her daughter.

"I saw you in the hall and wanted to see the babe at closer quarters. She is your image. I see no sign of me," he said.

Emma looked from her innocent daughter to William. They had the same flaxen hair, the same sky-blue eyes. Her daughter lay garbed in the coarsest of undyed wool. William's mantle and surcoat were finely made, their blue a clear match to his bright eyes. His clothing was clean and costly, his surcoat trimmed with rich red embroidery, his mantle with fur. He wore soft leather boots and thick warm hose. His daughter had strips of old linen from cast-off garments wrapped about her feet and little legs. The contrasts sent a knife-edge of anger through her.

"She is yours, nonetheless," Emma averred, the anger rising in her throat. She wanted to vomit from fear, not just fear of the coming winter and Angelique's small chance of survival to womanhood, but fear of William and what he represented. He took up all the space in her hut with his broad shoulders and audacious manner, sucked the air away so she could barely draw breath. She would not kneel in this man's presence. She would not make herself vulnerable to his ugliness in her home. She forced herself to stand upright and to square her shoulders.

He, too, rose and looked about with disdain. "I deny the child. You have no proof. As I said before, you probably spread your legs for many men."

"Nay!" Emma drew away from his ugly denial. "Nay. Surely you know I was a virgin!"

"Many women have difficulty accommodating me," he sneered.

She took a deep breath. As much as she despised this

man, he was her husband. "You may deny it ten times and still you are her father, I your wife. Even the church recognizes a marriage when two people speak vows to one another and consummation takes—"

"I spoke no vows. You seek to assure yourself of a better life." He tapped his finger on her cheek. "What would a man of my station want with a woman of yours, save the obvious? You were not even much amusement, truth be known."

Emma realized there was no reasoning with him now, just as there had been no reasoning with him when first she had found herself with child. She covered Angelique with her mantle to shield her in some small way from William's scrutiny. With a clarity of vision she'd not had when William Belfour had first come to the marketplace and noticed her, Emma realized she no longer desired his attention or acknowledgement. "Have it your way. 'Tis your loss, not ours. Why have you chosen this day to speak to me? You scorned my love and repudiated your babe a long time ago."

William stared Emma in the eye. What blindness had assailed her that she had not seen this man for what he was? Emma held open the battered wooden door that separated her from humanity. "Be gone."

"Nay. I saw you swishing your skirts before Lord Gilles and thought mayhap you'd gained some experience and might be worth a second try." William gripped Emma by the arms. He lowered his mouth to hers and claimed her lips. He tasted of a rich red wine.

Where once Emma had thrilled to William's touch, now she shivered in fear. His strength frightened her. He pressed his hips to hers and she felt his heated manhood growing hard against her stomach.

Emma bit his lip.

"Promiscuous bitch!" William pushed Emma away, his hand on his mouth. His surcoat bulged from the press of his desire, and he put his hands on his hips, emphasizing his state. Emma refused to look.

"I will be back, mark my words. We have business unfinished between us. Tempt not my anger, for I have influence here. Many may buy your cloth now, but a word in the right ear and your custom would dry up. You will find yourself assessed a penny here, a penny there until you must offer yourself for food." William left her with a quick swing of his mantle.

Emma sank to her pallet and scooped up Angelique, who'd slept through the confrontation. Her hands shook as she smoothed her daughter's curls. "He would not dare. His threats are hollow. There is always need for good cloth; we will never starve." She said the words aloud, repeated them again and again to convince herself and hold back fear.

A chill wind whistled down the chimney of Hawkwatch Keep. The hunting birds lifted their wings to protest the disturbing eddies of air. Garth moved closer to the fire.

"What is it?" Gilles demanded without turning to see who approached him. The fool would receive the sharp edge of his tongue for disturbing him. He lifted his tankard of ale and drank it down as he flexed the stiff fingers of his cold right hand.

"My lord?" a soft voice said behind him.

Gilles recognized the voice. It drifted like a gentle visitor through his dreams. He rose from his seat and turned. "Mistress Emma." Gilles swept her a courtly bow, his ill temper banished in one instant. "How may I be of service?"

"My lord, I do not require any service. I have brought

you a gift to thank you for saving my life and that of my daughter."

"A gift?" Gilles, nonplussed, groped for words. He could count on one hand the gifts he had received in his many years.

"Aye, my lord." Emma extended a package wrapped in clean linen.

He stepped down from the dais and took the bundle. For a moment he just stroked his thumbs over the coarse wrapping.

"I hope it will be pleasing to you, my lord," Emma said into the silence.

As Gilles plucked off the twine that bound the bundle, he sought to excuse his curt behavior. "Forgive me my churlish nature. I have just returned from a most unfortunate afternoon. One of my men wounded a horse in careless play with a sword—a prized horse's tendon was severed. What seemed but a careless accident resulted in the destruction of a valuable mount. I had need to cut the horse's throat." He ground to a halt, unsure why he had explained his foul mood at all.

The wrapping parted. Gilles did not know how to describe the pleasure he received from the length of intricately woven cloth in his hand. He unfolded it and saw that one end was stitched about a humble iron buckle. Humble could not describe the belt itself.

His gaze skipped from the belt, to the woman before him, to the floor. Words lodged somewhere in his throat.

She stepped forward, her child on one hip. "I tried to capture the carving of your chair, my lord, and the decorations of your chimneypiece." Her voice dropped. "I hope you are not displeased."

In fact, she had taken the Norman motifs found on his chair and painted about his whitewashed chimneypiece, and woven them in the colors of fire and storm clouds. The colors were more vibrant and alive than any he'd ever seen. He turned the belt. The interwoven designs became a string of hawks in flight. "Displeased? This is your work?" How could he be so stupid? She'd just said as much.

"Aye, my lord." She bobbed a low curtsy.

"I am more than pleased. This is beyond fine. I have never seen the like." Gilles held the belt in both hands and stroked his thumbs over the intricate pattern. Each motif entwined and linked to another, endlessly. An unfamiliar feeling came over him. A gift linked the giver and the recipient as the designs linked along the cloth. Did she intend such a thing?

He turned the belt in the light. The shades of color changed and shifted as did the color of her mantle as she moved.

"You must join my weavers." The words barely made it from his mouth. He raised his gaze to hers and thought he saw in her eyes what he felt coursing in his own blood. No matter the sounds that might surround them, no matter how many men and women were busy in the hall, only the two of them existed at that moment. "You must join my weavers," he repeated. "Today."

"Do you mean that, my lord?" Emma asked. "You offer me a great honor."

"On the contrary, the honor is mine."

Emma's heart raced, her palms dampened. *To weave for him!* She and Angelique would never starve, nor feel the chill of a winter storm blowing beneath their door. Angelique would grow with straight bones and a full belly.

She need not make excuses to Widow Cooper.

Then she frowned, turning away from Lord Gilles and

looking down the long hall at the folk who lounged about on benches to avoid the bitter wind outside. Just as the harrowing of the coming winter wind would be a torture, 'twould be a torture of another kind to be near William Belfour and feel his contempt and ugly scorn, to be within reach of his displeasure.

And to be within hearing of his words. 'Twas his poetry and song that had first drawn her. Poetry he had composed just for her. Words that she had thought were a window to his soul, a soul she'd mistakenly believed was as golden and fair as his face. Instead, they'd been false words raising false hopes. Listening to his poetry and song would be unbearable.

Starving would be unbearable. Beatings from Widow Cooper's son would be unbearable.

Emma lifted Angelique's hand and studied the dry tips of her little fingers and the chapped skin upon her downy cheeks. A mother should not put her fears before the health of her babe. She squared her shoulders and looked up at the man who offered her the world, frightening though it might be. "I will weave for you."

Chapter Five

Gilles strode down the keep's high wooden stairs to the bailey. Sourly, he looked around at the bustling activity in the courtyard, fully prepared to find fault with whomever should cross his path. He'd slept poorly, dined on turnips—which he hated—and spent the fine morning closeted with his punctilious cleric in discussion of the millage rates. The business of lord of the manor weighed heavily upon him.

If he closed his eyes, he could almost imagine spring was coming, not winter. The promise of rain filled the air, but the banks of dark clouds were still far off over the bay. A path parted for him as he made his way in the direction of the armory.

She sat on a stool in a patch of sunshine, a wooden device in her hands. His steps slowed. For long moments he watched only her hands as they moved with agile grace. A belt, or perhaps a length of trimming, grew apace on what he determined was a hand loom. The colors draped across her lap and, slipping through her fingers, reminded him of the sea, rippling and undulating as she worked. Occasionally, she lifted her face to the warmth of the sun. He sensed contentment. It showed in the set of her shoulders, the gentle smile she gave to her child who slept in a large basket at her feet, and in the soft humming that drew him near.

But he could not linger, could not indulge this inexplicable whim to pull up a stool by her side and watch her hands more closely. He admitted he wanted to know the touch of her hands. He imagined her hands brought joy.

Shaking off the desire, he forced himself to continue through the crowded bailey to the armory. At the last moment, he could not resist a nod to her as he passed. She stood and dipped into a curtsey. Her smile warmed him and the day no longer seemed wasted.

Moments later, his armorer scratched his head that Lord Gilles had found no fault with his new sword. The master of hawks heaved a sigh of relief that Lord Gilles had not complained at the state of the mews, and Hubert nearly collapsed in shock when the quintain swept him from his horse and Lord Gilles made no caustic remark.

Hours later, a smile still on his face, he called to Roland d'Vare's wife as he crossed the hall on the way to evening chapel. "A word, Mistress Sarah."

Sarah was a tall woman of middle years, handsome and lithe, still capable of commanding a man's attention by her forthright manner and winsome smile. Her dark hair beneath her headcovering might be salted with gray, but more than one youth sighed as she walked by.

"My lord?" she said and waited for him to approach. She admired Lord Gilles because he was not so set on protocol as his father. Never, under Gilles's father, could she have risen to such a position as head of the weavers—a position traditionally held by a man. Nay, Lord Gilles had given her an unusual chance, saved her from endless days sitting with the other women, embroidering and talking inanities. Therein, he'd earned her steadfast loyalty.

"I want to know how the new weaver is settling." Gilles held himself rigid with tension.

She noted the clenched jaw and the jump of a muscle by his eye. Had Emma displeased the new master so soon?

"The new weaver's a conscientious worker, my lord. She has an uncanny knack for the cloth; she's quick, and her patterns are unusual. Her work is unparalleled. She has shown us a new way to tie up the yarns before dyeing that makes its own pattern, resists the dye as it were, then when woven—" Sarah halted. "Forgive me. My tongue runs away with me. She is satisfactory."

"Excellent." He had restrained himself from inquiring about Emma for three days. They had been three days of expectation and tension. The lord of the manor did not visit the weaver's building. That chore fell to his steward, Roland. Emma had not taken her meals in the hall when Gilles was there, so he had not had a glimpse of her since her arrival—until this day, in a ray of sunshine, with the sea rippling through her fingers. "How fares her child?" Gilles hoped he was not further betraying his interest to his friend's wife.

"Oh, Lord Gilles, what a beautiful babe. She is like her name—an angel in every way. She has a sunny disposition and we enjoy her happy company. She does not hinder the work." Sarah finished in a rush. "Please, do not think the child hampers our work."

"Be at ease, Mistress. I have no reservations about the

child," he said. "I wish the new weaver to weave exclusively for me."

"My lord!"

So, 'twas pleasure not displeasure that drove him to inquire. Never had such a directive been given. A holding such as Hawkwatch was filled with hundreds of people. The looms of the village worked as hard as the looms of the castle, and still some cloth must be purchased farther afield to provide for all their needs.

"Mistress?" Gilles did not raise his voice, but the line between his brows grew deeper and his eyes snapped fire. No one questioned the master with impunity.

How could he explain that he wanted no one else to sample the fruit of Emma's labors? That he could not bear it if he saw another's surcoat belted in the colors of the sea?

"As you wish, my lord." Sarah huffed off to the outbuilding in the middle bailey that housed the weavers.

Lord Gilles could not have proclaimed his feelings any louder than if he'd shouted them from the ramparts. So . . . the master was enamored of the new weaver, Sarah thought.

Not such a beautiful woman, save for her eyes and hair, and perhaps her figure. She patted her own still slim hips. She thought it was interesting that Emma did not yet share Lord Gilles's bed but rather had a pallet with her babe in with the spinners, as most of the other weavers were men. This should prove an interesting match to observe.

For a moment, Sarah wondered if Angelique was Lord Gilles's babe, but decided not on the basis of the lord's startling black coloring, which was in such sharp contrast to Angelique's. Lord Gilles could have passed for one of Saladin's men with his sun-darkened skin. He wore his hair overlong for Sarah's taste, but as most men of his years were balding, her own dear Roland included, she did not fault him the small vanity. His black eyes and dark straight brows gave him a fearsome scowl, but she found him more bark than bite.

A sweet, fair child like Angelique was not likely to be produced by such a man. Granted, round apple cheeks did not mean that future high slashing cheekbones and a long haughty nose would not emerge, but she decided that some other man had fathered the babe. It would prove interesting to watch Emma's waistline over the next few months and see if Lord Gilles put his claim on her, Sarah decided, as she hastened to give Emma her orders.

"He said I was to weave only for him?" Emma looked down quickly lest the flush on her face betray her. Her hands stroked the belt she'd just finished. A belt she'd imagined looping about his waist. Her face flamed hot.

How enthralled she'd become!

She must avoid his lordship, avoid such thoughts. They led only to heartache. The distance betwixt lord and weaver was as far as that from earth to moon. She was a servant in his household, nothing more, pledged by loathsome vows to another.

But the thought of moonlight sent her musing on her weaving. She ran a hand along the smooth wood of her hand loom. Her mind conjured the shimmer of moonlight, molten silver, reflecting off a pool in the darkest hours of night. Abruptly, she rose and fled to the dyeing hut to have a special batch of wool prepared—wool for a surcoat.

Angelique's quick tug at her hem caught her attention. Her back ached and her fingers cramped. She had not noticed how much time had flown by as she worked.

79

Ann Lawrence

"Ah, sweet. Are you hungry?" She slipped her shuttle into the threads and hefted the babe to her lap. She kissed the small head as her daughter fed. "I have not forgotten you." When Angelique finished, Emma hastened to the hall, then paused and looked about. "But I have forgotten my place." Quickly, she made her way to a table where several spinners sat in deep conversation. Cradling Angelique in her arms, she ate from the communal platter of venison that fed a dozen workers, from spinners to dairymaids. She tore up soft pieces of bread for Angelique and crumbled cheese. Not once did she look toward the high table. As always, she kept her eyes downcast.

Despite her efforts, however, she could not ignore all the activity in the hall. This evening, men from the Duke of Norfolk's household dined with the company. William regaled them with song. She made every attempt to pretend indifference when the hall fell silent and his rich voice filled the vast space.

Truly the voice of an angel, Emma thought. Each note clear and fine. She looked about. Even the men sat enthralled, watching William. The man on her right leaned across the table and whispered to another. "One can always tell when Sir William's taken a new wench—he composes a new song!" The men laughed loudly over their jest. Emma sat frozen and sick. What simple devices men used to lure a woman. How simple of women to be snared so easily.

William took a long drink from a tankard and waved off calls for him to sing again. When the crowd grew insistent, he strode among the tables and bodily lifted a small man in colorful garb from his seat. Emma watched the ripple of muscles along William's back and arms as he hoisted the man overhead. She shivered and remem-

80

bered the strength of his hands as they'd bitten into her arms and held her immobile.

Cheers rose. William deposited the man on the table before Lord Gilles, and going again amongst the people, grabbed up apples and empty tankards. He tossed them to the man, who deftly snatched them from the air and began to juggle.

Emma did not see the objects whirling over the juggler's head, for he offered her an excuse to stare at the head table and the men who sat there. She examined them all, comparing them to William. They ranged from young to old. Nothing stirred within her as she examined their faces—until she settled her gaze on Lord Gilles. He watched the entertainment with a smile on his face, much like one he'd bestowed on her that very day in the bailey. That simple smile had knotted her stomach and caused heat to flood through her.

She flicked a glance from William to Lord Gilles. William was roving the company, bending and whispering to women as he moved about. Emma saw blushes and hopeful glances. Lord Gilles gave his attention to the juggler. An apple flew from the juggler's control and landed in a pitcher of ale. Ale splashed the face of a short stocky man who rose in a roar to chase the juggler. The juggler nimbly leapt from table to table, avoiding his pursuer. Lord Gilles rose and watched to see who won the race. Wagers flew. Emma found herself caught up in the moment. The juggler disappeared out the door. The company subsided, voices dropped, conversations resumed. When Emma looked at the high table, Lord Gilles was gone. The hall seemed colorless and empty without him.

Cease this senseless dreaming! Can you not see how far you sit from his table? She hoisted Angelique into her

81

arms and forced herself to leave the hall. She must avoid Lord Gilles and his enthralling presence.

Avoiding Lord Gilles should not be difficult. He kept warriors' hours, up at dawn. He did not carouse with the younger knights, but rather retreated to his chamber early of an evening or remained only to play a game of chess with one of his men—most often Mistress Sarah's husband. Lord Gilles did not wander the hall as William Belfour did.

To avoid William Belfour took a much greater effort, but she had swiftly learned that the man was tiresome and predictable. Emma had only to mark which women of the keep were most comely and stay away from their places of work.

It had become her habit to rise at dawn and work first to allow Lord Gilles and his men time to leave the hall before she ventured out. She waited for the sounds of the men's morning work at arms practice, then broke her fast.

'Twas usually only at prayers that she saw Lord Gilles. 'Twas sin she knew to stare at him so, instead of concentrating on her own prayers. Many prayers of thanksgiving had she offered in her few weeks at Lord Gilles's keep. 'Twas a miracle that her life was so blessed. No one scorned her for the child, or not in her presence, anyway. Mistress Sarah was a hard taskmaster, and she brooked no gossip or nastiness among her workers.

As Emma passed through the hall entry, a voice called to her. "Wench." It was an order as well as a greeting.

She turned and put down Angelique, who clung to her skirts and hid her face. Her babe had been fussy and irritable all day. 'Twas time she sought her bed. The short, burly man before her was battle-scarred and bullnecked. He was missing one eye, and the empty socket made Emma's skin crawl. She waited patiently, however, to hear what the man wanted. "Sir?" She recognized him as one of the duke's visiting knights.

"Come." The man crooked a finger and turned abruptly away.

Emma hesitated, but realized that a knight must be obeyed as surely as the lord himself. She lifted Angelique, protesting, to her hip. Her stomach danced. Mayhap he was to take her to Lord Gilles. Her free hand rose to smooth her headcovering and fuss at the wrinkles in her worn gray overgown, aware she looked unfit to stand before Lord Gilles.

She followed the man's swiftly retreating form as fast as she could with Angelique on her hip. The man led the way to a narrow stone staircase that led into the bowels of the keep.

The stair opened to a dark hallway lit only with two rush torches. The smoke stung her eyes. Off the hall were dark alcoves headed by stone arches. The scent of mold and damp pervaded the chilly hallway. At the bottom of the staircase Emma peeked around the corner. She set Angelique's twisting, wriggling form on the floor. The man disappeared into a side alcove, and she followed. The man cuffed Angelique away with one sweep of his arm as he engulfed Emma in a strong embrace.

"Angelique!" she cried, but her words were muffled by the knight's wet mouth. He leaned her back over stacked sacks of grain. His hand groped over her breasts, his fingers pinching, kneading, grasping. She fought, twisted, dislodged her headcovering, flailed her head about. Her eyes searched frantically for Angelique as she clawed at the man's questing hands.

Angelique set off a wailing so pathetic and loud as to wake the dead. Her cries echoed off the dank stone walls. The man bit back his ardor long enough to try to silence

Angelique with a raised boot. Emma took advantage of the lessening of his grip and brought her knee up between his thighs. He roared in pain, and stared at her in disbelief. Emma swept Angelique into her arms and fled. What had she done? This was not Ivo, a village dolt, this was a knight, a duke's man.

Gasping with fright and her rapid pace, Emma burst from the stair, careening into the broad form of William Belfour. He snapped a sharp rebuke at her before he saw clearly who had run into his back. Recognizing Emma, he grabbed her arm and drew her aside.

"Jesu, you are a mess." His hand was huge and his grip strong.

Emma placed a hand to her head. Her headcovering was gone. One of her braids had begun to unravel. She decided to try to enlist his help, although it pained her to do so. "A knight . . . a brute . . . he hurt Angelique," she gasped, stroking a hand over a red welt on Angelique's cheek. "He put his hands on me."

William pulled Emma against a wall and out of view of the company of people lingering after the meal. "Silence the child," he growled. Without thought, Emma did as he directed. She wrapped Angelique tightly in her arms and rocked her and murmured endearments.

Angelique's sobs subsided, and her thumb journeyed to her mouth. She settled.

William raked a hand through his blond hair, then touched the braid that lay across her breast. "Did you invite his advances?"

"Nay! He accosted me! He hurt Angelique."

"It didn't take you long to start lifting your skirts."

Emma's gasp of disbelief turned to a choked-back sob. How dare he insult her so? He, who'd had her virginity, he, the father of her child. "I did naught to tempt him!" she cried.

"Just as you did naught to tempt me?" He reached out, but she jerked back from his hand. "A whore's a whore. The men know you have no protection. They see the babe in your arms, know you have been well bedded. They want a taste. They will take what is offered."

"I offer nothing!" She batted away his hand again.

"Really? You twitch your hips as you go by, you smile sweetly to anyone who greets you. What are the men to think? Complain not of your lot. The men see a new whore—"

"Wife! I am—"

" . . . whore and they all wish to taste her, and many suspect that taste will be sweet." He spoke over her as if her words were mist on the air. "Your status as a free woman will not hold them off for long." William lifted a loose lock of Emma's hair. She snatched it away.

"Where are you off to? Mayhap we could take this opportunity to taste of passion's sweet kiss once more?" William threw back his head and roared with laughter when tears ran down Emma's cheeks. "Weeping? Spare me. You think yourself better than the others who sport a bastard? Think again. You carry your shame in your arms." William chucked Angelique under the chin and turned away, still laughing.

Emma fled into the night. She stumbled on the slick stones and slowed her pace. Clouds blanketed the sky, and all about her was silent and midnight-black. Head down, eyes on her feet, she hastened to the weaving shed, where a dark form appeared suddenly before her. She stifled a scream and clutched her daughter. The apparition became a large man—the last man she wished to see at that moment.

"Mistress Emma." Lord Gilles stood before her. His hair and black mantle made him one with the night.

Emma quickly forced her features under control. She could not let him see her anguish. She dropped a deep curtsey. "Lord Gilles. Forgive me. I did not see you."

Gilles realized he had almost touched the weaver. He glanced about, but only the sentries on the wall stirred. The wind whipped Emma's hair. One of her braids had come loose. A break in the clouds sent a sudden gleam of moonlight into the bailey. Molten gold, he thought. Molten gold flowing over her shoulder. Then he saw the silver gleam of a tear run down her cheek. "What ails you?" he asked, stepping closer to her. Her face was ravaged from weeping. Her hair no longer looked windblown, but disheveled.

"Nothing, my lord. Please. 'Tis cold." She took a step away from him, a step closer to the shadows.

He followed her, unable to ignore the hitch in her voice. "Something has happened. Tell me."

A sudden overwhelming need to lay her cares on him made her open her mouth. But fear stopped her. William's words echoed in her mind. *Whore. Whore. Whore.* Lord Gilles would only believe as William did.

" 'Tis nothing. Nothing." She fled past him.

Gilles stared after her. Her hair streamed, unbound, down one side of her back. In a moment she had disappeared into the spill of light from the weaver's building. He stood rooted to the spot. Anger burned through him. He did not know how he knew it—but he knew someone or something had hurt her badly. The light of the moon disappeared behind a bank of scudding cloud. In a swift turn, he too disappeared into the shadows.

Emma spent the night tossing on her pallet. When she took her next meal, it was suddenly apparent to her that some of the men were watching her. She looked long about the company and saw that most were battle-hardened men. What was in their minds was obvious now.

How had she been so blind? These men had no need of the many knives and daggers that graced their belts if they wished to handle her. They had only to exert their superior male strength and they would have her. She realized that the one-eyed knight would never have approached her if she'd had a man's good name to protect her.

No good man would have her.

There was no Widow Cooper here to defend her. In the long night she had also convinced herself that Lord Gilles would not protect her either. What were her wishes in comparison to that of his men and their needs?

Men took what they wished. Some, like William, might use pretty smiles and false vows to woo a female. Others would do as the one-eyed knight had—use a fist to stun. But when the moment arrived, false words or cruel fists, there'd be naught from the man but rough, hard hands and pain.

Chapter Six

"I seen ye speakin' wiv Sir William." Beatrice, a serving maid, stood by Emma's side at the table and offered her a platter of boiled eggs.

Emma looked up, then hastily captured her daughter's hands, which were taking as many eggs as her fists could hold. "You little swine," she murmured in Angelique's ear. "Aye. I was talking to Sir William."

Beatrice set her heavy platter on the edge of the table. Her simple woolen tunic was taut over full breasts. Her blond hair curled in fine wisps about the edges of her headcloth. "Are ye wantin' 'im?" Her work-roughened hands selected an egg and rolled it to Angelique, who squealed with delight. No longer just something to eat, the egg became a source of amusement.

"Ball," she squealed and quickly rolled it back to Beatrice.

Emma smiled up at the young woman, her cares

momentarily forgotten. "I have no interest in Sir William."

With a nod, Beatrice plucked up another egg, peeled it, and offered it to Angelique. "She's a fetchin' mite, ain't she?"

With a possessive stroke over Angelique's brow, Emma nodded. "Aye. She is everything to me."

Beatrice hefted her platter to move to another table. As if remembering something, she turned back. "Mistress Sarah'll stripe yer hide if ye dally wiv them's as is above ye. Took a birch rod to May fer layin' wiv Sir William just last week."

Emma said nothing. She had no wish to imply that William held any of her interest. May and any other maid of the keep were welcome to the knave, but a part of her wished someone would take a birch rod to him.

"Ye can 'ave them's as is sittin' o'er there." Beatrice thrust her chin in the direction of two stable grooms who were staring at them. "They's poor sport, though. Naught but babes if'n ye ast me, but Mistress Sarah won't begrudge ye the likes o' them."

A shiver coursed down Emma's spine. The grooms had only eating daggers, yet there was no mistaking the same lascivious looks on their faces as she'd noticed on the knights and men-at-arms. Cheeks still downy and bodies unformed into manhood, and yet, she could read the bent of their thoughts as if they'd called across the table and offered her coin for her favors.

A man, Mark Trevalin, came to stand at their side. He was of middling height, barrel-chested, and plain of face. His best feature was his thick brown hair, streaked with gold. "You have duties?" The words, though mildly spoken, were orders. Beatrice rushed off. Mark Trevalin gave

Emma a curt nod, then joined a group of men by the hall entrance.

Emma studied Beatrice's retreating figure as she moved down the long, crowded tables. Why would Beatrice give her such advice? Could it be that Beatrice thought her of easy virtue, just as William had implied?

That afternoon, Emma sought out Sarah.

"Mistress Sarah, I need to speak with you."

"How may I be of service?" Sarah asked. "You're pale, child. Are you ailing?"

Emma shook her head. "I have need to gather some bark for dyeing. May I have your permission to leave the keep for a time?"

Sarah nodded agreement. "The walk will do you good, put some color in your cheeks. Take the boy, Ralph, with you. He'll tend Angelique for you whilst you're gathering."

"Aye, I will take the boy." In fact, she would agree to anything to be away, though lying sat ill with her. Sarah summoned Ralph from the kitchens, and Emma followed him across the hall after she removed her pack from the weavers' building. If anyone inquired, she would say she was gathering. In her pack was her leather purse of trea- sures and the worn hand loom.

Dark eyes tracked her progress across the vast chamber and noted the eyes of many that also were drawn as moths are to a flame. Dark brows drew together in displeasure.

Another set of eyes, the blue of the summer sky, noted her progress and smiled.

Ralph, a gangly youth of two and ten, fell into step with Emma and prattled about the day. Emma knew the boy liked going outside the castle walls and so would not question their destination. He ran in circles about Emma

91

making faces at Angelique and causing her to giggle and hide her face in her mother's neck.

They made their way down the steep hill to the base of the castle wall. Turning east, they walked until they came to Emma's hovel. She halted and looked the boy square in the eyes. "Ralph. You are to return to the keep. I'll be staying here from now on, and if Mistress Sarah asks why, you may tell her it is none of her concern."

Mouth open, showing the gaps in his teeth, Ralph stared at her. He was a simpleminded boy. He shrugged and left Emma alone.

Emma laid Angelique on her pallet and surveyed her surroundings. From humble to shabby they had gone. Someone had stolen the stool she had left behind, so Emma had only her pallet left to her name. She ought to be thankful, she supposed, that the thief had not moved in instead. With a sigh, she sank to the covered bed of straw, and after several moments, allowed her shoulders to slump in despair. To have come so close to comfort and have it snatched away was crushing. But in her heart, Emma knew each day would become a challenge for her virtue, if not from William, then from some other man.

"I said vows! He said vows! I am virtuous!" she said into the silence of her home. "I gave myself for what I thought was love, and I will not be shamed by the outcome. 'Tis William who should hang his head in shame!" Tears rolled down her cheek. Angelique touched her face and frowned. Her little fingers rubbed at the tears. "Nay, child. Do not fret."

But the tears would not abate. They ran in rivulets to stain her mantle and finally she dropped her head to Angelique's shoulder and sobbed. "I gave my virtue to a liar." Poor luck it was that she'd so misjudged the recipient of her gift.

Lord of the Keep

*Who is she that looketh forth as the morning, fair as
the moon, clear as the sun . . .*

The words of the song William had composed for her
ran through her troubled mind. How his words had
touched and beguiled her, drawn her to him.

*Her mouth is most sweet:
yea, she is altogether lovely. This is my beloved.*

How his words had remained with her, taunting her
after his cold, scornful rejection. She could not shake
them off. False words, false heart. Other words also
taunted her, for another reason. The words of her dinner
companions: William composed a song for each new
lover. What a fool she'd been.

But Emma's thoughts were not of William as she rose
and set aside her daughter, ignoring the child's mewling
protests. She pressed her cheek to the rough stone wall of
the hut. Blinking back tears, she placed her palm flat on the
stone as if pressing her hand to feel a heartbeat. Lord Gilles
was in there and she would likely never see him again.

What was the uncanny pull she felt when near him?
How could she explain the attraction she felt? Simple.
The oldest one in the world. Then she shook her head.
Nay. That attraction she had known with William. This
was as different as moonlight from madness, a stunning
blast of something for which she had no name.

Emma forced herself to change the direction of her
thoughts. What mattered was the loss of a steady diet of
nourishing food. Naught else should matter.

But she lost the battle with herself as cold crept under
the door. She forgot her hunger and mourned the loss of
him, for his nearness had nourished her dreams—childish

dreams. She would never again trust in a physical longing. This flutter in her belly, this ache in her loins would not lead her into fancies that had not a chance of fulfillment.

"I have no notion of Lord Gilles's character," she said softly, pushing thoughts of him away. "I know naught of the man. Mayhap he, too, composes false songs and poems for his lovers. I know only that he is not of my world and foolish fancies will only make life more difficult. 'Tis better not to dream." She wiped her face on her mantle and dropped to her knees. She dug a hole in the corner and buried her father's spurs and her mother's cross. With them, she buried her dreams.

"Ralph." Sarah gestured the boy to her. She slid over to allow him to sit by her side at the table. "Where's Mistress Emma? I haven't seen her since she left the keep."

"Mistress Emma told me to tell ye she were stoppin' there . . . in that place . . . by the wall." Ralph stuffed his mouth with a bun topped with sticky honey.

"Stopping? Whatever do you mean?" Sarah cuffed Ralph when he reached for another bun. It was several moments before he was able to speak. His cheeks bulged with dough.

Gulping, he eyed the next bun but decided 'twould be folly to try to reach past Mistress Sarah. "She said 'twas naught of yer concern."

"Not my concern?" Sarah rose and excused herself to those she bumped in her hurry to exit the keep. She drew her shawl about her shoulders to fight the winter chill in the air as she hurried across the middle and lower baileys. At the gate she waited for a team of bullocks to enter before she hurried across. She stood indecisively at the edge of the village. Against the castle wall was all Sarah could remember about Emma's story of her home. It took an hour, but Sarah found Emma.

"Explain yourself." Sarah blocked the doorway, stealing away the meager sunlight.

"There is naught to explain." Emma rose from her loom and clasped her hands calmly before her. She had been prepared for this, but was just surprised it was Mistress Sarah herself who had sought her out.

"Since I will surely have to explain to *him*, I suggest you explain to me. I'll not be going until you do." Sarah stomped to the pallet and sat, her hands clamped on her knees, determination on her face.

Emma sighed. " 'Twas only a matter of time until I would have been ravished by one of the men in the keep." Emma's knuckles turned white as she tightened her fists to calm herself.

"Ravished? Were the men after you already?" Sarah did not sound surprised.

"Aye. What am I to do? I'll not become what they think of me." She wiped at the corner of her eye with the hem of her gown. "I fought off a man, a one-eyed knight, but 'twas only a matter of time. I was . . . afraid."

"One-eyed? Aye, I know him—a careless brute. I understand, dearie." Sarah slapped her knees and rose. "There will be hell to pay." She swept past Emma.

Frantic, Emma flew after the older woman and snatched at the flapping tail of her shawl. "Wait. What do you mean—hell to pay?"

Sarah turned and considered Emma. A cry made both women lift their eyes. A hawk coursed the sky. They watched it float on an eddy of air before it disappeared over the keep's high tower. Sarah broke their contemplation. "Lord Gilles, is what I mean. The man is not to be thwarted." Sarah turned and began the long walk back to the keep.

Emma stared at the castle wall so high overhead.
Thwarted.
Whatever did Sarah mean?

Sarah approached Lord Gilles when his page stepped away to fetch a new pitcher of ale. The two knights on his left were engaged in a heated discussion of the afternoon's hunt. Her husband, on Lord Gilles's right, was sound asleep. She spared Roland an indulgent smile before speaking. "My lord, may I have a word with you?"

Gilles raised an eyebrow and nodded. "Speak." He raised his tankard and took a long swallow of the cold ale.

"For your ears, my lord." Sarah eyed the men at Gilles's side, then jerked her head to the crowd behind her and met his steady gaze.

"Hmm." Gilles rose. After finishing what remained of his ale, he set the tankard on the table and strode from the hall, through the stone arch leading to the chapel. He turned, crossed his arms on his chest, and waited.

"My lord, your new weaver is gone." Sarah cringed as she waited for the explosion.

"Gone?" He spoke mildly, deceptively so. In truth, he could only say the one word. He didn't know what emotion he felt, only knew it was stark and painful.

"Aye. I went to see her because she failed to return from an errand outside the walls. I questioned her, as she seemed determined to settle herself in the village." He felt Sarah's scrutiny, but could do naught but stare. "Emma said she was threatened here. Feared ravishment."

"Ravishment?" Gilles whirled about, turning from Sarah to face the dimly torchlit altar at the fore of the chapel. In truth, ravishment was so close to what he wanted to do that Gilles thought Emma must have read his mind.

"Aye, my lord." Sarah spoke to his back. "From at least one of the duke's men—the one-eyed brute. The cur trapped her in a storeroom below stairs."

"Thank you." Gilles dismissed Sarah with a sweep of his hand. How he wished he'd trusted his instincts when he'd seen Emma in the bailey. Her hair, half unbound, her tears, they should have alerted him to her fear. Instead, he'd allowed himself to focus on his lust, the sensual gleam of her hair. Had the one-eyed knight hurt her?

His thoughts sent him to the bailey, where he scanned the crowd. He did not see the knight among the Duke's men, who were loitering at ease. He called Hubert and told him to find the man.

When the one-eyed man stood before Gilles, he felt satisfaction at the knight's trembling voice and evasive eye.

"My lord? Y-y-you wanted to see me?" he stammered.

"Aye. I have heard you were bothering one of my weavers."

"Her." The man's posture eased. He spit in the rushes.

Gilles stepped forward and grasped the man by the throat, striking with the swiftness of the hawk carved on his chair. "You knave." Gurgling sounds of protest issued from the man as he hung from Gilles's steely grip. "I do not want any woman in my keep to be cornered and pawed by the likes of you, be she serf or highborn. Never do I want a member of my household to walk in fear. Never. You have overstepped the bounds of propriety, and you will take yourself back to the Duke's, from whence you came—now."

Gilles thrust the man away as if he weighed no more than a sack of feathers. The man bounced off the far stone wall and fell to his knees, clutching at his throat and gasping for life-giving air. With legs spread and fists on hips,

Gilles watched the man recover himself. Scrambling to his feet, the knight fled.

That night Gilles paced his chamber, considering the many ways he might somehow entice Emma back to his keep. In truth, he had never been at ease with the seduction of a woman. Crooking a finger usually sufficed. The courting of his wife, a score and more years before, had been done by his father and the king's men, with little care for his wishes and needs—or hers. He combed his fingers through his black hair and summoned his friend Roland.

Roland sat himself down at the table and propped his feet on a stool. Watching him pace, Roland waited patiently to hear whatever Gilles had on his mind.

Gilles halted before his friend. "Since the knight who accosted Emma is gone, think you she might return?"

"Emma? Knight?" Roland peered at Gilles, eyes wide in innocent wonder.

"Do not pretend ignorance. I'm sure Sarah has told you all about the new weaver."

"Aye." Roland placed the tips of his fingers together. "I'm sorry, friend, Sarah doubts your weaver will return. She seemed sure others would be similarly inclined as the duke's man."

Gilles resumed his pacing before the fire. "Others?"

"Mayhap," Roland continued, "if the wench were assured of your 'protection'? Or you could wed the wench." The words hung in the air between them.

Both knew what protection Roland implied. The other Gilles dismissed with a sharp slash of his hand. "Barons do not marry their weavers."

"Aye, tongues would wag if you were to wed Robert of Lincoln, despite his skillful hands and fine cloth."

Gilles grinned, then frowned. "Barons wed for land

98

and power—not to satisfy some basic urge. We jest, but mayhap a leman would not be such an ill-conceived notion."

Roland leered and propped his boots on the table. "I thought you had no use for a leman."

With an answering leer, Gilles shoved Roland's boots to the floor. "A man may have a change of heart."

Moments later, he paced in a turmoil of agitation. For all his outward show of humor, his insides seethed. To have Emma near to him! His footsteps paused at the bedside. He stared at the luxurious furs and linen draperies. His imagination placed her there on the furs, draperies drawn, the scarlet linen aglow around them, lit from the hearth as if on fire, whilst she warmed the inner space with the heat of her body. And she would be very warm. He would see to it. He would warm her with the conflagration of his passion.

A cold thought quenched the embers of his desire. What hope had he of enticing such a young woman when men such as William roamed the hall?

Roland interrupted his thoughts. "If I may suggest, Sarah believes Emma will need to return to her usual method of feeding herself and her babe. She will need to barter her handwork at the market. If you were to seek her there, you would not need to go to her in the village. Sarah thinks it would shame her, should you go there."

Shame. Aye, if he was seen alone with her, word would spread like seed scattered on the wind. It would harm her. But in the marketplace all could mingle and speak without censure.

Roland continued, "Once you have her inside the keep, 'twill be child's play to have her in your bed."

Gilles nodded and dismissed Roland with a vague wave of his hand. The marketplace. How simple. Emma could be back within two days' time.

Ann Lawrence

Gilles stripped off his clothes. He slid between the cool covers and vainly sought the relief of sleep. His fevered mind and fevered body did not relent until the wee hours before dawn.

As if by magic, the morning's cold winds fled. Warm ones replaced them with just enough of a hint of the autumn past to bring the crowds to market. She found a spot where she could set out her work, next to a butcher's stall. Swarms of flies raised by the stink of blood nearly made Emma return home. More time was spent flapping at flies buzzing about Angelique than entertaining offers on her work.

Sarah had left a bundle on Emma's stoop—the belt she'd left behind. With shaking hands and prayers of thanksgiving, Emma had held it to her chest. There had been little to eat since the day she'd left—naught but bread and fresh water. Soon she would need to spend the last of her pennies. Emma's stomach felt squeezed back against her spine. Her breasts felt drained dry. Mayhap from the tension of her life, or mayhap from Angelique's growing diet of other foodstuffs, Emma found her milk supply almost gone. Now that the bountiful food of the keep was gone, she had not the milk to take its place.

She'd soon need to seek Widow Cooper's help to aid Angelique. Her mind shied from thoughts of Widow Cooper's son. To go to the widow would be to admit defeat and seek charity, begging. Emma was not yet ready to beg or wed—or pretend her vows to William did not exist.

If not for Sarah's kindness, Emma would have had nothing to barter at the market. Now she would be able to earn a few coins to keep them in food and warm clothes for the winter. The belt was made of the finest of thread,

100

the best of dyes. She'd chosen them with Lord Gilles in mind; it should fetch a high price. But should she fail to sell it, she would lodge Angelique with Widow Cooper and walk to the nearby port of Lynn. There, heartrending as it might be, she would sell her mother's cross or her father's spurs. Pride truly could not abide in the same house as starvation.

Two women approached—Ivo's wife and another woman she did not know. They fingered Emma's work while gossiping. Neither acknowledged her. They did not buy. Ivo's wife spat near Emma's feet. The other lifted the belt, slipped it through her fingers, then let it drop into the dust. An inauspicious beginning to the market day. With unsteady hands, Emma brushed off the belt and arranged it again to catch the light and show the surface sheen. Two more hours passed.

Emma knew when he entered the row of stalls.

She had no need to actually see him. A tingling in her spine, some change in the air, alerted her. When his shadow fell over her lap, she raised her eyes.

He was resplendent in black and scarlet. His richly embroidered tunic and black mantle suited him well. He wore his mantle thrown back over his shoulders, held in place by a gold pin inset with blue enamel. The hand that caressed the belt she was selling had a vivid scar across four fingers. She wondered if he'd suffered when he received it.

As if reading her mind, he spoke to her. " 'Twas nothing."

Angelique stirred against Emma's breast. She attempted to still her wildly beating heart by stroking the nimbus of curls that rose about her child's head.

Gilles watched Emma's hands, and for a moment it was he she stroked. He could almost feel the warmth of

101

her palm and the press of her fingers on his body. Desire hammered him unmercifully so his words sounded harsh and complaining.

"How may I persuade you to return to your duties?"

"Meaning no disrespect, my lord, but I cannot return."

"Ah, you prefer this," he said with a gesture encompassing the area. His mantle slid over one shoulder. Impatiently, he flung it back.

"To fear and pain, aye, I prefer it." Emma shot to her feet and clasped Angelique tightly to her chest.

"Mistress Sarah told me of your fears. You should have confided in me that night, Emma. I demand total obedience from each person under my care. If you were being accosted by some unworthy, then it was to me you should have come. Why did you run from me, from telling me your troubles?"

She met his eyes. "I am sorry, my lord, but I did not want to make you choose between one of your knights and . . . a weaver. Surely, you would think ill of me." Emma could not say that to accuse a knight might bring the lash. She'd not lived in a cloister. William Belfour, too, was unlikely to earn censure for his behavior toward a mere weaver, so well-favored was he, sitting as he so often did at the high table.

"A cur is a cur. I don't allow the forcing of any woman, no matter how humble her station."

Her voice almost a whisper, Emma tried to make him understand. "There are those who would be most subtle in their pursuit."

"I offer you my protection." He couldn't banter words with her. He had to say what he wanted. She would say aye or nay, but it must be brought to that point—*now.*

"Protection?" Her eyes searched his face. Just the night before he had appeared vividly in her dreams, a dark image jumbled together with hawks soaring into the heavens. She had jolted awake aching with desire. Her thoughts painted a rosy blush on her cheeks.

"Aye. You do understand *protection*, don't you?"

His implacable demeanor and his fierce scowl made Emma feel slightly faint. A nervous sound escaped her throat. His scowl melted into a smile.

"Nay, my lord. I don't think I do."

His smile deepened the lines radiating from his ebony eyes, and she thought of smoothing those lines of care with her fingertips. Then she realized she'd never be in a position to touch this man. Only a light-skirt could touch a lord, and then only at his behest, not hers.

"Then I will explain it to you." Gilles clasped the length of cloth in his hands and sighed. If she refused him, he knew the pain of it would be like that of a suppurating lance wound, unlikely to heal, always weeping. "My protection would mean no man would dare accost you, speak to you with impropriety, touch your hand even, without your permission."

"That is a formidable statement, Lord Gilles." Her voice was a caress of his name. Desire was a tangible web being woven around them. He offered her safety in his lofty world.

"I am a formidable man," he said.

Chapter Seven

The desire to touch him was overwhelming. Emma reached for the belt that lay between them and took it from his hands, brushing against his knuckles. A shiver coursed through her.

"Again, Emma. Do you understand *protection*?"

"I must think first of Angelique," she began.

"The child will be protected as well."

Emma searched his face for guile, for some telltale sign to guide her. He held her gaze and did not look away, nor did he begin to babble reassurances to persuade her— or spout pretty words. He waited in silence. She took a deep breath.

"Mama?" Angelique raised her head. "Hungry!" Her little hands tugged at the front of Emma's mantle.

They were in a world of their own. Time and sound receded to a gentle buzz. Who watched, who spoke, she wouldn't later be able to say. It was as if time stood still for her reply. After Angelique's words, there could be but one answer.

Emma nodded agreement. Her eyes filled with tears. They fell unheeded down her cheeks and dripped on the soft wool of her mantle. Gilles reached out and caught one silver droplet on the edge of his finger. He brought it to his lips, tasted the salt, savored the moment. He had no doubt the tears were from an excess of emotion. He hoped the emotion was joy.

"Forgive me. We are hungry and tired." Emma dashed the tears away with the back of her hand.

Gilles snapped his fingers and his squire appeared as if by magic. "Hubert, escort this woman and her child to the keep. See that Mistress Sarah feeds them both." He swept up the belt and strode away.

Roland looked about the hall to see what had turned his wife's mood sour as poorly made wine. She was stiff and abrupt. He supposed it was the weather. Gloomy and dark, the hall had taken on the dank, wet scent of the rain-swept outdoors.

She shook off his soothing hand. " 'Twas only a matter of time," Sarah muttered to her husband, and nodded in the direction of the lower tables.

He saw William Belfour teasing the new weaver. The weaver, whose name he'd forgotten, was not smiling or enjoying whatever jest so amused Belfour.

"Be she blind or simple?" Roland asked, draining his tankard and wiping his mouth with the back of his hand.

"Humpf. More like the brightest of them all, or the clearest of eye—to give that one the cold shoulder."

"No other wench here would agree with you."

Sarah turned on the bench and contemplated her husband. He, too, was gray now. He was a fine man, firm of limb, strong of wit, and a generous lover. He'd given her three fine sons, sons off fighting with King Richard. She tempered her black mood with a smile, and touched his thigh. "There are many women here who see through that one. They wish to warm his bed anyway." With a sigh, she rose. "I will see to Emma. Lord Gilles would not want her annoyed."

Roland d'Vare watched his wife cross the hall. She went directly to the young people, intent on her task. She did not, therefore, note that Gilles had entered the hall, come from the bailey. He noted Gilles's scowl, noted that the hem of his mantle was thick with mud and stained with wet. Roland rose and headed in his wife's direction. Should there be trouble, he wanted to be there to smooth the rough edges.

"Sir," Sarah said to Belfour. "You take advantage of your position."

"How so, Mistress?" William rested his forearm on his thigh and looked Sarah up and down.

" 'Tis obvious Mistress Emma wishes you to leave her alone."

"Emma?" William turned from Sarah to Emma.

Emma felt the warmth drain from her body. Her hands were icy, her throat dry. Over William's shoulder she saw Lord Gilles approach. William had been describing to her what she must do to get back into his good graces—meet him behind the granary or the dovecote.

She swallowed her fear of him. Lord Gilles had promised her protection, but to need it so soon made her sick with apprehension. *Courage*, she bid herself, *courage*.

William moved his leg an imperceptible inch toward her arm and pressed against her. 'Twas time to put Lord Gilles's promise to the test, when few could hear her words. If William persisted, the time might come when she would need to speak before a larger company. "Aye, William, Mistress Sarah has it aright. I wish that you would be gone."

Gilles wore a fierce scowl. As he passed through the crowded hall, the men and women fell silent. Many had heard the rumors of Lord Gilles's protection of the new weaver, though none were privy to any actual time they spent together. But here was William Belfour with the weaver, a man notorious for taking what he wished. Surely, sparks would fly.

Emma's hands were cold and her throat tight. She had angered William, could see it was so in the tight line of his jaw and the hand he fisted on his bent knee. What if William shamed her before Lord Gilles? What if Lord Gilles did not come to her aid?

"Problems, Mistress Sarah?" Gilles stripped off his gauntlets. There was a pain residing in his belly. It had flamed there when he'd seen William, one powerful thigh so near Emma's face, his boot propped up at her side on the bench. He trusted himself to speak only to Roland's wife.

"Nay, my lord." Sarah met Gilles's eye and smiled a smile that let him know *she* was capable of handling any problems between these two.

"Excellent. William, Roland, come. Gather the men." Gilles strode away.

William stretched out his fingers, gave Emma a baleful stare, and hastened after Gilles, who had returned to the bailey. William had no wish to anger Gilles. He, too, had heard the rumors. As one of Gilles's knights, he had power here at Hawkwatch Keep. He would have less at some other. A dispute over a wench was foolish if it meant being sent to some hellhole, like Seaswept Keep on the godforsaken coast, with its weeping stone walls and unknown steward—Gilles's son, Nicholas d'Argent.

Emma allowed the tension to ooze from her body. Her neck ached. She rubbed it with the tips of her strong weaver's fingers. Lord Gilles had but to raise a brow and all acceded to his wishes. His power was as tangible as a scent in the air. Emma lifted a brow and practiced Lord Gilles's stare on a potboy. The child scurried away. She giggled.

"What amuses you so?" Sarah used the edge of her apron to wipe the spot where William had planted his boot before seating herself.

" 'Tis naught." She watched as men hastened from the hall after Lord Gilles. "What has happened to rouse so many men from the hearth in this beastly storm?" She stood and shook out her skirts; she'd been sitting on them lest they touch William Belfour's muddy boot. She wore a woolen overgown of russet wool. A linen kirtle to match could be seen at hem and neck. They were her first new clothes in three years.

Sarah followed Emma's gaze. "The rain caused a slide. Part of the north wall collapsed. I will see if we may make ourselves useful."

Emma could only stare after Sarah. The north wall. Widow Cooper lived at the north wall. The five grand-children, too. Emma ran from the hall, heedless of the rain, sweeping up her mantle. She jumped puddles on her way to the weaving building where the spinners slept.

"May! Thank God. Please, could you see to Angelique until I return? 'Tis said the north wall is collapsing. I've a friend there. She might need me."

"Aye. I'll be pleased to see to yer babe." May nodded. Wisps of fine brown hair had escaped from her cap. Her

109

gentle doe eyes made her seem as guileless as a child, but Emma knew May was quick as a fox. Emma bussed her child's cheek and dashed off.

The cobblestones in the forecourt were slick with wet and mud. She held her skirts above the mire. Disaster filled the air. Men ran through the gate, pushing her to the side. She became just another person pulled along in a tide of people heading to the north wall.

The sight that met her eye chilled her bones. Rubble, mud, and water took the place of homes and businesses. She stood in stark fear for her friend, her hands clutched in her skirts, the effort to protect her new garments forgotten.

A shout drew her attention, and she saw Lord Gilles, mounted on a black horse, calling orders to other mounted men who circled the rubble. The sight of him made her freeze. He looked magnificent atop a horse that must have stood at least seventeen hands. His harsh features somehow reassured her. He was not a romantic courtier. He was a man to whom the milling people turned for succor. The very breath in her lungs heated.

In the next moment, he leapt from his horse to stay the hand of his squire Hubert, who shifted stone with a long wooden rake. From out of the pile he lifted a muddy bundle. In one smooth motion, he mounted his horse, the bundle close against his chest. The huge horse high-stepped amongst the people to the edge of the crowd. A keening cry rent the air. A woman burst from the mist. She tore at her hair, shrieked, then threw herself on the stones.

The horses shied and pawed at the commotion. Lord Gilles rode straight at her, controlling his horse's agitation. When he reached the woman's side, he spoke sharply, and to Emma's amazement, the woman clutched at his mantle and kissed his hem. Two men-at-arms rushed forward, but Lord Gilles waved them off. Carefully, he leaned down and offered the woman the bundle in his arms.

Emma gasped, for the woman tore open the wrapping and a babe's flailing arms beat the air. The weeping mother clutched again at Lord Gilles's mantle and babbled words of gratitude for the saving of her child. With a brusque wave, Lord Gilles wheeled his mount and edged his way back to the men frantically casting stones aside.

"Sweet God," Emma whispered as their efforts revealed a poor soul; his clothes proclaimed his low station. Lord Gilles dismounted and crouched at the man's side, momentarily going down on one knee and bowing his head. Emma reeled away from the sight of death. She must find Widow Cooper. The muddy bundle could have just as well been one of Widow Cooper's grandchildren.

She searched the crowds who had gathered to help the keep's men shift stone. Slick mud hampered their efforts. Rain pelted their shoulders. Emma ignored the chill drops and moved through the throng, her eyes alert for anyone familiar.

Gilles's stomach lurched as another body was revealed. A woman, full with child, broke from the crowd to fall on her knees at the young man's side. Unlike the mother whose child he'd saved, this woman's sorrow was deathly silent. Gilles placed a gentle hand on her shoulder. "Come," he said, and urged her away from the pitiful sight. He glanced about and saw the captain of his guard, Mark Trevalin. "Take this young woman into your care." Trevalin nodded, wrapped his own mantle about the woman's shoulders, and led her away.

As Gilles turned back to mount his horse and see what

else needed doing, he caught sight of a familiar color bobbing at the edge of the crowd. "Jesu," he swore. He swung into the saddle and nudged his horse through the crowd. "Emma!" he shouted. She whirled about and stared up at him, her face a pale oval in the sodden shadow of her mantle's hood. "What are you doing here?" he roared. "Do you value your life so cheaply?"

She stared up at his angry face. "My friend, my lord. Widow Cooper—"

"Get back to the keep. Now." Mud had dirtied her hem, rain had plastered her hair to her face. At worst she might be caught in a further slide. At best take a chill.

"I cannot!" she cried up at him. She gripped his hand where he held it clenched in a fist on his thigh. "Would you have me abandon a friend?"

He leaned over and swept an arm about her waist. Breathless, she found herself before him in the saddle— held by an iron grasp to an iron chest. Still, she could not let him take her away. She shifted, turned, and raised her eyes to his face.

His glower told her she would not easily persuade him. "I must find my friend. She birthed Angelique, saved me from starvation. Please, my lord, I beg of you, I must find her."

His expression softened. He slid back in his saddle and made more room for her. His hand at her waist eased. "Allow me a moment and I will see to your friend."

Emma scanned the crowd as Lord Gilles maneuvered to a large group of men. Emma stiffened in his arms as William Belfour separated from the crowd to stand at their side. His swift and contemptuous leer swept over her as she sat in Lord Gilles's embrace.

"William. I want every homeless villein taken to the keep, the injured put in the chapel. Have Father Bernard

112

gather as many braziers as he can find to keep them warm. Have the leech see to the injured in the order of the severity of their need, and not by his estimation of the number of pence in their purse. Do you understand?"

"Aye, my lord." William saluted and strode to his men.

Gilles did not wait upon the completion of his orders, but rode back to where he'd lifted Emma from the ground. "How shall we know this widow?" he asked her, his mouth close to her ear. The sharp contrast of the warmth of his breath on her cheek and the wet of his beard raised gooseflesh on her arms and sent a shiver through her.

She felt the press of his body against hers, felt the shift of his thighs and arms as he urged his mount along the perimeter of the disaster. Her tongue seemed clumsy with her words. She gripped his horse's rough mane and attempted composure. "Widow Cooper is most likely issuing her own orders, arms akimbo, my lord." Her voice dropped. "Unless she has been—"

"We will find her." His confidence soothed her.

Emma leaned forward, assured of his hold, and searched the sea of faces. Their search was continually interrupted as men and women snatched at Lord Gilles's mantle, beseeching his attention. He stopped for each and answered calmly, directing them to the keep or the chapel depending upon their need.

"There!" she cried, pointing to a knot of men and women who were shifting the remains of some poor soul's shattered home. "Widow Cooper!" She searched the crowd frantically for the five grandchildren.

The widow paused in her labors and turned, her face fiery red from her exertions. Emma heaved a sigh of relief when she spied the widow's son, moving among those who rendered aid. Huddled nearby, the familiar

113

faces of his children gaped at the rubble like a row of crows on a branch. "Thank God," she said to Lord Gilles. "They're safe."

Gilles stilled his mount as the gelding shifted and danced when Emma leaned over to touch her friend's cheek. He forced his mind from her bottom wriggling against him. He tightening his grip to hold her still as she clasped her friend's hands. A shiver, not brought on by the chill wind, coursed through his body.

"Praise God, yer not part o' this," the widow said, kissing Emma's hand.

Emma felt the heat on her cheeks. What must her friend presume from her position in Lord Gilles's lap? She stammered an excuse for her actions when Lord Gilles cut across her words.

"Have you need of more help, Mistress? Is anyone trapped beneath yon building?" He flexed his fingers about Emma's waist, drawing her tighter against his chest. Heat flashed up her cheeks.

"Nay, my lord, there's naught but a few goats lost here. But we're in need of a few more hands to shift the stone, as these people counted on the goats to see them through the winter. Can't let them rot."

"You shall have what you need."

Emma had but a moment to lift her hand to bid her friend good-bye when Gilles wheeled his mount and made his way back to the crowd who worked at the wall. In moments, he'd commandeered men who were doing naught but gawking at the mountain of rubble. He sent them to aid Widow Cooper, then turned his horse again.

Emma sat in the shelter of his body. Warmth radiated from him. He'd drawn the edge of his mantle over her. Every inch of her body was aware of him, aware, most especially, of the nearness of his hands as he tugged at the reins. He wore no gauntlets. His hands were red from the cold, and she almost gathered them to her to rub them back to warmth. 'Twould be an impertinence . . . nay, a madness.

There was nowhere to put her hands. The most likely place, the horse's mane, had put them in his way as he plied the reins, shifting the horse skillfully through the crowd. She kept them balled in fists instead, or clutched her mantle's edge. But the constant movement of the horse as Lord Gilles rode about, calling orders, directing the workers, made her wobble against him constantly. She wanted to hold onto him, but didn't dare.

Again, he seemed to read her mind. " 'Twould be safer if you held my arm. Should you fall off, you would suffer a grave injury."

Gently, she locked her fingers about his forearm. She felt the strength of him through the wet cloth of his sleeve, and knew immediately that she had not the right to touch him. " 'Twould be safer yet to put me down, my lord."

"Aye," he agreed. Emma wanted to bite her tongue, for he looped his reins in one hand and wrapped his other arm securely about her waist. In a moment, she was sliding back to earth. Her skirts tangled on his boot and she fought them down. "Thank you, my lord, for helping me search for my friend."

Gilles reached out for her hand. Her fingers were cold as they met his. "Go back to the keep and see that Mistress Sarah gives you a warming drink and dry clothes. Tell her that if others have the same need, the chests in Lady Margaret's chamber should at least clothe the females."

Lord Gilles held her hand as if she were a fine lady and he a courtier. She felt breathless and, despite the disaster, she did not want to relinquish her hold. "Rest assured, my lord, I shall do your bidding."

She looked at her hand in his. An urge to bring his fingers to her cheek made her draw back as if a snake had bitten her. Head down, she whirled away. Lifting her skirts, she ran from him, her heart wild in her chest.

Gilles, disconcerted, stared about the hall, which held twice the normal number of folk. Roland joined him. "Quite a spectacle, is it not?"

Gilles nodded, stripped off his sopping wet mantle, and tossed it to Hubert. "I had no idea my wife had such a colorful array of garments." Dotted about the hall from high table to low, women sat in bright silks and woolens. "Well, well," he muttered.

"My Sarah was loath to take the weaver's word that you wanted to rifle Lady Margaret's coffers, but when Sarah saw the pathetic garb of the villeins you sent here with William, she did not really care if you had offered the suggestion or not. You did suggest Lady Margaret's clothing for these unfortunates, did you not?"

Gilles nodded. "Aye. 'Twas done as I directed." He smiled with satisfaction as a yellow gown he had particularly loathed on his wife went by on a wench who most likely sold her favors at the village tavern. "That gown always made my wife look bilious."

Roland snorted. "I hope Lady Margaret does not return to haunt you when she sees who is wearing it. The bodice does strain the—"

"Imagination?" Sarah finished with a cuff to her husband's arm. "You'll keep your eyes in your head."

Roland grinned, hugged her close, and nuzzled the warm skin of her neck. "Aye. I've eyes only for you, my love. Could you not find some filmy silks for yourself?"

"I've no need of silks," Sarah said, sighing and leaning against her husband.

Gilles coughed. Sarah slipped from Roland's arms. She turned her attentions to other matters with a grin. "Hubert has seen to a hot tub in your chamber, my lord."

"My thanks." Gilles bowed, then crossed the hall. He looked neither right nor left. His strength had been tested. Not the strength of his body, but of his spirit. He wanted to hear no more of misery for a few hours. In truth, he had need to cleanse his spirit before cleansing his body.

With that in mind, he made his way to the wall-walk that encircled the high stone keep and connected with another walk running atop the outer defensive walls. The wooden walk was four feet wide. He propped himself on his forearms in a crenel, the gap between two merlons, and stared out to the waters of the bay. The parapet was his favorite spot for thinking through a knotty problem. The sentries did not trespass here when he appeared. They respected his need for solitary silence.

The rain still fell in a light drizzle. Every muscle in his body screamed with fatigue, but he dreaded sleep. He would see the dead in his dreams, he was sure.

He breathed deeply and imagined a hint of lavender on the air. A ghostly flutter of cloth caught his eye—not the sentry. He knew their every step, their hours, their habits. From the dark shadows, a woman appeared. The weaver. A flush of heat crept up his cheeks as he remembered how warm and supple she had felt in his arms. How shameful to have his mind on his cock when so much misery had been all around them.

"Mistress Emma." He said her name softly. He nodded.

"Lord Gilles." She dipped into a low curtsey.

She'd changed into a worn gray woolen gown. It was ill-fitting and frayed at the hem.

Ann Lawrence

"Forgive me for trespassing on your privacy," she said. She made no move toward the arched entrance and the winding stone staircase that led past his chambers to the hall below.

"You do not trespass." He returned to his contemplation of Hawkwatch Bay. He felt rather than saw her move close and stand on tiptoe to look through the neighboring crenel. His thoughts spilled from his lips. "Does not the bay appear as if it were a silver island?"

Her voice was a soft whisper in the night. "Aye."

He imagined her saying aye to him in just such a way when he asked her to come to his bed.

Emma cleared her throat. "My lord?"

He turned and faced her. They were near enough that he could smell the wool of her gown, the harsh soap she'd used to bathe. "Emma?"

"You saved so many this day. Should no one else say it, I must. Thank you."

"I but did my duty." His voice felt rough, raw.

"Nay, you acted from within here." She touched her hand to the center of his chest. "Many would not have cared for some poor serf's death."

A flame of passionate agony burst where her hand lay on his chest. It was all he could do to stand still. They locked eyes.

Emma could not move. What had she done? She had touched him. Yet she could not remove her hand. Her arm trembled. Slowly, Lord Gilles lifted his own hand and covered hers. She felt the hard beat of his heart, felt the warmth of him through the damp wool of his tunic. He pressed her hand against him.

The flickering, smoky light of a nearby torch cast his face in harsh shadow. She knew what character of man he was now. A man who thought of others. A man who com-

118

manded, yet did not crush those beneath him under his boot.

"Do you remember accepting my protection?" Gilles asked her.

"Aye." She nodded. Her mouth dried.

"I want you in my bed."

A cold pain washed through her. *William said much the same. Yesterday. And today.* She jerked her hand from under his. A quick step back and she bumped into the hard stone wall. With trembling fingers, she clutched at the soft wool of her damp skirt. How could she have made such a mistake? Tears rose and blurred him into a dark, formless shape.

The measured cadence of a sentry's boots neared, then turned and moved away. "He will not trespass here," Gilles assured her. She listened to the fading sound of the man's departure. The night became still save for the whistle of the wind and the drip of rain from the roof.

Gilles blocked her flight by stepping in close. He cupped her cold face in his hands. "You are lovely." He rubbed his thumbs over her soft cheeks. "Sweet. Yet loveliness and sweetness I can resist. 'Tis something else you have, some spell you've woven about me that makes me want you." He released her and turned away. How could he possibly tell her how drawn he was, how captivated? "Nay," he said quietly, almost to himself. "Nay, it makes me need you."

Emma stood as if bolted to the wooden walk. Nothing lay between her and the archway to the hall, but she could not move. Of all the reasons he might have offered, need she could not have guessed. He appeared to be a man who had everything. Mayhap his words were ones of calculation, as William's had been. Before she left, she must make him understand. Just in case. Just in case it was

119

need that had made him speak. "My lord, I believe I have misunderstood your protection. I paid my sixpence fine. It makes us even. My crime is paid for. Do not seek to enter my name in your rolls again."

Gilles jerked around at her words. "Is that what you think? I want to shame you? I want to honor you."

She shook her head slowly. A pain pounded in her temples. "There is no honor in what you offer. If my father and mother lived, I would feel no pride in my position. You see, I said vows I thought were forever, so there is no role I can play here save mistress. It's a fool's role."

He had forgotten her background. "I meant no insult. On my honor, on my good name, I had no intention to sully yours." They stood there in silence for a moment. Then her words penetrated his utter disappointment. "Vows? What vows did you say?"

She bent her head and folded her hands, yet he imagined the flush on her cheeks. "I offered myself once, in exchange of a promise of marriage, not, I regret, before others or a priest. Needless to say, the father of my child now denies his vows, denies his daughter." Her chin came up, her eyes met his. "See, my lord. I have already played the fool's game. And though he may deny his words, I said mine. And meant them. To say anything else makes of my daughter a bastard. Pray, my lord, let us forget what has happened between us."

She turned and fled.

Gilles cursed himself for a clumsy fool. He'd botched the offer, insulted her. He'd held her in his arms, touched the silk of her cheek, breathed in her womanly scent. Madness would claim him if he did not have her.

The wind rose. It carried the salt scent of the sea. It neither soothed nor cleansed. Nay, it swirled about him as his passions and disappointment swirled through his mind.

He understood all about making a child a bastard.

Vows. Bloody vows. Pledged for eternity—to another.

Emma watched Angelique from the corner of her eye as she worked at a loom in the far corner of the room. The men had accepted the child. She tumbled in and out of a basket of yarn. Emma's back ached. She worked from dawn to darkness and fell into a troubled sleep each night. Lord Gilles visited her dreams. She dreamt she could feel the heat of his skin, the touch of his hands. There was no peace. She wanted him as much as he wanted her. Time had eased nothing, in fact, had made it worse. Each day strengthened her conviction that he was a good man, one who cared for those beneath him.

"Sarah," she asked her friend one day, "what think the people of the keep of Beatrice?"

"Cock-struck. She's little on her mind save what's between a man's thighs. Poor Trevalin—and Hubert—they pant after her but haven't enough between them to hold her attention." She held up her fingers spaced a few inches apart and laughed.

Emma nodded. Cock-struck. Was that what she'd be called if she gave in to temptation?

"Why do you ask?" Sarah swept Angelique from the wool pile and dandled her on her knee.

"A woman has no respect if she lies with a man out of wedlock."

" 'Tis more like she has no respect for herself." Sarah began to tickle Angelique. The child's squeals and shrieks drew all the other weavers' attention and allowed Emma a moment of red-faced shame.

121

Sarah brought Angelique close. She went down on one knee at Emma's side. Emma ignored her and threw her shuttle as if naught else concerned her.

"Forgive me, Emma. I did not think when I spoke just then."

Emma's hand trembled. "No need to apologize for truth."

"Stop." Sarah captured Emma's hand. "I've insulted you. Please, forgive me."

Emma shook her off. She retrieved her shuttle and set to work. The words her friend had spoken merely reinforced her own conviction that to give in to her desires for the lord of the keep was folly. She had made her vows.

Desire him she might, have him, she could not.

Chapter Eight

To shake off his dire mood, Gilles threw himself into the restoration of his castle wall. For the next few weeks, he labored alongside his men, and drove them and himself to exhaustion. Each night, when he returned spent and the younger men rallied and turned to wenching or dice, he was reminded most sorely of his age. His rewards were few, physical or mental. At the end of one particularly fruitless day of labor, he entered his chamber, wet and filthy.

He turned on Roland, who'd followed him there. "This damnable sandy soil! It will not surprise me should we wake on the morrow to find we've sunk into the sea itself. Are we built on a bed of quicksand? And why is *this* winter so capricious? Yesterday bitter cold, today as warm as spring."

"Have the men determined what caused this latest slide?" Roland asked, settling himself at Gilles's table.

"Aye. 'Twas merely shoddy work done decades ago. Poor excavation, impatient building. 'Tis a bloody waste and naught to be done about it. God's holy blood, when will this damnable rain end?" Gilles stripped off his sopping wet clothes. He tested the water of the tub that stood steaming by the hearth, then sank into its soothing depths. He closed his eyes on the memory of the flattened skull he'd seen when he helped lift some fallen rocks. As several weeks had passed since the man's death, there was no blood to be seen, but the sharp shards of bone had turned his stomach. The youth of the dead man saddened his heart.

"Why, Roland, is one man chosen and another passed over?" He did not wait for his friend's reply. "Like myself? I stand at the end of life's road burying dead men who should have one foot at the start."

"I have no answer, my friend."

When Gilles heard Hubert gathering the filthy clothes, he opened his eyes. "Bring me plain bread and some of that Rhenish wine." Hubert hurried to his duties, and Gilles scrubbed his hair and body of the mud and memories. When he had rinsed clean, he turned to look at his friend. "You are not here to scrub my back. What do you want?"

Roland d'Vare rose and strode to the hearth. He traced the painted designs that bordered the chimneypiece with his fingertips. "My Sarah plagues me. I fear for my manhood should I try to bed her in her present mood."

Gilles grinned up at his friend. Roland and he were friends from childhood, when Roland had been a page to Gilles's father. "What ails the termagant now? She seemed amiable enough this morning." Gilles closed his eyes and rested his head back on the tub edge.

"William Belfour." Roland had no need to say much

more. "He oversteps himself. He is causing a furor among the spinners and weavers."

"Weavers!" Gilles sat up. "How so?"

"Constantly about. Pestering one and all. Nearly had my Sarah spitting blood."

"Jesu." Gilles surged from the tub.

"You'll have need of your skin on the morrow," Roland remarked as he watched Gilles dry himself.

"Speak plainly. I am sure Sarah can handle William's arrogance. She certainly handles mine!" Gilles swept up a flowing robe from the bed. The embroidery that edged the sleeves and front was as black as the silk it graced. It had been a gift from old King Henry. Roland jested often that it made Gilles look like the very devil himself.

He tied the robe closed with the blue-green cloth belt made by Emma's hand, then flung himself into a chair by the hearth. The contrast of the cold silk and the searing heat of the fire made him shiver. He idly stroked the belt.

"Sarah would have me speak plainly. You may hide your interest from others, but not from us." Roland drew a second chair to the hearth. "Claim the wench before William does."

The two men stared at each other. Gilles did not need to hear more. "I see." Gilles stretched his feet closer to the heat of the flames, rested his elbows on the wide oak arms of his chair, and steepled his fingers. "So . . . William plays his usual games of seduction."

"Aye, 'tis a shame you may not speak more plainly to William," Roland said into the silence.

"Nay." Gilles leapt to his feet. "Spare me the old arguments."

"If William knew he was your bastard, he would be less likely to trespass where your interests lie."

Gilles paced before the fire in agitated silence.

Roland's words simmered and steeped in his mind. Finally, he halted. Legs spread, arms crossed on his chest, he faced his friend. "I will speak to William as lord to vassal and he will listen and obey."

"If you say so." Roland looked skeptical and sighed.

"Jesu. I have kept his parentage from him for these twenty-odd years. I'll not speak now. He will have coin enough when his mother dies. I settled a fortune on her to take herself from this keep and never return."

"Aye, she could not help but kiss your hem when she saw what a few times in the hayloft had earned her."

"Damnation, Roland, I could not shame my wife. What a callow youth I was to bed the wench when Margaret was swollen with child. Jesu, Nicholas was but six months old when William was born. I did what I thought was best."

"Don't flail yourself so. William's mother was beyond beautiful, and Margaret stirred your lust no more as a virgin bride than when she was great with child. No one would blame you for taking your pleasure with a beauty such as Alice Belfour."

"*I blame me.* I've been ensnared with William's mother in one way or another since first she lifted her skirts. I've provided well for her, found her a worthy husband, and truthfully, who's to say that William is even mine? Yet I took her word for it at the time. He has not the look of me, but it matters not.

"We have this same discussion once a year. I will not change my mind. William's mother agreed to her silence, and I have agreed to her keep. I have fostered William, made a knight of him, trained him well. Spared him bastardy. *It is enough.*"

They fell silent as Hubert entered and set a tray of bread and wine on the table.

"We have wandered far from our path," Roland said when the youth had gone. He poured wine for himself and Gilles. "Sarah thinks William will soon tire of May. Should he turn to Emma . . . well, the maid has not the nature of a leman. Marry the wench."

"Again, I have no wish to wed." Gilles stared down his friend.

Roland sipped his wine and smiled.

"Marry. *Mon Dieu.* I've neither the inclination nor the need to wed. Especially a woman half my age. And what has she to increase my wealth or power? What could she bring me? Her spindle?"

"And what of love?" Roland asked.

"Love is a jongleur's game. We speak here of lust, nothing else." Gilles could not tell Roland that Emma considered herself pledged, out of reach. He personally thought little of words spoken in bed; they meant only that the heat of the moment had addled one's brain, but Emma might take some time to come to that same conclusion. She was very young, her abandonment new— and there would always be the child who would be naught but a bastard if Emma denied her vows.

A thought, more painful than any yet considered, swept through him—mayhap Emma still loved the man who denied her. Nay, she had stated to him she no longer believed in love. But what woman did not believe in love?

"A woman that young will find an equally young lover if you don't take a step to prevent it, Gilles. She may seem uncommonly innocent, and more gently born than her circumstances, yet Sarah thinks—"

"Enough." Gilles thumped his fist on the armrest. Innocent and possibly still in love, and yet . . . alone.

It was Emma's gentle and ladylike manner that kept

127

him from speaking to her—and her youth. How young she had looked as she'd spoken of her vows. Too young to know that little said in passion lasted beyond the spasms of physical satiation.

Yet, here he was, lying awake each night, thinking of her like some besotted page. He conjured her face, the sound of her voice. He imagined he could scent her, taste her. The last few weeks had been torture.

"I'll tell Sarah I did my best." Roland sighed. He rose and drained his cup. "She'll plague me to death one day."

"Roland," Gilles said. Roland stopped at the door, his hand on the latch. "I *will* claim Emma. She will come to me—vows or not."

When Roland was gone, Gilles began to pace. He was a turmoil of anxiety within. For all his commanding words, he did not know how to approach Emma after their last conversation.

Roland's remarks about William had touched a raw nerve. How could he expect Emma to resist a man such as William? No woman whom William decided to pursue, be she highborn or low, resisted him for very long. He must assume William visited the weavers for May— whose thighs his son had ridden a score of times.

Flinging back the door to his chamber, Gilles sought the wall-walk. He must make his claim on Emma before William's attentions to May began to wane.

The rain had stopped, though the wind still whined wildly around the stones. He barely heeded the cold, slick wood beneath his bare feet as he turned his face to the wind, breathed in the scent of damp, mossy stone, and wished fervently for what he could not have—that she would come to him.

For he could not go to her.

* * *

Emma set her hand loom on the table and lifted Angelique from the basket at her feet. She walked slowly to the long room housing the spinners. There, she moved quietly to the last pallet and the woman who sat there cross-legged, mending a worn shift.

"May, would you consent to watch Angelique? I'd like to see if I might be useful in the hall. I cannot sleep."

"Oh, aye, but this is becoming a habit. You will become ill if you don't have some rest." May tucked the sleeping babe against her, smoothed her curly hair, and looked up at Emma. "Go now. She will be safe here with me—as long as need be."

Emma thanked her and left her child in May's capable arms. Bleakly, she realized that since her milk had failed, Angelique seemed just as content with May, who played and jested, as with her mother, who toiled every hour of every day. She worked to fight temptation.

Her heart beat in her throat. She did not look to the left or right as she climbed the steep stairs to the hall door. The sentry there opened for her without challenge.

Restless, Emma wandered the hall, stepping quietly by the men and women wrapped in blankets and sleeping on rows of pallets. A small boy she recognized from the village caught her eye, a boy whose parents had died the previous spring and who Emma suspected existed through thievery. He crouched by a knot of men who sat near the fire, talking softly among themselves.

"Robert?" The boy turned and stared up at her. He had deep brown eyes that were dark holes in his thin, nearly starved looking face. "Come, find a pallet. Rest."

He ignored her, flapping a hand at her as if she were a burdensome fly, then turned once more to the men. A burning look of concentration was on his face. She dropped at his side and followed his gaze. A massive man

129

with arms like tree trunks was holding forth on some matter. The armorer—Big Robbie. "He is a kindly man," she whispered to the boy.

"Who cares of kindness? He makes the best swords in all of Christendom." The boy duckwalked a bit closer to the group.

Emma smiled. "In all of Christendom! Well, well." With a smile, she rose and shook out her skirts. The boy barely subsisted in the village. How little of joy must he have in his life. She would not take this small time of hero worship from him. Thoughts of another man, another who could be called heroic, entered her mind.

As she moved about the hall, she realized there was little to do save join the beggarly eavesdropper. The fatigue of the busy weeks had taken its toll on young and old. Yet she could not return to her bed. Her eyes searched feverishly for the sight of him. He was not in the hall.

She paced up and down the aisle of the chapel. Finally, she found herself at the foot of the stone stairway to the castle tower.

He slept above. He was from another world. He wanted a leman. He needed her. Whenever their eyes met, she saw it there, as tangible as the need she felt within herself.

Inexorably drawn, her mind in a turmoil, Emma mounted the stairs. Her heart warred with good sense. She passed his chamber door on soft footsteps, lest she disturb him, and continued on to the arched opening of the wall-walk to seek the night air and its cleansing peace. How could she banish this wild ache she felt for him?

He merged with the black night, but she instantly knew he was there. Had she known all along? Had some intangible thread between them brought her here to this place at just this moment?

Even if she had wished it, she could not have stilled her progress toward where he stood. His hair lifted and blew about his shoulders like part of the dark night as his robe billowed and swirled about his body. Emma halted beside him.

Gilles turned and saw her. His chest felt suddenly tight. A need for her burned low in his belly. He raked his hair back from his face with his hands, then extended them to her.

Her hands were very strong, and he measured their strength as she entwined her fingers silently with his. Staring at her, oblivious to the whip of the wind or the beads of moisture that collected on his skin from the light mist, he drew her hands to his mouth and caressed her palms with his lips, breathing his warmth on her. He stepped closer and watched her as he gently held her fingers to his mouth. All the words he could not speak crowded in his throat.

It was she who broke the silence. "I tried to stay away."

Her words were whispered. Sorrowful. They raised an ache in his heart. He understood. He, too, had tried to put her from his mind. "You will never be sorry." He kissed the backs of her hands, first the right, then the left.

Slowly, she turned hers, covering his in turn, and traced the scar across his fingers. She visited the pads of calluses on his palms from years of wielding a sword. He lifted her hands and placed them on the edges of his robe. He felt the heat of her fingertips as she discovered the intricate stitches that edged the silk. His heart pounded like a warhorse racing to battle. He drew the edges open wider, bared his chest, placed her hands on his skin. When her fingers moved to explore the shape of him just as she had traced the embroidery, the pleasure of simple arousal gave way to a fiery need. A look of innocent wonder crossed her face.

His eyes never left her as he watched her expressive face—so sweet, so gentle. Her hands spread over the shape of him, sought and found his tight nipples in the hair on his chest. A groan escaped him when she used the pads of her thumbs to stroke him in gentle circles.

His nipples were on fire, the pleasure bordering on pain. He encircled her wrists, held her loosely, and guided her hands downward, then abruptly released her before he made a mistake and took her beyond where she wished to go on her own.

Emma could barely breathe. She raised her eyes to his black ones, the same black ones that had beguiled and taken possession of her soul—drawn her to him with an inevitability she could no longer fight. She read the need in his eyes.

The wind blew his hair and hers, mixing the gold with the black, entwining the strands like lovers embracing. Her hands, with a will of their own, went to the belt of his robe, the one she had made in the colors of the sea.

"I could not let another have it," he said as she touched the design on the belt with her fingertips.

He guided her hands to the knot. Together, her fingers trembling beneath his, they loosed the knot. He let her hands go.

"I made it for you," she whispered.

She set him free.

The wind took the edges of the fine silk and blew it back from his body like the huge wings of a hawk.

Stunned at the madness that suddenly swept through her, she gripped the belt to anchor herself. He was naked to her eyes. Her first glimpse of a man fully naked. She drank in the look of him, like a pagan god, strongly muscled, black hair dark on his chest and thighs. His legs were spread and he stood braced against the elements, exposed to whatever would come.

She could have stared at him forever. Despite the chill wind, her cheeks burned at the thoughts and desires that swirled through her. She wanted to lay her hands on him, lay her mouth on him, tell him every thought that was within her. She stood in silence, clutching the belt.

Gilles had never felt so naked—or so gloriously alive and free. He relished the feel of the mist beading on the hair of his body, relished the way she stroked and caressed him with her eyes. 'Twas a powerful thing, her looking—a looking that touched him everywhere as tangibly as the silk swept and flew about his sides.

Every fiber of his body had strung itself taut from the first moment when he'd held her in his arms. She was the weaver that could make whole cloth of his desires. He wanted her to touch him and somehow make real what had hitherto been but a wild wish in his imagination.

He took her hand and pulled the belt from her fist. He pressed her hand to his lips, then with jerky motions, clumsy in his need, he pressed her hand to his chest. "You are mine," he whispered, his voice hoarse.

"Aye." Her hand spread to cover his heart.

How his heart pounded against her palm. How her own heart's beat rose to meet his. Soon their hearts beat as one rhythm, hard and fast, inflamed and urgent.

He could not bear it, closed his eyes, and lifted his arms—braced his hands between the stone walls to his right and left. He could not look at her . . . not when she used the misty beads of moisture gathered on his skin to slick her way along the ridges and valleys of his chest . . . not when she pushed the silk from his shoulders to savor the warrior strength that lay in wait in the stretched muscles and taut tendons . . . not when she swept her wet fingers over his nipples to tease his heart's beat from rapid to racing.

Nay. He could not look at her. He would ravish her, he was sure, if he saw his own stark passion mirrored in her eyes.

Her heartbeat became frantic with his. A quick, intense twist of sensation pounded in her loins. An answering quiver passed along the muscles of his belly. Her hands sought lower and closer to intimacy.

Her journey of exploration visited every ridge, every hollow, every hard surface of him. She learned him from shoulder to thigh, finally spreading her hands on his hips, so close to his manhood, that thrust like forged steel from the black hair of his groin. He groaned and she looked at his face. His head was thrown back, the tendons of his throat stretched.

Then his robe lifted and wrapped about her legs and his, caressed her thighs and calves like a hand, invited her to come closer.

And she did.

She used her fingers to explore the length of him, explore the hard heat of him. He clasped his hands over hers and thrust into their warmth. He was on the edge of madness.

"Your skin is like precious silk, my lord, silk over fire." As she spoke, she learned every heated inch of him.

He felt like a green squire with his first maid. Out of control, frantic. He finally opened his eyes, met hers, and saw what he wanted and needed desperately to see. He breathed slowly, deeply, trying to regain his wits.

"Emma." His voice was rough on her name. The wind whipped his hair and his robe until they stung—a counterpoint to the pleasure of her hands.

"Gilles," she answered him. Then there were no words. Their mouths touched in a wet whisper of warmth. She tasted him—a first taste of restraint breaking from its reins.

She tasted him and wanted more.

He tasted innocence—sweet, untried innocence.

Their joy in each other tangled their tongues and captured their breath. His hands snatched hers from his manhood as his every desire poured from him like a molten, burning stream of liquid pearls, poured out in pulses that tore at his insides.

She moaned and shuddered in response to his release. Her nails dug into his palms. He reveled in his release, her response, their heated passion.

He wrapped his arms about her and embraced the feel of her body pressed to his. He took her lips more forcefully, claiming ownership. When they pulled apart, their breathing was ragged and frantic. He had never before been so spellbound, so enthralled by the caress of a hand or the touch of a woman.

"You will be with no other. *Ever.*" He said the words. He still stood exposed and naked, the wind still blowing his hair and robe wildly about him. His words were a command.

She wanted no other.

"And you—you will be with no other—*ever.*" It was audacious, a woman commanding a man, a man answerable only to the king.

"So be it," he said.

"So be it, my lord," she returned.

Chapter Nine

When he extended his arms, she fairly leapt into them. He wrapped his robe about them both and hugged her to his heart.

Had he ever felt a joy such as he felt at that moment? *Never.*

He whispered against her temple. "Forgive me. I took all tonight, gave nothing."

"You gave me yourself, my lord. What more could I desire?" She locked her arms around his waist and clung to him.

Large, cold drops of rain struck his shoulders, but he was loath to relinquish his hold on her. When she laughed up at him, pulling on him, he grinned back and let himself be drawn through the stone arch to the shelter of the staircase.

Together, arms about each other's waists, they stumbled to his chamber. He felt drunk, drunk on her scent and the feel of her body pressed to his. Laughing, they fell side by side on his bed. Then a laden silence fell over them. When she bit her lip and looked away, Gilles leaned over her.

With a gentleness he rarely showed anyone, he grasped her chin and turned her face to his. "I will not hurt you."

Her eyes widened. "I do not fear you," she said softly and touched his hand; the touch became a caress.

"Then what is it?" he asked.

"My heart says to yield you everything; my mind tells me I will be forever labeled . . . fallen."

Blood throbbed in a vein in his temple. "You are mine. Should any man or woman speak one word against you, I shall flay the skin from their back! Do you understand? You are mine." His fingers gripped her chin fiercely.

For a wild moment, she thought to protest. He didn't understand. Unacknowledged though they might be, she was breaking her vows, denying the promises she'd made.

Her eyes searched his face. The shape of his bones, his long nose, his fine straight brows told her he had generations of ancestors of quality behind him. He had not one coarse feature, one flaw. Even his teeth were straight and white. Her gaze flickered away. One did not propose vows to a lord when his ancestors had come with Duke William and conquered hers. She swallowed hard.

He pulled her tightly against him. "You are mine." He kissed her gently. The taste of him, the press of his body on hers shredded her thoughts. Her utter fascination with him allowed her fears to scatter like chaff on the wind.

He did not do as William had, toss up her skirt and shove her thighs apart. No, he skimmed his fingers along her throat, gentling her, soothing her agitation, murmuring reassurances. He made no move to bare her skin. As their mouths feasted on each other, his hand journeyed over her as calming as if he were settling a skittish mare.

They lay side by side for what seemed hours to Emma, slowly bringing their bodies together until every inch touched—and every fear dissolved to nothing.

Soon, she could not bear even the separation of their clothing. Her hips arched against him, her arms locked urgently about his neck. His robe lay open between them. Everywhere his hands or mouth touched, she burned with frenzied need.

Finally, he rose on one elbow and lifted a heavy curl of her hair to his lips. "I wish to touch you as you touched me."

Although the many beeswax candles in the chamber would expose her to him, Emma slipped from the bed and dropped her clothing in a pool at her feet. The chill in the air tightened her nipples, and for a moment she felt exposed and frightened.

She hesitated. To touch was to go forward, to be unable to return to what was before. Nothing would be the same. Ever.

She had already touched.

When her hands crept to cover herself, Gilles came off the bed and wrapped his arms around her, drawing the edges of his robe about them until they were both enclosed in the soft silk. He held her still against him, let her feel his desire. "Don't be afraid," he whispered against her brow.

He felt her body slowly relax. He sheltered her, tried to calm her fears. Her hands fell away. With words congealed in his throat at the wonder of her, he lifted her into his arms and placed her on the bed. He discarded his robe and came over her. Every inch of her skin glowed in the candlelight. He ached to be in her immediately, but did not want the moment to end. Never had he wished to linger—until now, until this woman.

Never had he been with a woman who was so innocent. Her kisses were unschooled, and despite the way she had touched him, he knew instinctively that she had been exploring a man for the first time.

He wondered if she'd woven her tale of wedding vows to spare her child bastardy and herself the need to admit to abuse. The thought made him even more gentle. He whispered the warmth of his breath on her shoulder, and skimmed his fingertips over her soft skin for many long moments.

Her skin flushed at his touch, her breath quickened against his throat. Slowly, he ran his hand over her until he came to where he wanted to be. When he touched her, she moaned and arched to him. The way was well prepared; she was soft and ready. Her hands urged him on; wordless sounds came from her throat. He joined his mouth to hers as he joined his body.

All doubts fled Emma's mind. The touch of him, his scent, the feel of him filling her made her embrace him fiercely, her arms locked about his neck. She gave herself to his movement, met his rhythm. Sensations swirled madly through her. His movements escalated, swept her along. Beneath her fingers, the muscles of his back and buttocks tensed, bunched, arched. A final time he thrust into her, gave himself to her.

Every touch of his skin to hers, every sweep of his tongue in her mouth made her wish to scream. In an explosion of undiluted sensation her body shuddered fast upon his release. Her thighs trembled. In frantic motion, she heaved against him again and again and again. She moaned his name, her fingers scraped helplessly along his back as she collapsed.

They panted in each other's arms. Emma's shock held her immobile beneath his body. This joining had been as different from her one time with William Belfour as silk thread from coarse wool. Her legs trembled from her release. Her mind trembled from the knowledge of how this man had cherished her.

Gilles gathered her even closer and used his palm to soothe the jumping muscles in her thighs. He whispered a kiss on her brow. "Stay with me the night. Lie here by my side."

"Nay." She struggled from his embrace. Thoughts of where she should be, what others might think, flooded in. She snatched a pillow and held it tightly before her breasts. "I must return to my pallet. I have Angelique to see to." She evaded his hand and leapt from the bed. Her hands shook as she hastily dressed. She felt his seed on her thighs.

Gilles sat up in the pillows at the head of the bed. His body ached to have her back in his arms, but the hectic flush on her face told him he needed to move slowly with her. "I want you by my side. I will have Sarah find a nurse for Angelique, so you may attend me without fear for her."

"My lord . . . please. Wh-what will Sarah think—" Emma stumbled over her words. She wrung her hands.

She touched his heart. "Aye. I understand." He thought a moment. "Seek a nurse yourself. Come when you are able. But please . . . come." She smiled and a shaft of pure desire plunged through his body. "I want you," he said, "but willingly, not in shame at what we will do here."

Emma approached him warily and put out a hand to

141

him. "I have but one experience with a man to judge what happened here, my lord. I found ecstasy with you. I cannot find shame in what we did." She bit her lip. "Others, my lord, they may gossip—"

He entwined his fingers in hers. "I want only your comfort. Do nothing that makes you uneasy."

Her fingers gripped his. "I will come as soon as possible."

Relief broke on the hard edge of his desire.

"I just do not know the way of it"—she swept a look about the curtained bed—"the way of lovers."

He kissed her fingers. "Emma. I must have you near."

And that was that. It took but a sennight for her desire for him to outweigh the nagging doubts about becoming his lover.

Emma's meager belongings were moved to a brass-strapped chest beside the bed with the sky-blue draperies, two rounds up the keep's tower from Gilles. At the very bottom of the chest she hid her precious leather pouch. Straightening her two gowns and her one shift, Emma marveled that her life should be so changed. Carefully, she lifted Angelique from where she slept on the linen-draped bed, cradled her in her arms, and mused on her good fortune.

The warming fire was a luxury she'd thought never to have again. For the last two years, she'd had naught to warm her child but coals in a brazier, or wood scraps. Truly, the only roaring fires she'd encountered at Hawkwatch were in Lord Gilles's hall, and craftsmen and women certainly did not sit so high at the table as to feel its heat. Granted the hall was quite comfortable, but Emma liked knowing there was no end to warmth and its accompanying luxuries for her child.

Her fingers stroked gently through the silk of

Angelique's hair. "You'll not have chilblains this winter, nor cracked lips," she whispered. "I'll not need to use precious fuel to thaw rainwater to make the thinnest of pottage. In fact"—she smiled—"we've no need to dine on pottage ever again." Angelique stretched and yawned, opened her eyes, and thrust her thumb into her mouth.

Emma tickled her stomach. "Good heavens, this belly's quite full, my little lady." Then she frowned. *Heaven.* She'd made vows to heaven—vows scorned by William. Would she roast in hell for putting them aside and seeking Lord Gilles's bed?

She shook her head and hugged her child close. Tears pricked her eyes.

How could such ecstasy be sinful? How could such caring in a man's eyes be wrong?

Her own hands caught her eye. Weaver's hands. Callused, nails worn low. Not the soft hands of a lady. How long would she have with Lord Gilles before a woman more gently reared caught his fancy?

She had become Lord Gilles's leman. The word frightened her, but having known his touch, been enfolded in his embrace, she feared the loss of him more.

She could be nothing more to him than a mistress. Her life was bound to William—unto death. To declaim their vows would make her child a bastard. To say aloud what she had done would be to shame her mother's memory. Had not her mother walked into the North Sea rather than become Simon's leman. She soothed her conscience with the fact that if she pleased Lord Gilles, Angelique would live past three summers. She touched her fingers to her breast, a breast that no longer yielded milk. There was healthful food and goat's milk to take its place here in his keep. Better Angelique's mother be called wanton than the child starve.

She would not regret her decision. In truth, how could she have resisted him? Her head bowed. Tears welled. Mayhap he would love her enough to keep her by his side—at least until Angelique grew straight and strong.

"I must do this. It is best for you, my child. You are all I care about. I will stay here as long as you are cared for."

Gilles stepped quickly from the doorway. He'd come in a rush when Sarah had informed him Emma no longer slept with the spinners. But her words cut through him like the icy wind that harrowed the land.

She came to him for the child.

Rain splashed and streamed against the stones of her narrow windows. The shutters rattled and banged loosely in their frames.

Sighing, Emma rose, drew a soft blanket from her bed, and went to the warm pallet that had been placed by the wall. She settled the blanket about May's shoulders and kissed Angelique good night. May had little liking or talent for spinning, and a great affection for small children. Smiling, Emma realized that attending Lord Gilles had benefited more than just Angelique.

As she rose, she smoothed her hair with nervous fingers. Her mouth dried. Despite a day in her new surroundings, Emma still marveled at one inescapable fact of her dwelling in this chamber here at Hawkwatch Keep. She could touch Gilles whenever she wanted, could taste his mouth, hear his heartbeat.

Silently, cloaked in her mantle, Emma waited in the shadows for a sentry to make his rounds, then descended the several steps of the spiral stairs to his chamber. Not a sound did she make as she lifted the latch. The scent of wet, mossy stone filled her nostrils.

Disappointed, she saw that his chamber was empty,

the bed deep in shadows. Crossing rapidly to the bed, she dropped her mantle and outer clothing, then, clad only in her shift, climbed into the center and knelt there in nervous anticipation. Would he still want her? William had not wanted her after just one time.

Was she too bold to be here? She certainly did not want Lord Gilles to come to her chamber with May there—and Angelique.

His bed was piled high with furs and fine linens. She made a nest in the center with her knees. Her heart pounded in her ears, and she closed her eyes to conjure him in her mind. She breathed deeply and slowly as she let the image of him, naked to the night, rise in her imagination. She breathed in the scent of his chamber, the scent of fine beeswax candles, applewood, warming wine—and him. She would forever remember him as she'd seen him—standing in the dark night, black hair blowing—waiting for just her. She would forever remember the taste of his mouth and the scent of his skin. She would forever remember the liquid rush in her loins as she thought of what this night would bring.

"Gilles," Roland said and snapped his fingers.

"Hmm?" Gilles idly traced a design on the tabletop with the point of his dagger.

"You have heard naught that I've said these last few moments. Be gone." Roland rose from the chessboard. He clapped Gilles on the shoulder, then strode off in the direction of his wife.

Gilles watched Roland hug his wife in a warm embrace. He felt quite warm himself. Heeding some silent call and a tangible need, he headed for the tower steps. With his hand on the latch to his chamber, he hesitated. Something made him pause and look up the winding staircase in the direction of her chamber, then back down at his hand. How he wished he'd not heard her words to her child.

He lifted the latch slowly and silently. She knelt in the center of his bed clad only in her shift. Her hair was unbound and the small residual light of the guttering candles turned the honey to gold, cast her face in deep shadow. The dusky hint of her taut nipples dried his throat. The deep contrast of shadow and golden skin brought a sweat out. As he stood and silently watched her, she raised her arms over her head in a stretch, lifting her breasts. Her eyes were closed. He watched her luxuriate in his bed, her arms descending, her hands stroking the linens and furs. She shifted her hips to settle more deeply into her nest.

He craved the caress of her strong fingertips on his skin, craved her innocent explorations of his body. Watching her, aroused by her, he could forget why she came to him.

With a sense of being in a dream, he approached the bed to stand at the foot, so close he had only to bend slightly at the waist and stretch out his hand to touch her. Her every movement was a silent invitation for him to take what was offered.

Emma opened her eyes. Obsidian ones met gentian, like night possessing a spring flower.

Their hands met midway between their bodies. She clasped his long fingers in hers and directed them to the crest of her breast, which strained against the soft linen of her shift. A tiny sound escaped her throat, and her eyes squeezed closed as he fondled her.

Gilles had spent seven days unsure if their first night had been a dream—one from which he might awake and find himself alone. Her soft sigh reassured him.

Was he too rough? He'd not cared about a woman's

needs for years. Doubts of his prowess as a lover rushed in. He'd bedded many women, rarely bothering with any one of them for long. His mind had never been engaged, let alone his heart.

Would this woman again find pleasure with him? How long before a man such as William noticed her, sensed her awakening to bodily joy? How well he remembered Margaret's wandering eye, her pets at court, once she'd learned the ways of men and women.

His eyes traveled over Emma's innocent face. With a ruthless will, he thrust his doubts aside. As he let his gentle stroking become stronger, her nipple grew even harder between his fingertips. He clasped it and tugged. Her eyelids fluttered; she moaned her pleasure. Satisfaction warmed him.

He climbed onto the foot of the bed and knelt tall and straight before her. Their eyes locked. He was unable and unwilling to break the contact as she reached up and put her hands on the backs of his thighs. Her strong weaver's fingers dug deeply into his muscles. As she kneaded his flesh, he moved his hands to rest lightly on her shoulders. He drew the thin straps of her shift down to expose the upper swell of her breasts. Her skin was smooth as satin, and he stroked his fingers back and forth on the gentle swell.

Her hands grew urgent on him. His entire concentration lay on how to control his breathing, how to prevent himself from crying aloud with the sheer ecstasy of her hands running over him. When she slid them under his tunic and up his hips, he lost both his voice and his breath.

She made short work of his ties, and he stood long enough to pull off his clothing and fling it aside. Her hands returned to her task, now on bare flesh. She wove a web of desire about them. He didn't want her to see his desperate need, so he closed his eyes. They tumbled on the furs, hurried, wanting.

Cool breezes from a loose tapestry near the window dried the sweat of his brow as she put her tongue, hot like a brand from the forge, to his throat. A string of prayers and oaths hissed from his lips, as she first licked then kissed his pulse.

He growled and held her beneath him. When she clasped her legs about his flanks, an expression of passion crossed her face and then transmitted itself to her hands. She clutched and kneaded his flesh. He wanted this night to be for her as their first night had been for him.

His mouth worshipped hers. His hands caressed and swept over her full breasts. His manhood sought its place.

"Guide me," he gasped out against her lips.

For a brief instant she did not understand; then she took him and held him, did as he bid.

He thrust in.

The heat of her burned him. He groaned aloud as he drew back and repeated the fierce plunge to ultimate pleasure. With agonizing slowness he moved. A nearly complete retreat, a pause of a heartbeat, a body-possessing plunge. He owned her mouth as he owned her body—at least for this moment, in this place.

She touched him so deeply he wanted to shout, yet only hoarse moans escaped their locked mouths. The throbbing and beating built to a crescendo. He craved it. Sought it. Held it in check and waited for her. Sensation streamed through him as he kept his deep rhythm, kept the thrust the same. Her hips knew his pace without tutoring. She deepened his thrust with her own lifting hips.

When Gilles saw Emma's eyes widen and glaze, when he felt the involuntary twist and churn of her hips, he changed to quick stabbing thrusts, claiming her in the same unconscious rhythm of their two heartbeats. In hot, near painful bursts, he gave her his seed.

In total silence she rose up against his body one last time, flung her arms about his waist, her mouth hard against his chest, her cries lost against the thump of his heart.

He captured her wrists, shackled them with his hands, and spread her arms wide, chaining her to the mattress. Where they touched, flesh burned.

Held immobile, she bucked her hips and arched her back off the mattress. Her nipples burned him like flames as they grazed his chest. The lingering pulses of her sheath held him captive, hardened him anew, enticed him to another body-shaking climax, quick on the first, something he'd not experienced since his long-ago youth.

Gilles released her and knelt between her thighs. Her eyes met his as she remained outstretched, unable to move, though no longer fettered by his passions.

Then she was on him, her hands locked around his neck, her mouth on his. "I felt your power. You gave it to me," Emma whispered between the caress of his lips and the sweep of her tongue.

" 'Twas just your woman's pleasure," he said into her mouth, kissing her back.

"Nay," she cried. "I felt it. I felt it to my soul. 'Twas your power and it burned through me. I never dreamed such ecstasy could exist."

Silently he hugged her to him and urged her to sleep. Emotion choked in his throat. He was not an object for adoration. He was but a simple man.

In their first dawn together, Gilles rolled carefully from the bed. He went to the window and opened the shutters

Ann Lawrence

to let in a dull gray light. The rains had ended. He could not decide on a course of action. He had never given himself so completely, nor had a woman given so much of herself to him.

Turning back to the bed, Gilles swept aside the blankets and stretched himself atop Emma. No urgency drove his caresses. He woke her to gentle touches and warm kisses. Their lovemaking was protracted. They lingered over each touch. Each kiss was a slow and easy slip and slide of tongues that explored and learned instead of conquering and possessing.

Gilles rolled to his back and drew Emma over his hips. She rocked gently and felt the quiver of his muscles tensed between her thighs.

"I have never met such a man as you," she whispered into the bright dawn morning as her fingers touched his forehead, lips, throat, traced the lines radiating from his eyes. His body gathered itself for completion, his chest tight, his heart pounding. Then she rested on him, still as a statue.

He trembled, his body shuddered, so near . . . on the edge of a precipice. She held him there, ready, aching.

When his breathing slowed and his hips relaxed beneath her, she began anew. The feather-light brush of her fingertips about his eyes was as arousing as the skimming touch of her breasts, or the heated place that sheathed him. Finally, beyond what he could bear, he entangled his hands in her hair. He pleasured his hands and arms with the silk tresses. He cupped her head as she found her completion, tightened his fingers to hold her to him while his own heart roared and his passions were mightily spent.

She fell into a heavy slumber; he stroked her shoulder. His hand, sun-darkened and scarred, contrasted sharply

150

with the alabaster satin of her skin. An old man's hand, a young woman's body.

His throat tightened. What had he done? She deserved the vigor of youth. He clenched his hand into a fist. The knuckles ached.

A score of years ago, he would have wed her. Nay. He'd still have married for wealth and power; he'd not have known what he was missing, nor valued it if he'd known.

Carefully, he settled her within the crook of his arm. He could not forget one fact today, here in the stark light of day. She was at the beginning of her life, he, at the close of his. He stared overhead at the scarlet canopy of his bed. She stirred, opened her eyes for a moment, then closed them and burrowed into his side, a smile on her lips.

I love you. He said it silently.

Chapter Ten

Emma stroked her hand on the fine wool that grew apace on her loom. It was perfect—*he* would wear it. The silence around her made her start. "Angelique!" She bolted from her stool and noted the sun was high. In a whirl of skirts, she fled across the bailey.

At the hall, she calmed herself before lifting the latch and entering the forebuilding. The sentries parted for her, their faces impassive. Still, hers flamed as she imagined that they did not challenge her because she was Lord Gilles's favorite.

"Beatrice," a voice said against her ear as hands encircled her waist. She struggled and turned in the man's arms.

"Mistress Emma!" Mark Trevalin set her aside. "Forgive me. I thought, you looked j-just l-like—" he shuttered, face red.

She patted his shoulder and moved past him, scanning the faces that crowded the hall for May.

"Do you seek your babe?" Trevalin asked, following her, still offering apologies.

"Aye." She nodded. "Wherever can she be?" Emma stewed in a turmoil. It was hours since she'd last noticed Angelique. The babe's presence among the weavers was now so commonplace that Emma had relaxed, stopped fearing some offense might be taken by another weaver. In truth, Emma had grown so relaxed, her weaving grew swiftly upon the loom. It was knowing Gilles would wear her cloth that made her work so diligently, that had allowed her to forget the child in her work. Now, she was wracked with guilt.

"She is where she has been each morning these past three days, whilst May helps in the kitchen." Trevalin gestured to the end of the hall.

Panic surged as Emma pictured Angelique wandering into the huge fireplace. Her feet flew as she ran the length of the hall. Her eyes searched among the men gathered at the dais.

Gilles watched her come. He reclined in his oak chair, pretending she did naught unusual. At his side, William Belfour and Thomas argued the accounting of the villeins. Bored stonemasons awaited their turn to hear what task Gilles would set them in the restoration of the north wall. It had further collapsed, luckily not injuring any villagers this time.

Emma skidded to a halt, aware she had made a spectacle of herself before the company.

Silence fell. Heat surged into her cheeks as she spied Angelique. The child was curled in the crook of Gilles's arm, her thumb firmly planted in her mouth. Her feet batted the air. An unnamed emotion assailed Emma as she watched the scarred warrior hand caress her daughter's silky head.

"My-my lord," she stammered. "Forgive my interruption. I'll take Angelique. Surely she's a bother."

"A bother?" Gilles's mouth stretched to a wide grin. "Mayhap it is this rough company that may be a bother to her."

"Oh, never," Emma disclaimed, stepping up on the dais.

"Then let her rest. She is quite spent from chasing poor Garth's tail." The men drew back from Emma as she sidled past them to Gilles's chair. Her eyes rested on the old hound at Gilles's feet and then rose to meet his. "Let her rest," he repeated.

Emma's hands dropped from their outstretched position. She curtseyed. "As you wish, my lord." She was acutely aware that many observed their byplay, William among them. She whirled and fled.

William watched Emma cross the hall. He smiled for a fleeting moment. Gilles watched his bastard son watch his woman. Angelique shifted on his lap, reached out, and with an impish grin, snatched at the rolls of parchment on the table. Gilles laughed at his men's dismay, and pulled the documents from her busy hands. Angelique giggled and turned her smile on him.

Like a bolt from a crossbow, pain struck him in the heart. He gasped at the searing pain. The room was suddenly cold—nay, icy like the grave. Sweat broke out on his body, yet he was chilled. He looked from Angelique to William Belfour and back again.

William.

Gilles immediately knew that William must be Angelique's father.

How could he have not known?

It took all his self-control not to howl with the pain of it. Gently, he urged Angelique to sit down in his lap. His hand trembled as he stroked her silky hair, hair as flaxen as William's, not golden like Emma's. He stared at the curved bow of Angelique's lips, seeing the child William in the babe in his arms. His vision blurred a moment in his grief.

Of course William would have pursued Emma. He remembered her words, spoken so sincerely at the manorial court. She had given herself for love.

Love of his bastard son.

William was the man who denied his vows. Oh, not vows said on the church steps, or recorded in the manor records, but vows just the same. Vows of love. Some priests recognized such a troth as being as binding as a marriage sanctified by the church.

For Emma, denying them meant making a bastard of her daughter.

What a fool he was. He had worried William would notice Emma now she'd been awakened to passion! Awakened! She'd been taught by the master—long before ever he, Gilles, had touched her. Unschooled? Innocent? Never!

That evening, Gilles snarled at all about him. Emma followed her usual schedule, which did not include being in the hall when he was about. His eyes searched for her anyway.

" 'Tis shoddy work," he snapped at Mark Trevalin. "We've many mouths in need of food, and you've no idea how much grain lies within?" He snatched the tally sticks from the man's hand. "I will see to the count myself."

He strode away to the staircase leading deep into the bowels of the castle and his storerooms. The harvest had been fat. He knew the sticks should indicate a far greater surplus of grain. Was there naught but incompetence surrounding him? Sourly, he moved along the rooms, counting the sacks of grain. A sound teased at the periphery of his attention.

He stood still, listened. It came again. A muffled cry. Someone in trouble. Gilles hurried to the end of the storerooms. There he froze. William stood, his braies and hose about his knees, grunting over a wench. In times past, Gilles would have snapped something rude and departed. This time he stood in the shadows and watched his bastard son.

The girl was bent forward over some of the very sacks of grain Gilles wished to count, her skirts up, her buttocks plump and white in the torchlight. It was May, Angelique's nurse, he realized. William stood behind her, and Gilles again felt that surge of heated jealousy as, with each thrust, the girl writhed and squealed and clawed the sacks of grain. Gilles watched it to the bitter end. He tortured himself with what he saw. It wasn't the huge size of his son's manhood, the frantic shrieks of the maid's completion, or William's triumphant shout that twisted the knife and honed the pain. Nay, it was his imaginings that substituted Emma's sweet form on that of the wench. That was what rent his soul. It became Emma bent over the sacks of grain. It became Emma who panted and cried for more.

Reeling, Gilles hurried from the storage rooms. He needed to use one hand to guide himself in the dark corridor. When he emerged, as if from a tunnel, he stumbled on the worn stone steps that would take him to the bright light and crowded hall.

Finally, he came to his senses. Choking back his bile, he stood like a statue on the top step, got a grip on his envy, got a grip on the murderous need he felt to draw his dagger and relieve William of his most prized possession.

In his anger, he snapped the tally sticks like so much light kindling. Emma had shown no favor to his bastard son. None. In fact, she seemed to actively avoid William. It took all his mighty fortitude to shake off his envy and control himself.

As he tended to his duties, he realized he could not lie with Emma in his present mood. He could not bear it should he sense she yearned in some way for a man more youthful than he—more handsome, more virile.

It did not help to know that William intended a marriage alliance with a powerful family, one wealthy enough to allow him to live at court. Everyone knew William's ambition. For what other possible reason had William not wed Emma and claimed his child? A weaver brought nothing of power or monetary value to a man of William's overweening ambition.

Gilles did not sleep in his chamber that night. Instead, he gathered some men and made the ride to Lynn. There, along with his men, he drank himself into a stupor at a dockside alehouse.

Emma wondered at Gilles's mood. She'd waited for a few hours in his bed—alone. As the moon gleamed along the floor of his bedchamber, she realized he was not coming to her. After the sentry made his rounds, she climbed to her own chamber, plucked Angelique from May's arms, and slept restlessly until dawn.

He was not at prayers.

'Twas midday when she heard the sound of numerous horses entering the middle bailey. She rose from her loom and stood in the doorway to watch the men dismount. Gilles strode with Roland and Mark Trevalin across the bailey, not looking in her direction. Something in his stride, the set of his shoulders, told her he was in a great hurry. He joined a group of his men, and their conversation was low, agitated, with much hand gesturing and show of exasperation.

Silently, she returned to her loom. When her work was done, she took Angelique and went to the hall, trailed by May. Heat swept her cheeks as she noted eyes following her progress to the tower stairs. At Lord Gilles's doorway, she handed Angelique off to May with a kiss. When they disappeared, she raised her hand and knocked.

"Enter," he called. Emma slipped into the room. Hubert nodded to her, gathered up a hauberk and helm, and left them alone.

"You look tired, my lord," she said. In truth, he looked more than tired; he looked angry.

"I am not tired," he snapped. "I am busy." He wrapped a leather belt around his fist before shoving it into a saddlebag open on his bed.

Emma recoiled from the tone of his voice. "Forgive my intrusion, my lord," she said, and fled from his chamber. She stumbled on the worn edge of a tower step, but his hand was there to save her from a nasty fall. She twisted in his grip.

"Nay, Emma. Do not run away. I am not angry with you. Come."

She followed him reluctantly. When he released her, she stood close by the door.

He sighed and resumed his packing. "I am off to York. I heard in Lynn that whilst traveling home from Crusade, Richard had the ill-begotten luck to be taken prisoner by that damnable Duke of Austria and he, in turn, has delivered him up to Emperor Henry. No one seems to know Richard's whereabouts!"

159

Ann Lawrence

"Oh, Gilles, will he kill King Richard?"

"Henry is likely to do anything. We barons will meet to discuss offering a ransom. 'Tis all that is needed—Richard in prison—to bring Philip of France and John sniffing after his dominions."

"Would Prince John do that? To his own brother?"

Gilles stopped his packing and smiled cynically at her. "My sweet. If John and Richard could conspire against their father—why not one another? 'Tis why we barons will meet. To prevent chaos from following these ill events.

"It was Richard's charge to me to see to the loyalties of certain of his lesser barons whilst he is gone. This coil will surely bring every grasping fool from the woodwork to snatch what he may of Richard's."

Emma rushed forward and touched his arm. "Will you be fighting?"

He looked down at her hand and she snatched it back. He caught her fingers and drew her close. "Aye. Mayhap. Political turmoil breeds unrest at all levels. Remember the massacres of the Jews of York? England does not need a repeat of such a disaster."

Massacre. A chill entered the warm room. What if he fell in battle?

"Will you send me with your blessing?" he asked.

He kissed her, and all thought of his anger or her position fled her mind in the fear that he might be injured or killed. "Aye, my lord. Go with God." She held him tightly to her. She tried and failed to say she loved him. A man who talked of emperors and kings did not love his weaver. The most she could offer him was her prayers.

" 'Tis a chore," Gilles sighed as he oversaw the disposition of his men.

"Aye. 'Tis a chore to ride and fight and wield a sword again." Mark Trevalin grinned. "You and Roland have missed such a chance, I beg to say. Your swords grow limp with inactivity."

Gilles joined Roland in a guilty smile as Trevalin continued to taunt them with references to old swords. Both Roland and Gilles itched to be gone. Despite the gravity of King Richard's position, both hoped for a skirmish to test their skills. Roland clapped Gilles on the shoulder and went off to make his farewells to Sarah.

Gilles went to the hall for a final adieu to Emma. He watched William move about the hall, laughing, teasing the serving wenches, buffeting the young knights and squires. Gilles's chest tightened. William's every move was followed by the females of the hall. Each woman watched him for a different reason, though all seemed to admire him for his comeliness. Gilles had to admit that William was a fine warrior.

Emma came from the chapel, and although she appeared to be oblivious to William, Gilles saw that William's body had tensed at her presence. With great subtlety, William worked his way to the side of the hall by Emma and her table. Gilles could see that whatever William was saying to Emma, she was persistently shaking her head in negation. Gilles could not stop himself, he strode to the young people.

"Damnation, Emma—my lord. Are you ready to depart?" William straightened at Gilles's approach, yet 'twas obvious to Gilles he'd cut off some personal conversation between the two.

"See to our mounts, William. I'd like to leave as soon as the horses are ready."

Gilles watched Emma. Her face was flushed and she avoided his eyes.

161

"Emma, we leave within the hour. Is there anything you need before I go?"

"Nothing, my lord. It is most kind of you to inquire. I will be safe here."

"Look at me." Gilles hated the sound of supplication that colored his words. Emma looked up, rose to her feet, and gave him her total attention.

"Go with God, my lord," she said into the silence. "The hours will be empty with you gone."

A flush of satisfaction replaced his apprehension. "Come," he said. Then added, "Please."

"Such soft words, my lord, how could I refuse?"

William watched them walk out of the hall. He cursed softly. He hadn't given Emma a thought until he'd noticed Lord Gilles's interest. Envy gnawed at him. He wanted to wield the power of a Gilles d'Argent. One day barons would listen to *him*. He only needed a wealthy wife. With a fat purse and a place at court, he could be a man of influence.

In the meantime, as a small child wants what he cannot have, William wanted Emma. He'd had her once. He'd have her again.

Emma followed Gilles into his chamber. She was so close behind him that when he turned she was almost touching him. He ran his knuckles down her soft cheek. As he studied her flawless skin, watched her eyes watch him, she turned her head and kissed his palm.

"I am sorry, my lord, that you will miss the Christmas celebrations," she said.

He shrugged. Hard on Christmas came Epiphany. "I hold little liking for the trappings of the season."

She wrapped her arms about his waist and laid her head on his chest. " 'Tis said your hall is decked with pine, and delicacies from the Holy Land will grace even the lowest table."

"I will miss only the scent of your skin," he whispered against her hair. "Yearn only for the taste of you."

Emma lifted her face and studied his. "Do not go," she said softly, her arms unconsciously tightening on his waist. "It will all be but empty revelry without you."

For a moment, they said nothing, then he kissed her forehead, gently, but with a possessiveness he could not conceal. "Why me?" he asked. Her answering smile warmed his bleak heart.

" 'Tis a mystery, my lord. I just know that I have but to see the shape of your profile, the line of your shoulder, your hand upon the table . . . and I want to touch you. I know when you have entered a room, long before I see you—I feel it deep within my body."

Gilles's mouth went dry. Her words struck him silent.

After many moments, he found his voice, licked his dry lips, and searched for some hint she wanted William. "Surely there are others who have much more to offer you."

Emma shook her head in vehement denial and squeezed her arms about his waist. "No man has offered me more. No man is your equal. You are cool, calm, still water. You are sleek strength, like oak carved for a great purpose. You are sweet reason to my madness. I see you and I want to touch you."

He groaned at the power her words had over him. He clasped her tightly to him and knew the last place he wished to spend the night was on the road.

A fortnight later, William Belfour rode across the draw-bridge and onto the slick stones of the bailey. Behind him rode seven men-at-arms. They were weary and wet, sent on a mission to gather more men. Gilles could not do it himself. He'd been forced to lay siege to Castle Woodleigh in an endeavor to oust a baron who was determined to take advantage of Richard's imprisonment to seize as much property as he could.

The vassal had refused to accept terms and, with stifled delight, Gilles had set his siege in motion. William had volunteered to marshal more forces. He'd ridden to the d'Argent vassals and called upon those who owed their forty days. Next, he'd traveled down the coast to Seaswept and summoned Nicholas d'Argent to his father's side.

How he hated the man who possessed a wealthy manor for no more reason than the luck of paternity. Mayhap Nicholas would fall to a sword or eat tainted meat at the siege site, and Lord Gilles would need another to command Seaswept.

William knew there were no more men to be had at Hawkwatch, but when the weather turned brutal, William used it as an excuse to make his way there, rather than travel the extra miles to the siege site. He'd justify himself later.

Tweaking the cheek of the serving wench who'd just breathed a blatantly sexual invitation, William smiled. "Have a bath brought to Lord Gilles's chamber and . . . come yourself, Beatrice."

"Aye, sir." Beatrice hurried off to obey his request, thrilled that she had been so favored. When the deep wooden tub was filled with steaming water, she stood hesitantly in the shadows until the kitchen boys were gone and then stepped forward. William stood naked by the tub, one hand drifting back and forth in the water, boldly aroused.

"Well?" he asked. Beatrice hurried forward. She shivered a moment as she sank to her knees by the side of the tub. His eyes were cold and distant, as if his thoughts lay elsewhere. That he knew she was there, however, was evident as he locked his hands into her hair and pulled her roughly to face him. "There be few as privileged as you, Beatrice, yet you are easily replaced. Please me well and I may call upon you again to assist me."

William's words frightened Beatrice. His tone and words were not gentle or inviting—they were hard and coldly spoken. She desperately wished for a life far from her father's mill, but scrubbing Lord Gilles's floors was not far enough. Mayhap with Sir William she would find a future of ease. She took him in her hand and tried her hardest to please, but her nervousness made her clumsy and rough with him.

As many women before her had been mistaken, so now was Beatrice. William would never seek a common maid's attentions for long. He used her merely to assuage his ache. If ever he wed, he'd reach for wealth and position. 'Twas the reason he'd scorned Emma and her child.

"Enough," he ordered, as Beatrice continued her ministrations even after his release. He turned abruptly away and stepped over the side of the tub, sinking into its still steaming depths. "Bathe me," he ordered abruptly.

Beatrice stared at him, bewildered. He had closed his eyes. She took up a cloth and soaked it before reaching into a nearby pot of soft soap. She worked up a lather and started to scrub his chest.

"Jesu!" he exclaimed, snatching the cloth from her hand. "You're as rough as a wild boar. You're no better at washing than you are at pleasuring. The calluses on your hands are rivaled only by the clumsiness of your tongue. Be gone."

Beatrice shot to her feet as if burned; indeed, her face

flamed and her hands shook. "But, William, I-I wish a chance—"

"Can you not obey, either? Do you need a strapping? I'll need to find another to service me, since I feel ill-satisfied with this encounter. Mayhap you could redeem yourself by finding me another—one more gentle, with smooth hands and soft lips. Be gone."

If he'd shouted the words, they'd have hurt less. Beatrice was used to her father's cuffs and shouted orders. It was the cold quietness of William's words that sliced her to pieces. As she flew to the door, he repeated his last request.

"Bring me another wench, quickly." Out the door she ran, and took the stairs two at a time, tears obscuring her vision. She stopped on the last round of the staircase and looked wildly back up whence she'd come. Surely everyone would know she'd been favored and discarded—as she was so soon back at her duties from Lord Gilles's chamber. And whom could she find to replace her? Everyone would scorn her if she had to summon another to take her place.

Emma rounded the turn in the stair and nearly ran into Beatrice, who sat on a step, face buried in her hands.

"What's the matter?" Emma dropped down beside her. She picked up the edge of her apron and wiped away tears and grime dislodged by the unexpected cleansing.

"That one! 'E angers me so."

"Who?"

" 'Im. 'Im!" She flung an arm up toward Gilles's chamber. Emma suddenly knew to whom Beatrice referred. She'd seen the girl trailing William up the stairs not so long ago. "Dry your eyes and tell me if William hurt you."

" 'E . . . 'e said my lips were chapped, my hands rough and clumsy. 'E found me unworthy." Beatrice laid her head on her knees and choked on her sobs.

"Don't, child." Emma tucked Beatrice's fair hair into her headcovering. "Go back to the kitchen and have some warm milk with a little honey. You'll feel much better."

"Nay, nay, ye don't understand. 'E bid me find another . . . another . . . one with softer hands—" Beatrice sobbed. " 'Ow could 'e do this? 'E wrote me a song." She buried her face in her apron.

Emma's heart ached for the girl. She knew the power of William's songs.

Beatrice lifted her red eyes to Emma's. Her voice was a strangled whisper. " 'E sang to me. Fair as the moon, 'e said I were."

"Oh, Beatrice." *So much for a new song for each new wench.* Emma lifted Beatrice's head and again wiped her cheeks, looking into her large blue eyes. She took up one of Beatrice's work-roughened hands. "These calluses have been earned honestly. Don't let him shame you so. You must not be lured by honeyed words. Save yourself for a more worthy man—a man as good as Mark Trevalin. I think he shows great interest in you. Did he not show you favor at the Christmas feasting? Did he not present you with a token?"

Beatrice sniffed and wiped the back of her hand under her nose. " 'E did. A ribbon wiv a lock o' 'is 'air." Then she looked above. "Mark is not so 'andsome as Sir William."

Anger surged through Emma. "William is not worth Mark Trevalin's right arm. I will deal with Sir William."

She patted Beatrice on the shoulder and climbed the stairs. When she reached Gilles's chamber, she was so angry she pounded the door fiercely. *How dare William presume to take the lord's chamber whilst he was gone?*

"Enter." William stood naked before the fire, warming his hands. "Surely you are most eager," he said, turning to see which maid came so demandingly to seek him. A grin lit his face as he saw who stood in the open doorway.

"Eager is not how I would describe my mood, William. You are the lowest, vilest man I have ever met," Emma said from the doorway. His casual nakedness further angered her. She was about to slam the door and leave the sight of him when, like lightning, he was across the room, snatching her into the chamber. They struggled a moment, William holding her with only one hand as he shut and bolted the door. When he was able to use two hands, he trapped Emma against the stout oak. The iron latch dug painfully into her back. She fell still to give herself relief, and became aware that William was panting, not from exertion, but from exhilaration.

"Nay, Emma, fight me more. Fight me." He bent his head and claimed her mouth, silenced her protests. Despite the sharp pain of the latch, she fought him. But he was a seasoned warrior, and she, a woman skilled only at weaving. He had her skirts up and his hand between her thighs before she could stop him. He whispered erotic words and groaned in her ear as she fought his questing fingers. Emma took advantage of being held by only one hand to slip her own hand to her belt. She slowly drew forth her eating dagger, gritted her teeth as William groped more forcefully for entrance, and slashed out at him.

"Bitch!" he roared, and released her. He stepped back and examined the deep slice Emma had carved in his upper arm.

Emma put one hand on the latch.

"Open that door and I'll pursue you just as I am and proclaim you *my* whore to all below. I am sure Lord Gilles would take exception to such news."

Emma froze. Satisfied as Emma stood motionless, he smiled. "Ah, I have your attention."

"William, you surpass all that is evil." Emma shook inside, yet held the knife steady before her.

"Me? Evil? You sought me here, Emma. Now what would Lord Gilles think if I told him you sought me in his chambers and took your pleasure of me?"

Emma could only stare open-mouthed at his audacity. He stood squarely before her, arms outstretched. Blood dripped from his wound to puddle on the wooden floor. "Come, Emma. Put aside your knife and temper and let me make you scream with delight. Surely, 'twill be far more pleasurable to lie with me than with an old man." He took a step forward, but stopped when Emma lifted her knife.

"I know how to use this, William. Stand back." She avoided looking at his heavily aroused body and took in instead the face that had once held her in thrall. She recognized the guile in his smile now, saw the menace twist his lips as he whispered.

"How will you explain drawing my blood here?" He lowered his arms and then coated his fingers with his own blood. He stepped forward and raised the bloody fingers to her as if in invitation. "Come, sweet Emma, lick this blood from my body." He laughed and drew his bloody fingers across his belly and over his manhood.

Emma frantically searched for words to stay his progress, for he drew ever nearer. She knew she could do serious damage with her blade, but she also knew their contest would have only one possible victor. He was Angelique's father.

She had not the will to harm him.

Chapter Eleven

"Come, sweet, I shiver at the thought of you lapping up every red drop of blood you've drawn."

"Stay!" Emma ordered. "What makes you think Gilles would believe you over me? He treasures me. He would not hesitate to punish one whom I accused of rape." Her words reached him. William froze and tilted his head. The fire cast his hair into a silver blaze. It gilded his body, made him beautiful, powerful, masculine. But Emma could see beyond his fine face and form now. She saw the coldness in his eyes. She saw a man driven by desire and ambition.

"If he treasures you so greatly, why are you naught but whore to him?"

His words sliced into her heart as surely as her knife had sliced into his arm, but then she remembered the way Gilles had looked at her before he'd left. Her words carried the sure ring of conviction. "I do not think Lord

171

Gilles thinks of me as a whore. Shall I tell him instead to think of me as your wife?"

William sneered, but his words lacked heat. "Leman. Whore. Wife. What is a name? But mayhap we should call this contest a draw—but only this once. Come so boldly to me again, Emma, and I'll know you do wish to resume where we left off. I'll have you beg for it, on bended knee, you bitch. I vow it."

"How easily vows come to your lips." Finally, she felt some measure of control over him.

"Get back to your bastard." He turned, strode to the tub, and splashed water on his wound.

Emma edged to the door and was through it in a trice. She sheathed her knife with a quick thrust of the blade. She stood at the head of the stairs where the sounds from the busy hall drifted up to her. For the first time she walked boldly down, head up, ready to challenge any who might look at her with derision. What had been her heartache, now had become her weapon.

She had spoken the truth, she must believe it. Gilles treasured her, vows of love or not.

Gilles put aside the aches and fatigue of his body as he rode into the bailey, his horse snorting plumes of steam, hooves striking sparks. His caparisons were streaked with mud, his men weary of their siege, yet elated at finally returning home. Crowds surged about his party. Wives and lovers, friends and children spooked the horses as the people sought their men. Gilles grinned as he controlled his horse's behavior; his eyes searched the crowd for his beloved Emma.

She stood in the shadow of the hall entry, aloof to the throng. Her eyes avidly searched over him as if seeking to find a wound or some evidence he'd been hurt. He felt her glance as if she'd actually touched him.

Gilles tugged off a gauntlet. His hair, now a month longer, and loose about his shoulders whipped in the wind to sting his cheeks. Without showing the urgency he felt inside, he lifted a hand to her in acknowledgment of her presence and then turned to the man at his side.

"Nicholas, see to your men and mine." He turned back, but Emma was gone, had disappeared from the steps like a dawn mist flees the sun. "I will see you—anon."

It was but moments later when he reached his chamber.

"Gilles, Gilles. You've been gone for weeks." Emma threw herself into his arms. Her encounter with William had made her frantic for reassurance. His arms tightened about her, stole her breath.

"Aye, I understand." They didn't wait for him to bathe the sweat and grime of weeks from his body, they didn't even wait until they undressed. They made love immediately and urgently. Emma could not stem the tide of her words. They flowed from her lips in soft whispers against his ear as he held her. She told him how much she'd missed him and needed him. He was moved beyond words—indeed could still not say what lay in his heart, could only absorb her care and strength into his being.

Distance had not, however, erased his jealousy that William had loved her first—or his fears that she loved William still. Nay, the long nights on a cold pallet on the hard earth had convinced him Emma came to him only for her child's sake.

I must do this. It is best for you, my child. You are all I care about. I will stay here as long as you are cared for.

He must somehow make her want to stay for her own sake, not just her child's. Lying in her arms, he reveled in

173

her touch and accepted whatever she offered—for now.

When both of them were too sated to endure another kiss, Gilles pulled from her arms. He opened the door and asked the posted sentry to call for hot water and food. For once he looked forward to the rich fare of the keep. He was tired of Hubert's meager repertoire of roasted meat and, in truth, his insides had been complaining for the past fortnight, as he had his aching back. He looked at Emma, smiling up at him from the nest of pillows she'd made for herself. He considered asking her if she knew of some potion to relieve his discomfort, but could not bring himself to show that weakness to her. He would call for the leech later.

While he waited for his bath, he paced restlessly, rubbing at the small of his back. When the tub and the accompanying servants arrived, Emma was nowhere to be seen. She had taken herself behind a screen, and he knew she would not appear until they'd left. She always hid herself from the servants' scrutiny and always stifled her sounds of passion lest the sentry on duty hear her. At any other time, Gilles would have smiled to himself at her reticence, for surely all knew that Emma was his lover. Yet, she did not wish to flaunt the fact. He had, heretofore, shielded her as she wished.

Tonight, fatigue and the long siege made him impatient. He was short with the servants and peered critically at the food arrayed on the tray. He lifted the linen napkins and grimaced at the venison in rosemary and thyme. He'd had enough of venison from Hubert. He then sneered at the roasted turnips. He'd been forced to eat endless mounds of turnips at the siege site as well. He was damned if he'd eat them at Hawkwatch.

Pouring himself a flagon of wine, he stood with one hand on his hip and waited for Emma to reappear. When she peeked from behind the screen, he was short with her, too. "They are gone."

His anger disintegrated when Emma placed her hands on him. She unlaced his filthy shirt, fit only for burning. As she eased it up his body, her hands trailed over him. She plucked open the tie of his chausses and danced away, evading his questing hands. He stripped off the rest of his clothes, stepped over the edge of the tub, and sank into its depths. Emma dropped to his side and gently kissed his shoulder.

" 'Tis time to make you sweet smelling again, my lord." She opened a pot of soft soap, scented with cinnamon and cloves, and lathered a cloth. Bathing became a sensual pleasure that set Gilles to groaning. At the finish, Emma was as wet and sweetly scented as he. They entwined themselves in the many furs and pillows and gave themselves to their individual dreams.

It was dark night when Emma awoke. The tapers had extinguished themselves in pools of wax. The fire had died. Thousands of stars glinted through a gap in the shutters. She stretched cautiously so as not to disturb Gilles, but discovered the bed by her side empty. She sat up and searched the gloomy corners of the chamber, but he was not tending the fire. She knew a momentary stab of fear. The door opened.

"Where did you go?" Emma rose and held a fur to her chin as he slowly closed the door.

"I went to visit another female, to give her my kisses, to see to her good health."

Emma swallowed. A lump formed in her throat.

"Don't look so stricken. I speak of Angelique. I found I missed her almost as much as you." Emma's relief was tangible. "She could sleep here, with us," he said, striding to the bed and touching Emma's cheek with the back of his knuckles. "May says she misses her mother in the night."

"Oh, Gilles!" Emma rose on her knees and put her arms around his neck. "You always know what is within my heart!"

He pressed her back into the pillows and drew her close. She searched over his many scars with her fingertips, learning each one anew.

"What are you doing?" he laughed as her quest tickled along his ribs.

"I am making sure you were not injured. Hubert is skilled with a needle, as I well know, but I do not trust anyone to see to your care save me."

"I am flattered." He lay back and stared up at the canopy over their head. He savored the clean scents of his chamber—fresh rushes scattered with sweet herbs, applewood in the hearth, soap from the bath, the musk of their lovemaking—and sighed. " 'Tis glad I am to be home."

Emma propped herself on her elbow and continued to scrutinize him for bruises and scrapes. "Is Richard free now?"

He tweaked her cheek. "Nay, you innocent. It has not even been determined where he is being held. 'Twill be weeks or months of intrigue until a ransom is settled and delivered. In the meanwhile, we will have skirmishes here and abroad. Pray they do not fall within my sphere, or I shall again be gone from you."

She felt ignorant. What did a weaver know of royal ransom? "I prayed in the chapel four times a day that you might be delivered home unharmed." *And that William would go away.*

"Four times," he said, amused. He sat up and threw off the coverlet and inspected her knees. "Aye. These knees seem much worn!" He kissed each one.

Desire swept through her. His playful kiss became a caress. The sight of him, the flicker of light playing over his broad shoulders, as he bent his head to touch his mouth to the soft inner flesh of her thigh, made her tremble. The fire threw a red gloss on his hair, cast shadows on his cheeks. She reached out and sifted her hand through his hair.

He looked up. Their eyes locked. Her small tremor became a quiver. He turned his gaze to her long legs, and his hand traveled slowly in long sweeps from her knee to her hip. Over and over again. "I desire you only," he whispered.

The warmth of his words sank into her vitals. It might be the closest she ever came to love. Her breath caught. Her hands moved on him to tell him she felt his desire. There was a scar on his back, a long puckered mark. She oft felt it as she embraced him during lovemaking. She traced it now with her fingertips, her eyes closed, and felt his muscles ripple in response to her caress. She knew his body by heart. The scar now beneath her fingertips, the curve of his ribs, the furrow of his spine, the cleft of his buttocks, the soft furring of hair on his thighs and chest— every inch of his body fell under her exploration.

He was resilient muscle, hard-edged bones, smooth skin, roughened scars. The myriad textures of his body made her insides flow warm and liquid.

His hand slipped between her thighs. "I desire this and only this." He bent his head to press a kiss to that part of her that ached for his touch. She arched to his mouth, gasping and shaking from the tantalizing caresses. The intimate kiss tore away all restraint from her. She returned his bold touch, kissed his shoulder, his chest, and on down to his hip. She traced the rise of bone with her tongue, followed the swath of black hair to his belly and lower. She inhaled his scent, tasted him, aroused him.

She drew back and raised her head. "Come to me."

"Jesu," he whispered, and did as she bid.

Later, he stroked his hand along her shoulder and trailed kisses in its wake. "I know 'tis past Epiphany, and I could not be here to celebrate the Christmas season, but I wish to give you a piece of jewelry to grace your beauty."

Emma sat up abruptly, reached for her shift, and drew it over her head.

Gilles sat up, too. "Does the offer of jewels offend you?"

She shook out her hair. The golden mass slipped over her shoulder. With impatient fingers she quickly plaited it. "Nay, 'tis just that others will see, and know—"

Gilles grabbed a braid and tugged until she faced him. "What is this? Shame? Shame that someone will see you wear a token of my affections?"

Emma shot off the bed, jerking her hair away from his grasp. "A weaver does not wear jewels, my lord." She pulled on her gown and tied a leather girdle about her hips: weaver's clothing, simple, sturdy, warm—not that of a fine lady, worthy of gems.

His title on her lips pained him. It was easier from his place at the table to forget the differences that lay between them. "Forgive me. I did not think. Is there nothing I may give you, no token it would not shame you to wear?" He said it in a rush, lest she pursue the topic of the distance betwixt lord and weaver.

"There is something, my lord." She dragged her toe through the rushes.

Her tentative manner made him sit up straight. He clasped his arms about his knees and grinned. "Come. Do not play the shy one. Name it. An emerald for your navel? Bells for your toes? Toes may be hidden from view in your slippers."

Emma giggled. Her eyes met his, shining with amusement, and he thought of sapphire seas and lapis skies. She was more precious than any jewel, more worthy of them than even Queen Berengaria.

"Nay, my lord. I've no wish for such things. Do women wear jewels in their navels?" She cocked her head to the side.

Gilles's blood boiled as her braids fell over her plump breasts. " 'Tis said they do in the sultan's harems of Arabia."

"Hmm." She seemed to consider the idea. "Nay, my lord. What I wish is very simple." She climbed onto the bed by Gilles's side and knelt there, her hands clasped in her lap. "I have a cross of my mother's that I cannot wear for lack of a chain."

With a nod, Gilles rose from the bed and went to a coffer. He dug about for a moment and finally brought to the bed a soft leather pouch. Drawing the thong that held it closed, he poured a cascade of glittering jewelry across the bedding.

Emma stared at the pile of gems. She did not gasp as he expected. With her lip between her teeth, she stirred the pile with a single fingertip. She rejected a fortune. Then, finding what she wanted, she drew from the tangle a delicate chain of silver. Although of fine workmanship, it was of little value.

"Take what else catches your fancy," he urged her, but she shook her head.

He saw tears in her eyes as she slipped the chain over her head. "This is all I need."

* * *

179

Gilles stepped over Angelique as he drew on a long linen shirt. He toed a stuffed leather ball in her direction, then reached for his surcoat, but Emma stayed his hand. "Wear this instead, my lord." He took the bundle from her. A small thrill ran through him as he touched the beautiful cloth she'd handed him. His long fingers stroked the pewter-colored fabric. He unfolded and shook out the garment.

"I thought the color would suit you . . . Gilles."

He looked sharply in Emma's direction. His hands stroked the cloth. His eyes held hers. He watched a stain of pink rise up her cheeks. His own face felt hot and flushed.

" 'Tis in thanks for the chain." She touched the spot where her mother's cross lay between her breasts. "Could you watch Angelique whilst I fetch May?" He nodded and she left him.

He gently laid the surcoat on his bed. The sheen of the wool was so lustrous he needed to stretch out his hand and touch it. He walked about the room and inspected the cloth from many different angles. From some angles it appeared to be molten silver flowing in waves across his bed. From others, it took on the dark sheen of moonlight reflected off a stormy lake.

The cloth was fluid, strong, sensual like the woman who wove it. Without shame, Gilles allowed himself to pick it up and hold it to his face; it was meant to be touched and savored. He knew without any prompting that it was the right and proper color for his black looks.

Arousal came hard upon him, because the cloth held Emma's scent. He pictured her at her loom, her hands weaving this cloth. His pleasure was as ripe as any new pain could be. He drew on the tunic. Opening his coffer, he brought out the first belt she'd woven for him, the one with hawks in flight—linking one to the other, end to end, and settled it on his hips. Garbed as finely as any king, he thought. He should not wear such a garment except at some great occasion, yet he knew he must have it on, next to his bare skin even. He resisted the urge.

A sharp tug on his hem brought him back to the here and now.

Angelique.

He bent and scooped her up. "What is it, my child?" he asked, nuzzling her neck and taking in the scent of innocence. She had become his child in his mind. She *was* his grandchild, and he loved her to distraction. His son, Nicholas, had no children yet, so Angelique was his first—albeit through William's loins. Though he could never acknowledge her, she was his, and his grip tightened possessively as guilt assailed him. He bedded his grandchild's mother. Somehow it seemed incestuous, though Emma and he shared no common blood.

"Gilles," Angelique squeaked at his tight grip. She had just learned to say his name. In fact, she practiced it by bellowing it down the hall whenever she wished. That such a small set of lungs could give forth such volume of demand amazed him. He thanked God she'd not been swaddled and placed with a village woman. With a grin he rewarded her with a kiss and loosened his hold, tossing her aloft and changing her squeak to a shriek of delight.

"She will vomit on your head," William said from the threshold. Gilles clamped his lips on a sharp retort and bid him enter, putting Angelique down in a nest of blankets arranged for her comfort. May would soon come to feed the child. Emma no longer nursed her. The image of Emma with her child at her breast sent a bolt of possessive agony through him.

"What do you want, William?" Gilles strolled to a

hearthside table and poured himself a cup of wine. He strove for the impassive, cold demeanor for which he was known. A wretched thought occurred to him. If William sought to claim Angelique, he might not have this time with her. He let the cool liquid slip down his throat as he listened to William's litany of complaints about an elusive band of thieves who had been taking advantage in Gilles's absence.

"You should seek the thieves yourself." Gilles carefully pulled Angelique back as she toddled too close to the hearth.

"You don't wish to hunt them, my lord?" William cocked his head to the side and studied Gilles in surprise. "You love a good hunt, be it man or beast."

"I think I'll remain here. Take whom you wish and . . . good hunting." He watched Angelique try to sneak back to the forbidden hearth. For the first time, Gilles understood how Roland could be content to remain by the fire with the family he loved.

He had never sat at the hearth with his wife—nay, he'd avoided her, and having fostered Nicholas early, had seen little of the boy.

Nicholas. His son would return to Seaswept in a day or two. Gilles felt guilty he had taken his son away from his new wife throughout the season of celebration and feasting.

He also felt guilty he'd not mentioned Emma to Nicholas. Nor mentioned Nicholas to her.

What did he fear? Disapproval from his son? Or the look on Emma's face when she met his son and the realization struck that to have a son of more than a score of years, he must be near or more than two score years himself. Another thought intruded. Like William, Nicholas was a comely man. Women sought him. Gilles thrust the thought aside.

William paced the large bedchamber. He looked for signs of Emma about the room, but saw none. He was beyond curious. Emma ignored him at every turn. She didn't meet his eyes. She didn't acknowledge his words. He had to have the haughty bitch. As his eyes took in the huge carved bed, the luxurious furs, the scarlet bed curtains, he grew hard thinking about subduing Emma on those soft furs, tying her down, mayhap, with the golden bed cords. Envy that she lay on such finery consumed him. Needing to take a wench in some dark corner rather than on a feather bed made him more resentful.

"I'll mind leaving for only one reason." William climbed the low dais on which the bed stood and flopped back onto the fur coverlet to savor its feel. He closed his eyes and stretched, missing the glint of anger that coursed over Gilles's face at the audacity of William, lying upon his lord's bed. "This wench I'm bedding, I've just taught her the ways of a man's tongue. 'Twould be a pleasure to have her kneeling, plump ass in my face, on this fine bed, my tongue and hers busy with each other."

"Take your muddy boots from my fine bed—now." Gilles's words were softly spoken, but the menace in his voice was real.

Angelique, sensing his displeasure, slipped her fingers into his, and hid her face against his knee as he spoke. William rose hastily and swung his feet to the ground.

"Forgive me, my lord. I forgot myself."

"So I see." He lifted Angelique into his arms. The images that had risen in his mind tormented him—Emma kneeling over William's huge phallus. Her carnal kiss of the previous night had stunned him. Now he knew her tutor.

Chapter Twelve

Gilles found no joy in the fine supper of sauced partridges and leek pie. A traveling troupe of mummers did not amuse him either, for they baited the women of the hall. Their ribald songs and poems chafed at him. He was not pleased at the women's blushing discomfort, or Emma's in particular. Worse, William entered into the amusements. His rich voice held every woman of the keep enthralled. Silence fell whenever he sang. The room was mesmerized by his words, the richness of his voice.

Gilles lifted his hand. William caught the barely perceptible gesture, gave a nod, and brought the song to a close.

One woman wept as William's song ended. Emma sat stone-faced.

"A voice to match the face," Nicholas d'Argent remarked to the company as he lifted his tankard of ale.

185

"I would imagine he's had every woman worth having hereabout," he added for his father's ears alone.

Gilles bit back a sharp retort. He shifted his gaze from his bastard son to his legitimate one. The two men held little resemblance to one another save height, breadth of shoulder, and fierce fighting ability.

Nicholas had blue eyes, too, but a soft blue, like his mother Margaret's. His arched brows and full lower lip also reminded him of Margaret. Only Nicholas's black hair, long reach, and sure foot were his. And mayhap his sharp tongue and quick temper.

Beatrice leaned between them and refilled Nicholas's tankard. She issued him a silent invitation. His son seemed oblivious. It pleased him. Gilles liked Catherine, his son's wife, very much. It would sadden him to know that so soon after the nuptials, Nicholas sought another woman. A few months ago, he wouldn't have cared if Nicholas was constant; a few years ago he wouldn't have known it mattered.

"Will Catherine ever forgive me for calling you away over the Christmas season?" Gilles asked, smiling as he pictured the tiny woman who had captured his son's heart.

An answering smile lit Nicholas's face. "Aye. As she still stands in total awe of you, she would forgive you anything. But I should soon return. How can we get you your first grandchild if I am here and she is there?"

Gilles's face stiffened. He already had a grandchild—one he could not acknowledge. "Then, by all means, provision your party and take to the road."

Gilles left the table abruptly. But a few moments after he had gained his chamber, the door opened and Emma slipped in as silently as a wraith.

She took his hand and led him to a seat by the fire.

Acting the part of squire, she eased his clothing off, taking each piece and laying it carefully aside. She slipped out of her own clothing and wrapped his black silk robe about her. The sleeves hung inches too long at the cuff, the hem trailed like a train behind her. She returned to where he sat naked, feet outstretched to the leaping flames at the hearth. Slowly, she skimmed her fingertips along the tendons knotted in his neck. Gooseflesh broke out on his arms.

He captured her hand and pulled her around to stand between his thighs. Very slowly, she sank to her knees, then sat back on her heels. Her breath felt hot in her chest, her heart seemed to stutter.

Here, kneeling at the fire before him, she felt the full weight of his scrutiny. All about them receded—the sounds in the hall below, the call of a sentry overhead. He leaned forward and pulled the knot at her waist. With a soft smile, he opened the silky material and slid it from her shoulders, baring her breasts. Cool air swirled across her skin, tightened her nipples. A heady, powerful feeling swept through her. She desired him, only him, saw in his eyes, the flare of his nostrils, that he met her desire, wanted her with an equal ardor.

Flames leapt in the hearth, reflected in his black eyes, bronzed his skin. He lifted his hand, but she shook her head. With a low moan, he let his hand fall back to the armrest.

Emma placed her hands on his knees and using the same light touch as she'd used on his neck, she skimmed her fingers down and up his calves, behind his knee, and then finally came to rest, hands spread high on his thighs.

"Mon Dieu," he gasped.

"Gilles," Emma whispered, "I felt every moment of your absence, here." She touched her breast, then

187

returned her hand to him, tightening her fingers, feeling the leap of his thigh muscles.

"Emma," he said. "I—"

The door swung open. "Father?"

An icy breeze swept the room. Emma froze, then fumbled the robe closed. Gilles leapt to his feet, stepped in front of her, and snatched up his tunic. "Nicholas!"

Nicholas! Emma quailed. *Gilles's son!*

The young man standing in the chamber doorway flushed red and backed hastily through the door. "Forgive me." The door banged shut behind him.

Gilles swore, pulled the tunic over his head, and jerked the door open. "Nicholas. What is it?" he called after the swiftly retreating figure of his son.

Nicholas turned on the stairs. He shrugged and held up a stoppered skin one might use to hold wine. "I had forgotten in the confusion of the siege. Catherine sent this for you. She said, that is . . . I just . . . " he stammered.

Gilles decided to act as if naught were amiss; he went to his son. "What is it?"

"Oil. For your back. She knows how your back aches. . . . "

Emma hid behind the screen in the corner of Gilles's chamber until the men's murmured conversation ended. The door opened. She bit her lip and buried her face in her hands. Her face flamed.

"Emma?" She opened her eyes. Gilles hung a skin by the fire, then turned to her, his expression wary.

She flew into his arms, clutched him fiercely. "Oh, Gilles, what must he think? Finding me on my knees, t-t-touching you—"

His grip grew painful; he jerked her away from him and held her at arm's length. "I care not what he thinks."

For a moment they stood in silence, the only sound the crackling of the fire. She looked away first. "Of course. It . . . it matters not."

Gilles knew she was lying. Her face was pale, two bright spots of color high on her cheeks. "He will know to send a servant next time he wishes a word with me."

"I must go." She dropped the robe and fumbled for her clothing.

He snatched her shift from her hand and threw it on the bed. "You must go? Why? Lest my son think what is truth? You service me here?"

He wished the words snatched back into his mouth.

"Service you?" He saw the muscles of her throat work. "Is that all this is to you?" she asked, her words barely a whisper.

"Of course not. But you have told me quite clearly, you are free for nothing more."

Her cheeks flushed a deep red. "And do the king's knights offer more than this to their weavers, my lord, should they be free, that is?" She swept a hand to the bed.

He committed worse folly. "You come for your comfort."

"Do I?" She backed away and groped in the bed-clothes for her shift.

Her question kindled a fire in him. Fatigue and jealousy, a dangerous mix, drove words from his lips. "You give me no indication of anything more."

Every jealous thought that had crossed his mind since meeting Emma reared its head to be examined anew. Every gesture, every glance in William's direction, every word she spoke came under scrutiny. Lastly, he condemned himself for wanting the mother of his grandchild.

He knew he would soon be half-crazed and take her with violence if he did not gain control of his envy. He might never know if Emma came to him by choice or by the necessity of William's rejection of her.

She jerked her clothing on with agitated hands. In a trice, she was gone.

He would never ask.

He would never know.

Emma found Gilles in a small chamber off the chapel, a room with real glass in the windows. The walls held several shelves filled with rolled parchments she supposed were castle records. To her amazement, she saw a number of books, too. One lay open on the table before him. He intently studied one page.

"May I ask what you are reading?"

His head came up, and his eyes widened as she closed the door behind her. "What are you reading?" she asked again, going to his side.

Gilles frowned. "I am looking over this old book, a gift from Abbot Ramsey to my father for a window my father donated to the abbey. A collection of the Abbot's favorite psalms, and so forth. Of no importance." He made a move to close the book, but she placed a hand over his.

"What beautiful work." Emma leaned over his shoulder. Her scent filled his head, distracted him, but he desperately wanted to close the book. "What is the meaning of this lovely work?" Her finger hovered over the large 'C' that began the page.

He cleared his throat. "It represents man's journey through life." At the lower hook of the letter a babe rested; climbing the curved back was a young man, hand outstretched, as if to claim a prize; and at the top of the letter, hair grizzled, clung an old man, his life done.

"Read it to me." She leaned on his shoulder as if no harsh words had come between them.

He stalled. "You cannot read?" The room was stifling, kept overwarm to dry the air and prevent decay of the documents. Sweat bloomed on his body.

With a quick touch, she tapped his cheek. "Oh, aye, I can read, but ill. I would prefer to hear the words from your lips."

Gilles cleared his throat. "Cast me not off in the time of old age; forsake me not when my strength fails." How the words tore at him. How could he have been reading just this page when she'd arrived?

"Beautiful. You have a wonderful voice for reading."

Before she could ask for more, Gilles closed the book. He redirected her attention by pointing out the marvelous gilding of the leather cover. " . . . Had you need of me?"

Emma moved around to the front of the table and faced him. "Nay. But I regret our angry words. Forgive me?"

He smiled. "There is nothing to forgive. I fear I was out of sorts—too long from Hawkwatch."

For a moment, they just smiled at each other. Then she frowned. "There is a boy from the village, Gilles, he has nowhere to go; his parents are dead." She knotted her hands.

"Shall I take him in?"

Her eyes grew round. "You would do that? Take the child into your household?"

He shrugged and reclined back in his seat, stretched out his legs, and stroked his mustache. "If it would please you, aye."

"I fear he is a thief." She rested her hip on the table and laughed. "Yet, he might make you a worthy page if you lock up that pouch of jewels you have in your coffer."

He loved the way her eyes gleamed like sapphires in the afternoon sunlight that shone through the window.

"But I have another plan," said Emma.

"Pray tell." Impulsively, he rose, circled the table, scooped her into his arms, and returned to his seat. She settled into his lap as if she'd always curled there.

"The boy worships your armorer." Gilles stroked his hand from her knee to her ankle. When he tried to slip his hand under her hem, she slapped his wrist.

"Big Robbie?" Gilles accepted her rebuke and linked his hands about her hip. "He is a man much to be admired—and he and his wife are childless. Do I understand the turn of your thoughts?"

"Perfectly. And the child's name is Robert—"

"Soon to be called Little Robbie."

"Big Robbie can teach the boy his craft; the child need no longer steal—or starve."

Gilles kissed her neck. "You are as lovely inside as out." This time when he slid his hand beneath her hem, she did not stop him. Her skin was warm and silky against his palm.

When duty called Gilles away, a few minutes later, Emma blushed at how boldly he'd touched her. She sat in his chair, chin propped on her hands. They'd not discussed what had passed between them, but at least the thieving little boy would have a home—and a chance—before he must forfeit one of his hands.

The beauty of the book lying on the table drew her. Before she touched it, she wiped her hands down her skirt, then tried to find the page from which Gilles had read.

Another artful page caught her eye, where delicate shades of greenery entwined a letter 'W'. Her throat constricted.

*Who is she that looketh forth as the morning, fair as
the moon, clear as the sun, and terrible as an army
with banners?*

Army? Banners? That was not the way William had
sung it. And how could William's song be here? Her
stomach lurched.

She turned the pages rapidly, looking forward, back-
ward.

*His mouth is most sweet: yea, he is altogether love-
ly. This is my beloved, and this is my friend, O
daughters of Jerusalem.*

His mouth? Anger filled her. "What a fool you are,"
she said aloud to herself in the small chamber.

Each page of the holy book, each verse, seemed to be
from the scriptures. She didn't understand the words—
they were surely not meant to be understood by mortal
woman, but some things were now as clear as spring
rain. . . . William was not only a liar, and a seducer of
women, he was also a blasphemer.

And she was a fool.

Chapter Thirteen

Gilles paced the perimeter of Hawkwatch near the hour of midnight. He disliked the frost that touched everything on his manor with a rime of white. The wood beneath his feet was slick and treacherous like the nature of relationships.

He disliked the touch of frost that had come between him and Emma. Despite their words of conciliation, he sensed a tension festering and growing between them. Envy of William tainted their lovemaking.

Gilles waited until the change of sentries, barely noting their presence, though he greeted them. Far below, a small shadow darted after the hulking armorer as the man passed through the bailey to the hall.

Gilles realized he would find his manor running more smoothly if Emma sat at his side. He found her council invaluable. She knew the villagers, knew their ways—who cheated, who dealt honestly. Gilles frowned. But to seek her, he must wait until the dark of night, hide behind a closed door.

He must wed her. The thought felt right and good. He had a barrel of silver coins, four manors under his care, a strong son who would give him strong grandchildren. Only the matter of her vows to William stood between them—vows to a man who would never claim her. Even now, William was picking out his bride.

Gilles found himself on the spot where he and Emma had stood the first night she'd come to him. He felt her presence there as if her ardor had imbued itself into the very stones, as her dyes colored her cloth. He remembered the words they'd said, and knew he wanted to hear her say them before every person of the manor, before God, too.

William would not have her.

He would not have Angelique, either.

How could he convince Emma that her vows to William meant nothing? Only a woman would hold to such nonsense. Her fears of gossip would not taint their lovemaking anymore. As to Angelique's bastardy, he would find her a suitable husband one day who, for the right marriage portion, would not cavil at an unfortunate birth.

When he returned to his chamber, he found only Angelique curled asleep in a ball, like a kitten in a nest of furs that had slipped off the foot of the bed. Impatient to see Emma, he hastened to the hall in search of her. Rows of sleeping families filled the cavernous space. There in the far gloom, near the stairs to the lower level, stood William and Emma.

Too close.

They turned and disappeared into the dark well of the steps.

In the early years of his service to King Henry, Gilles had received a near mortal thrust of a sword in his back during a tournament melee. The blow had pierced his mail, laid open his flesh to the bone, but even that deadly stroke could not compare to the pain that now filled his chest.

He took the stairs to his chamber slowly, feeling like an old man. Once there, he occupied himself building up the fire, filling the room with light and heat, for he was cold to his marrow. For what seemed an eternity, he waited for her, staring at the bed, allowing his imagination free range.

She came in quietly, easing the door shut as he had, then she turned and tiptoed to the bed, lifting one corner of the bed curtains and peering in.

"Are you looking for me?" he asked from his seat by the fire.

"Gilles, you startled me! I was looking for Angelique," she said, coming around the bed. "Ah, here she is." Emma paused a moment at Angelique's side and touched her child's brow with a kiss. "Have you been waiting long, my lord?"

"In some ways but a moment, in others years."

She lifted a brow and cocked her head. "I beg your pardon?"

"That is not all you should beg." He rose, feeling one hundred years old. How young she looked in the hearth's light. "You appear flushed." He moved to the table and poured a cup of wine, but his hand shook, so he set it down abruptly.

"Am I?" One hand went to her cheek, the other to her hair. "I fear I ran rather quickly—"

"Pray tell why? You had no pressing business *here*."

"I did not want to leave Angelique so long alone; you were busy, Roland said, and May was—"

"Do not explain. I understand, you came for your child's sake." He moved to the fire, and toed a burning log closer to the flames.

He caught her scent before he felt her touch on his back. "I came for you."

With a shrug, he threw her off. "I saw you." The words burned in his throat as the flames burned the wood.

"Saw me? Where?"

But he could see from her expression, she knew of what he spoke. He arched a brow. "Where? You tell me."

"Below. In the hall." She bit her lip. Color flooded her face.

"Aye, in the hall, but not for long. William much enjoys a few moments in the storage rooms below—the third chamber along; you are not the first—"

"Stop!" she cried. "He took me only as far as the shadows. He—"

"He had not the courtesy to seek privacy for your tryst?" Gilles felt the acid rise in his throat with every word.

"Tryst! William is a loathsome, vile—"

Gilles snatched a pillow from his chair and threw it against the wall. "I do not believe you! You went below stairs with him."

Emma's heart began to pound, sweat gilded her brow. "Only to try to reason with him. He is constantly about, brushing up against me, touching me, making base suggestions." Her chest tightened as she realized he did not believe her. "Please," she whispered. "Please, believe me."

The cold hard tone of his voice reminded her more of a lord commanding his men. "Few women object to William's touches."

"Well I do!" she retorted, but he continued as if she'd not spoken.

"You will put him from your mind. I will not have him in your thoughts or dreams."

"I do not dream of him! You are wrong!"

"He can do nothing for you, nothing for Angelique."

Suddenly, her whole body ached. His face was a study in fury, his words cold and heartless.

He loomed over her. "I am your protector—not he. Whatever vows you said to him mean nothing if he never acknowledges you, and acknowledge you he never will. His every moment is spent assessing dowries, tallying the benefits of one daughter over another as a bride. Your name is not among them! Only a total fool would believe such a ruse."

"Only a fool?" Emma could barely raise her voice above a whisper. "Is that what you think of me?"

"Aye. Foolish as are most women. You lie to yourself to justify what you do."

A shiver of ice spangled down Emma's spine. "A liar as well?" The chamber was frigid despite the roaring fire. She spun away from him.

"Stay where you are!" Gilles stepped between her and the door.

She froze in place.

He punctuated each angry word with a sharp slash of his hand. "You are alone on God's earth save for Angelique. You are my chattel as is the lowest swineherd. You'll obey me, yield to me." He came so close she saw the flames of the hearth flicker in his ebony eyes. "You will never touch him again."

"Nay, I did not touch him." She tried to thrust past him.

He shackled her upper arms with his hands. "You are mine!"

Her heart screamed at his harshness.

"Understand me," he demanded. "Understand that you

are never to touch him again. Wipe him from your thoughts. Eradicate him from your dreams. Do you understand?"

Slowly she nodded. Her eyes smarted with a torrent of unshed tears. She pulled from his grip and sank into the chair. Gilles leaned over her, his white-knuckled hands on the arms. His intimidation oppressed her and destroyed any hope that she could reason with him.

"There will be no more hiding that you sleep here. He would not dare trespass on what is acknowledged by all to be mine! You have nowhere to go and no one to protect you—save me. You may deny it if you wish, but you are mine. You will stop pretending you do not lie in my bed! *Everyone will know*. You will do as I wish, when I wish, before whomever I wish. If I demand you sit at my side at the table, you will do it! Truly, if I ask you to attend me naked on your knees, son or no son to see you, you will do it.

"You gave him up when you sought my protection, and now you will give him up in your heart and mind as well." To punctuate his words, he prodded her chest, then her forehead with his index finger. "You are *my* woman, *my* leman."

Leman. The word was said aloud. *Simply another name for whore.*

A fool, a liar, and a leman.

Despair ran through her, chilling the warmth of her love. She could not contain the small moan that issued from her lips.

For a moment the look on his face hovered somewhere between pity and regret, then in the next instant, it disappeared, replaced by the mask of the man who spoke of kings. She realized she was with the warrior who could cut a man's life off with a single stroke of his sword. Lost was the man who gentled and caressed her, held Angelique on his knee, told the child stories, fed her sweets.

Her moan became a hiccuping. No other sounds came from her throat. She held them in, though they burned her chest and throat.

"No more silence! No more stifling moans so others will not know that you are in passion's thrall. I want them to know what we do. I want no doubts; I want William to know what a chance he takes trespassing on what is *mine*."

She sat in silence, withheld the torrent of words she wanted to scream at him—for the words would end anything between them forever.

Her silence enraged him further. He whirled away from her. He ripped the covers from the bed. He stripped it bare, dragging the mattress from the ropes and heaving the lot to the rush-strewn floor. He swept his arm across the table, smashing goblets and plates to the floor. As the last plate clattered to a stop, Angelique's wails filled the air.

He spun toward the sound. The babe's cry drew his rampage to a halt. For a brief moment a look streaked across his face—shame, despair . . . regret? He stormed out, leaving Emma silent and humiliated, Angelique clutched to her breast.

When Angelique had quieted, and Emma could breathe calmly, she searched his coffers for her sturdiest shoes and her blue mantle, and donned them hurriedly. Then she wrapped Angelique in several warm blankets and cautiously opened Gilles's door. At the bottom of the stairs a sentry blocked her way and said that at Lord Gilles's orders she was not permitted below. Meals would be sent to her. Emma backed away from the contempt in the man's voice and the sneer on his face, and hurried up the winding stair to the highest chamber. A sentry stood there, too, and blocked her entrance to Lady Margaret's former bedchamber.

Footsteps dragging, she returned to Gilles's chamber. She looked about her and decided to leave the devastation as it was.

"Lemans earn their way on their backs, not on their knees scrubbing wooden floors," she said to Angelique. Dragging a mound of furs and linens to the hearth, she made a pallet for herself and the child. She remained wrapped in her mantle as she lay down by Angelique with her back to the room.

Sleep eluded her. Every word whirled and spun through her mind. *Fool* hurt far more than any other name Gilles had called her. She'd called herself a fool enough times to know the truth.

The keep fell silent, the rustling of night creatures the only sound to be heard.

How she wished she'd been able to explain how William delighted in pestering her, even as he wanted nothing truly to do with her or Angelique. Why had she not ignored William tonight of all nights?

It did not matter. In truth, a noble, a great lord, had no need to tolerate the misbehavior of his leman—he had merely to cast the old out and take on a new one.

At last she wept.

Gilles rode across the drawbridge and far from Hawkwatch. He skirted the pine forest and drove the horse to a hard gallop along the ancient paths through the marshes, his way lighted only by the moon. Ahead lay Hawkwatch Bay in an eerie shimmer of white.

Eventually, the horse labored, foam flying from his

flanks. Gilles reined him in and slid from the saddle. He stood on the sand and faced the mouth of the bay, where it gave onto the great North Sea. Across the curved bay, at low tide, lay the short way to Lincolnshire if a man dared cross the treacherous sands. Treacherous like a woman's heart, sure to suck you in and drown you.

A bank of clouds covered the moon. Black night blended with the black water, one inseparable from the other. Waves foamed white, surging out of the darkness, then retreating. Sand beneath his feet shifted precariously, recalling to him the dangers of the change of tide, the number of people who had perished in this morass of shifting sand over the years.

Salt spray bathed his face; the rush of water soothed the fever of his mind. He led the horse to firmer ground and confronted his shame.

How would he ever face her? What man of honor would so treat the woman he loved?

He did not want to feel this painful, wrenching guilt. To cleanse himself of guilt he had only to remember Emma's deep flush when he'd mentioned William.

Her words at the judging when first he'd met her came back to him. She'd given herself for love. She loved William. She merely serviced Gilles as any other leman might. He should not feel guilty for ordering about a leman.

To admit that what he'd done was unjustified would be to admit the depths of his fears and envies. By the time the horse was rested, Gilles had convinced himself that Emma only stayed with him for the warmth of his hearth.

Dawn painted the stone walls of the bedchamber rose pink. Emma watched two maids giggle as they put the chamber to rights. Beatrice, who worked at their side, shot Emma sympathetic looks which Emma ignored. They whispered about her, stole glances at her, until Gilles entered. They finished with alacrity under his ill-concealed impatience. When they were gone, he ordered her to sit by the fire.

"You will not sleep on the floor."

"I'll not sleep with you," she returned.

They stared at each other. How could he undo what he'd wrought in but a few maddened moments?

"You will not sleep on the floor," he repeated.

"I beg leave of you to allow me to return to a pallet in with the spinners then, my lord."

"And when I require your 'services'?" he asked acidly, pain flaring in his chest at the aloofness of her words, the formality of her address.

"You need only command, my lord. Just as you would should you have need of your *swineherd*." She met his gaze head-on. There was little point in hanging her head, but she felt a deep flush of shame spread across her cheeks.

"As you wish," he replied, noting her high color and wishing he could reach across the distance between them and beg her forgiveness. But to do so would make him appear weak.

Emma rose with great dignity and scooped up Angelique. The child began to cry and stretched out her arms to Gilles. Emma whirled away, ignoring her daughter's entreaties, and left him. Angelique. He had lost her, too.

May touched Emma's shoulder. "Have you need of me tonight?"

Emma shook her head. "I have no more need of your help, May. Go. Join the other women." Emma did not hear any of Sarah's words, nor May's either. The two women exchanged knowing looks as Emma curled about Angelique and turned her back to the other spinners sleeping amid the looms that were scattered like small trees about the long, warm room.

"Leave her," Sarah whispered as May made to go to them. Sarah's solicitous care only honed the knife edge of Emma's pain. She knew quite well how the castle tittered over the devastation Gilles had wreaked in his chamber.

Emma did not sleep. She stroked her hand over Angelique's curls. She was out of tears. They no longer dampened the wool of her pallet. She listened to the snoring of one spinner and shifted impatiently on the scratchy wool bedding. How soon one grew used to the luxury of privilege—or the illusion of it. At least the scents here of wool and work were familiar and comforting, and those of honest living.

She knew in her heart what ailed Gilles. Everywhere she turned, there was William. He stood too close and whispered what he would have her do to him when Gilles grew bored and withdrew his protection. Surely it had been only a matter of time before Gilles imagined there was something between them.

How could she make Gilles see it was not so? What if he sent for her? She knew she would go. She could not bear to think that he did not want her. She was his—but she was afraid.

I mean no more to him than any other of his servants.

Nay, that was not true. Her heart told her it was not true. No man ever looked at a woman with so much concern or ardor. She must believe it, else she was what he'd called her, and nothing more.

Was keeping her vows to William a fruitless attempt to

spare her child bastardy? Or did she secretly know a lord would never pledge himself to a lowly weaver, and so weaved a tapestry of reasons she was not free, could not have him even if he so desired?

His passions were as easily aroused to anger as they were to lust. The passion of his anger frightened her. What if he struck her? If he did, he might kill her with one well-placed blow. His strength was huge. He had lost control of himself, and how she'd savored his loss of control when he'd made love to her. Why had she not seen that his incredible passion could also spawn incredible jealousy?

Emma wavered between anger with Gilles and utter shame. She deserved his treatment for yielding up again that which should have accompanied sacred vows.

Angelique stirred and shifted in her arms. Angelique. What if the child provoked his anger? Her body tense, every muscle tight, Emma spent the night awake, uncalled.

During the day, Emma kept to her weaving, Angelique close at her side. She ate little, as her stomach churned with anxiety.

"What ails the two of you?" Sarah asked as Emma threaded the heddles of the loom.

Emma could not look her friend in the eye. "Leave it be. It is of no consequence."

"Humpf. Lord Gilles storms about the keep, berates all from lowest villein to my beloved Roland, and you say leave it be. How may I help?" The words were kindly spoken and brought tears to Emma's eyes.

"There is naught to be done." Emma bent and continued to thread the yarn that would form the warp of the fabric she would weave. Her hands were clumsy at her task, for her eyes were suddenly blurred with tears.

"You and Lord Gilles have fallen out." Sarah was relentless.

"Lord Gilles despises me." Emma broke down. She fell back to the low stool behind her and pressed her head to her knees. "Nay," she whispered, her voice barely audible. "Nay, despise is not strong enough. I had convinced myself I went to Lord Gilles to spare Angelique the hard life. In truth, I went to him for the basest of reasons. He has forced me to see myself for what I am—"

"Oh, child." Sarah gathered Emma to her ample bosom and patted Emma's back.

Emma raised her head. "I am no better than the women who sell themselves at the village alehouse. I barter myself for Angelique's food and warmth—and to gratify my own desires."

"I do not think Lord Gilles feels that is so. I think his rage bespeaks his love for you."

"Love!" Emma shot to her feet. "He has never said the word! He speaks only of desire. He has mistaken what is between William Belfour and me, and it has made him blind. I thought he esteemed me enough to trust me, but I erred. He holds me in contempt."

"William Belfour? I wondered when his attentions would draw the master's eye."

"Aye. I could kill William for taking what was sweet and wonderful and making it naught but filth and sin."

"Hush," Sarah shushed Emma, for her voice had risen and drawn the attention of the other weavers.

"Hush! Aye! Let us hide my sins. 'Tis my own fault." She fell to her knees by her friend. "Oh, Sarah, Lord

Gilles will take another to his bed and I . . . I will die from the pain of it."

"It might be better if you stayed out of Lord Gilles's sight for a while. Mayhap with distance Lord Gilles will see that you are everything to him. My Roland believes him completely besotted with you . . . and the little one. Is William her father?" Sarah dared to put the question no one else had asked.

"Aye." Emma nodded. "I was so lonely. I convinced myself that I loved him, when I only saw his face and form—"

"And believed his honeyed words!" Sarah interrupted.

"Aye, I believed his honeyed words. He denied me, denied Angelique. I counted myself one hundred times blessed that he did when I met Gilles. Oh, Sarah, Lord Gilles, he is . . . the air I breathe, the food my body needs, the very soul of me." Emma could not continue; she could no longer weep either. Emma could not tell Sarah that trust was gone—gone in one brutal instant.

Gilles allowed five days to pass before he gave in to a need he refused to name. He had neither looked for Emma in the hall, nor acknowledged her presence in chapel. The immense pride that had fueled his anger now kept him equally incapable of reconciliation or apology.

But standing on the wall-walk at night, when the stars blazed in the inky sky, in the place she'd first come to him, he felt the ache of her loss. Finally, he told himself 'twas just lust that made him feel so wretched—and lust was easily gratified.

He took the tower stairs two at a time and wove his way through the hall to find a willing wench. He watched Mark Trevalin wrap an arm about a serving woman—one of William's castoffs—and lead her from the hall. Were they all—himself included—doomed to sup at a table only if William had finished first?

William sat by the hearth with two men-at-arms, tossing dice. Three women, Angelique's nurse among them, leaned over the men's shoulders making suggestions, cheering William's luck.

Angelique's nurse looked up, saw Gilles, and offered him an invitation, squaring her shoulders and at the same time thrusting her breasts forward. He had hardly noticed the woman beyond her solicitous care of the child. That she thought little of trespassing on Emma's territory annoyed him. Then he cursed his own folly. A serving woman's loyalty lay with the lord, not his leman.

He ignored May's invitation and others that presented themselves as women sought the man who was master. None met with his approval. His footsteps neared the long stone building where the weavers and spinners slept. As lord of the manor, all men, women, and children in his care must obey him. He had planned to order Emma to his bed, but now he realized he could not face her refusal, and returned to his chamber, angry and taut with leashed desires and envies.

With a few terse words, he sent a sentry for Emma, unable to ask her to come himself. When she stood silently by his closed door, her head down, her shoulders bowed, hands clasped tightly before her, her posture told him all. He had shamed her, cowed her wonderful spirit, mayhap crushed it irreparably.

He stood confounded for a moment, unsure how to proceed. He'd let too much time pass for words to come easily.

All their moments of lovemaking had been a mutual coming together, with her often reaching out to him. He knew only how to command men.

His voice sounded harsh in the silent room. "You know why you are here, remove your clothes."

"And if I do not?" her voice trembled. "Will you beat me?"

He did not believe his ears. He whirled to the hearth. "Get on with it," he ordered.

The spinners, when they'd thought her asleep, had whispered wagers on whom Gilles would favor next. It only twisted the knife deeper that May was considered the most likely choice. Emma had tried to tell herself it did not matter—if he called for her, she would refuse.

But when the summons came, she went, a tiny part of her heart sure he wanted to beg her forgiveness.

Foolish heart.

Emma did not look at Gilles as she walked to the bed. Every night for days she'd rehearsed the words she thought might heal the rent between them, but his brusque manner struck her silent, held the words deep within her. She lost the will to say them and knew only a bleak despair. He was treating her like a leman.

Although a free woman, she could not disobey him. To do so might mean she and Angelique must leave. She was not yet ready to sever the tenuous connection she had to this man and make the trek back down the hill to the village.

With her back to him, fingers shaking, Emma unlaced her gown and dropped it in a heap. She sat down and slid her shift off her shoulders, then pulled up the covers. Her heart raced and her palms were sweaty.

She heard him strip off his clothing. Her eyes began to smart with tears. How could she endure his touch, grant his demands, if he treated her with cruelty?

She loved him, could not bear to have him touch her merely to gratify some base urge. How could she show him she loved him? How could she ever say the words aloud?

The bed dipped as Gilles climbed in beside her. She felt a trembling in her legs from tension and fear.

Gilles leaned over her. The coarse weave of the linen sheets mocked him, for they were from a less skilled weaver's hands.

The mattress quivered with the trembling of her body. It was fear of him, he felt. It shamed him. He would not be shamed by a woman who was but a servant. "You know why you are here. Do you so soon forget your duties?"

His words killed any hope in her heart. She froze as his arms closed about her. He buried his face in her hair, his breath warm against her skin. She shivered. Then he ran his hand over her and, before she could prevent it, she rose to his touch, moved into his embrace, clung to him.

Whatever she had expected, it was not this, this gentle caress. He made love to her with all the skill he had at his command. He worked upon her senses, tantalizing, teasing, licking, kissing. She closed her mind against him. She willed her mind somewhere else, but could not stem the liquid rush of desire that flooded through her body. 'Twas shameful to be so enflamed by a man who held her in contempt.

Gilles claimed her. When finally he fell upon his back, his heart racing, his body drained, he knew a deep pain that might never be assuaged, for as he'd spent himself, he'd faced a terrible truth.

Despite the fiery response of her body, his Emma was not there. He'd killed some precious part of her and, in so doing, part of himself.

Words spilled from his mouth before he could stop

211

them. "You will not hold back from me what you so willingly gave him."

Something within Emma snapped. She rolled from his embrace and slipped from the bed, then jerked on her clothes, tearing laces. "What I gave him? What tales have you heard? William, aye, let us name him, had nothing from me!"

She knotted her hands before her. "William Belfour! Let's be done with pretense. Aye, he was my lover and I thought my husband. And aye, he is Angelique's father. Did he claim her or me? Nay. Did he ever help me? Nay. I birthed his babe in Old Lowry's stable, with rats eating the birth sac as I lay in a faint.

"Widow Cooper saved me, not William! Why should I feel any loyalty, any caring for him? I was just a vessel for his lust. And why do you, his lord, not take him to task for his behavior? Because he is a man—*your man*—and I am but a woman?"

Gilles sat up. She looked him over. The bedclothes pooled about his hips. Just a few moments before, his beguiling body had claimed her, driven sense from her, maddened her. Now, the fire painted harsh shadows on his face. Hard man. Hard heart.

"I erred in first love." Her voice dropped from frantic anger to whispered sadness. "I have erred in my second love, too." She tipped up her chin, defiant again. "Well, my lord, I will not err again. I refuse you your satisfaction, save this—I never knew passion with William because he sought only his pleasure, never mine."

Gilles stared at her as she turned away.

Could she be telling the truth?

She left him with a bang of his chamber door—left

him to cold, coarse sheets. Her words ran like a litany in his mind.

Second love . . . second love . . . love . . . love.

A knot of ice lodged in his chest. She had loved him. His eyes burned with tears he denied, as he'd denied their love.

Chapter Fourteen

The next morning, Mark Trevalin roused Gilles from a restless sleep. His head pounded as if he'd had too much ale.

"My lord, I beg leave to disturb you. The village . . . I fear 'tis in flames. The smoke is everywhere!"

"Mon Dieu!" Gilles rolled from the bed. "Summon the men. Saddle the horses." He snatched at his discarded clothing. In moments, he was striding through the hall, looking neither left nor right as he called for his horse.

Roland caught up with Gilles near the stable yard as he talked to the village lad who'd originally sounded the alarm. "What is it?" Roland asked, gasping for air.

"A thief, likely one I trusted William to string up, has fired an abandoned cottage. These damnable winds have cast the embers to others. The village is in turmoil. Again! Order all the men available to help carry water from the village well. I want to see to the matter myself."

At that moment a groom arrived leading the mare Gilles favored for short rides. He swung into the saddle. "Trevalin will see to the gathering of the men. Attend me, Roland."

"Is there fear of the fire spreading?" Roland asked, looking up to Gilles.

Though Gilles's hair was tied back with a leather thong, the high winds tossed the loose strands about his brow. That brow was deeply furrowed with anger. "With my luck of late? Be sure of it."

Roland's horse was brought forward. From the vantage point of his saddle, he saw thick smoke billowing skyward.

Gilles's mount thundered over the drawbridge, Roland on his heels, and scattered people, who barely had time to escape the hooves. They swung off to the west, toward the plume of smoke rising beyond a cluster of cottages.

As they neared the conflagration, their mounts sidled and reared in fear.

Gilles slid off his mare and soothed her until she quieted, then he turned her reins over to a stout man who hurried to assist him. Roland ran after Gilles through the frightened clusters of people passing buckets of water. They aimed to soak the thatch of the roofs of the nearest cottages threatened by the flames. The fire, larger than Roland had anticipated, made him swallow hard. His mother had died in a fire.

Gilles pulled off his mantle and offered it to a woman who stood and stared, tears running down her face. She shivered in naught but a shift. Her feet were fiery red. He spied Roland and turned her over to him.

"Find a woman to care for her. We need you here." Gilles disappeared into the swirls of smoke that enveloped one end of the line of people who fought the flames.

Roland felt the woman quiver in his arms. He looked down and saw what Gilles had seen. The woman must have walked across one of the patches of burning hay. Her feet looked painful, though the woman seemed oblivious. Roland looked wildly about until he saw an old woman.

"Grandmother. Take this poor woman. She's in need of care; her feet are burned."

"Aye. Mistress, come with me." The villagers nearby surged forward and offered their help, glad to be of some assistance rather just standing and watching their homes burn. The lines of men passing buckets made little headway. The winds were too strong.

Gilles strode out of the smoke, his face streaked with grime, and spoke with Roland. "There's little help for that end of the village. We've soaked the thatch here, and we can but hope. Most surely, the gods are punishing me." He shook his fist at the azure sky overhead. "Where are the rains now?"

Then he was engulfed by a throng of panicked people. He promised all shelter at the keep, and help for those burned. He soothed and calmed. He shepherded the people away from the lines of men passing the buckets. He issued directives to the able. Finally, he and Roland joined Trevalin, where he stood with a line of men who were trying to save the alehouse. "I've assigned tasks, more to keep the idle busy and panic down," Gilles said to the men, "but there's little to be done." *And little to return home to.* He sighed. "I'll stay until the fire is out."

Word of the devastating fire's consequences raced through the village, over the drawbridge and into the keep. Emma hurried to join the crowd in the bailey to hear news of the village. As villagers once again thronged to the keep in the age-old seeking of shelter, as they would in a siege, Emma searched their faces for friends. Widow Cooper, hair windblown, soot on her plump cheeks, trudged in her direction from the inner bailey. Alone.

Waving frantically, and unable to breach the throngs of people, Emma caught her friend's attention. "Thank God you're well." Emma clutched the kindly woman to her breast when they finally found a way to each other.

"Aye. I am. But others were not so fortunate." The widow swept her hands down her skirts, spotted with soot.

"Your son? The children?" Emma asked, her eyes searching the crowd again. She would never have admitted it was Gilles she sought.

"The young ones are settled in the chapel. Eating their 'eads off. My boy's fine. Able, 'e is, and thus Lord Gilles has set 'im to fight the fire. There's a one!"

"Who?" Emma took the widow's arm and led her through the masses of people toward the hall.

"Why, Lord Gilles. Other nobles would 'ave let the village burn and sent their steward to assess the losses, with a mind on taxes to cover 'em, too, no doubt."

Emma tried to keep her voice even and calm. "Did you see him?"

"Aye. I was close enough to touch 'is 'and if'n I'd so desired. There's one not too proud to pass a bucket o' water with 'umble folk. God love 'im."

How easy, Emma thought, to forgive him in light of the widow's report. He'd behaved in an admirable way. It was such behavior that had made her love him, but he had

218

another side, a dark side, one he'd hidden from her. Angry words might occur daily in the village, but Emma had elevated Gilles to another plane. She'd made a god of him in her dreams and in her life. Now he'd fallen from grace. She choked back tears of anguish as the widow rambled on about Gilles.

"Come, help me with the children," Emma urged the widow.

"Nay. Take me to the kitchens. I'd be 'appier 'elpin' prepare a meal for this vast crowd than watchin' babes. They'll surely need extra 'ands in the kitchen, don't ye think? Ye could watch the babes 'til my son comes."

Emma had to agree. She sighed. The last thing she wished was to bandy words with the widow's son. Emma left the widow in the kitchens in Beatrice's care, and went into the chapel to see what she could do. In short order she was bathing grime from children's faces and helping to entertain them while spouses found their partners and groups of adults gathered to tell their own separate tales of the fire. The villagers seemed sure that Lord Gilles would come to their aid as promised.

No lives had been lost, so the atmosphere was not one of great sorrow. The greatest loss, deserving of much mourning, appeared to be a goodly number of kegs of ale.

She looked about. Smoke wreathed the high beams overhead as torches burned in the chapel's wall brackets. The cross at the front mocked her. She touched the one about her neck. A servant hastened by her with a tray of loaves of bread, which he handed to Father Bernard to distribute. A mother soothed her crying child. The stink of smoke clung to everyone's clothing and hair. The widow's son lay asleep in a tangle of his children's arms and legs, Angelique among them.

219

Carefully, so as not to wake her, Emma lifted Angelique into her arms. Another would need the space. But when she came to the building that housed the spinners and weavers, she found every available space taken. Her pack hung from a peg on the wall. She lifted it and tiptoed away.

Chapter Fifteen

Sarah removed the bandages from Gilles's hand and, with Roland peering over her shoulder, inspected the burns on his palm and fingers. " 'Tis healing well, my lord, but the leech should see it."

He shrugged. "He will do naught but bleed me. I am burned, not feverish." She coated the wounds with goose grease, then wrapped his hand in clean strips of cloth. When it was done, Gilles rose and cleared his throat. "Mistress Sarah, may I have a word with Roland?" He stood indecisively before the couple. He'd never known their closeness; in truth, had never before sought it, or realized it was missing from his life—until Emma.

"Aye, but not for long, my lord." Sarah gave her husband's knee a squeeze and slid silently from the chamber.

"Gilles?" Roland hooked his foot on a rung of Sarah's stool and pulled it toward him. He propped his feet up and began to pare his nails with a small sharp knife.

"Roland, we should seek those villagers tomorrow who are capable of speaking for the rest. We need to assess how the rebuilding is going."

"Aye." Roland nodded.

Gilles took an apple from the table and took a bite. He frowned. It was hard and mealy, tasting of ashes, as did all he ate these days. "I know nothing of thatching cottages. I am better suited to determining Richard's ransom!"

"Aye. But you'll soon learn." Roland settled back into a lazy posture again.

Gilles sat on Sarah's stool after pushing Roland's boots to the floor. He was now at eye level with his friend. Roland returned to his nails, with apparent lack of interest.

Silence reigned. A log fell in a shower of sparks and fragrant smoke. A child cried out for its mother and Gilles thought of Angelique. Anguish smote him.

He rested his elbows on his knees and clasped his hands. "Emma and I, we have had a falling out."

"Tell me something the entire keep does not know." Roland snorted.

"Jesu. Must you make of everything a jest?" Gilles turned his anger on his friend. He leapt to his feet and made for the door.

"Gilles, stop. I did not mean to offend you." Roland also rose. He stood in stiff anticipation before the hearth. "I have promised Sarah I would lend you an ear should you broach the subject yourself. There'll be domestic hell to pay if I let this opportunity slip by."

Gilles stood, taut and angry, by the door. Suddenly his shoulders slumped. He had no other of whom to seek advice, no one whose advice he valued more, no one to whom he could speak frankly.

"What I am about to tell you, it must remain here. It is not for Sarah, either."

" 'Twill be hard to keep any secrets from her." Roland sheathed his knife and approached Gilles. "Secrets between husband and wife foster distrust and make for acrimony."

"Then only Sarah." Gilles felt raw and on edge. He felt at sea, a feeling new to one so used to command. "I know all about secrets."

"Then sit and tell your tale."

Gilles strode past Roland and slammed a fist on the sturdy table, causing goblets to leap, and apples to roll. "Angelique is William's babe."

"Never." Roland grasped Gilles's shoulder, spun him around. He saw the stark truth in Gilles's eyes. And he saw deep pain.

"She believed herself in love, made vows with him."

"What kind of vows would William offer a woman?" Roland sniffed.

"The kind that would hasten the lifting of a skirt."

"What can I say, friend?" Roland gave Gilles's shoulder a squeeze.

"Nothing. There's nothing to be said. *Mon Dieu*, I have said it all—already—to Emma." He let the pain burn up his throat again, and had to turn abruptly away to hide his emotion. Bracing his hands on the table, he confessed. "It ate at me. *Mon Dieu*. It tore me apart. One night I let my jealousy get the better of me." Gilles could feel the blood rise to stain his cheeks.

"Did she wish to hold William to his pledge?" Roland asked.

"I think . . . not." Gilles raked his fingers through his hair. "*Mon Dieu*. I do not know. Jesu, Roland. He is but a

223

score of years." He whirled to face his friend. "I cannot fathom why she would want my company, other than the obvious reasons."

"What are the obvious reasons?"

"My position . . . William's rejection of her . . . my ability to offer Angelique a better life . . . " He burned with leashed emotion.

"Mayhap she seeks you because she sees much to admire and loves you."

It was Gilles's turn to snort in derision. "Loves me? Aye, loves the benefits of whore to the lord of the manor." He punctuated his pain by slamming his fist on the table again.

"You just called her a whore." Roland frowned. "Am I the only one to whom you've called Emma a whore? I tell you, I like the wench, and do not approve of what you would make her."

Gilles paced the chamber. "I was angry. I called her my leman when only she was there, but . . . I was shouting. It is possible others heard. I made her out to be nothing, when she is everything to me."

"So . . . we have the heart of the matter. She took exception, justly so, and shuns you."

"Shuns me?" Gilles began to laugh. It was an ugly sound. "She despises me. Yet I know if I command her to me, she will come." He again turned away from his friend and stared into the fire. It burned as they had burned, but now he had naught but ashes. "I summoned her once. 'Twas an agony to have her . . . nay, she was not there. She inhabited my bed, but her soul was not there. What use is that—to know she comes only in obedience, or worse, fear?"

"Gilles. Decide how you feel about the wench and act upon it. It is unlike you to equivocate on any subject."

Thrill to the most sensual, adventure-filled Romances on the market today...

FROM  LOVE SPELL BOOKS

As a home subscriber to the Love Spell Romance Book Club, you'll enjoy the best in today's BRAND-NEW Time Travel, Futuristic, Legendary Lovers, Perfect Heroes and other genre romance fiction. For five years, Love Spell has brought you the award-winning, high-quality authors you know and love to read. Each Love Spell romance will sweep you away to a world of high adventure...and intimate romance. Discover for yourself all the passion and excitement millions of readers thrill to each and every month.

Save $5.00 Each Time You Buy!

Every other month, the Love Spell Romance Book Club brings you four brand-new titles from Love Spell Books. EACH PACKAGE WILL SAVE YOU AT LEAST $5.00 FROM THE BOOKSTORE PRICE! And you'll never miss a new title with our convenient home delivery service.

Here's how we do it: Each package will carry a FREE 10-DAY EXAMINATION privilege. At the end of that time, if you decide to keep your books, simply pay the low invoice price of $17.96, no shipping or handling charges added. HOME DELIVERY IS ALWAYS FREE. With today's top romance novels selling for $5.99 and higher, our price SAVES YOU AT LEAST $5.00 with each shipment.

AND YOUR FIRST TWO-BOOK SHIPMENT IS TOTALLY FREE!

IT'S A BARGAIN YOU CAN'T BEAT! A SUPER $11.48 Value!

Love Spell ✦ A Division of Dorchester Publishing Co., Inc.

GET YOUR 2 FREE BOOKS NOW–AN $11.48 VALUE!

Mail the Free Book Certificate Today!

Get Two Books Totally
F R E E —
An $11.48 Value!

▼ Tear Here and Mail Your FREE Book Card Today! ▼

PLEASE RUSH
MY TWO FREE
BOOKS TO ME
RIGHT AWAY!

Love Spell Romance Book Club
P.O. Box 6613
Edison, NJ 08818-6613

AFFIX
STAMP
HERE

Roland crossed the chamber and placed his hand on his friend's arm. "An apology may be just what is needed. I apologize for much—whether I am to blame or not. It soothes the womanly spirit. And, for what it is worth, my Sarah and I believe that Emma feels naught but contempt for Belfour."

"Contempt?" Gilles asked doubtfully.

"Aye. The man is relentless. There is more than one maid in this keep who has cause to despise him for his heartless rutting. Believe your Emma. If she says that naught is between them . . . then it is so. She has confided in my Sarah that 'tis you she loves. I believe she said some ridiculous nonsense about you being the very air she breathes, or some such jongleur's words fit only for wenches and jakes."

Gilles began to pace. "I must speak to her. 'Tis difficult—"

"Aye—especially since she is no longer here." Roland stepped back from his friend's ire, hands raised. "I only bear the tale."

"Where is she?" Gilles asked. "I assumed, when I did not see her about the hall, that she was avoiding me."

Roland shook his head.

Gilles thought he had felt the limits of his pain, but Roland's words took him to a dark place he did not want to visit.

Emma had left him.

"Sarah says the wench has returned to what she was—whatever that means." Roland's words were lost as Gilles stormed from the chamber, and clattered down the stairs. Men scattered as he ran across the cobbles of the bailey. He burst into the chatter of the weavers. "Sarah," he roared. "Where is she?"

Sarah rose from her place and laid aside her hand-

Ann Lawrence

work. "Now you wish to know!" She spoke loudly, near as ever a person might be to impertinent without the punishment of a whipping. Both ignored the interested stares of the other weavers. " 'Tis four days, my lord, since she left this place. Four days. Much harm may befall such a sweet and guileless woman as Emma in four days, especially in a village half-burned and in turmoil. She said that by going she made more room for those in need. 'Twas just an excuse. How could you have let this come to pass?"

"Consider me suitably chastised," Gilles thundered. "I thought I was practicing patience and forbearance. Where is she?"

"You will treat her with care, my lord?"

Sarah's audacity went unnoticed. Gilles was in a fever. "Aye. Where?"

"Against the wall. Go east."

Gilles went to his chamber and snatched up a mantle. He sought her on foot, thrusting past everyone in his path, unseeing. Snow filled the air, swirling about him, laying a white blanket over the scars of the fire.

It took him no more than three-quarters of an hour to find her place. The loom betrayed her to him, though she was not there.

He could pace her hut in two strides. The space was cold. He touched his fingertips to the stone wall and shivered. In moments, he'd lighted her brazier. Its scant heat did little to warm him. The thought of her sleeping here, of Angelique, made him pause. As he fed her small store of sticks to the meager flames, he sensed she'd returned.

He rose and faced her. She studied him in silence and then gestured to the gray world outside. Snowflakes clung to her mantle.

226

"Please step without, my lord." Her words were calmly spoken, but were as cold as the winter wind.

"I do not want to talk with you before the whole village, Emma." He stood silently by her loom until she shrugged in resignation, entered, and seated herself on her stool. The space was barely warmed by the small brazier.

"Your presence will merely confirm what all suspect of me."

"Then we shall leave the door open so the curious will have their questions answered." He flung the door back. A gust of wind threatened the weak flames of the fire. "Where is Angelique?" He dropped into a crouch before her, pulling his dagger from its sheath and playing its point over the beaten earth floor, tracing random designs.

"Is the knife some means of intimidating me into telling you where she is, my lord?" Emma asked.

"Forgive me, Emma, it is just a habit of mine," Gilles said, rising and sheathing the knife. "Where is she?" He hid his real purpose behind his concern for Angelique. Just being in Emma's presence robbed him of his ability to articulate, robbed him of his composure. He felt raw and exposed.

"Safe."

"Safe? What danger has her lodged somewhere far from her mother?" Gilles was astounded. "What do you fear?"

"She is safe from your anger." Emma knotted her hands.

"My anger?" Incredulity streaked across his face. "I mean no harm to Angelique. How could you think I would harm her, an innocent child? I have only affection and concern for her. Nay—I would never hurt her!"

227

"I thought you would never hurt me, my lord. I was very wrong. There is ofttimes as much harm in words as in a fist."

A deep flush heated his cheeks as she stared at him. "It is hardly the same thing," he said.

"I beg to differ—it is the same thing. When you are angry, you lash out. Angelique is mine . . . and as you said, the only thing I have in this world. I'll protect her from you and anyone else that may harm her. Promise you'll never come here again, never speak to her, and I'll bring her home. She will have a safe and contented life here with me, and I with her."

Only the sound of their breathing pierced the silence that followed her words.

Never to see Emma or Angelique again.

Gilles cleared his throat and looked away first. "Emma, I was wrong to lash out as I did. It was a grievous error in judgment. I would have your forgiveness."

"Nay, Gilles. I'll never forgive you. All knew what was between us. All knew you had me at your leisure." Emma's voice broke. "I was a fool twice. The first time the foolishness was of my own making. Yet I have Angelique to compensate me for that error. She is my sign from God that surely He forgave me my foolishness. But I erred again. Only this mistake has no compensation—only pain and more pain." Her eyes glinted with tears. "How foolish I was to degrade myself to be with you, to lie with you without vows. I had no pride. I told myself that I could put aside the words I'd said to William, could pretend I did not make my child a bastard in the doing. You brought me most brutally to my senses."

Never to be forgiven. The pain was enormous, a stone in his throat, a burning conflagration in his belly.

Her voice dropped to a whisper. "There is no forgiveness necessary. Did you know that I'm referred to at the well as Lord Gilles's cast-out whore? I do not need to forgive you, my lord, for treating me as a man treats his whore. Your behavior was appropriate in every way. I was beneath contempt and you treated me thusly. Do not seek forgiveness for acting on the truth. Just go away and let me be. Never come back. Ever."

"I can't promise. I can't stay away," Gilles said softly. His guts burned. How efficiently he'd destroyed her. How efficiently he'd made his own future a hell.

Emma sank back to the stool and began to cry. She held her hands stiffly in her lap and let the tears roll down her cheeks and wept openly. She didn't care if he watched. She was defeated. How could she have imagined that a baron would heed any wish of a weaver? How could she have imagined that he would honor her request? How could she have imagined how bleak life would be without him, without his love?

"Emma." Gilles went down on one knee before her. He touched her bowed head with a tentative hand. "Don't cry. I never meant to hurt you, but I must see you."

All the days of upset congealed into a ball of fury within her. Each day, just drawing water was an exercise in her defeat. Each walk through the warren of hovels and stalls that crouched at the castle's base was a torture of proposition and lewd suggestions.

Each day was a lesson in a woman's place beneath the heel of man. She shot to her feet; the tears gleamed on her cheeks. "You must see me?" She yanked at the lacing of her gown. "Are you willing to pay me? I could get tuppence from the mercer for a look at my breasts. Sixpence to lie on my back for the alehouse customers," she taunted.

He stumbled back as she jerked open her woolen gown

and kirtle, baring her breasts to him. "See me, my lord. See me." Her naked breasts heaved as she gulped in air. "Have me, have me if that is your will. But first, let me close the door." She slammed it with all her strength. "The village harlots hang a rag on the latch as a signal they are occupied. Have you a piece of cloth? Mayhap your belt will do!"

Gilles held his hands palms out. He could not bear the words she spoke. "Catch hold of yourself, Emma. Stop this."

"Haven't you sixpence, my lord?"

"Stop it!" He grasped her wrists and pinned her to the rough stone wall. She fought wildly against his strength, bent and bit his hands, kicked his shins. He wrapped his arms about her, held her tightly against his chest, ignored any pain she inflicted, until she went still in his arms, sobbing and heaving gasps of breath. He lifted her and carried her to the straw-stuffed pallet and placed her gently there. He stretched out beside her, his arms still tightly holding her in case she flew out of control again.

She lay stiff as an iron pike in his arms. Tears ran over her cheeks. There was a streak of blood from his hand on her cheek. Every muscle in her body quivered against him. Her eyes gleamed dark blue, filled with her shame.

As if a bolt of lightning had struck him, he felt what she felt, knew what it had cost her to come to him as a lover. A tremor ran along his arms to his hands where they held her. There must be an answer that would allow them to be together.

Darkness fell and still he held her. He stroked her hair and held her loosely against his chest. He did not speak, and eventually her head fell against him.

He rose once and went out to the side of her hut to relieve himself. 'Twas then he noticed the stench of refuse that lay on the misty night air and the stink of charred wood. That she must daily take in these scents added to his guilt.

When he returned, he gathered her back into his arms and held her close, stroking her hair, which smelled of a soap he knew was poor stuff. She was clean, but no essence of flowers scented the soaps she used. He did not like the thought of harsh soaps against her skin.

He dozed, and woke finding that dawn had broken. He eased from her arms and shut the door, closed them into the small space. When he returned to the pallet, he saw that she was awake. He stretched beside her and began to speak. "I am no longer young, Emma."

"How does youth enter into this?" She was calm now, had been awake a long time, listening to his heartbeat. She was no more sure of what to do now than when she'd attacked him. Her whole being flooded with humiliation at how she'd lost control, just as he had . . . and how she'd blamed him, held it against him.

"He is but a score of years." He fisted his hand and smacked the earth beside them. "I have lines on my face, scars on my body. I cannot compete with such youth."

"You have no need to compete." She rose on her elbow and looked down at the stark honesty on his face. How could this have escaped her? He envied William in a way she couldn't understand. "I see the power in you, the many facets of your character. Aye, I also see the smoothness of William's youth, the facile nature of his being. Were he three score he would not have your wisdom or caring. I don't compare you, Gilles. Please believe me." She pressed her palm to his chest, felt the rapid, agitated beat of his heart. "I care not for your age."

"I feel like the old men of jests who are helped to

231

climb on their wives. I may not be there now, but in a few years . . . "

"Nay. I will not have it!"

"If you still love him—"

"I love *you*. I want nothing more than to be with you. I believe you interpreted my ardor as experience—experience I gained with William, but I never found passion with him," she whispered. "He took me but once, and 'twas over before I knew what had happened. What I had with you cannot compare.

"Only you have made me feel passion. Anything William told you is a man's bragging—swelling his prowess before one more powerful than he. You are all that is powerful to me, Gilles. It is an intangible that all in your presence feel. When you saved me in the forest, I thought 'twas the devil come to claim me. I wanted only to be swept into hell with you. And I have been to hell, Gilles, the hell of wanting you, needing you, and knowing I'm but a vessel for your lust."

"How can I take those words back into my throat?" Gilles's hand was unsteady as he stroked her cheek with his knuckles.

"You can't take them back; they will always be there."

"Always?" He could barely say the word.

"I don't know." And she didn't.

"You were never just a leman to me. I love you, Emma. I have been wracked with jealousy at William's knowledge of you. Wracked with guilt that I had the power to make him acknowledge you and Angelique—and yet I did not. Did I know even at the judging that I would one day want you for myself?

"When I saw you at the stairs with him, I thought you had lain with him, but I should have listened, and believed in you. To do anything else was to deny what it is I love about you—your sweetness, your caring, your inner beauty." He looked away. "I thought you wanted him in your bed. I was the fool, not you."

Emma rose above him, bent down to him, and stroked his cheek. "I want only you. I see you in my dreams. I see you in my mind's eye as I weave, the shuttle flying in patterns it knows by heart, weaving you into the cloth of my life."

When he did not respond, she hurried on. "I met William and saw only his beauty. Nay, 'twas his words—his songs that lured me in. I was so lonely, and he offered what I had lost when my mother died. I thought I loved him, when, in truth, I knew nothing about him. When I met you—at the judging—I felt struck by some disease, a fever to be near you, to know you. I beg you to understand—you are like the warp of my fabric, woven into my life. The cloth is not whole if you draw those threads. It falls apart. When I'm with you—flesh to flesh—I am like a person possessed."

"I cannot live without you," he said, his hand slipping into her hair.

"I promised before God I would be with no other."

His black eyes roamed her face. "But you are not really free." He touched her breast. "Not here, not within your heart."

Silence stretched between them. Finally, he rose on one knee, and pulled her to sit before him. He lifted her hand and spread it open, palm up on his right hand. With his left, he touched each finger, traced the calluses there at the tips, stroked the lines of her palm. When her fingers curled about his, captured his caressing hand, he lifted their joined hands to his mouth.

"Forgive me," he breathed against her skin. "There is naught to my life without you—free or not."

She fisted her hands in his hair, yanked his head back, and studied his face. "Even if I were free, a weaver may not wed a lord."

"She may if the lord wishes it."

Her hand trembled as she traced the shape of his brow. "You would say vows with me, at the church?"

"Aye. If we can free you, will you wed me?"

"Free me?" Her voice trembled.

"I have been thinking all night. We could see the Abbot. Seek a dispensation from the archbishop, if necessary. It would benefit everyone." He smiled and captured her hand. "I could purchase a great window for the abbey, with the Abbot's face as St. Peter or some such."

She could not prevent a smile, but then just as quickly as it had appeared, it died. "And if freedom is not possible?"

"It is possible. I feel it in my bones; I believe it." His voice became rough with emotion. "I promised you I would be with no other."

Peace flooded through her. The dawn no longer looked a dull gray, but silver—precious, foretelling a day worth living. "I, too, promised to be with no other."

Their lips touched in a gentle caress, his tentative, and fearful of frightening her with the sheer power of his need. Her fingers traced the shape of his face, skimmed his throat, his chest, and flattened over his groin. Her caresses there set him to groaning, and he cupped her face as his mouth grew hungry and urgent. She met his ardor, degree by fevered degree, stoking the flames to a conflagration. Painstakingly, Emma unlaced and removed his clothing until he was naked.

On her knees at his side, she kissed him as lightly as a butterfly sips nectar, from his shoulder to his knee. She visited her favorite places, the hard male nipples, the black wings of hair across his chest, the sleek muscles of his arms and thighs that shuddered with leashed power beneath her touch. She examined his bandages and kissed the tips of his injured fingers.

Every place she touched, burned. The golden skeins of her hair slipped across his shoulders and arms. He shivered with anticipation. He pulled her into his arms and atop him.

Together, they slid sword into sheath, and then were swept away. His hands snatched her down, breast to breast as their hips and mouths met in a clash. She took him and he took her. They burned at the same moment, and quickly, like a spark to dry straw. Emma tore her mouth from his just as the incredible heat of her release swept her. Her cries of ecstasy were her gift to him. He pulled her mouth back to his, his kisses gentle now, to soothe her lips. He touched her soul; she possessed his.

The sunlight striped the dirt floor, mice rustled through the thatching. They lay entwined on the pallet in a fierce embrace.

Gilles swallowed hard and linked his fingers tightly with hers as he spoke into the charged atmosphere—said it all so no more stood between them.

"William is my son."

He held his breath as he awaited her response. Would it be condemnation? Would it be horror? How he wished he'd said the words before they'd made love.

Emma slowly withdrew her hands, reached across him, and drew his mantle up and about her. So much was now explained, she thought. 'Twas more than simple envy of youth, 'twas envy of a youthful son. An unacknowledged son.

"Why have you not claimed him?"

He heard curiosity in her voice, not censure. When she spread the mantle to include him and rested her head on his chest, an incredible tension loosened in his body.

"His existence would have caused great pain to my wife. Margaret and I were a match of land and power. She cared little for me, I suppose, yet it was inexcusable to have dallied elsewhere whilst she was . . . Nicholas is only six months older than William, if you understand. I am ashamed of my behavior, even now, twenty years later."

"Did you love William's mother?" Emma asked, listening to the rapid hammer of his heart.

"Nay." Gilles rolled from the pallet, disentangled himself from her arms and the mantle, and drew on his clothes. He'd been naked enough. He bent and lightly touched her cheek. "When William's mother came to me, I doubted I was the father of her babe. Others had lain with her, too, habitually. But my honor said I should help her, for I had had her a number of times, and was old enough to feel the responsibility.

"We bartered over him. A worthy husband and her silence for my wife's peace of mind. I found her the husband, and paid gladly every year for William's keep whilst Margaret lived. She may not have loved me, but she cared deeply for her good name and her place at Henry's court."

"Oh, Gilles." Tears pricked Emma's eyes, and he caught one, and wiped it away with his thumb.

"It somehow felt incestuous to lie with my son's woman, the mother of my granddaughter. I felt so old . . . and yet lacking in the wisdom I should have gained with those years. I understand now that I cannot demand what is in your heart. You must give it freely, or it is worth nothing." He knelt before her. "Whatever comes, let me love you, and Angelique."

Emma felt his pain. It was as tangible as the love he'd poured into her but moments before. He was stripping himself bare before her. What knowledge he was giving into her hands. How much she understood of him now. How easy it was to forgive him.

"Aye, Gilles. You may love me . . . and Angelique."

Chapter Sixteen

Emma stood in awe of the Abbot. He did not once look at her or appear to be aware she was present. She felt beneath his notice.

The wealth of the Abbot's apartment amazed her. He lived far better than Gilles. Tapestries hung on the walls, silk covers graced the stools.

The Abbot rubbed his chin. "I will not speak merely to please you, Lord Gilles. The simple folk of the village ofttimes say their vows in bed."

Emma felt her cheeks heat. Her stomach churned.

"Emma and William are not 'simple' folk." Gilles rose and paced the elegant apartment.

"No. It seems obvious to me this William Belfour sought to lure an innocent to sin. Shameful." The Abbot closed his eyes and tipped his head back against the high headrest of his silk-covered chair. A few minutes later, he sat straight, and Emma knew a pronouncement was coming. She held her breath. The Abbot would say aye or nay, and from that moment, they must abide by his word. She would be a true wife, or forever but a mistress.

Suddenly, she did not care. Surely, God had sent Gilles to save her in the forest. How could He then condemn their love?

The Abbot impaled them with a sharp look down his long nose. "Our beloved Holy Father wishes that every marriage be consecrated by a priest. I, personally, believe a marriage is not valid without such a blessing. Indeed, I do not recognize the marriage of this"—he swept his thin hand in Emma's direction—"weaver and Sir William. Be at ease. I shall have a dispensation drawn for you this very day for the archbishop's attention. You may then marry at any time. In fact"—he impaled them both with a glare—"I suggest you do so immediately, to give her child a name."

Gilles took Emma to fetch Angelique from a ploughman's home, where she had lodged in return for a length of cloth.

Together, they went home to the keep. He strode through the crowds in the hall to the high table. He drew her close to his side. Before them all, he rapped his dagger on the edge of a metal goblet. A hush fell over the hall.

"We have had enough of tragedy these past few weeks—the collapse of the north wall, the fire . . . " A murmur rose at his words. Heads bobbed in agreement. "In a fortnight, I propose to give us all a moment of joy in this dark time—a celebration. You are all invited, every man, woman, and child of the village and manor, to a wedding feast."

A thunderous shout rose. There had not been a feast at

Hawkwatch Keep in many years. Gilles waited for the tumult to subside. He saw anticipation and hope on faces that before had seemed drawn and discouraged. He saw his son William standing at the periphery of the crowd, arms crossed on his chest, puzzlement on his face.

"I offer you my future bride." Gilles lifted Emma's hand and, before them all, kissed her fingers. Angelique strained in Emma's arms to reach for Gilles. He laughed, snatched her from Emma, and tucked the child into the crook of this arm. The crowd cheered as he leaned over and kissed Emma with a passion that caused her face to flood with heat.

Grinning, Gilles faced his people. And they were his people, he realized as he looked over the upturned faces. He was as responsible for their happiness as for their pain. It no longer seemed a burden, but instead, a privilege.

When the long, exhausting day finally ended, Gilles mounted the stairs. Emma sat on a stool by the fire rocking Angelique. A tenderness welled in his breast. He stood there in silence and watched mother and child.

She looked up and smiled. "I hope one day to nurture your child, Gilles."

He turned away and went to the window embrasure. He threw open the shutters. "I must send for Nicholas. I want you to meet him in better circumstances . . . and, of course, his wife, Catherine. She is wonderful. An artful healer."

Emma watched him warily. No smile lit his features. "What is it? Have I said aught amiss?"

With an abrupt shake of his head, he turned back to her. Leaning against the stone window ledge, he seemed one with the black velvet sky behind him. His features were solemn.

"There should be only honesty between us, my love. That is why I must tell you a child between us is unlikely."

She tilted her head and gazed at Angelique's downy cheek. She placed the sleeping child gently on the fur pallet by their bed. When Angelique settled, she went to stand at Gilles's side. "Explain what you mean."

With an infinite sadness, he lifted his hand to her cheek. "I was two score this Epiphany. Did you know I was so old?"

A fierce anger coursed through her. "You could be three or four score and I would not care," she almost shouted. "I love you. I will not hear this talk of age again."

Gilles wrapped his arms about her waist. "You are as fierce in your defense of me as in your anger. But you must listen. A man of my age has had . . . women, my love."

She leaned back to better see his face. "Many, Gilles?"

He nodded. "Many. Only after my wife died, I swear it. It has been eleven years since her death. I've never fathered a bastard in all that time. Never."

"What of William and Nicholas?" she ventured, puzzled, unsure what he was saying.

"I was ten and seven when I fathered them. In the years since, I've never left a woman with child. Do you understand?"

Emma studied his face. "You only had barren women?"

Gilles moved away from her and smiled ruefully. "I know 'tis the belief of most men and women that 'tis the woman who is to blame when no heir is born, no child conceived. In the early days of my marriage, my wife and I worked most diligently at giving Nicholas a brother. Do I need to say more? Another reason to wed a younger man."

Emma touched his back. The muscles were rigid beneath her hand. "Make love to me, Gilles. I care not if a babe results. You have no need of an heir. I have Angelique. We have each other. 'Tis enough."

He bore her to the bed and made short work of their clothing. Rising on his knees, he drew the bed curtains tightly closed, cocooning them in their private space. When they lay facing each other, he spoke. "I have laid bare my soul to you as I have never done to another person in my life. What is it about you?"

"What is it about you that makes me turn liquid inside? Makes my heart beat so, makes life seem empty without you?"

He smiled and cupped her face in his palms. "That night—on the wall. I have never been touched in such a way. I do not mean your hand on my body. I mean in my heart."

Emma captured his hand and placed it on her breast. "Touch me, my lord, here."

He felt the rapid beat of her heart. "I felt your fear that day in the woods. With the dogs. I felt it the moment you received the wound on your leg. You are somehow a part of me."

She drew his fingers slowly along her breast to the tight crest. It ached for his caress. He bent his head and took the swollen tip into his mouth. She moaned at the exquisite feel of his warm, wet tongue on her. As he caressed her, she wrapped her hand around his manhood. With slow, gentle strokes, she offered him pleasure, wringing a moan from deep in his chest.

When he would have moved atop her, she held him back. Instead, she lay facing him, her hands on him, savoring the satiny smooth texture of him. She rubbed her palms over him, then down his thighs, between them, up and over him again. Sweat gilded his skin. She bent her head over him.

With a strangled oath, he pulled her forcefully back, and all gentleness between them disappeared. He plundered her mouth. He mounted her in a near brutal plunge. She welcomed him, bore his ardor, returned it with savage pleasure.

When they fell back into the pillows, chests heaving, mouths open and gasping for air, she felt the tears well up in her eyes at the shattering pleasure he'd wrung from her. She fell instantly to sleep.

Gilles did not sleep. He thought of what lay ahead. A visit to the archbishop. A possible need to offer a suitably large gift to the church.

A few hours later, Emma shifted closer to him and he realized the room had grown cold.

He slipped from the bed, folding back one curtain to allow the light to enter the bed. Emma opened her eyes and smiled at him. Before going to the fire, he looked her over, sprawled in his furs. "I thought of you here, warmed by my passion, but it is you who has warmed me."

He moved to the fire. She gasped.

"What is it?" He hurried back to the bed.

Emma touched a long scrape on his upper arm. He looked down and shook his head. "I've had worse wounds. 'Twas gained in loving combat. Do not concern yourself." He watched the color flood her face. "In truth, the wound I dealt myself that night I accused you of preferring William pained me more than any wound I've had from dagger or sword." Then he smiled and kissed her nose before tending the fire.

The sight of him at the hearth, the muscles of his back moving as he worked, sent her from the bed. She knelt behind him and traced the ridges of muscle that edged his spine.

She urged him to his back, there upon the rush-strewn floor. Astride him, hands planted on his shoulders, she possessed him as the flame possessed the wood, burning in a lick of searing heat, each movement of her body meant to seal their troth, bind him to her, and wipe the doubt from his mind.

The next morning, feeling rather dull from a night with little sleep, Gilles accompanied Sarah to the armory. Big Robbie nodded when they arrived and handed over a sword and belt. Gilles weighed the sword in his hand. He swiped the air a few times, then sheathed it. "I like the balance. You've done a fine job." He unbuckled the sword belt. "Mistress Sarah will require it within the sennight." Big Robbie grunted assent.

Gilles gave Sarah a smile. " 'Tis a fine gift. Roland will treasure it." Little Robbie rushed forward and reverently held out his arms for the sword. Gilles placed it on the boy's palms with equal gravity.

The heavy clatter of hooves distracted him from the boy's devoted attention. He stepped from the armory and looked toward the gate that separated the lower bailey from the middle. A party of men rode through the gate a moment later.

They bore the royal colors. Something dark and forbidding seized Gilles's heart and squeezed. Several grooms rushed forward to assist the riders to dismount. When one groom pointed to where Gilles stood at the armory door, he strode to the party.

"My lord Gilles d'Argent?" inquired a well-dressed man, a courtier from head to toe.

"Aye." Gilles nodded. "And you are?"

"I am Stephen Monkfort, emissary of the king's justiciar. I have come with important documents drawn by the king"—the man coughed—"before his, shall we say, journey on the continent." Monkfort placed his hand on the parchments that protruded from a leather satchel.

"Present them." Gilles extended his hand. "These precede Richard's imprisonment?" He was too tired to dance over semantics. It was obvious at this time that Richard had been imprisoned somewhere and a ransom would soon be demanded.

"Aye, Lord Gilles." Monkfort nodded and offered the sealed papers. Gilles drew his dagger and slit the seals. He rapidly scanned the first document, turning slightly away so his face would not betray him to anyone watching. When he had read it, he crushed it in his hand, and slit the seal on the next. He disposed of three others, treating each as contemptuously as the first.

Pain bloomed in his chest, clutched his throat, and caused a muscle beneath his right eye to jump. In the first document, King Richard had betrothed him to Michelle d'Ambray.

She was ten and three.

Chapter Seventeen

With an ingenuity born of necessity, Gilles avoided Emma for the rest of the day. He found much to do in the village. He also discovered from a few terse questions that the emissaries had no real knowledge of the content of the documents. They would rest the night and depart in the morning. With no answer. No answer was necessary, Gilles had told them, with no further explanations.

Now, alone in the small chamber where Thomas, Roland, and he discussed the business matters of the manor, Gilles read and reread the betrothal papers. The other documents were the marriage settlements—vast in number—to encourage Gilles to wed again. Michelle d'Ambray's father was a powerful Marcher baron to whom Richard owed a favor. D'Ambray was also a man with seven daughters. He held far-flung estates from the dispositions of William the Conqueror. To secure his barons' loyalties where Richard wanted them, Richard had betrothed Gilles to d'Ambray's eldest daughter. The king's personal message stated his devout wish that Gilles would obey.

Sweet Jesu, Gilles mused. Richard expected him to wed a child. But the awful irony caused him to throw his head back and howl with laughter. He laughed so hard, Roland and Mark Trevalin crowded into the small chamber in alarm. Gilles waved them off.

" 'Tis a madness," he said, and swept his hand out to the papers. "Read gentlemen, read, and tell me how I may wed the woman I love and still satisfy a king."

Roland leaned his shoulder on the stable wall and watched Gilles throw his knives. It had not taken Roland long to find him. When Gilles had not been found contemplating Hawkwatch Bay from the wall, Roland had guessed he would be here, away from prying eyes, thinking. Each blade Gilles threw found its mark, dead on. "What are you going to do about this betrothal? Have you told Emma?"

Gilles flicked a glance at his friend. He tossed a knife from hand to hand, then let it fly.

" 'Tis ludicrous." Roland shook his head. "Richard knows you have no wish to wed."

"Aye. Do you think he will reconsider?"

"Not from afar. You were Henry's man, not his. A simple refusal will not work. You could cross the channel, look for our wandering king, and when you find him, negotiate his ransom. He might be so grateful he'll release you from the betrothal, head intact."

"Jesu," Gilles swore, and glared at his friend.

"Or, you could marry them both. Of course, an old man such as you may find it difficult to satisfy two wives."

"Would you like me to plant this knife in your back?"

Gilles snarled. He strode to where Roland leaned so indolently. His steps slowed. "Ah, I see, you think 'tis time I told Emma of this dreadful coil."

"Sarah and I think you have waited overlong."

Gilles sheathed the knife he held in his hand. He nodded.

"Sarah also suggested you speak with Father Bernard. He may be a tiresome flea, but unlike the Abbot, who is a political animal, Father Bernard cares little for the machinations of state. He might know of some practical way to thwart a king—without spreading word of the betrothal about the kingdom."

Together, the men went in search of the good father. They found him over a trencher of mutton.

Father Bernard blinked an owlish gaze at Lord Gilles and cleared his throat. "You announced your intention to marry Mistress Emma before all the people of the keep, my lord. May I ask, um, that is, did you and she, that is, have you—"

"Have I what, man?" Gilles tried to conceal his impatience.

"C-c-consummated your love, my lord?" Father Bernard mopped his brow with the edge of his sleeve. A hectic red stained his round cheeks.

Gilles smiled at the man's hypocritical discomfort. The father kept a buxom hearthmate. "Oh, aye. Many times over."

Father Bernard shook his head. "You really must do some penance." He coughed. "Then you should tell the archbishop of your predicament. He can override a king's wishes."

"Can he?" Gilles arched a brow. "Why would the archbishop risk the king's wrath over such a petty issue as my marriage?"

Ann Lawrence

The priest eyed his dinner. He picked up a leg of mutton and began to gnaw at the bone. "Then find a willing substitute husband for the child. An equally tempting man—to the king, not the maid—one worthy of the match, your equal."

"By God. You are brilliant!" Gilles shot to his feet. He clapped Roland on the shoulder. "We have but to find a substitute. Magnificent. Roland, put your mind to it—immediately. I must see Emma."

In an instant he was gone, tearing up the stairs to his chamber. He startled Emma as she splashed water on her face. In the next moment Gilles had her in his arms.

"What is it?" she gasped as he swung her about, spraying water everywhere.

"Just joy, my love. Just joy." He kissed her soundly and tossed her on the bed.

An hour later, their passions spent, Gilles raised himself on one elbow. He took a mighty breath of air and slowly let it out. "King Richard has betrothed me to a powerful baron's daughter."

Emma stared at him, dazed. For many moments, she lay speechless, her mouth open. Her words were high and sharp when, finally, she found her voice. "You've asked me to marry you and you're betrothed to another? What cruel jest is this?" She shoved him aside and scrabbled about for her clothes.

"Hold." He jumped from the bed and grabbed her shoulders. "I am not going to wed the girl."

Emma jerked out of his grip. She quickly dressed. Then she seated herself at the table and tried to be calm. "Mayhap you should explain. You make love to me, then drop this news into my lap. I shall soon fear all lovemaking!"

Gilles drew on his robe. He sat at her side. Her fingers

250

were cold when he held her hand. "Do you remember the royal emissaries who arrived today?" She nodded. "They brought betrothal papers drawn by King Richard. My marriage is meant to reduce his brother John's power. I will not marry her."

"How can you possibly defy a king?" He watched her eyes fill with tears.

"I will not defy the king. I will present him with a willing substitute who will just as ably suit his purpose." Her face brightened. He swallowed hard.

"What if you cannot find a man who will do as you ask?" Fear struck deep and hard. Emma threw herself into his arms.

"If there are problems, we shall go away somewhere together and truly defy King Richard." His grip was hard and fierce.

Emma searched his face for the truth of his words. "You would take such a risk? For me?"

"Aye," he whispered against her lips. "Aye. There is nothing here for me if you are not by my side."

"I love you, Gilles." She pressed her cheek to his, felt the soothing silk of his beard, but inside, she was afraid.

The hunting birds were gone from the walls as the many men of the keep took advantage of the fine weather the next day to hunt. In fact, the hall was nearly deserted. Sun streamed in the arrow slits overhead and lay in pools of gold on the wooden floor. The scent of baking bread filled the air as Gilles contemplated the chessboard. He took one of Roland's pawns. "I cannot just pick any man. He must suit. Think."

"I am thinking." Roland retaliated by capturing Gilles's bishop. A highly significant move, he thought. "We've named every lad in Christendom!"

251

"Every lad, true." Gilles grunted as Angelique threw herself against his knee. He allowed her to climb into his lap, and kept her little hands from stealing the colorful wooden figures on the game board. "My little lady." He bent and kissed her hand. "Have you any names to suggest?"

Angelique shook her head as if she understood his question, snatched a pawn, and sucked it.

"You love the child." Roland's statement was met with a nod. "And does William? Does he love the child, too?"

"He repudiated Emma and the child. So Angelique is mine," Gilles retorted. He replaced the pawn with a bone ring that had belonged to Nicholas.

"My experience with William says he has but to hear you express that opinion and he will want the child with a singular passion that will tear us all to pieces."

"Ah, but I know him, too. He will be silenced with the offer of enough silver, doubt it not."

"As you say." Roland returned to the game board. He moved his knight. "Harold of Middlesex," he said into the lengthening silence. "He has a son. A rather homely lad, but his prospects are as formidable as yours."

"Aye." Gilles's face lighted up and he gave Angelique a quick kiss before setting her back on her feet. "I would be able to ride to Middlesex on the way to seeing Richard's justiciar with news of the change of groom. Michelle d'Ambray is far better than Harold could ever hope for his boy. Harold holds important border properties with the Scots, too. 'Twill be . . . a ridiculous match. The justiciar will roar with laughter." Gilles surged to his feet. He paced and fumed.

Roland arched an amused brow. "Too bad Nicholas is wed. He would have served very well. Mayhap you should acknowledge William and offer him."

"Damnation. This is not a jest." Then he froze. "I know! Nicholas's wife, Catherine d'Anjou. What of her brother Gabriel?"

Roland raised his hands in mock horror. "Gabriel d'Anjou! And who will drag him to the altar? You? Me? I value my head—attached to my shoulders."

"But he is perfect. He has no lands and so would benefit greatly by the match, and yet his relations are beyond formidable. Richard would get what he wishes— alliances that make a web of protection against John's connivance. Gabriel d'Anjou is perfect! He will forge a bond that John will find difficult to fight. At the same time, Gabriel will bring into Nicholas's sphere, and mine, those lands belonging to d'Ambray."

"Gabriel d'Anjou will never agree. He wenches from coast to coast."

"Eventually he will need to wed. As you said, Michelle is a child. He can—" Gilles stopped himself. He had almost said that d'Anjou could wench for years before settling and getting heirs on his bride. A few years ago, he'd not have realized there was anything wrong with the thought. A few months ago, he'd not have cared. Instead he said, "Richard will love it. He will enjoy d'Anjou's protests, but in the end, they both will see how perfect it is." Gilles reached across the chessboard and moved his queen. "Check."

Roland eyed the board. "You seem very sure."

"I am sure. I feel it in my bones. 'Tis an inspiration from God. All will be well!" He strode from the hall.

Roland sighed. "I am sorry, my friend," he said softly. "You left yourself bare." He lifted his bishop and took Gilles's queen.

Gilles burst from the hall and out into the bright sunshine. He flung open the door to the weaving building.

With no decorum, he snatched Emma from her loom and dragged her laughing behind him, up the stairs and into his chamber.

"Do I assume your happiness stems from finding a suitable replacement for matrimonial sacrifice?" Emma touched him lightly on the cheek.

"Aye. Gabriel d'Anjou. He is perfect. Handsome, young, well connected. He is brother to my son's wife. I will ride tomorrow for Seaswept—d'Anjou is frequently a guest there. If he is not there, they will know where I may find him. I shall then convince Gabriel of the superior opportunity a marriage to Michelle d'Ambray will afford him."

Emma gasped. So little time. She cupped his face with her hands and stroked her thumbs over his close-cropped beard. She studied every line of his face, to memorize it.

"Such a serious expression, Emma. Are you regretting your decision to wed me?" Gilles's laughing countenance grew stern.

She slid her fingers into his hair and drew his head down. "Nay. I have no regrets." She gently kissed his lips. "Make love to me, Gilles." He swept her into his arms and set her gently in the center of the bed. Though he was determined to go slowly and gently, it took but a moment for them to be mutually swept into passion's web. At the penultimate moment of his passions, he clasped her fingers to his lips and again begged her forgiveness for any pain he'd caused her. Again, she granted him absolution and then joined him in a soul-tearing completion that was as powerful as anything they'd yet experienced.

Emma remained awake for several hours, wishing she felt as confident as Gilles. That she knew none of the people discussed, King Richard or this Gabriel d'Anjou, did naught to help her. She drifted asleep, their names awhirl in her mind, twisting and turning, linking to each other in an endless spiral of confusion.

Gilles awakened, struck by Emma's flailing arms. She moaned, eyes tightly closed. Gathering her to his side, he hugged her and smoothed her hair, gentled her and urged her from her dream. Her skin was slick with sweat. She lay quivering in his arms, her face buried against his chest.

"What troubles you?" he whispered into her hair.

"Nothing." Emma did not want to put her dream into words. She wanted to banish it.

"Tell me. You will feel better and be able to sleep again." Gilles stroked his hand down her back.

Emma refused to acknowledge that she'd had a bad dream, and turned his questions aside by caressing him and drawing him into her arms.

All thoughts of dreams flew from his head, replaced by the reality of Emma touching, holding, and loving him.

When they were sated, she burrowed deeper into Gilles's side. She feigned sleep that he might not raise the issue of her dream again. As she lay waiting, his breathing deepened, and she knew he slept. Thus she lay awake until dawn, frightened of what she'd dreamt.

It took Gilles a day to prepare his party for hard riding. Emma wished it were longer. She was scarcely prepared, herself, when Gilles came to bid her good-bye.

"Take care, Emma. I have sent William to oversee the strengthening of one of my properties near Selsey. He'll be gone far longer than I, and needn't trouble you. Mark Trevalin and Sarah will see to your care. Do not hesitate to seek their advice."

"Gilles, don't go." Emma clung to him. "I have had a dream—a fearful dream."

255

"I wondered what made you so restless." Gilles patted her back. "Now, hush. A dream is not truth." He turned the subject. "You will think of me every day, will you not?" In truth, Gilles was as loath to leave Emma as she was to have him go.

"My dream, Gilles, I must tell you." She searched his face for impatience or derision. She found only concern.

Gilles drew her to an alcove and sat her down on a long, padded bench. "Tell me." He held her hands.

"It was very dark. I thought mayhap the fire had died, as there was no light. Then I realized that I was dreaming. I was in a dark room, no fire, no lamp, just darkness. I was so cold." She clutched Gilles's hand until hers hurt. "I woke in darkness, pain in my throat, cutting off my air, strangling me. Then it was gone. You were gone. 'Twas agony."

"Emma, it is but a dream. You are worrying about our future." He gathered her in close and held her fiercely. "I love you. I will return to you a free man and we will wed. You must put aside your fears."

"I love you, too." Emma did not pursue her fears. He needed to go. She wanted him to stay. She was afraid.

Gilles rose, drawing her up. He stepped away and turned to Angelique, who'd pursued them to their private alcove. He held her tightly and breathed in her sweet scent. "Be good, my child."

It felt wonderful to call her his child, for in his heart she was.

Together they went to the bailey. Just as Gilles mounted, William drew to his side on a magnificent gray stallion and bid Gilles good journey. Emma was heartily grateful that Gilles had seen fit to send William away. Seeing him as he now was, armored, trailed by his own men, she feared him anew.

A familiar figure darted between the great horses. "Sir William," cried Beatrice. He half turned in the direction of her voice. "I packed this jest fer ye." She held up a napkin Emma had seen her preparing that morning. Emma smiled, remembering the care with which Beatrice had selected fruit and cheese for her parcel.

William's gaze swept over the woman's offering. Without a word, he turned back to Gilles, bowed, and kicked his mount into motion.

Emma cried in dismay as mud splattered Beatrice's snowy apron. She hastened forward to help her, for Beatrice stood in the midst of the horses, arms upraised, frozen like a statue. "Come," Emma urged her as Gilles scowled, then drew his horse about to lead his men from the bailey. 'Twas another ill omen, Gilles leaving with a frown on his face.

Beatrice's body stiffened in Emma's arms as she awkwardly lowered her gift. " 'E dint see me."

Distracted by her last glimpse of Gilles riding out, Emma spoke half to herself. "He saw you."

With a wrench of her shoulders, Beatrice tore herself from Emma's grasp. "Ye know naught! 'E gave me a token last night. A token! A lock o' 'is 'air. 'E'd a spoken if'n 'e'd a seen me." Her eyes narrowed. "Ye flaunted yerself 'ere afore all 'is lordship's men, so they's eyes fer only ye. 'Ow's William to see me"—she thumped her chest with her fist—"if'n yer twitchin' yer skirts?"

The ire and bitterness of Beatrice's attack stunned Emma. Her clenched fist seemed poised to strike. Emma backed away, clutching Angelique close against her chest.

Sarah and Emma walked slowly about the bailey taking the air. Trevalin trailed them at a discreet distance.

Sarah sighed. "It has been a sennight and I don't mind

admitting I am missing my Roland. 'Twas necessary he ride with Lord Gilles, but still, I miss him."

Emma turned to her friend. "I have had my dream again. I want Gilles to come home."

"Aye. Dreams are powerful things." Sarah shook off her own shiver of fear. Anxiety had etched itself on Emma's face. Her eyes were shadowed and her skin pale. "Come, let us see what you might accomplish on the loom ere they return. You may tell me of your dream, and we will banish it from your mind. Mayhap we may lose this shadow." She jerked her thumb over her shoulder in Trevalin's direction.

Emma cared little who followed, watched, or heard them speak. She had little enthusiasm for any activity save caring for Angelique. They finally settled in with the spinners. May came to them and begged a few moments' privacy, leaving Angelique with the two women. They sat in silence, Sarah's spindle moving in a smooth rhythm, Emma knotting and twisting the silks she was using to weave a trimming for one of Gilles's tunics. Finally, frustrated with the tangled mess, she threw it aside and hoisted Angelique into her lap. She rested her chin on her daughter's head.

"I cannot shake this foreboding."

"Then tell me the dream again, and purge yourself of its poison." Sarah set her spinning aside.

" 'Tis always the same," Emma began. "I am in a dark, dark place. Night or day—I can't say, I just know 'tis dark and I am sleeping. It is pain that wakes me each time. A pain so piercing, so terrible, I need to scream, but fast on the pain I lose my air. No screams escape my throat because I can't breathe. I try, I grasp my throat, I struggle, but 'tis all for naught. Then, just as suddenly as the pain comes—it goes. In my dream I lie on some hard surface and know that this pain means something terrible, something fearsome. I'm so afraid, Sarah. I want Gilles."

Angelique thrashed in Emma's arms, responding to her mother's agitation.

"Be calm," Sarah warned, reaching for Angelique and pulling her from Emma's lap. "Do not let others see you so overwrought. You don't want to be an object of gossip. You'll be Lord Gilles's lady soon."

Lord Gilles's lady. Emma nodded, saw the curiosity around the weaving room, and choked back her fear. She plucked up the silks and bent her head over them, fussing at the snarls.

"This dream is disturbing, I'll grant you that," Sarah said when Emma had regained her composure. "But I see naught in it that would bode ill for our men. So try to put it aside."

Emma knew the subject was closed. She looked about the room at the other women spinning. There was no one to help her. She was alone.

Chapter Eighteen

William Belfour had made several quiet visits to Hawkwatch over the three weeks since Lord Gilles had sent him to see to the inspection of the outer walls at Selsey Manor. Lord Gilles had no wish to have the same tragedies repeated there as at Hawkwatch. The fortifications were of a like age.

Once William had determined that the builders knew their task well, he saw no reason to breathe down their necks, and, in truth, Selsey quite lacked in maidenly diversions.

This day, loath to bestir himself from his horse, William Belfour leaned his arms on his saddle and waited patiently for his mount to drink from the pond behind the mill that served Hawkwatch Manor. The day stretched lazily before him, pleasure only on his mind. A quick movement in the shadows cast by the morning sun caught his eye. Ah, she was early, eager. It boded well.

A woman walked from the copse of trees edging the pond. He frowned. Then a short jeering laugh caught in his throat. Dismounting and flipping his reins over a branch, he crouched behind some low hedges and watched.

He remembered well another day when he'd seen Emma searching among roots and reeds for plants to enhance her dyes. That she still came here amused him. Shouldn't a future lady of the keep be ordering jewels and ribbons, not grubbing in the dirt?

Emma slipped her heavy pack from her shoulder and settled herself on the hard ground. Painstakingly, she examined her finds.

"May I help?" William rose from concealment.

"William! You startled me." Emma scrambled to her feet, thrusting her gatherings into the pack.

"Did I? Startled is not the reaction I used to get when we met here."

Emma shouldered her pack and stepped back, widening the space between them, her eyes going to the silent mill.

"Surely you aren't leaving, Emma. You just arrived." He caught her arm as she turned to go.

"Why aren't you at Selsey?" she retorted. She snatched her arm away, watching him warily. He was resplendent in the morning sun, blond hair gleaming, fur-lined mantle folded back over his broadly muscled shoulders. It was the ripple of those muscles that frightened her when she remembered their power.

Suddenly, the brilliance of the sunlight was concealed by the dark foreboding of William's contemptuous smile. "I know my duties," he said. " 'Tis none of your concern how I choose to perform them."

Emma edged along the frost-hard bank of the pond, trying to distance herself from him.

"Were you waiting for me? Is this not where I first had you? Mayhap you have improved your skills under Lord Gilles's tutelage. Of course, he is not so young as to be a very demanding lover . . . or are you here to ply your trade? Exchanging favors for a reduction in millage costs for the keep?" he asked with a quick laugh.

His words were softly spoken. Their import was ugly. William stalked her, step for step along the bank. He swept out an arm and encircled her waist. Quick as a snake striking a mouse he grasped her breast and squeezed.

"Leave off!" Emma struggled in his grasp. "You wretched knave," she gasped as he pushed her to the ground and straddled her body.

"I want to see your soft, white thighs." He shoved her flat with a hand spread on her chest, and dragged up her skirts.

Emma went wild. She thrashed beneath him and pummeled him with her fists, to no avail. She only succeeded in making him laugh.

"Aye, fight me. Fight me, you haughty lord's whore." He bent his head and took her nipple in his teeth and, as if swatting a fly, flung her hands away.

When his teeth closed on her tender nipple, she knew he meant her harm, for this was no caress, but a vicious bite. He stretched himself atop her, effectively ending her struggles. His tremendous weight stole her air. With little way to defend herself, she tried words, scraping strands of his hair from her lips to beg him.

"William, stop, please. Gilles will never forgive you. Please." Emma's last words were barely audible amidst her sobs, for William had pushed her skirts to her waist.

263

He thrust his thigh hard between her legs.

Emma's terror was complete. She struggled as William lifted his hips to free himself.

"Did he fill you as I did, sweet Emma?" he jeered, crushing his lips to hers, groping to find his way.

Emma flung her arms out to her sides, seeking with her hands for dirt to fling in his eyes. Her fingers dug, but the cold earth, impervious, yielded nothing. Then her fingertips met, encircled, and hefted a stone. Unthinking, she slammed it against William's shoulder. It was like hitting a boulder with a pebble.

The air filled with her sobs of anguish and his grunts of erotic anger as her struggles prevented him from seating himself. With a brutal push of his hands and hips, he laid her open. Emma smashed the stone on his brow.

Precious air gusted into her lungs as he rolled off her. Gasping, weeping, she struggled to gather her torn skirts about her.

"God curse you, William." Emma scrambled away on her hands and knees as William staggered to his feet, his brow dripping blood onto his tunic.

"You bitch." William's anger was very personal as he lunged for her, but she twisted away, raised her skirts, and ran for her life.

He swore as she ran into the woods. "I'll have you soon, I promise," he shouted. "You think you've won, well think again. Next time I'll have you in his bed. Aye," he muttered to himself, straightening and wiping the blood from his face with the back of his hand. "Aye, I'll make you beg for it."

She disappeared into the trees. He stared after her, then shrugged. Carefully, he fastened his clothing, pulling his tunic down, muttering at the smear of blood on his hand when he smoothed back his hair.

He tore a strip from an old shirt in his saddle pack, then knelt and dipped it in the icy pond. He dabbed at the cut on his brow and vented his ire in a stream of colorful words.

A shadow fell across him. He half turned. Pain exploded in the side of his head. He fell to his back in a tangled sprawl of limbs.

The jagged rock came down on his face again and again and again. He didn't struggle; he didn't protest. As the stone obliterated his features, he felt nothing, for the first blow had killed him.

Chapter Nineteen

Emma blocked the memory of William's curses as she ran. She was too intent on escape, running as swiftly as she could, stumbling over insignificant stones. She tripped on a root and fell headlong into a rotted pile of muddy leaves. Her headcovering came off, and her braids tumbled over her shoulders.

Frantic, she snatched up the muddy cloth, looked over her shoulder just once, then forced herself to run even harder. Her legs wobbled as she made her way through the winding alleys that separated the dwellings at the castle wall.

She could barely stand when she reached the gate, and needed to sit and gather her wits. Her skirt was torn and there was mud splashed across her bodice. Shame painted her cheeks red. Shame that she'd given herself to William Belfour so willingly without first seeking to know the man inside his godlike face and body.

"Mistress, are ye ill?" the gatekeeper shouted down to Emma from his high perch.

Emma couldn't answer, she just gathered her ripped skirts and ran through the gate, swept up the keep's steps and, avoiding all eyes, stumbled up the stone stair to Gilles's chamber.

She shot the bolt and tore off her gown. Shivering and naked, she took up one of Gilles's daggers and shredded the gown, reduced the ugliness of the day to tiny tattered scraps of wool that she flung into the fire. She searched out Gilles's robe and wrapped it tightly about her.

As she watched the gown turn to ash, she became aware that her right breast throbbed. Shaking off her fear, she rose and bathed William's touch from her body, and then curled in Gilles's bed, wrapped in his scent, surrounded by her memories for comfort, praying he would soon come home.

She bit the cuff of the sleeve to keep from weeping.

"Hungry." Angelique tugged at Emma's hair, waking her. "Hungry! Angelique hungry!"

"Oh, my child. I'm sorry." Emma roused herself, rose and dressed, muttering to herself. "Hiding will gain us naught. I must face him, for surely he is below awaiting us." She dug in a coffer and sheathed one of Gilles's daggers beneath her gown. "If I hide here, he'll have won. He'll know he has frightened me."

Why didn't I take someone with me to gather my plants?

Emma clutched Angelique to her breast as she paced the rush-strewn floor of Gilles's chamber. She resisted the urge to climb onto the high bed and hide in its soothing depths. "I will be strong. I'll not let him take my peace from me."

"Peas, Mama. Angelique wants peas."

Emma looked at her daughter. How could William have scorned such beauty and innocence? She pressed her face into Angelique's neck and her throat worked as she stemmed her anger and grief. "I can't hide until Gilles returns. I must face William now."

Shifting Angelique to her left hip, Emma groped in her skirt for the knife she'd strapped to her leg. Then, squaring her shoulders, Emma put her hand to the iron latch.

With but a moment's hesitation, she lifted it. She nodded to the sentry who stood guard at the base of the stair. When she rounded the last spiral of the stairs, she paused, then forced herself to enter the hall. She searched the many tables crowded with retainers, but did not see the man she sought. Heaving a sigh of relief, Emma made her way to an empty seat by Sarah.

"May I take her, Emma?" May asked, stopping at Emma's side. Emma handed a hungry Angelique to May and then helped herself to a partridge from a long wooden platter of birds.

"How quickly I've become accustomed to such bounty." Emma tore a piece of bread from a loaf at her place and slathered it with drippings from the partridge platter. Chewing rapidly, she kept her eyes on the various doorways, anticipating William's arrival at any moment.

"You seem ill at ease this evening. Are you feeling well?" Sarah asked, selecting a plump bird for herself.

Emma avoided Sarah's eyes. "I don't feel quite myself." *What a lie*, she thought.

She felt frightened and anxious.

"You must take care of—"

A cacophony of sounds in the bailey cut Sarah's remarks short. The two women rose and, with the rest of the gathered company that surged to the great doors opening into the bailey, they sought the source of the tremendous wailing and screaming they could hear from without.

'Twas a scene of turmoil that met their eyes. The miller had drawn his cart close against the steps that led to the great doors of the keep. He was instantly thronged with people. Men were pushed aside by wives and women servants as the form stretched out in the cart was glimpsed.

Women tore their hair and sobbed. Men were struck silent at the macabre scene. One old man with poor vision raised his voice above the noise of the crowd.

"What is it? What has happened?" he quavered, frightened and bewildered.

"Murder! William Belfour has been murdered!" cried the miller. He stood on his cart seat and addressed the crowd. As he spoke, the people fell silent, though weeping continued unabated. "I found him by my pond, his face bashed in, his blood staining the earth. Great evil this is!"

Emma pushed forward, shocked and dismayed. She'd seen William but a few hours ago in that exact spot. She reached the side of the cart. Placing her hands on the rough wooden edges, she looked over, then reeled back, choking down the vomit that threatened to spew from her lips.

'Twas beyond ghastly, the sight of him. If not for his blue mantle and well-known form, it could have been any fair-haired man. There was nothing of William Belfour's beauty left. He was a pulpy mass of broken bone, smashed teeth, and blackened gouts of blood.

The miller jumped into the back of his cart and lifted a brown leather pack from William's side. "Who recognizes this?"

Emma spoke before prudence could stop her. " 'Tis mine."

"Were you at the mill today?" He spoke in an accusatory tone and the crowd fell quiet around them, all eyes turning to Emma and the miller.

"Aye. I was. I was gathering plants for my dyes." Emma looked cautiously about her. The crowd was silent, not a listening silence, a malevolent silence.

"I saw that one run in the gate today. She had blood on her gown. Her gown were torn."

Emma stared at the man who spoke. She recognized the gatekeeper, didn't miss the excitement that lit his eyes as he swiftly became the center of attention, people parting to let him through to the cart's side.

" 'Twas not—" Emma began.

"Murderess!" screamed a frantic woman's voice. "Murderess!"

The crowd closed on Emma and she stepped back against the cart's side to avoid them.

"Nay, I would never hurt anyone." Hands reached for her arms, clasped her and held her against the cart. Two women snatched at her hair. Emma tried to raise her hands to protect her face, for the women in the crowd had whipped themselves into a frenzy.

"Stone her as she stoned him," a voice screamed above the crowd. The men stood by in silence while the women sought stones and dirt, flinging them in Emma's face, pelting her breasts and stomach. She screamed and bent to try to protect herself, but hands held her upright, tearing and stripping her gown and shift, turning her to face the bloody mess that was William.

Gasping with pain and blinded by the blood that dripped from her own brow, Emma began to grow weak, too weak to fight them. Held against the cart, her now

271

naked body was pummeled with stones while hands clawed at her arms, dirty nails digging furrows from her elbows to her wrists. Like a wounded animal, Emma began to slide down the rough side of the cart.

Sarah ran into the keep and up the winding stair, gathering the sentries she could find on her way. She had only to invoke Lord Gilles's name and future wrath to gain their instant support. Accompanied by three stalwart soldiers, Sarah forged a path to Emma, shoving men, women, and children aside as she moved. The sentries shouted for order and used the flats of their swords and the heavy edges of their shields to bash a path to the two men who held a now unconscious Emma against the cart. Intimidated by drawn blades, the men let Emma fall to the ground.

"Emma, Emma," Sarah crooned to her friend, who lay in her own blood at the wheel of the cart. "Please don't die," she sobbed. "Help me with her," she demanded of a nearby man. The armorer, ashamed of the behavior of the crowd and most shocked at the women's frenzy, welcomed the opportunity to atone for his silent fascination as the crowd lost itself in bloody sport, so he stepped up to help when summoned. He hoisted Emma into his arms and ignored the screams of a crowd deprived of vengeance. He stepped into the protective circle of the three soldiers. As a body, Sarah leading the way, they made their way to the keep.

At the first touch of a cold cloth to her bruised face, Emma moaned and stirred, and threw up her hands to shield her face.

She shuddered and shook in reaction to the horror of what had transpired. A shadow fell over her. Mark Trevalin bowed slightly at the waist. She clung to Sarah.

"Mistress"—he spoke to Sarah rather than to her— "I know this is difficult for you, this woman being your friend, but I must hear her story. The crowd is calling for her to be brought out, brought out to answer for murder. I must speak to her if she's able."

"Lord Gilles will have you stripped of your rank, should you hurt her!" Sarah spat. She bathed the blood and dirt from Emma's face. "You're safe here, Emma. No one will harm you."

Mark Trevalin's face paled. "Tend her, then I must speak to her, though you may remain while I question her. I will see to the dispersal of the crowd." He turned and left, and Emma could hear him shouting orders. She heard the march of boots, she heard what sounded like a small skirmish in the bailey, then silence fell.

Emma sat on a bench in Gilles's chamber. Arrayed before her were Mark Trevalin and three other men-at-arms.

"Aye, I saw him today," Emma said. Her face was puffed and bruised. Her eyes stung with unshed tears as she faced the men at the table. Sarah patted her shoulder to reassure her, but nothing really helped. Life was a nightmare. She prayed for Gilles to return and help her; she prayed to God to send Gilles swiftly home.

Swallowing audibly, she continued. "I was gathering plants when I met Sir William at the pond. We spoke a moment and then he tried to kiss me. I tried to get away but he is . . . was very strong. He tried to force himself on me." With a trembling hand Emma reached for a cup of water on the table. When she looked up she saw skeptical frowns on the men.

Mark Trevalin spoke in the silence. "Belfour had little need to force his attentions on any maid." His contempt for her words was barely concealed.

273

"Yet he did!" Emma loathed the panic and fear that cloaked her voice. "He did." She fell silent.

"Continue your tale." Trevalin waited for Emma to drink again from her cup.

"He tried to force me." This time she met Trevalin's eyes, defying him to sneer. "I found a small, small stone." Emma cupped her hand to demonstrate the size. "I hit him on the shoulder. When that did naught, I hit him on the brow. He let me go and I ran. When I looked back he was standing and shouting at me. I heard some of it. He was shouting that he would have me yet. I was so frightened—"

"So you admit hitting him with a rock," Trevalin interrupted.

"Nay. I admit hitting him with a very small stone, but I swear in God's holy name, he was alive when I left him! He cursed me."

"The gatekeeper says your gown was torn."

"Is that not proof that William was forcing himself on her?" Sarah interjected.

"Please, mistress, if you cannot hold your tongue, you must leave." Trevalin spoke sternly to Sarah.

"William tore my skirts, aye." Emma's face flamed red.

"And the blood the gatekeeper claims was on your gown?"

"There was no blood. It was mud. I fell on my face while running in the woods."

"May I see your gown, please?"

Silence reigned for a moment, and Emma felt her flush become a heat that surely could be felt like a flame across the room. "I can't show you the gown. I burned it."

Sarah's gasp was the only sound in the room for several moments.

274

"I see. Why did you do such a thing?" Trevalin spoke harshly and with disbelief.

"I hated the sight of it. It would have always reminded me that William tried to rape me. Even mended, it would have reminded me. I would have had to tell Lord Gilles. I could not face that . . . telling him what William had done."

"You hated William Belfour, did you not?"

"Nay. I did not like him, but I did not hate him."

"One of the weavers says he overheard you telling Mistress Sarah that you could kill Belfour. Did you say that?"

" 'Twas not what it seems. It is an expression, spoken by many who have no wish to harm. It is just an expression."

"Yet William Belfour is dead."

Emma did not respond. She was suddenly lethargic, and her head pounded with pain.

"There are those here who say Belfour is the father of your child, Angelique. Is that so?"

Emma looked up at Sarah. She'd not told anyone but Sarah, yet as usual there were no secrets in the keep. When Sarah nodded and squeezed her shoulder, Emma knew her friend would stand by her.

"Aye. William Belfour is . . . was the father of my child."

"And you tried to make him responsible for you? I found in the manorial records that your uncle brought you before Lord Gilles to ask you to name your lover. You paid a sixpence fine for bearing a child out of wedlock."

"I never tried to make Sir William responsible. That was my uncle's wish, not mine. I wanted naught to do with William when I learned his true nature."

God, please send Gilles home.

275

Ann Lawrence

Trevalin rose. The other men at the table did not meet Emma's eyes. They'd remained silent throughout the proceedings. "I am afraid there is too much evidence against you to let you go. I am also unable to decide a matter of this gravity. William Belfour was a knight of the realm, and therefore you must answer in the royal courts. They are convened at the Duke of Norfolk's castle, and I'll have a party gathered to escort you there. The court will decide your guilt or innocence."

"Nay," gasped Sarah. Emma said nothing. It was what she'd expected from the start. Silently she rose and faced Trevalin. When he nodded, two sentries, the same who'd come to her defense in the bailey, took her wrists and bound them.

Before they led her from the room, Emma turned to Sarah. "Send for Gilles. He'll know what to do. Look after Angelique. Kiss her for me. Care for her." Emma's voice broke on her words, and her eyes filled with tears. Before they could spill, she followed Trevalin from the room.

·276·

Chapter Twenty

Gilles woke, immediately alert, his heart pounding. He shot to his feet, groaning with stiffness from spending the night on the cold hard ground. A sense of urgency, of foreboding, made him shake Roland awake and kick out the embers of the fire. His wrists burned and he rubbed them as Roland checked the girth on his horse. When Roland was ready, they mounted. The two men nudged their mounts to a quick trot along the fog-shrouded roadway. The rest of their party was at least three days behind.

"I know Nicholas thinks me mad to leave so abruptly."

"You were just avoiding Gabriel d'Anjou's wrath," Roland snorted.

Gilles could not raise the expected grin—or response. He had not even waited for the loading of the wagons that would carry assorted goods he'd purchased for the displaced villagers back to Hawkwatch.

The eerie silence of the morning fog made each word

spoken seem loud and intrusive in the dawn. They rode in comparative silence for two hours, when suddenly the sun pierced the fog like golden knives cleaving the sky.

"Ah," Roland sighed, " 'tis a good omen, this sun. It warms the spirit."

"I am beset with a mad impatience to be home. Whatever good omens you may perceive, I have this gnawing in my gut. I feel uneasy, almost as if . . . I know 'tis foolish, but I feel as if all is not well."

" 'Tis just deprivation, or your usual distaste for my cooking. You should have bedded that little redhead— Juliana, I believe her name was. She was practically undressing you before my very eyes. Ah, if only she'd looked my way!"

"And at the risk of having Sarah flay the hide from your bones, you would have bedded her?" Gilles asked, smiling.

"Nay, but a man may dream."

"Aye. A man may dream." And Gilles's dreams were all of Emma, the scent of her, the texture of her skin beneath his fingertips.

Gilles was not heartened by the sun. Each mile drew them closer to home, and each mile the gnawing in his gut became more insistent. He let his attention wander to Emma's dream. He'd tried to downplay his apprehensions, for to admit that dreams could foretell the future was to admit to a belief in sorcery, but it boded ill that she had dreamt an evil dream.

"A race!" Roland kicked his mount to a gallop when the tower of Hawkwatch came into sight. Soon the two men were thundering along in reckless disregard of the sheep populace. Gilles was first over the drawbridge and into the bailey, sliding from his saddle and tossing the reins to a groom. He took the steps of the keep two at a time, Roland close on his heels.

An ominous silence greeted them. No one smiled. No one hurried forward to greet the lord. The oak door crashed back on its hinges as he strode in. The people gathered there froze in their various positions as if turned to stone. Gilles's frown deepened as he strode up the center aisle of trestle tables set for the midday meal. His eyes searched, but found no pleasure in the journey over the many faces.

The gnawing became a searing, stabbing pain in his stomach and chest.

Roland skidded to a stop at the door. Unlike Gilles, he could not make himself walk into the trouble, for only trouble could have painted such expressions on the faces before him. His eyes also searched through the crowd and came to rest on Sarah. When Gilles stopped before her, she sank back to her bench, her hand clutching the table's edge. Roland hurried forward, knowing instinctively that she needed his support.

"Speak." Gilles's voice was a near shout. A servant dropped a knife and several eyes turned to it, for the sound pierced the silence.

"Speak!" he thundered, and smashed a fist on the tabletop.

"W-W-William Belfour. He is dead."

Gilles reeled away. He tore off his leather gauntlets and stepped up to the dais. He braced his hands on the mantelpiece, and drew on his vast control. "How? Was there trouble at Selsey?" He turned back. He was not wholly surprised; warriors died. But then he saw the faces in the hall. Eyes slid from his. No one spoke. No one moved. "How?" he repeated, returning to stand before Sarah.

279

She rose on shaky limbs and met his eyes. She was aware of Roland's approach, and put out her hand to him—a hand that trembled. Roland took it and squeezed, gave her his strength.

"William was found two days ago at the mill, murdered. Someone had . . . stoned him . . . his face. A bloody rock was nearby." Sarah had no tears for William, had loathed him, but she cried for what more needed to be said.

"What villainy is this? Has the murderer been found?" Gilles swallowed. He couldn't betray his sorrow. It was too late to acknowledge William now. Revenge was all he would have.

"Aye." Sarah's voice caught on a sob and her nails dug into Roland's hand, her eyes round and frightened.

Gilles searched her pale face, the sudden way she'd aged. Her face had grayed to match her hair.

"Nay," Gilles roared, whirling away. He knew what Sarah wasn't saying. He hurled himself up the tower stairs and away from the hall. Roland dragged Sarah after him. They watched in mute distress as Gilles flung open his chamber door, and took in the empty room.

Sarah stepped in behind him, clinging to Roland's strength. "Aye. Emma. Trevalin took her away, to the Duke of Norfolk's. She denied the murder, but she admitted hitting him."

"Nay and nay and nay." Gilles went wild. He whirled through the chamber, smashing and destroying everything in his path. He couldn't think and couldn't feel. A crowd gathered at the doorway, and Roland enlisted two hefty sentries to tackle Gilles. They pinned him against the wall until his struggles weakened. Roland and the men dragged him to a chair and pressed him into the seat.

"Tell me. Everything." Gilles voice trembled with

leashéd fear and rage. His eyes were burning black coals in his pale face.

Sarah dropped to her knees before him, frightened, but wanting to help him. She tentatively touched his hand, but he snatched it away.

"No one knew William had returned, my lord. He must have stopped at the mill pond on his way here. The miller found him, and Emma's pack was nearby. A hue and cry rose when William was brought here by the miller.

"We all hastened out to see what the fuss was, and in front of all, Emma claimed her pack. Many women were wailing and . . . and when Emma took up her pack, they turned on her."

"Jesu." Gilles tried to rise, but Roland held his shoulder in an iron grip.

"God was not there!" Sarah began to weep. "They tore at her and blamed her. The gatekeeper told the crowd he remembered her coming over the bridge, her skirts torn and bloody. She had no chance. Your men took her. No one knew when you were returning. I sent a messenger to bring you home, but the guards took her to Norfolk's, to the royal courts." Sarah clutched his hand. "You must not believe she did it."

"Never. . . . Emma . . . she would never." His voice was a harsh whisper.

"You must help her, my lord. The women were crazed. William loved them all so indiscriminately. In death, they all claimed him by turning on her. They snatched at her hair, stripped off her gown. She was naked when your guards were finally able to stop them."

"She didn't do it." Gilles spoke calmly. This awful stillness frightened Roland more than the wild rampage. Gilles's lips were pale and bloodless. His hand shook as he offered it to Sarah, helping her to rise. "Emma would not hurt a fly."

"She was bruised and bleeding. I tended her wounds, but she was like the walking dead. She couldn't explain herself, just said she had been gathering plants for dyes when she met William. She said he tried to force himself on her." Sarah's tears wet the back of Gilles's hand. "She fought him, hit him with a stone. But she said when she ran from William he was standing, dabbing at his head and yelling obscenities at her. I believe her. I went to the mill pond and there was a small stone with what might have been blood near the . . . place." Sarah closed her eyes on the memory of the large stain of black where William had bled his life into the dirt. The other rock, the one smeared with flesh and hair and blood, had gone with Emma to the royal court. "I kept the small stone."

"I must go to Norfolk's. Now." Gilles began to pace. He couldn't think coherently. He had no grief for William now, had only fear and anguish for Emma. The thought of her stripped and abused by a crowd brought him close to the edge of madness.

Gilles turned to action, hurling orders. Less than an hour after he had ridden into the bailey, he rode out, with naught but a small stone with which to defend the woman he loved.

Chapter Twenty-one

The Duke of Norfolk's great hall was paneled in English oak, the walls adorned with ranks of weapons, attesting to the prowess of the Duke as a warrior.

Daniel Tucker, the Hawkwatch Castle gatekeeper, licked his lips and gazed about, awed by his surroundings. He didn't meet Emma's eyes, but then he didn't meet the eyes of the men who sat on the panel of judges either.

"What evidence do you have to present?" The lawyer paced before the panel of judges. He was bored. He flicked a small piece of lint from his hose and adjusted his jeweled belt. It was close on midday, and he mused on braised lamb in rosemary sauce.

"I saw the weaver come arunnin' in the gate, my lord."

"And how did she appear?"

"Appear?" Dan licked his lips and twisted his cap.

"Appear. Look. Was she upset? What of her clothing?"

"Oh, look. She were upset. Running. She sat a

283

moment and that's what made me notice, like. She sat on the railing. Was getting her breath."

"And her clothing?" the lawyer prodded.

" 'Twas torn about the skirts." His face flushed hot. It was the view of her long, shapely legs that had drawn his eyes. "Her legs be showing."

"Anything else?"

"The front part, on her—" He gulped.

"Breasts?" the lawyer supplied.

"Aye. Her breasts, 'twas all blooded."

"Nay!" Emma shot to her feet. All day she had listened to the testimony, most of it exaltations of William's prowess as a knight, a fact that Emma felt had naught to do with what had happened. She was not permitted to speak. No one had asked her what happened. She could no longer remain silent. "Nay, 'twas mud, mud!"

"If you cannot keep the prisoner quiet, remove her," one of the judges said to a nearby guard. The guard stepped before her and she lost control.

"I want to speak, I have to speak. I didn't kill him. 'Twas not blood!"

"Remove her," the judge ordered the guard. Emma had to be dragged away. She knew she was going to be found guilty, did not understand this travesty of justice that a woman could not speak in court, could not offer up some defense for herself.

The guard was less than gentle as he heaved her along the corridor. That she was unbound was a testament to how little they feared her. She was shoved back into her cell and the door shut.

Her meager cell held only a slops jar and a moldy straw pallet. It had neither window nor ventilation. The only hint of air was a thin cold draft that crept around the ill-fitting oak door. There was no candle to light her way. She used her hands to locate the pallet and stretched out. She wept. She prayed, first to God, then to Gilles. Her only hope was for Gilles to return and save her.

The Duke of Norfolk's personal apartments were as rich as a king's. His walls were carefully painted to resemble marble. The leather benches that lined the wall were hand-painted and dyed. "This is highly irregular, Lord Gilles." The Duke of Norfolk rose and greeted his guest. "Please, rest your bones." He indicated a seat before the fire.

Gilles remained standing. The Duke of Norfolk was a hard man and Gilles was not about to put himself at a disadvantage. A head taller than the Duke, Gilles knew he'd be giving the advantage to the Duke if he sat. "I did not come here to rest. You have one of my weavers here."

"Aye, the murderess." The Duke did not smile.

"She did not kill William Belfour." Gilles tried to remain calm.

"The royal court has decided she did—but an hour ago." Norfolk said it gently. He had heard that the weaver was once d'Argent's mistress.

"An hour ago?" Gilles sank to the bench he'd shunned. He couldn't take it in. He was too late. Pain burned through him, stole his breath.

"I understand she was your leman. I am sorry." There was a slight hesitation, then, "The hanging will be in a sennight."

"Hanging?" Gilles repeated it like some dull-witted fool.

"Sir William was well thought of. He curried favor in the right places. Richard's men rule now." It was a subtle warning that Henry's men were no longer in favor and could expect no special treatment.

The duke poured wine into a silver goblet. He put it in Gilles's hand and watched him drink, though he suspected Gilles didn't taste the wine. Color flooded back into Gilles's ashen complexion.

"I am too late." Gilles slammed the goblet on the table and, ignoring all protocol, rose and stormed from the room.

Roland, waiting in an antechamber, had only to see Gilles's face to know the news was of the worst sort.

"Gilles, what can I say?" Roland reached out to his friend, but Gilles avoided his touch.

"Send for Nicholas, immediately, then send a man home to see if any evidence can be found that will save Emma. I'll not be too late." Gilles squared his shoulders and focused on his friend. "I will think of something."

"Gilles. There is nothing—" Roland began.

"There will be something. Pick the best of your men—not Trevalin—he sent Emma here. But find someone. Something. Anything. Anything that will stay this madness."

Roland bowed at the waist and hurried from the antechamber. For a moment, Gilles was alone with his grief. He shut his eyes, and fought the pounding blood that made his temples throb and his vision blur.

"God in heaven, don't let him fail," Gilles whispered.

The clink of metal alerted Emma to a presence. When the door opened, Emma threw up her hand to ward off the light, a light she'd not seen in three days. Then she was leaping across the room, for she knew the silhouette in the lighted door, knew the scent of him.

"Gilles," she cried.

He embraced her, crushed her in his arms, sought her mouth. They were aware only of each other in the dark space. The stink of the slops jar, the mold and damp of the chamber retreated. For Emma there was only Gilles and his strength.

"Ahem." They ignored the noise behind Gilles and continued their frantic kisses, and when Gilles tore his mouth away, his cheeks were as wet as Emma's.

Lord of the Keep

He tilted her head back and looked her over in the dim light of the torch behind him. He saw a ravaged countenance. He saw fear. He saw despair.

"My lord?" The priest tried again. "My time is limited."

"Just so." Gilles turned to Emma and crushed her against his chest again. "This priest will wed us."

"Wed us?" Emma struggled in his grasp. "You can't possibly marry a murderess."

"There are still four days, Emma. I am seeking an end to this madness. You have only to trust in me. Now . . . I wish to be married."

"I don't understand." Tears streaked her dirty face and he raised the edge of his hand and smoothed them away.

Gilles's voice was light, seemingly unconcerned. "I will not be apart from you another day." He gently kissed her cheek.

"You cannot mean it." Emma searched his face.

"Would I dress just so, only to visit?"

Emma stroked her hand down his chest, savoring the weave of his silver tunic—her magnificent gift. "I remember every thread of this cloth, Gilles. I wove it with my dreams and my love."

He pulled her around to face the light, blinking rapidly to hide his emotion. He urged Emma to her knees. Neither noticed the damp, nor the look of distaste on the priest's face; they only had eyes for each other. The gaolers moved near, to stand as witnesses.

"Say your vows, Emma." Gilles caressed her wrist, maintaining his lightness of manner when inside he was broken, devastated, and near to his own limit of endurance. He had envisioned her as she was when he'd left. He'd not prepared himself for what she had become—abused, purple bruises on her face, dirt on her skin and clothing, hair in greasy hanks about her shoulders. He would not react. He needed her to have hope.

287

Ann Lawrence

In a near whisper Emma repeated her vows, pledging herself to the one man who held her heart. She watched as Gilles slipped a wide band on her finger, gleaming gold woven with a dull black metal.

"This represents my love, my eternal love," he said. "The gold for you, the rarest of women, and the other—naught but base metal for me, who is unworthy of you." The priest inscribed the sign of the cross over their heads and pronounced them man and wife.

"Be gone." Gilles shoved the priest from the cell, tossed a purse to the gaolers, and kicked the door closed. He drew her into her arms and rested his chin on the top of her head.

Lust had no part in their embrace. It was an embrace of hopelessness. He held her and she wept on his chest, and choked out between long pauses what had occurred.

"Gilles, I could not bear it if you thought I did this terrible thing."

"Shh, I know you, my love—know you are as gentle as a new fawn. Be at ease."

She pounded his chest in frustration. "They would not let me speak. I could only watch in horror. It all looked so awful. If only I'd not burned my gown, I could have proved 'twas just mud, not William's blood. Please, my love, help me."

"Aye, I will help you. This is only temporary, my love, until I may see the Duke. You will shortly be gone from this place. I have left a purse with the gaoler so he will better your circumstances."

Gilles held her close and soothed her with softly murmured words, and knew he lied. He'd fought and railed and threatened and stormed, yet he'd not been able to change the verdict. William was a knight who'd endeared himself in all the right places, Emma but a weaver, a lord's leman. She would hang in four days' time.

288

Chapter Twenty-two

Gilles watched Nicholas from Norfolk's doorway. He hesitated. His task was an onerous one at best.

"I am here to see my father, your Grace." Nicholas d'Argent stood at stiff attention before the Duke. He still wore his mail and had not taken time to wash off the dust of travel.

Gilles was pleased that, as ever, Nicholas had not wasted even an hour before riding out to his filial duty. Gilles already knew from Roland that Nicholas's wife, Catherine, had accompanied his son.

Gilles froze in midstride as the Duke spoke. "Your father has been waiting most anxiously for your arrival, my boy. Mayhap you can dissuade him from his madness." The Duke thumped his fist on the armrest of his chair.

"Madness?" Nicholas arched a brow in question. Gilles moved forward. He did not want Nicholas's opinions tainted by the Duke's.

"Aye," the Duke continued, "your father is about to marry . . . here he is. You dissuade him." The Duke rose and left father and son alone.

They did not embrace. Nicholas shoved his gauntlets into his belt and straightened his shoulders. "Father, Norfolk says that you are going to wed."

"Have wed. Just now." Gilles locked his fist about Nicholas's arm and practically dragged him from the chamber, down the steep stone steps to the terraced gardens. When they were as far from the hulking stone edifice as possible, Gilles released his son. He paced back and forth, stroking his beard, trying to think of how to explain. "You must hear this from me. There is no way to soften this, make it less . . . ugly. I summoned you because I didn't want you to hear this tale from any lips but mine."

"Father, I've just arrived. What tale?" Nicholas shoved his hands through his thick hair in exasperation, causing it to stand on end like a rooster's comb.

His appearance reminded Gilles of the way his son had looked as a child, when his hair defied his nurse's best efforts. The feeling that accompanied the thought was bleak. "When your mother was full with child—you—I took a mistress," he said.

Gilles waited, but Nicholas didn't interrupt. He stared as if stunned.

" 'Twas despicable. Oh, I know 'tis accepted practice, to take mistresses, but still 'twas dishonorable. Your birth was followed six months later by another. God forgive me, I had another son, by name William Belfour."

"Belfour!" Nicholas spat the name. He marched away, and turned his back on his father. His stiff posture, the long strides, bespoke an angry man. Nicholas made it as far as the crushed stone border of the gardens before he wheeled and came charging back. He attacked, pummeling his father with his fists. Gilles did not defend himself.

"Why?" Nicholas wiped the blood from his knuckles, then extended his hand to his father, hauling him back to his feet when madness settled to a simmering anger.

Gilles pressed the back of his hand to his split lip, then bent and spit blood to stain the purity of the white stones on the path. "Why? For the same reason all men give. My marriage to your mother was arranged. She had little affection for me, or I for her. Surely, *that* is not a complete shock." He was glad that Nicholas seemed to have calmed. There was so much more to say, and little enough time in which to say it.

"Nay." Nicholas rubbed his grazed knuckles and stared at them as if amazed he'd raised his hand to his father.

"I never meant to hurt your mother or you. I don't think she ever knew of William, or William's mother. William's mother was not exactly constant to me, so I have oft doubted that William was mine, but the fact remains that I bedded the wench and she gave birth. I found her a husband and have paid them dearly for their promise to keep William's fathering a secret."

"Why are you telling me this? Am I supposed to accept this bastard son now? I despise Belfour." Nicholas's face suffused to a deep red.

"William is dead. You've no need to accept him." The words did not make William's death any easier to bear.

"Dead?" Nicholas studied his father's ravaged face. "Had you love for William?"

"Love? Did I love William? Jesu, I can't possibly tell you how I felt about William." Gilles sank to a stone bench and breathed deeply of the harsh cold air. He could not bare his soul too much. He could not let his pain show in this cold, cold light of day, could never admit that William was more rival than son, more enemy than ally. "Suffice it to say, he was my son. I paid for his keep, had him raised to be a fine warrior, just as I did for you. I took him into my own household when I sent you to be fostered at King Henry's court, and made him a valuable knight."

"Why are you telling me this?" Nicholas's words were hard-edged with anger.

" 'Tis a long tale, and I would ask your forbearance to hear it through." Gilles waited in impatient anticipation. Nicholas gave a curt hod and Gilles began.

"When your grandfather died, whilst I was on the continent, I sent a contingent of my men to Hawkwatch Keep to see to its management until I could come myself. Do you remember?"

Nicholas thought on the events, the passing of a grandfather he barely knew. "Aye. I remember."

"One of the knights I sent was William Belfour." Gilles waited for the explosion.

"Sweet Mother of God. You had your bastard by your side in France, whilst I was at Seaswept?" Nicholas raised a fist, then let it hang at his side. "Go on, the tale grows ever more interesting." He arranged his face into an impassive mask, and Gilles realized there was more hurt here than he'd expected. And how suddenly, for the first time, he saw his own harsh face reflected in his son's.

"As I said, William Belfour was in that company, and during those early days, William met a young woman by name of Emma." Gilles looked down at his hand, at the ruby winking in the sunlight. Just the thought of William lying in Emma's arms was terrible; to say it aloud was to flay his soul. "They said vows together, though William denied it."

"Hardly a surprise with Belfour," Nicholas interjected.

Gilles nodded. "It seems he made many promises and kept few." He sighed. "William got Emma with child, then abandoned her."

"Like father, like son," Nicholas sneered.

"Aye. Your contempt is well placed, but I again ask your patience to hear me out."

"Continue," Nicholas snapped.

"William scorned Emma, relinquished his . . . claim. She had the child, Angelique, to support—a child William would not claim. Don't say it. 'Tis the same." Gilles forced himself to be calm. He looked over the bare canes of the Duke's rose bushes and thought that surely his life would be like those thorny branches if Nicholas did not believe him. "I was drawn to the child. I fell in love with the mother first, but I love the child, too."

"*Mon Dieu.* A grandchild?" Nicholas strode away, paced back, wheeled, and turned in exasperation. "What of William? Did he accept your attentions to this—this—this leman?"

"She went to him with love, not as a leman. They said vows, though William denied it." Gilles realized he was getting sidetracked with William. "I will not bandy words with you; it wastes time. William didn't care for her love or the child. No matter. It was over between them ere I came on the scene."

"How convenient for you. From son's bed to father's." Nicholas leaned on a stone wall and crossed his arms on his chest in a belligerent posture. "I suppose 'tis the woman I saw on her knees before you that night? Moving up, was she? From simple knight to baron."

Ann Lawrence

Gilles bit back a bitter retort. "I have married her, Nicholas. She is my wife now, have some shred of respect."

Nicholas said nothing.

Gilles sighed. "There's more." Gilles knew Nicholas was in some ways a guileless soul, and he watched as Nicholas's every thought flitted across his no longer impassive features.

"More?" Nicholas raised his hands heavenward. "How could there be more? You had another son, one you kept at your side, trained yourself, and now you've married that son's whore—excuse me, wife. There's nothing more to say, for I'll hear no more." Nicholas strode away.

"Wait. Please." Gilles hated the pleading note in his voice. Nicholas stopped in his tracks. He turned back and stood in silence, arms loose at his sides as his father approached him.

"I told you William was dead. William was murdered, and Emma suspected. They have tried her, Nicholas, and found her guilty. She's to hang in four days."

"Did she do it?" The question caused Gilles more pain than any other, for each word was imbued with the certainty she had.

"Nay. Emma is . . . I can't explain it. She gives life. She is honorable, kindly. She didn't kill William. Although I have done all I can, I haven't been able to postpone . . . haven't been able to influence—" Gilles could not finish.

"How may I help?" Gilles's head came up. He searched his son's face. Nicholas spoke harshly. "It is why you sent for me, isn't it? To help you? Not just to confess the sins of your youth?"

"Nay. I don't need any help. I just needed to tell you

294

what I intend to do. Had to tell you to your face. It is not something you should learn from a messenger."

"What are you going to do? Bury her next to my mother?"

The sarcasm was back. Gilles took a deep breath. "Nay, son. I am going to confess to William's murder. I'm going to say I killed him in a rage after he attacked Emma."

"Nay!" Nicholas's face blanched as white as new milk. He clutched his father's arm.

"Aye. I've lived my life. What more may I truly expect? Another five years? I can't let them take her life. Angelique needs her. She must have a chance to live."

"You can't do this for some leman!" Nicholas's fear was as stark on his face as his anger.

"She's my *wife*. I would die for her, aye, willingly."

Nicholas stared in horrified dismay as Gilles's determination became evident to him. "I will stop you!"

Gilles gripped Nicholas's arm and led him back to the stone path. "I won't have it. My mind is made up, and tonight I will see the Duke to confess. I ask but one thing—"

"What?"

"Take care of Emma for all her days, and Angelique as well. I must know she's under your care, and will reap the protection of being my wife. I ask this and only this."

Nicholas's look was mutinous.

"I love her, Nicholas. Would you ask less of me for your beloved Catherine?"

They stood a moment in heavy silence, then Nicholas spoke. "Of course not."

"Then do this for me. Make me a promise you'll look after Emma and Angelique."

"You can't hang for this woman!" Nicholas cried.

"She is my wife! Would you not give your life to save Catherine? Answer me!" Gilles waited in tense anticipation, knowing that if Nicholas's love of Catherine was not the all-encompassing passion he felt for Emma, he would never understand—or help.

Nicholas locked eyes with Gilles. His throat worked. "What you propose is monstrous . . . but aye. I would give my life for Catherine."

That night, in a bedchamber in Gilles's rented townhouse, accompanied by the sounds of merriment from a nearby alehouse, Catherine d'Argent drew her husband down into her arms. She was a small woman, dark-haired, bright-eyed. Something lay coiled tightly in her husband. His body did not lie at ease; he stared at the ceiling.

She would wait until he was ready to speak. She was a healer. When the cause of his discomfort became clear, she would heal him.

Nicholas stroked his hands over Catherine's silky skin. "You are so beautiful. Sometimes I feel unworthy."

Catherine sat up, and let her thick brown hair fall forward to cover her breasts as she leaned over him and studied his face. "I sense pain, Nicholas. What has happened? Why were we summoned by your father?"

"Not now." Nicholas slid his hand into her hair and drew her mouth down to his. "Not now," he whispered against her lips.

Later, Catherine lay awake waiting. A candle guttered in a dish, and she rose to light another. She wrinkled her nose at the rank stink of tallow and wished she had brought her scented beeswax candles with her.

She pulled her bedrobe tightly about her against the cold. There'd been an edge to her husband's lovemaking, a near violence that had never been there before. If he didn't speak soon, she would have to badger him into it. Nicholas was an introspective young man, and it oft annoyed her that he kept his troubles to himself. She curled at his side. They both stared at the ceiling.

"My father intends to be hanged in four days." Nicholas's voice cracked on the words, and a sheen in his eyes told Catherine he was not jesting.

"Hanged? I think you need to explain." The cool air had no part in the shiver that coursed down Catherine's spine. She lit more candles and put them by the bed. She sat at Nicholas's side and picked up his clenched fist.

"My father has fallen in love with a woman accused of murdering a man named William Belfour." Nicholas lifted her hand to his mouth, and kissed each of her fingers. Catherine could not see Nicholas's face, could only hear the anguish in his voice. "My father swears she did not commit the crime. He loves her, has married her, and now he intends to confess to her crime to save her from the hangman."

"Oh, Nicholas." Catherine drew him in. It was like finding out a loved one was mortally wounded. "Is there no way to dissuade him? Surely, the courts will not allow this?"

"Allow it? My father is a powerful baron. He is respected. Who will doubt his word?"

"Had he any reason to kill this William Belfour?"

"Oh, a wonderful reason. The man is Father's bastard son, the former lover of this Emma, and father of her child."

Catherine's mouth fell open. "Surely, you jest!"

"I had a brother, Catherine. I never knew it. Forget for

a moment that I despised the man, still he was my half brother. Now he is dead!" Nicholas rose, naked, and paced the room. Catherine trailed after him, trying to get a bedrobe on his arms. "All these years I thought I was Father's only child. How could he have betrayed Mother that way? He's as dissolute as any other member of court. And why couldn't he have told me once Mother was dead? It wouldn't have hurt her then. I'd not have condemned him." Catherine bumped into him when he suddenly stopped. "Nay. That is not the truth. I condemned him today. I said hurtful things."

"You are rarely hurtful with your speech. I noticed it is a trait of your father's. You temper it well, but sometimes it appears. If you hurt him, you must apologize."

"Never. He betrayed his marriage vows. He never recognized his bastard son. He married a murderess!"

"Hush. You'll wake his man Roland."

"Roland! He has been Father's friend since childhood. We must wake him. Surely he'll know a way to stop Father's madness!" Nicholas yanked the robe from Catherine's hands, wrapped the belt tightly, and then stormed out. He had but a few steps to go to find Roland d'Vare's chamber. He didn't think of the hour; he just pounded the wooden door.

The door crashed back on its hinges. Roland's hair was pillow-tossed. His frown made Nicholas pause.

"I hope you have adequate reason to disturb me." Roland stepped aside. He slipped the knife in his hand back under his pillow and then covered his own nakedness with a robe and lit a taper. He watched Gilles's son warily, then smiled. "Come in, Catherine." Catherine slipped in the door. She encircled Nicholas's waist with her arm.

"So, take a seat and tell me what needs saying in the

darkest hour of night. What couldn't wait until dawn?" Roland did not remark that he, too, had been unable to sleep.

Nicholas poured himself a goblet of wine from the skin Roland had warming by the fire. For many moments no one spoke.

"Take your time. I find the hours weigh heavily when I'm away from my Sarah."

"Sarah." Nicholas squeezed his wife's hand and his eyes lit up. "Aye, Catherine, because of Sarah, Roland will understand." Nicholas turned eagerly to his father's friend. "Surely, I need not tell you that Father is besotted with love. This woman he loves has been condemned to be hanged in four days." Nicholas looked at the dark night, seen through a narrow window. "Three days."

"I know full well your father's love for Emma," Roland said carefully. He crossed his arms on his chest and studied the young people.

"Father's madness, love, or whatever it may be, has made him marry this woman today, in her cell."

Roland nodded. "I know. I had charge of obtaining the marriage ring. Your father wanted Emma to have the protection of his name."

Nicholas shook off his wife and began to pace. "And did you also know that Father's bastard son was this Emma's lover and the father of her child?"

Roland nodded, but kept silent.

"And did you know that he intends to confess to William Belfour's murder and take her place?"

In startled disbelief, Roland gasped. "Nay."

"Aye," Nicholas spat. "He says he loves this whore enough to give his life for her. We must stop him!"

"*Mon Dieu*. This is beyond belief." In two strides

299

Roland reached Nicholas and gripped his robe in a balled fist. "What you say is surely mad."

"Then let us see him, talk sense to him," Nicholas pleaded.

The balled fist tightened. "Should you call Emma a whore, you young whelp, son or not, your father will gut you and feed your entrails to the hounds."

For a brief moment, Roland thought Nicholas would strike out. His face was suffused with deep red. He nodded. "As you wish. My opinion of his woman will not dissuade him from offering up his life for her."

"We will speak to him, but I imagine he will not change his mind."

Catherine piped up. "He will most likely repeat what he told Nicholas."

Roland pulled on his braies and his linen undershirt, heedless of Catherine's presence in the room. She yelped and turned her back. Roland donned his tunic and sheathed a dagger at his waist. "What did he say to you?"

"He will but ask you if you love your Sarah, could bear to see her die."

Roland paused, looked out to the night. "Nay, I could not bear to see my Sarah die." He flung open the door. "But before I offered up myself, I would think of some scheme to save her. Let's put our heads together with Gilles and see what we may hatch."

Gilles was not asleep. He had no need to cover his nakedness with a bedrobe. He'd never undressed. The late night visit did not surprise him.

He sat in stubborn silence as his son and his friend pummeled him with questions and exhortations to change his mind. He barely spoke.

"How can you convince the duke that you killed

William when you were away at the time?" Catherine demanded.

"I will say I rode ahead—and that is the truth—Roland and I were ahead of our party of wagons by several days. The carts moved too slowly for me; I grew impatient."

"What of motive?" Nicholas asked.

"I imagine the duke will believe me that I became maddened by William's attack on Emma. I will say I saw William attack Emma and then when she ran away, I beat him to death."

"You have the coolest head in Christendom. Who would believe that muck?" Roland began to pace, throwing out his hands in derision. "If William had been skewered on a blade, mayhap, but stoning? No one will give credence to such a thing."

"Then I shall simply say I did not want anyone to suspect that the murderer was an accomplished fighter. And I had the best of motives, one not mentioned here yet." They all stood still and looked at him. He swallowed hard. Honor had guided him all his life. Once he had acted without thought for it, and down through the years the ripples still spread in the pond of his deceit. This confession would sully his good name for all eternity. Yet for Emma's life, he would do it. "Many, especially in the village, hold with the idea that saying vows, whether before a priest or not, is a binding marriage contract." He took a deep breath. "Despite our dispensation, many will still believe Emma's vows to William should stand." He took a deep breath. "By killing William I cleared the way to an undisputed marriage with her."

Roland threw up his hands. "But what of me? I was with you and know 'tis not true!"

"You will lie for me, and say I rode ahead of you as

301

well. You will say I was gone at the crucial time. I will say that I backtracked to you, so that we could arrive at Hawkwatch together."

"Nay. I will not be a party to this!" Roland drew his sheathed knife and flung it at the wooden mantelpiece. It quivered in inanimate testimony to its owner's turmoil.

"Aye. You will agree because you would ask the same of me to save Sarah's life."

The fight went out of Roland. He nodded. "Then we must think of a scheme that will allow Emma to go free and you to live."

"There's no time," Gilles said. Every muscle in his body felt stiff and aged. Just a few months ago, he'd rued the end of the second score of his life. How precious every day seemed now. "It is too late."

"It is too bad we cannot make it appear that you are dead, Gilles; you know, trick the hangman somehow," Roland mused.

Gilles just shook his head. Nicholas shrugged.

"'Tis possible," Catherine said into the silence.

Chapter Twenty-three

The three men turned to look at Catherine. She smiled at them. "I know herbs and their properties, men. There are several potions that would render a man quite like the dead. The mixtures I make are delicately weighed and portioned out, my lord. Many have soporific or deadly properties. When they are taken just right, healing and easement take place, but too much results in death."

"It matters not." Gilles flicked his hand in dismissal. "They will not offer me a cup of hemlock to end my days. It will be a tight knot and a swing."

Catherine's face paled at Gilles's stark description of his fate.

"A tight knot . . . " Roland said. He suddenly smiled and patted Catherine gently on the shoulder. "I believe I know a way. Now, I think we should all get some rest."

Grateful when they finally left, Gilles stretched, fully clothed, on his bed. He was not afraid to die. He could just as easily have fallen in battle. Certainly, it could be no more difficult to hang than to take a sword in the chest.

Catherine rose and discarded her embroidery when Roland and Nicholas walked in.

"What news?" she asked.

"News? What news?" Gilles came down the ladder that led to the second floor.

"I've been to see the hangman, Gilles." Roland poured a goblet of wine and strode to his friend.

"How ghoulish." Gilles's tone was light. In truth, since making his decision, he'd felt oddly at peace. Emma was all he cared about.

"It seems Master Dobbins is soon to give up the hanging business and live in idleness in York." Roland handed the wine to Gilles.

Gilles just arched a brow.

"For a princely fee, he is most anxious to help us in our game."

"What game?" Gilles frowned at Roland.

"Catherine here will mix you a most vile-tasting brew—or so she claims—and you will drink it. When Dobbins, the hangman, slips the noose about your neck, you will be feeling no pain. He will tie it loosely, or he will reap no reward. He will cut you down immediately, and you will lie in your coffin like the dead until Catherine's potion wears off."

Gilles watched the reactions of those about him. Catherine, nearly as white as Nicholas, was clutching her husband's waist as if it were all that kept her standing. A bright spot of red appeared on each of Nicholas's cheeks, and the hand that held his wine trembled. Gilles's face heated with anger. "This is nonsense. I will go to my fate without your interference!"

Roland rested his hip on the table. "So anxious to die? Do you not wish to hold your wife in your arms, to make love to her again?"

Gilles whirled about, his mantle flaring in anger behind him. He was abruptly halted at the door. He struggled with his mantle and realized he was pinned by a thin silver knife to the jamb.

"Now. Seat yourself and tell me why you object to my offer of life." Roland strode to his friend and released the knife, slipping it back into his boot.

" 'Tis not life I object to, 'tis the foolishness of it all," Gilles said as he stuck his finger through the thin slit in his mantle. He was no longer angry for some reason. "What is gained?"

"You will be dead," Catherine said before Roland could. "No one notices a dead man. You could return home and discover who really murdered William. You could gather the evidence and see the man held account-able. Then you and Emma would be free to live your lives together."

Gilles touched Catherine gently on the shoulder, a rare display of affection. "Sweet, sweet child. What if I can't find evidence, or am unable to discover the murderer?"

"You will discover the evidence," Nicholas interjected, a genuine smile lighting his face for the first time since Gilles had told him of his brother. "When have you ever failed at what you have taken on?"

"Your faith is touching," Gilles said sardonically. "But if I fail?"

Roland raised his goblet as if in a toast. "You and Emma can go quietly off somewhere and live as peasants until the end of your days, with no one the wiser."

"Hmm." Gilles liked it. "I could shave my beard!"

"And your head," Catherine offered. A stunned silence met her remark. Gilles's hair was his vanity, and all knew it. "Well, you're far too distinctive a man with that ebony hair!" she said in defense of her comment.

"I will do it." Gilles smiled at the gathered group. He slapped his hand on the table. "Come, let us see to the details."

"First, you must tell Emma of our plan," Roland said.

Gilles shook his head. "She will never allow it. She will confess herself. She'll . . . *Mon Dieu* . . . I don't know what she'll do, but she'll not let me risk my life for her. The Duke has promised to hold her in her cell until after the deed is done. There's no way you could convince her to go along with this." Gilles raked his hands through his hair. He knew Emma, knew she would reverse her plea and stand by it, confuse everything.

"Then we'll not tell her," Nicholas said. "Let her think as all others do that you are dead. She'll present the proper demeanor."

"Nay," Catherine protested. "Proper demeanor? What of the shock? The grief? Her pain?" Catherine grasped her husband's hand and pressed it to her cheek. She was a sprite of a woman and came scarcely to her husband's shoulder. "I cannot imagine the pain if Nicholas were to die," she said to all of them.

Nicholas gripped her hand. "I care naught about her grief. 'Tis father's possible death I fear." Nicholas let his antipathy for his father's bride take control of him. His words were harsh, and nearly shouted.

"Nicholas," Catherine said sharply. "You cannot mean it. She will grieve, painfully so. Do not be so heartless."

"Aye, Nicholas. I would have you give Emma your sympathy, not your anger. Save your anger for me." Gilles stepped between husband and wife.

"She causes your death! She will live on . . . will most likely spread herself for the first—" Nicholas found himself stretched across the hearthstones, his head throbbing, his father looming over him.

"You speak of my wife." Gilles's face flushed with his effort to control his own anger. The desire to strike again was nigh impossible to resist.

Roland stepped in to make peace between father and son. "There is naught to be gained by this. No one need die. Catherine will make her potion and Dobbins will do his part. Emma will grieve but will find future joy in Gilles's eventual return."

"What if I can't get the potion right?" Catherine's fear about her part in the plot showed vividly on her face.

Gilles turned to her and offered her his hands. He knew he'd intimidated his son's wife from their first meeting, and he sought to reassure her. Gilles slipped her hands into his and squeezed them.

"Catherine, if your potion is wrong, it will matter naught. I am prepared to die. I am a knight. I would gladly give my life for my king and my country. Why not for love?" He was not speaking to Catherine, but to Nicholas, who still did not understand. It was Nicholas he'd charged with Emma's care, and Nicholas who must have compassion.

The pain came in her sleep. Emma sat bolt upright, her hands clutched to her throat, unable to get her breath, the pain so acute there were no words to describe it. Her skin became clammy with sweat as she fought the pain. Then,

307

just as suddenly as it had come, the pain vanished. She lay back, shaking, and fear of what was to come swept in to replace the pain. The darkness of the cell was absolute.

It was her dream come true.

She was overcome with fear, then fixed her mind on Gilles and what he had said to her the night before.

Angelique would be loved and cared for always.

She had never believed that she would be released. Oh, she believed that Gilles worked to see it come true. Why, even last evening, as he'd held her in his arms, he'd promised her this moment would not come. But come it had.

As she thought of Gilles, her heart rate slowed and her fear began to retreat. She spent the final hours before dawn thinking of him and Angelique, knowing they would be her last thoughts.

The scrape of a key brought her heart rate back to a thundering crescendo, surely audible to those on the other side of the door. She knelt quickly and asked forgiveness for her sins, straightened her spine, and folded her hands.

A burning torch preceded the sentry who stepped into the cell. The torch's smoke burned her eyes and clogged her throat. The man waved some of the smoke away as he gestured her to follow him.

For a moment Emma thought she would faint. But she sucked in her breath and followed. The passage through the bowels of the Duke's castle was black as night. No windows pierced the stone to allow the wan light of dawn to show the way. Emma thought it could as likely be midnight as morn. The guard moved slowly, occasionally looking over his shoulder to check that she followed.

Her legs began to tremble. Could she do this with dignity?

Finally, they reached the end of the stone passage. Emma had been aware of a slight rise in the passage, and the footing here was drier, less slick with damp and mold. The air smelled fresher, and a breeze touched her cheek.

The sentry turned and opened a stout arched door, strapped with iron, then stood back to allow her to pass. He closed the door behind her. She looked about. The room, bare of furniture save a wooden stool and a table, was cold. She shivered. A scrape of a key made her whirl to another door opposite the one through which she'd passed. The room tilted a moment. A hum filled her ears. She swallowed and breathed deeply. She still could not take a deep breath, her throat still burned.

A cry of surprise escaped her lips when a man entered the room. *Nicholas d'Argent!*

She swayed, then gripped the edge of the table. His unexpected appearance robbed her of speech.

"Do you know who I am?"

She nodded, utterly confused. With a wary glance, she looked at the door he'd left open. No sentry was in sight. For a brief moment she thought of dashing past him, escaping . . . fleeing her fate. No. That would be dishonorable. She must do this with dignity. "I don't understand why you are here," she said. "Where is Gilles?"

"Gilles is dead."

Chapter Twenty-four

"My father is dead," Nicholas d'Argent repeated, his voice harsh as icy water.

She did not understand. Gilles dead? She stared at the young man, speechless. Finally, she found her voice. "Nay." She stated it emphatically. Gilles could not be dead.

"Aye, he was hanged this dawn as punishment for the crime of murdering his bastard, William Belfour."

"Nay!" she shrieked. She leapt from the stool, her devastation complete in that instant. She threw herself at the man before her. She pounded his chest, screaming in her agony, beyond pain and conscious thought. She had been unable, for days, to eat, to sleep; now she felt the world recede to gray and black. She slid down his body to her knees, a terrible pain expanding and pulsing through her being.

He crouched before her and gripped her arms.

"Aye, Emma, 'tis done." He tried to break through her sobs. When her cries became silent gasps, he spoke. "Father asked me to take charge of you. Roland's wife has Angelique at Hawkwatch, and there we will care for you both as long as you live." His final words were more spat than spoken.

Nicholas tried to remain hard against her, but her pain was tangible in the room, a living, screaming thing. He held her as she wept. This woman was nothing like he'd expected. She was not beautiful, although a few weeks in prison could take their toll on the most fair of face and form. What gave him pause, however, was the depth of her agony.

After what seemed hours, Emma had no more tears. Her throat ached from vomiting, and her eyes burned with her tears. She held her chest and gasped several times, trying to get a grip on her emotions. She looked up at the man crouched by her side. He asked a question with his eyes and she nodded. He lifted her up onto the stool, then hurried to the door. He spoke to someone she could not see. He turned back to her and took her arm. Unaware of her surroundings, she followed docilely to another chamber, more comfortably furnished. He settled her on a padded bench and poured her a goblet of wine.

Emma choked on the strong warm wine, but it did serve to steady the tremor in her hands and the roil of her stomach. She clutched the goblet's stem and looked up at the chilly man who was Gilles's son. He seemed as cold as winter.

"Tell me." It was all she could manage.

"My father came to me several days ago. He told me of your plight—"

"Nay," she cried. "He knew he was to do this each time he visited me? *He knew!* My God, he hid this from me . . . " Emma could not continue. Suddenly the fierce embraces, the gentle promises, took on new meaning, were not just promises that he'd look after Angelique, were not just empty hope that she would soon be released. Nay, they were not as she'd imagined. She'd thought them just the painful delusions of a man who loved her very much. Now she understood they were promises, promises he'd kept with his life.

Nicholas began to pace. "My father swore that never would you have lied. He insisted you left William alive and another killed him. He said there was no time . . . no more time to discover the truth, as you had been found guilty and were to hang today." He took a breath; Emma's face had drained to an ashen white. He took a step forward to catch her should she faint, but she gestured sharply and he withdrew.

"He said he could not bear your death. He said he was going to confess to the murder." His voice became even harsher. "He said he had lived his life." Nicholas had trouble continuing. The magnitude of his father's sacrifice had kept him awake all night; his own fear for him was a painful thing.

Tears welled and fell from Emma's eyes. How could she still cry? Yet the tears continued.

"I want to see him." Her voice was hoarse.

"Of course." Nicholas shrugged. "Come." He extended his hand.

She ignored it. She wanted to shun him. There was no comfort in him. Just cold hard accusation. 'Twas obvious to her he blamed her for Gilles's death.

She blamed herself for Gilles's death.

As she rose, she wobbled on legs barely able to support her.

When they left the Duke's prison cells, Emma stepped

313

into dazzling sunshine. It must be near midday! She looked about in wonder, drawing to a halt, causing Nicholas to stop and turn back to her.

"The pain," she moaned. "I know the moment. I woke, thinking it deep night, but I see it must have been dawn. I know the moment he died." She could not speak again, her breath sharp and cold in her chest. She clutched Nicholas's fingers tightly as she staggered at the knowledge. She no longer noticed if he held her hand or paid her any heed.

Nicholas led her to a small chapel in the lower crypt of the Duke's palace.

A priest, the one who had shriven her the night before, met them. Nicholas handed her off to the man and strode away without a word. The priest clucked and patted her hand. " 'Tis his lordship's wish that he be laid to rest beside his father in the family crypt at Hawkwatch Castle. I was preparing him to be taken. Come, my lady."

For a moment the name did not register. Then she realized that she had become a lady, and that the man she was to view was not just the love of her life, not just her soul, not just her reason for life itself, but also her husband. It took both of the stout priest's arms to support her into the dimly lighted chapel.

The man lying silently at the fore of the altar looked like a marble effigy in a great cathedral. She walked as if in a trance to his side and reached out her hand.

He was cold.

Grave cold.

Chapter Twenty-five

Gilles appeared merely asleep. The priest had covered him to his chin with a coarse blanket to hide the mark of the hangman's noose. Despite her wish to find him but slumbering, she knew there was no question—Gilles was dead. The hand she held to her cheek was icy. She traced the scar that crossed the back of his fingers, knowing it well.

She turned to the priest. "I want to be alone." The man patted her shoulder gently, bowed assent, and withdrew.

Roland watched from the curtained alcove of another side chapel. He did not want Emma to do anything harmful to herself, and he prayed that Gilles would not choose the next few moments to stir back to life. Roland suspected that such a happening would be too much for Emma.

As he watched, she drew the blanket from Gilles's body. Roland turned away, his cheeks flushing red as

Emma bent over Gilles's naked body. He turned his back, leaned against the chapel wall, and fervently wished they'd not promised Gilles to keep their plans a secret from Emma. In truth, his promise to Gilles held him silent whilst he suspected Nicholas's agreement with his father was for nothing more than spite. But the result was the same. They were bound to silence.

Emma knelt by the side of the slab on which Gilles's naked body reclined, and pressed her head to the cold stone. For many moments she remained there, lost in prayer. Then, rising, she stood and looked over her beloved's body. She touched each scar on him from his feet to his face, trailing her fingers lovingly over him. She covered him with the blanket to his shoulders and broke down. She railed aloud at him and fate. She cursed him for leaving her, then begged his forgiveness. She cupped his face and pressed her lips to his cold ones, breathing her warmth on him, trying for one frantic moment to bring him to life.

Roland rushed forward and touched her on the shoulder. She whipped around and stared, disoriented. When she finally focused, she gave him a wan smile and turned back to her dead husband. *Husband. For but a few hours.*

"Ah, Roland. Why, why?" She would never understand, never know what lay at the heart of Gilles's sacrifice. She pressed her hand over his heart and stroked from the rise of his chest to his strong shoulder, remembering how she'd caressed him often in love. "He is so cold, and I know 'tis madness, but somehow I sense his presence. Do you believe in the soul, Roland?"

He touched her hand. "Aye."

"I feel his soul. Here with me." She swallowed hard. "It gives me no comfort. He was so proud, Roland. Now, he will be remembered always as a man who murdered his own son. I don't understand. I know he didn't kill William. Why? Why? Why . . . " her voice trailed off into sobs.

"Gilles said you would ask me just that. He said to say that he was a sworn knight, that without thought or regret he would have laid down his life for his king, so *why not for love?*"

Why not for love?

She stared at Gilles's face. She could almost hear him saying the words. She knew now why he had done it. She understood. It was just as it had been at the manorial court when first she'd seen him. She could hear his voice as if it were but a moment ago.

"Emma, did you not realize the consequences when you took a lover? Why did you give your most precious possession away?"

Her voice was very soft, but not as anguished as she spoke. "Oh, Gilles. You, too, have given away your most precious possession, your honor—for love." She groped for his hand and pressed it to her cheek. "He did this for Angelique and for me. He gave away his name and his honor. I will try to be worthy of such a sacrifice." Reverently she smoothed the blanket over his body, her hands lingering for a last touch. She brought her lips to his a final time, then turned to Roland.

"I want him dressed in the surcoat in which he was married."

Roland went for the priest. Emma bathed and dressed Gilles herself, the priest and Roland only helping her to shift his body when it proved too heavy for her. Roland hovered in the background, no longer embarrassed by her reverent care for Gilles's body, but fraught with nervous tension that during her loving treatment and frequent pauses to caress Gilles's hand or to arrange and rearrange his garments, Gilles might begin to wake.

Emma clothed Gilles in the silvery gray coat she'd woven with her own hand, and looped at his hips the first belt she'd given him. It was woven in the colors of heat, and represented the flame-hot love she felt inside. She groomed his beard and hair herself, stopping every few minutes to take a deep breath, and wipe the tears from her cheeks as they fell to splash upon his skin, ashen and waxy in death.

When there was no other excuse to linger over her beloved, several monks laid him in a wooden casket, ornately painted with hawks in flight. 'Twas like no burial cask she'd ever seen. Before the lid was lowered into place, Roland laid Gilles's sword upon his breast and folded his hands about the hilt.

"Nay," Emma cried as they made to place the lid upon him. She darted forward and, groping in her gown, she withdrew her mother's cross. She took Gilles's scarred hand and wrapped the chain about his fingers, then folded them so the cross lay clasped in his palm.

"Now," she whispered. She took one last look. "Wait in God's holy love until I come to join you." She kissed his hands, his face, and then stood back to finally let the monks secure the lid. She almost screamed at them to stop, almost screamed at them to let her have another look, but she was restrained by the strong hold Roland had on her shoulders. There was nothing left to say.

"I am ready, my friend," she said.

Roland took her arm and led her away. He was beyond agitated. He feared the worst, that his friend would never regain consciousness, for 'twas an hour past time for Gilles to rise.

Chapter Twenty-six

Gilles awoke in darkness. He stretched and met the wall of his confinement. Confused, not able to see, he felt naught but walls about him. Panic rose in his throat.

His throat. His throat burned and ached. To swallow was agony. Just as he almost lost control of himself in the small dark space, he remembered.

He was dead.

He heaved his sword aside. Something was tightly wrapped about his fingers. Breathing deeply, stilling his thundering heart, he ran one bare hand over the other. In an instant, he recognized what held his fingers prisoner. A delicate chain, a cross.

Emma's cross.

So all they'd planned had come true. Pressing carefully on the lid of his coffin, he pushed. Nothing. He pushed again. His arms trembled, and in a moment of near panic he realized that they'd not thought he might be too weak to open his coffin.

Gilles turned his head and saw pinpricks of light coming in from small holes hidden amid the ornate paintings on his coffin—a coffin he'd chosen for himself. At least he had air. He made another attempt to lift the lid and felt a small shift in its position. Then it flew off and bright light blinded him.

"Thank God. We were about to take you out, servants about or no servants about to see you." Nicholas reached in and grasped his father's arms. With Roland, he dragged Gilles to a sitting position.

"Don't move him," Catherine admonished. "I do not like his color," she whispered to her husband. She placed her hand on Gilles's chest and felt his heartbeat. " 'Tis too slow. Get him out and lay him down."

"Take his feet." Nicholas grasped his father's ankles and, with Roland, shifted him from his coffin bed to a chair by the fire. They stood back and let Catherine take over.

Gilles felt curiously lethargic. He could barely bestir himself, was not even embarrassed as Catherine swept her hands over his body, touching him, lingering especially over his throat. He tried to speak but could not.

"Gilles, please squeeze my hand." Catherine took his hand in hers and chafed his wrist. With a sigh of relief, she felt the strength of his grip. "Now, can you speak?" Catherine had had two fears about her role in this scheme. One that Gilles would die and two that he would have lost his senses—suffered damage to his mind—even if he did awaken.

Gilles opened his mouth and a croak issued forth. After several tries he could rasp out a few words.

"Honey." Catherine snapped her fingers and Nicholas

put a stone pot in her hand. Nicholas held Gilles's shoulders while Catherine spooned some of her honey mixture down his throat. "There's more than honey in the pot, my lord."

It cost him dearly to swallow, and he held the concoction in his mouth as long as he could, stalling to avoid the pain. Finally he let the warm, sweet mixture slide down his throat, and was pleased that it hurt less than he'd anticipated.

Catherine examined him for a moment, turning his head this way and that, then peering into his eyes and laying a hand on his chest. "Now, tell me how you are."

His voice was a whispered rasp in the silent room. "I feel quite marvelous for a dead man."

Emma paced the small bedchamber Lady Catherine had led her to in the rented townhouse, fingers busy with her spindle. As she spun and walked, round and round, back and forth, she yearned to hold Angelique. She needed the comfort of her child's embrace and innocent scent.

She went to a chest, where Catherine had placed a cup of wine containing a sleeping potion. She lifted the goblet and swirled the deep red liquid. Her throat seemed hot and scratchy, mayhap from her weeping. And when she'd dozed, she imagined she heard Gilles's voice. Far away, echoing in her head as if in a cave. Her hand trembled. In the lower reaches of the house, someone laughed.

"How dare they!" she whispered, and drank the drugged wine to block out the laughter below. "How can there be pleasure when Gilles is lying cold in a box?" The thought made her throat tighten, her eyes burn. She stretched out on the bed and waited for blessed sleep to claim her.

* * *

Roland lifted his sharp knife and severed a long lock of Gilles's hair.

"Emma will sleep away the night?" Gilles asked.

"So Catherine assures me. 'Tis a powerful potion. You will be gone before dawn, and we'll take your box to Hawkwatch and bury you with all due ceremony on the morrow."

"I fear for her. Mayhap this is a mistake."

Nicholas and Catherine drew near. "We have gone round about this a dozen times," Nicholas said. "She must appear grieved."

Catherine stepped in. "I, too, worry for her, but I have come to think the men are right, my lord. Whoever killed William wished her ill, too. If she does not display the proper demeanor, the killer may wonder. That wonder might extend to more deadly thoughts."

Gilles sat with no energy, curiously detached and outside himself with his troubled thoughts as Catherine and Roland prepared his beggarly appearance.

Was it right to leave Emma in ignorance?

When Catherine swept the long hanks of his black hair into a pile, gathering them to be discarded, he rose shakily to his feet.

"Wait," he managed. His voice was still hoarse and barely audible. He accepted the offer of Nicholas's arm and walked slowly to where Catherine stood patiently waiting. He stooped and plucked up a lock of his hair. He leaned on the table and fumbled about his chest, sweeping his hand along, searching.

"What is it?" Catherine came close.

"I had a . . . a—"

"Is this what you want?" Catherine understood, rushing to a pack by the door.

"Aye, 'tis what I sought," Gilles whispered, accepting

the lock of golden hair Catherine extended to him. "I cut this from Emma's hair myself in the prison. She didn't understand why I wanted it. How long ago was it?"

Catherine rested her hand on his arm, alarmed at the anguish in his voice. "You've no need to speak of it."

"When was it?" he asked again, smoothing a thumb over the loop of silky hair.

"You were senseless for more than fourteen hours," she answered.

Gilles laid the two locks of hair, the gold and the ebony, side by side. He untied the ribbon that bound the golden tresses and sifted the strands together with his fingers, like the wind had entwined them when first they'd kissed and come to each other as lovers. He bound them as one and offered it to Catherine.

"For her." He extended the token. Catherine nodded as she took it, then left the room. Roland and Nicholas stripped Gilles of his finery. "Have a care of the coat, for it is precious to me," Gilles said, in his new gravelly voice. He strode to them, near the limit of his strength. He took up Emma's belt and wrapped it about his waist, against his skin.

With a nod, Roland folded the coat in Gilles's linen shirt and tucked it into his saddle pack. The two men then dressed Gilles as if he were a helpless babe—indeed he almost felt like one. He'd used what energy he had, and found none left except to drop Emma's silver chain and cross over his head so they might lie upon his chest.

When Gilles was garbed to Nicholas and Roland's satisfaction, they called Catherine for her approval. She clapped her hands to her mouth then rushed to her own saddle pack and withdrew a looking glass of polished steel she'd brought for just this moment. She held it before Gilles.

323

The man who looked back at Gilles was a stranger. He appeared elderly and gaunt, half-starved. He wore tattered clothing and appeared to have a scabrous condition of his bald scalp. Gilles's heart beat frantically in his chest. He didn't know the man, didn't recognize himself. His heartbeat slowed and he began to smile. " 'Twill do," he rasped. "Now, dawn is not far off, and 'tis a long way to Hawkwatch. Roland—"

"Aye, I found just what you need. There is a party of pilgrims who travel near to Hawkwatch—they're off to the abbey and a viewing of the relics there. The pilgrims are in need of a few pennies and will take you that far if you will but present yourself at the city gate."

"And Emma—"

"I will guard her with my life," Roland answered as he opened the door for Gilles. A mist had risen and crept over the threshold with fingers of white.

He nodded once and disappeared into the mist.

Chapter Twenty-seven

Two weeks later, at Hawkwatch, Emma stared about the hall from her place at the high table. The food tasted of ashes on her tongue. All about her, the men and women of the keep moved through their lives. Hers felt over. Even Angelique's sweet smiles and pats did not raise her spirits.

Beside her, Nicholas d'Argent sat at ease. Had he no grieving feelings for his father? He'd stepped into his father's place with little disturbance. Indeed, the people wanted guidance, and as Roland remained as steward, the transition had been smooth, but Emma felt horribly out of place in her position flanking him at table with his wife on the other side.

She imagined many of the folk in the hall held her responsible for Gilles's death. She imagined the women believed her to have murdered William. Fortunately, Nicholas's speech on the night they'd returned to the manor had compelled the people to keep their speculation to themselves. Nicholas had announced to one and all that his father had killed William, effectively silencing the doubters—or silencing them when any of the family was present. Only Nicholas's further admonitions that his father's widow must be treated with due respect kept the braver sort from lashing out at her. They were as yet unwilling to test the new lord's limits.

Emma herself was unwilling to test the new lord's limits. She most wanted to remain in Gilles's chamber, near to his things, wallowing in her sorrow, but Nicholas demanded her attendance at all meals and at chapel. They'd exchanged harsh words over his dictates.

Indeed, his wife was just as hard as he. The instant Catherine had seen Emma spin, she'd demanded that Emma teach the village girls to spin a finer thread than what was now produced. Where Emma had been but another weaver in Gilles's time, now she was his widow, and so should see to the improvement of the manor's production.

She would go mad soon. Her back ached and her eyes were deeply shadowed. Sleep eluded her. The spinning lessons only kept her hands busy, not her mind.

She dreamt of him. In her dreams he was cold. How she wished they'd buried him beneath a field of flowers and not in the stone crypt beneath the chapel. At least then, she could imagine him with his face to the sun.

Abruptly, Emma rose from the table. She ignored Nicholas's demands to know where she was off to and strode to the blue chamber that was now permanently hers. She donned her oldest clothing. When she reached the hall again, the occupants of the high table were deep in an intent discussion, heads together. It was child's play to slip out unseen.

For a few moments, she wandered the baileys. She had no direction, but the crisp, cold air cleared her head. Overhead, a hawk wheeled in the gray sky, floating on cross breezes, dipping, turning, wheeling. For a moment she watched it, then it blurred as tears filled her eyes and rolled down her cheeks.

"Beatrice." Mark Trevalin touched her shoulder.

She hastily wiped away the tears and turned. "You have mistaken me before—" She halted in midsentence. "What is it? Are you ill?" His skin looked gray and dry. An uneven stubble darkened his jaw. His eyes were threaded with red. She held his arm and examined his face. "Truly. You must see Lady Catherine. She is a healer far more talented than our leech."

"Naught ails me." He hastened off.

Emma watched him cross to the stables and disappear into their shadows. Nicholas would surely take him to task for his slovenly appearance when next he saw him. Gilles's men were always well turned out, garbed finely, with well-oiled leathers and gleaming sword hilts.

The thought of Gilles sent her eyes to the ramparts again, but the hawk was gone.

She walked slowly through the village from one end to the other, exploring each alley and byway, revisiting where she had come from—and at such a cost.

She examined a pile of rubble from the fallen wall and remembered sitting in Gilles's arms as he directed his men.

"I must stop this!" she chastised herself. With quick steps, she hastened from her memories. As she neared the well, a gathering of beggars burst into a relentless patter. With a shake of her head she spread her hands to indicate she had nothing for them. A ripple of laughter followed her. Gooseflesh broke out on her arms. A feeling that they stared at her as she walked along the path toward the castle made her glance quickly back, but they were haranguing another soul and seemed to have forgotten her.

Gilles watched her until she disappeared into the mist that now lifted and swirled about the drawbridge. He ached to call after her. It was all he could do to restrain himself.

He crouched by the well, leaning on his stick as if crippled. It concealed his height and served as a fine weapon. In but a few days, he no longer had need of Catherine's pots and paints for disguise. Dirt from the mill pond bank served just as well.

How he missed his sword and daggers. But if he were to be given one choice, he would most want to have back his fine leather boots. His feet hurt—as did his back. Sleeping on cold ground with naught but beggars as companions made him most appreciate his feather mattress and warm hearth.

Warmth.

He desperately missed Emma's warmth. As each morning dawned, he visited the mill pond to remind himself of why he had taken on this task.

For William. For his bastard son. A son who'd loved indiscriminately, from Beatrice the miller's daughter, to the alehouse keeper's wife, although the alehouse keeper had not had the opportunity to be loitering near the mill murdering his wife's suitors. In fact, Gilles suspected the man had pocketed a goodly sum in exchange for her favors.

Who had killed William, then allowed Emma to take the blame? Each night, as he strived for sleep in an abandoned stable, he seethed with indignation and faced possible failure. Just as he'd failed to prove Emma innocent

Lost of the Keep

Lord of the Keep

and legitimately gain her freedom, so he seemed to be failing at finding William's murderer.

The next day, Emma again felt drawn to leave the keep. The same lone hawk spun overhead, soaring high to disappear and reappear over the castle keep.

Exhausted from hours of teaching children to spin and then sitting patiently through meals of conversation that avoided mention of what all of them held close to their hearts, she trudged the hill toward the village. Candles glowed in a few cottage windows, and mist hung in the air. Occasionally, she caught the sent of charred wood as she passed a pile of damp refuse discarded after the devastation of the fire. The wind suddenly picked up, creeping beneath her skirts.

The hawk appeared, low in the sky. She found herself watching it and following to where it circled, alone, wings spread in majestic glory.

It settled on the roof of Lowry's abandoned stable and turned its head, looking at her, she imagined. The thought lured her near.

She stepped inside the rickety structure a moment. A sound startled her and she peered into the deep shadows. Three or four beggars crouched about a tiny fire. They turned their dispirited gazes toward her. She locked eyes with one. His eyes stared out at her from a grimy face, wrapped round about with rags. Unbidden, her heart raced and her breath came short. She whirled and fled.

Once in the bailey, she ran up the steps of the keep, burst into the hall, and sought May and Angelique. She snatched the child into her arms and held her close. The urgency and sudden flood of sensation that had driven her away from the stable set her heart to racing.

"Why am I afraid?" she whispered against Angelique's

neck. She took the child to her bedchamber and tucked her into the feather bed, then paced the chamber. She let down her braids and fussed at the knots. A few moments later, May quietly entered.

"May?"

"Aye, my lady?" May pulled her headcovering off and kicked off her clogs.

"I—I need air. You will be staying here again the night?" She tried to banish the breathy quality from her words.

"Of course." May took the ivory comb that had once belonged to Lady Margaret and ran it through her hair. "But 'tis damp and bitter cold. Ye'll freeze if ye go above to the walk."

"I won't be long." Emma drew on her mantle and stuffed her hair into the hood.

Sarah met her in the hall. "Where are you off to?"

For reasons she could not name, Emma lied. "I am only going to get some air." Sarah patted her shoulder and let her go.

Emma knew the gatekeeper would pull up the draw-bridge when full night descended. But for now, with the light just waning, a few horses and men were still coming across the bridge. Unable to stop herself, she slipped out as a cart lumbered in.

The mist crept in tendrils along the ground before her. The stable loomed as a ruin in the night, almost appearing to float above the earth with its wreath of mist. Hesitating, sidling up to the dark, yawning doorway, she glanced in. The beggars lay in a knot in the center of the main portion of the building, snoring and murmuring restlessly in their sleep.

A glance and she found the one she sought. Stepping over legs and arms, she knelt by the man's side, willing him to wake. She crouched there like one in a trance, drawn to this place, drawn to see those eyes.

As she knelt at the beggar's side, a wave of heat suffused her body. Her gaze took in his hand, resting on his breast. A scar, so like *his* scar, crossed the beggar's fingers. The moon ran from behind a cloud and an errant beam of light gleamed on something at the beggar's throat.

She reached out and touched it. Her fingers traced a delicate silver chain caught on the edges of the rags at his throat.

Her cry startled him awake. Their eyes locked.

He grasped her arm in an iron grip and hauled her to her feet. Silently, he dragged her to the black shadows of the rear of the stable.

They faced each other, unable to see clearly. The inky darkness was thick as velvet cloth. She wrested her arm from the man's grip. With shaking hands she groped out and encountered the rough wool of the beggar's clothing. Slowly, she spread her fingers on the cloth, then slid her hands up.

Starved for contact with him, she traced the shape of his jaw, his cheeks, his brow. His harsh breath was all that broke the silence between them. He neither restrained her exploration, nor returned her touch. She shoved back the rags that covered his head and scraped her fingers through the rough stubble of hair on his head. She knew the shape of him, knew him by heart, and had no need of light to confirm what her hands told her. Her breath shuddered in her chest.

"Gilles," she whispered, her hand shaking as she raised it to touch his lips.

Then she was on him—pounding his chest in a terrible anger, fueled by her grief. She snatched at his clothes, baring his throat, tore at his arms. He held her off, his hands becoming entangled in her hair, unbound and flailing him like some silken whip. She punished him silently in her agony. Her disbelief drove her to near madness.

He wrapped her tightly in his arms. Slowly, his hands gentled her. He whispered inarticulate sounds against her ear. Her hair was silk, her warmth an unbearable reminder of their times together. His eyes burned.

Emma collapsed in his arms. Every inch of him was so real and so familiar. Each sweep of his hands tortured her, each touch of his warm breath at her ear drove her mad. She opened her mouth to cry out to him her anger and her joy.

He covered her mouth with his. This was the man she knew. 'Twas no crippled beggar who kissed her. She knew his mouth, his taste.

Then she wanted all of him. She searched in his rags for him, touched his bare chest, flattened her hands on his pounding heart. Frightened that she was in some horrible nightmare and would wake to find him gone, she dug her nails into his skin.

Their mouths were hungry, never drawing apart to take air or speak. He held her breasts, learned the shape of her again, found her warmth beneath her skirts. He dragged her up, lifted her high in his arms.

Instinctively, desperate for what was to come, she wrapped her arms about his head and kissed him long and deep.

When he thrust up into her, she cried into his mouth, for 'twas like dying and finding heaven to be joined to him again. With her back against the rough wooden stall, he cupped her buttocks and gave himself to her, each stroke violent in its search for the deepest part of her. When she went rigid in his arms, he held her tight and poured out his love for her.

Lord of the Keep

Shaking, trembling with emotion, he lowered her and himself to their knees on the straw-strewn floor. Still joined, their lips were bruised and puffed. Emma didn't want to end the kisses, for to do so would mean words must pass.

Emma feared the words. Her mind remained blank, her body on fire with her passion.

At last, Gilles drew back. He knew he must speak first. The moon broke the clouds again. Faint light reached them. Enough that he could see her eyes were tightly closed. "I did it for love, Emma." He cupped her face, smoothed his thumbs over her cheeks. "Open your eyes."

"Nay," she whispered against his lips. "What if I do and you disappear?" Tears gathered and slipped from her eyes. He leaned forward and touched them with his lips. It opened the dam. Her mouth sought his and his hers.

This time the kisses were slow and careful. He let his hands float over her, touching gently. He drew her down beside him, her eyes still closed. Her hair slipped from her shoulder and he shivered at the feel of it on his skin. Arching into her, he took her, pressing slowly, drawing out the moment.

But she would have nothing of slowness.

She urged him on, hands busy, mouth sealed to his. He couldn't stifle his hoarse groans. Forgetting the sleepers nearby, he held her hips to him, tore his mouth away, and moaned his ecstasy.

Emma opened her eyes. He didn't disappear. He was hot flesh within her. Her tremors started, and she needed to close her eyes again, gasping with the power of it, the power of her passion and his igniting and burning at the same moment, joined as ever they were—not as two people, but as one.

333

Chapter Twenty-eight

"How? Why?" she asked finally, her voice shaking.

"I—" Gilles leapt up and blocked the swing of a stick through the air, taking the force of it on his arm, crying out in pain. "Sweet Jesu," he muttered. He snatched the stick with no trouble from the young mute beggar who'd come to his aid. Gilles realized their lovemaking must have sounded like a battle to his companions.

He took the boy by the arm and urged him to where the other two beggars cowered near the stable entrance. "I found a coin and bought a woman. 'Tis all. I thank you for defending me, but I've not yet had my fill of her," he whispered to them. With a sharp gesture that they should remain where they were, he took the stick and returned to the shadows and Emma.

She'd moved into the farthest corner. As he drew her into his embrace, he felt the hard shudder of fear running through her.

"You were not meant to know," he said.

"Your voice," she whispered, her hands going to his throat.

"It is as it is." He grabbed her hand. "Roland was to keep an eye on you."

"Roland! He knows? Who else? Catherine? Nicholas? Everyone save me?"

He silenced her with a fervent kiss. He attempted to turn her passionate anger, still her protests.

She broke away and held his obsidian eyes with her gaze. That was what had made him seem dead in the chapel, she thought. She could not see the flame of life in his eyes. "They all knew?" A sense of deep betrayal seeped into her being. "You agreed to this?"

Gilles clasped her stiff body to his. "We did it to protect you."

"Why?" She gripped his arms, squeezing frantically. "I suffered as if they'd hanged me! I felt as if my very marrow was being torn from my bones! How could you scheme and hide it from me?"

"We thought you'd not permit it—"

"Permit it? I would have forbidden it!"

"Exactly. We feared you would muddle it all, confess yourself, or not appear distraught . . . " His words drifted to a halt.

"You planned that I should be distraught?" How cold she felt, and yet inflamed, burning inside.

"We planned that I would live, that you would be free." The harsh scrape of Gilles's voice rasped in her ears. He folded her into his arms. "Trust that what we did, we did to spare your life."

"What can I say?" she whispered against his chest. "To object will make me seem. . . . heartless—ungrateful." The sound of the slow thud of his heart was so joyful, so completely perfect, she burrowed her nose against his rags and sighed. Feeling began to return and the tightness of her body eased.

"I hunt William's murderer," he said.

She clutched his arms. "Hunt? Are you mad? You are supposed to be dead."

"In that is my opportunity. Disguised as I am, I may investigate the circumstances—"

"I forbid it. You cannot conceal who you are. Someone will see you, they'll drag you away, hang you again!" Her voice rose, shrill and frightened.

"No one has recognized me but you." He attempted to embrace her again. This time, she thrust herself away from his beguiling body, from the lure of peace she found in his arms.

"Nay, 'tis madness!"

"I denied William in life, I cannot deny him in death."

Emma felt the tears rise in her eyes. "You will be the death of *me*. I have flooded my pallet with tears. To find you alive . . . and mayhap lose you again to possible death . . . " She choked. " 'Tis a cruel jest." She clasped her hands in supplication. "You cannot disguise who you are. Did I not find you? There is a—a quality to you no one else has. You will fail. I will lose you."

"Stop!" He combed his fingers through her hair, clearing her face, that he might look into her superb, compelling eyes. "I cannot deny William in his death. Am I not responsible for what he became? I was his father, but I took little part in curbing what was reprehensible in his nature. I set myself apart from it. And so must do this."

She knotted his rags in her fists. "You are not responsible for what he was. He was of his own making, nay, he was what we all made him, through indulgence, fawning adoration of his fair face. Do not hold yourself to blame.

Come away with me. In avenging William, you will be denying me. And Angelique."

He folded her tightly against him. "Nay, my love. I am denying you nothing. I wish to see your name cleared of suspicion. This I will do."

"How dare you!" She tore herself away. "How dare you risk your life?"

"It is my life to do with what I will."

"I ask you, beg you, as the woman who loves you. Change your mind. Come away with me. Forget William."

Silence reigned for long moments, then he answered, his words barely above a whisper. "How I yearn to grant your wish. But my honor demands I avenge William." He fisted his hand. "Someone stole his life from him, and in doing the deed carelessly considered yours forfeit, too! If you cannot understand my need to avenge William's death, then understand my anger over your endangerment."

He grasped her chin and forced her to meet his gaze. "He spread himself like a whore, Emma—here in the village as much as above." Then he took a deep breath and gentled his grip. His gravelly voice rasped harshly in the quiet of the stable. "It does seem, however, that he paid for that privilege. Those who might have objected to his behavior are more mournful of the loss of his coin than of the loss of their daughters' virtue, or outraged by their wives' deceit." He sought and found her hand in the dark. They linked fingers.

"Stop before you are found. Please, I beg of you."

He could not grant her wish. Each new fact he learned of William made him more angry, not just with his bastard son, but with himself that he'd not cared more, taken his son more to task. Had he taken on true responsiblity for his son, acknowledged him, he would not need to hunt his killer now. To distract her from her pain and his rejection of her wish, he drew her into his arms and spoke another truth instead. "Warm me, I am so cold."

She immediately looped her arms about him and pressed her body to his. "Oh, Gilles. Shall I bring you blankets?"

"Nay," he said against her ear. "A beggar has only what he stands up in."

"I fear for you. And what if you sicken?"

He let his mouth drift to her throat. "Do not fear for me—I am dead already."

Emma gave him a sad smile. "What a bitter punishment for my sins! To have the man I love within my grasp, then cruelly snatched by death."

Gilles tried to speak, but she violently shook her head and he held silent.

"And now—resurrected, but still lost to me. And for what? A disagreement of philosophy? You are a man, you must have your vengeance, spill blood to feel complete. I care only for peace. Choose, Gilles. Choose now. Bloodshed or peace. William or me."

"Emma—" Gilles began, one hand lifted; then he let it drop to his side. The low whisper of his voice made his words somehow more potent, more final. "It is not one over the other. I am compelled to do this. My honor demands it. He was my son and I denied him. Do not ask me again to choose."

She pulled herself from his arms and knelt before him. "I am asking. I am begging."

He shook his head.

In the long silence that followed her words, she looked him over, barely able to see him, save for the pale gleam of his throat and shoulder where she'd bared his skin. Her heart could not believe he would not give up his search. Her disappointment was a hollow pain in her breast. With shaking fingers she touched the chain of her mother's cross. "Go then. Go with God."

He heard but the rustle of her skirts to mark her departure. The stable was doubly cold without her.

With an oath he rushed after her, shoving aside the other beggars to stand at the stable door. He almost called out. But he was too late. There was naught to be seen of her. Clouds blanketed the moon, mist shrouded the lanes.

Emma's anger only sustained her for a day or two. How much longer could she hide from Roland and the others that she knew Gilles lived? Mayhap he was right. She could not prevent her eyes from roaming the faces of the keep. She concocted errands to take her into the village. She did not see him.

Then fear took anger's place. If she recognized him, others might, too. One moment she wished Gilles to the devil for his stubbornness and the next she found herself on her knees offering prayers for his safety.

"There is only one way to bring him home to me. I must learn who killed William myself. Then nothing will stand between us!" Once she had determined on her course, she no longer felt lost.

She watched everyone. William's women most especially.

May talked little of William, but was heard to sing a song or two of his when rocking Angelique or another babe to sleep. Beatrice burst into tears as forceful as the water gushing from Gilles's spigot whenever William's name was mentioned. But Emma felt no secret guilt in either.

On her way from her spinning school, she detoured to

the smith. There was one who knew the villagers from a different viewpoint—the thieving child. He was running to and fro for the armorer, handing him tools. They both nodded to her as she entered their domain. She sat beside the child on a bale of hay and watched Big Robbie hammer out a lance point.

'Twas said children did not lie. Emma crossed her fingers. "Were you here the day Sir William was killed?"

The boy eyed her, then darted forward to work the bellows of Big Robbie's forge. When he returned, he wiped sweat from his brow. "I seen him dead. Proper bashed he was."

She swallowed hard. She, too, remembered how William had looked the day of his death. "Do you know who did it?"

"Me? Why would I be knowing anything?" The boy shrugged. His dark eyes were shrewd, old beyond his years.

"I've a sweet bun for anything you can tell me of that day, of who might have killed him."

The boy grinned.

"I seen him, Sir William, earlier that day. In the village. Riding the alehouse keeper's wife, he were, behind the mill."

"How old are you?" she asked.

He shrugged and held up both hands with four fingers spread on each. "So young," she murmured. "When was this?"

"Missed me midday meal, I did, watchin'."

"What the boy says is truth." The armorer rested his hammer for a moment. "I fetched him here. He'd no business being at the alehouse, scrounging for scraps to sell. I swatted him good for watching Sir William at his pleasure, begging your pardon, my lady."

341

Emma felt her face flush at Big Robbie's solicitous tone. "Fear not to offend me."

"We were all surprised to learn Sir William were his lordship's bastard. And I won't believe his lordship killed his son. 'Tis against nature."

"Who do you think did it?" she asked the man.

"Not you, my lady."

She went to where he stood, tall, massive as an oak. "Thank you, Big Robbie. I want to find out who did it. I have to clear Lord Gilles's name."

He nodded and returned to his work. The muscles rippled in his arms as the hammer rose and fell in an ancient rhythm. "Look for a man. A powerful, angry man. Strong." He lifted an old wooden cask whose iron strapping had rusted. With a swift twist of his wrist, he smashed his hammer on the chest, splintering it into a dozen pieces. "Worse were done to Sir William than this hammer did to this chest, and with naught but a rock."

Emma swayed.

"Now easy. Forgive me," he cried and rushed to where she stood, her eyes locked on the smashed pieces of wood. "I weren't thinking. Should I have the boy fetch someone for you?"

Emma shook her head. Big Robbie was right. It must have been a man. No woman could have wielded such strength. She could no longer keep her thoughts to herself.

She tapped lightly on the door to Gilles's chamber. When Catherine opened it, she slipped in. It pained her to see Nicholas sitting in Gilles's chair, his feet stretched toward the fire in a posture so like his father's.

"He is cold," she said to him.

Nicholas shot to his feet. "Who?" His incredulous tone made her smile ruefully.

"Gilles. I know it all. How dare you keep this from me?"

"Fetch Roland and Sarah," he ordered his wife. She dashed to do his bidding.

With a shake of her head, Emma went to stand before him. "You have your father's imperious nature, but he tempers it with courtesy. He ordered me but once, and that in anger, so I must forgive him."

Color flooded Nicholas's cheeks. "You think to instruct me on how to treat my wife?"

Emma sat on a low stool by Gilles's chair. She stroked her hand along its arm. "Nay. Forgive me, my lord, I've not the right. I overstepped myself. Did I not steal your father's life and deprive you of his presence?"

"As to that—" He broke off as Catherine entered with Roland and Sarah.

"I have found him." Emma stated it simply.

"I am somehow not surprised," Roland said. He came to her side and touched her shoulder. "How is he?"

"He is cold. He is dressed as a beggar, his beard is gone, he has made a futile attempt to appear far older than he is—"

"Enough!" Nicholas cut her off. "It is now your duty to keep his secret as we have. He has a task, and intends to perish if necessary to accomplish it."

"You are an angry man." Emma stepped before him and fisted her hands on her hips. "Why, I ask myself. Is it me? Do I offend you?"

"Aye. You offend me. If Father had not become enamored of you, he would not have needed to defend you. Had you merely bargained some price for your services, he would not have paid for you with his honor!"

Sarah and Roland gasped. Nicholas wheeled on them. "Well. Did he not? What honor has he now? When the king is freed and finds me in my father's stead, he'll ask

343

the circumstances. What will be said of my father? He is a murderer—of his son!"

Whatever she might think of Nicholas's angry words, Emma knew she must remember that he, too, feared for Gilles's safety. "If you are so concerned for him, then help me solve William's murder. Can we not determine who is at fault if we put our heads together?"

"Excellent idea." Catherine clapped her hands. "We could each question William's men as to their whereabouts that day."

Before Nicholas could open his mouth to protest, Emma threw open the shutters and let the icy fog creep into the room. "He is cold. He will grow colder."

"Aye," Roland said, coming to her side, looking out over the mist-enshrouded land. "His back pains him when he sleeps too long on the ground."

Catherine lifted a skin from a hook on the mantelpiece. "I sent these oils with Nicholas for Lord Gilles's ease. Take them to him."

"Nay," Nicholas said. "She must not look for him. None of us must."

"I think Gilles should have someone to keep an eye on him. In case he needs anything," Catherine said.

She offered the skin to Emma, whose face heated as she remembered the night Gilles had hung it by the fire, the night Nicholas had found her kneeling between his father's thighs.

"Thank you." She clasped the warm skin to her chest. "But though this may ease his discomfort, it will not clear his name and restore him to honor. That will take all our efforts. I spoke to Big Robbie today. He showed me that 'tis most likely a man who killed William. Let us draw up a list of William's companions—"

"Few of them could have killed him," Roland said. "A goodly number remained at Selsey whilst William shirked his duties and returned here. More were with Gilles—"

"We must look into those who remained. And what of his women? Had they not fathers, brothers, lovers who might object to his trespass?" Sarah interrupted, coming to Emma's side.

"Aye," Nicholas said. "I would kill any man who stole what was mine. I would slice off his jewels and feed them to him for supper."

Roland sat in Gilles's chair. He unrolled a parchment and studied it. "This is a useless document. Gilles's betrothal contract with Michelle d'Ambray. We can conceal the list of names among the words so no one learns of what we are doing. Who will make the list?"

"I write a fair hand." Sarah drew the parchment to her. "Let me. You men will better know who belongs on the list than I."

An hour later, they had exhausted their ideas. The formidable list was divided equally among them. An uneasy truce stood between Emma and Nicholas, forged with delicate links by the common goal of bringing Gilles home.

Roland escorted Emma to supper that night and sat at her side. "Separate him from his companions." He had no need to explain who *he* was. "You cannot talk to him in their presence, and he must be apprised of what we are doing. 'Twould be a waste for him to cover the same ground. Mayhap you can force him to set a limit on his folly, too, have him decide on a day to call a halt to this quest."

Beatrice placed a platter of boiled eels before them.

Roland served her. Emma's stomach lurched. She waved off the generous portion he extended to her and took a slow sip of her wine. "I know just the argument to persuade him to end his quest. I shall simply ask him if he wishes to see his babe grow to manhood."

Chapter Twenty-nine

Emma marched directly to the well and began to harangue the beggars for sitting idly by whilst others cleared the lanes and helped rebuild the village. Those with their wits about them hung their heads and shuffled off. Two who dwelled in their imaginations muttered and gestured wildly; Emma paid them no heed. One stayed where he was, leaning on his stick, a twisted smile on his grimy face.

"Well. Can you not help?" She fisted her hands on her hips.

He shrugged and lifted his stick to indicate his status as a cripple.

"Humpf. You use your infirmity to support idleness. Come."

She heard the stump of his stick following her as she strode east along the castle wall. Despite the lack of good housing, her hut stood empty. "This place looks in need of cleaning. Sweep it out. Gather fresh straw. Make it habitable."

"Why? No one will dwell here. 'Tis a haunted place," he said and spit in the dirt.

"Haunted!" she scoffed. "Who put about such nonsense?"

A few men who were replacing a nearby thatched roof paused to listen. They eyed Emma in a way that made her skin crawl. She recognized them as alehouse companions of Ivo.

She could tell Gilles had to strain his voice to make sure his words reached the workmen. " 'Tis said some murdered man's ghost haunts this place. He has no face they say."

"Why here? The man you speak of was a knight. This is no knight's dwelling."

"His whore lived here."

Emma slapped his face. He reeled back and staggered, falling to one knee.

Her voice shook as she stood over him. "Watch your tongue, you vile man, else I'll see it removed. Do you not know who I am?"

He bowed and scraped before her. "Nay, I am new here. I came with a party of pilgrims but a sennight ago."

" 'Tis a weak excuse. I am the late lord's widow. Lord Gilles's widow. Now clean this place—ghost or not—and do a fine job of it, you lazy man, or I'll see the reeve sets you on the road from whence you came."

He touched his forelock to her, an obeisance he'd received so many times in the past from peasants and never thought to deliver to anyone himself.

She concealed her smile as she walked away. Her step felt light. She had separated him from his companions and found a place to meet him.

Lord of the Keep

* * *

In the darkness of her hut, he pulled off his clothing. She'd been here first. A brazier glowed red and the air was filled with some spice he couldn't name. He drew back the blankets and found heated rocks between the layers. Setting them to the side of the pallet, he slipped into the warm bedding. He drifted in and out of sleep, anticipating her arrival. The scrape of the brazier being refilled startled him awake. He propped himself up on one elbow. "I feared I had misunderstood you and that you might not come."

"How is your jaw?" Emma asked.

"Sore. You are strong for a woman."

She laughed softly and checked the rags that blocked light from escaping the chinks in the walls and door and then knelt at his side. "Roland sent me. But first, lie on your belly. I've brought an oil to ease your back."

"Why would my back need ease?" he asked, but did as she bid and pillowed his head on his arms.

"According to Roland, you do not do well on a cold, hard bed."

"Without you, any bed is cold and hard."

She kissed his shoulder, then drew down the blanket to his waist. He frowned when the chilly air slipped over his skin, but forgot it when she dribbled warm oil along the furrow of his spine. An immediate jolt of arousal swept through him. His breath caught.

Gently, she spread the oil out from his spine in slow sweeping glides of her hands. Her hands floated over him, gilding his back with the sheen of warm oil. He buried his face deeper in the blankets and held his breath. Heat flooded through him.

The cadence of her motions changed. Her strong weaver's hands kneaded the knots from his muscles, start-

349

ing at his nape, moving with infinite slowness down each bone of his spine, along each rib, to the center of his back. Then she stopped. He felt more drops of the potion. The air filled with its scent. Musk. The scent of lovemaking. Her hands started anew, spreading the oil first, then working it in, one muscle at a time, from neck to . . . lower. A hands-breadth farther along. He groaned.

"Am I hurting you?" She snatched her hands away.

"Nay," he said, his words muffled in his folded arms. "Nay, 'tis so . . . good, I cannot bear it."

A subtle change occurred in her ministrations after his words. Her fingers still stroked and eased his muscles, but the sweeps of his spine were more caress than healing. He reveled in the myriad textures of her skin on his, from smooth to callused. He no longer noticed the cool air. His body was on fire.

She lingered over his shoulders. Every knot, every bit of fatigue disappeared. He arched off the blanket, begging for her hands to return to his back. A dribble of oil again slipped down his spine, some running warm over his sides. His breath grew short; his heart thudded in his chest.

Her fingers swept up and down, in longer and longer sweeps. Cold air kissed his skin as she drew the blanket completely off him.

His body shuddered when her hands ran from his back over his buttocks to his thighs. The essence of him gathered, hot and ready.

"Emma," Gilles gasped, and whipped over onto his side. He clasped her into his arms and pulled her down against him. " 'Tis not the oil that heals, but your touch."

The taste of her mouth on his chased all thought from his mind. The scent of the seductive oils, the feel of her hands as she spread them on his chest and down, cupping his warmth, brought another moan from his throat.

"Come to me," she whispered. "Come to me as you were wont to do."

He claimed her in a whirlwind of motion, possessed her with the fierce intensity of his need and desire.

When their passions had cooled, she drew the blanket close about their shoulders again and snuggled against his body, now hot and shiny with sweat in the small brazier's glow.

She traced tantalizing patterns in the hair of his chest. "Roland and Nicholas have drawn up a list of those who might have killed William." She sat up for a moment and dug about in their discarded clothing. "You kept this with you?" She drew out the belt she'd woven for him.

Gilles took it from her hands. He slipped his fingers along the pattern. "You wove this for me, these hawks, these symbols that link endlessly, one to the other. Did you mean something more than thanks for it?"

She bent and kissed the hands that held her work. "Aye, I did. I wove in my endless need for you, but did not know it at the time. We are joined, are we not?"

"Aye." His emotion was so thick in his throat he could barely speak. "I wear it against my skin to have something of you near."

His words reminded her that she was not there only to offer him passion, but to give him his list of names. She carefully folded the belt and searched her pack. "They sent you this." She handed him a tiny scrap of parchment severed from Roland's list of names. "They will ascertain the whereabouts of other suspects. These are for your attention."

Gilles propped himself on an elbow and peered at the

Ann Lawrence

list of names squeezed between some dowry figures. He
gave a soft laugh. "I see Michelle d'Ambray's betrothal
papers are finally serving a purpose." He glanced down
the list. "I have determined the whereabouts of most of
these men already—men love a gossip over a pot of ale,
I've found. Few evade a direct question. Hmm. The
miller. He spends all his time bragging of his role in dis-
covering William's body, but when challenged by others
admits that earlier in the day he was hauling a new millstone home from Lynn. I cannot go to Lynn to determine
when he left there. Mayhap Nicholas could—"

"I will ask him. The others?"

He snuggled her into the crook of his arm and rested
his chin on her head. "The alehouse keeper. Cross him
off. He was serving drink before three men at the time.
The baker: His wife and he were in near mortal combat
all that day over her slattern ways—or so a gaggle of gos-
sips claim. Big Robbie: Nay. Not possible—too gentle a
soul. But I will see to his whereabouts if it would please
you. These other two were with my party." He sighed,
folded the scrap, and tucked it into his beggar's coat.

"Roland and Big Robbie think 'twas a man who killed
William. If none of these men did it and it is discovered
that none of those on Roland's list did either, could it
have been a woman?"

"Women do not kill."

Emma stifled a laugh. "You are jesting. Women have
terrible passions, too. And this crime was passionate. If
done in the heat of the moment, would not a man draw
his sword or dagger?"

"So Roland says, too, but I think William angered a
man enough to fight him with fists. When William died
during the fight, the killer concealed the fact with a
stoning."

352

"A woman might wish to do it, but mayhap not have the strength."

"Women loved William."

"Passionately. Mayhap he scorned the wrong woman. The court did not think a woman too weak to kill a man of his size."

Gilles's embrace was fierce, bone-cracking. "Do not speak of it. Put it aside."

She waited until he relaxed against her. He needed to put it aside as much as she. "I want to believe a man did it, but it doesn't feel right."

Gilles slipped a hand from her waist and cupped her buttock. "It feels just right to me." He nuzzled her neck. "When I see you in the village, I cannot believe our time together is but a tempting dream."

He pulled her hips against his. "When summer arrives, I will take you out into a field of flowers and love you beneath the blue sky."

"We'll have no summer if you don't give this up. Please, I beg of you again, come away with me. Choose life, not death. Forget William. God will see to the judging of this crime."

"You asked me before to give this up, and I thought I'd never see you again. Yet I cannot. I failed with William by denying him. Daily, I learn more of his perfidy. He left debts at the alehouse. He rode his horse carelessly through crops, laying them to waste and mayhap causing a family to starve this winter. It—"

"Is not your fault!"

"Hush!" He pressed his fingers to her mouth. "Do you want someone to know we meet?"

Suitably chastised, or deliberately silenced, she lowered her voice until only he could hear her. "Give this up. Now. For the sake of our child."

He fell back and searched her face. As she leaned over him, he cupped her face in his hands. "Our child?"

"Aye." She clasped his hand and drew it down to the warmth of her stomach. "You will scoff, but I know 'tis true. We made a child that night in the stable. I have never burned so fiercely or felt your passion so deeply."

His throat ached, not from the indignity of the noose this time, but from the power of his emotion. He pressed his palm against the softness of her. "I cannot scoff. I love you too much, know how you found me with but your love for me to guide you." They embraced each other. He kissed her shoulder, her throat, her breasts. Finally, he pressed his lips to her belly, her hands kneading his shoulders. Her heat mesmerized him; her words gave him hope for the future.

Later, he held her in his arms and stared unseeing at the thatch overhead.

She spoke softly. He had not changed his mind, not even knowing about their child. "Men care for naught but bed and blood."

He sat up. "That is a cold assessment."

"And a true one. If it were not so, you would think first of this new life I nurture, instead of vengeance."

"Enough. It is not revenge I seek, but justice. I will not change my mind. We will have a lifetime together after William's killer is made to pay, a lifetime to raise Angelique and this child—in peace!"

She bit her lip at the pain his words caused. Her hands covered her stomach. "We have talked of how William died and who might have killed him, but we have not talked of what is more important. Why."

The rocks in the bedding and their passions had cooled. She shivered and he held her closer before answering. "Why? You mean why would someone kill

354

William? 'Tis simple. He made someone murderously angry. Or jealous."

She studied his face. The hard lines were harshly delineated in the brazier's glow. Without his beard there was nothing to soften his expression. "I mean why at that time, that place? Who would be so angry that William was forcing me? Oh, I would hope a good person would have tried to stop him, but to be angry enough to kill him? Nay. I cannot think of any man save Roland who would care so much about my fate. And he rode with you."

"Hmm." Her words, coupled with the news of their child, pitched his mind into a turmoil. He no longer knew if what he did was right. He knew only he could not forego his oath to avenge William.

"What man would kill William for attacking me? Who would care about my fate?"

"I would," he growled. "I cannot bear the thought of him hurting you. . . . "

She closed her eyes. "Don't think of it."

He pressed his forehead to hers. "Did he only have what is the worst in me?"

"Don't say that. Don't, please. What of his mother? The man who was husband to her? Had they no part in what he was?"

"You don't understand. He came to me for training at nine. There was no other place to foster him. I am responsible for what he was—no other."

Gilles moved over her, his body propped on his elbows to spare her his weight, and kissed her. She twisted her head aside. "What am I to you save this?" She cupped his buttocks and arched her hips against him.

"My heart. My soul."

He tried again to bring his lips to hers. She turned her face to the wall; tears ran over her cheeks.

Ann Lawrence

" 'Tis not enough," she whispered.

"My love, 'tis not true I care only for blood and bed. But the warrior in me will not allow this to pass. I must have justice—"

An eddy of cold air tickled Gilles's shoulders. He rolled to his feet as he threw the blankets over Emma. In a moment he'd snatched up his rags and stick.

A small face peeked in. "Are you a ghost?"

Gilles relaxed. He glanced behind him. The pallet looked like naught but a rumpled heap of blankets. "Do I look like a ghost, ye imp?" he rasped out. He leaned on his stick, diminishing his height. His thundering heart calmed.

The child crouched in the open doorway and glanced about. "I heard his ghost were here."

How swiftly word traveled. "Children should not listen to gossip. Where be yer mother? Yer father?" He shook the stick at the boy.

"Dead. They's not ghosts. They's buried in the field with the rest of the fever folk."

"I'll make a ghost of ye if ye don't disappear!" Gilles prodded the boy's belly with the end of his stick.

"You's an old man. You couldn't catch me if I decided to run."

"But ye are not running, and I've a mind to whip ye with my stick." The boy darted from the doorway. Gilles slammed it. He used the end of his stick to chop a small hole in the dirt, then jammed one end into the hole and lodged the other end against the door. "That should hold him. Next time, we will be more careful."

Emma threw off the blankets and scrambled into her kirtle and gown. "There will not be a next time. What if he recognized me? I'd surely be called a whore then, lying abed with a beggar."

356

Gilles reached for her, but she evaded his touch. Tears still ran down her cheeks. "He could not possibly have seen who was lying beneath me. My body concealed you, I am sure."

"But all know this was my place." She checked her pack and slung it over her shoulder. "They might assume . . . "

"Exactly." Gilles captured her hands and held them in his. "Think, Emma! We see what we expect to see because of where we are. Anyone opening that door and seeing a man making love to a woman, would assume the woman was you—"

Emma bit her lip. She refused to acknowledge the seduction of his hands, the nearness of him. She concentrated on his words. "And who might a person expect to see at the mill pond? Beneath a man or not?"

"The miller's daughter," Gilles said.

"Oh, sweet God." Emma stared at him.

"What? You have thought of something."

Emma paced the tiny space, biting her lip. "Trevalin has mistaken me for Beatrice on a number of occasions. What if"—she swallowed hard—"what if Trevalin thought 'twas Beatrice that William tried to rape?"

"What care would Trevalin have for Beatrice?" Gilles tried to close the space between them, but each step he took, she took one away. It hurt in an intangible way.

"He cares deeply for her. It could be him."

"You wear a mantle unlike any other."

She shook her head. "Not that day. The sun was shining so, I wore but a heavy woolen gown." Her voice grew more confident as she mulled over the idea. "And Trevalin feels guilty—'tis preying on his mind."

"Why do you say that?"

"What is your assessment of him?"

"He is an able if not inspired warrior. I would trust him to guard my back. Nay, he could not have done it."

She nodded. "I, too, would have dismissed him as a possibility, save for two things. His captivation with Beatrice and the fact that suddenly he looks slovenly. His skin is an ill color. He looks as if he is suffering."

"Suffering?"

Emma watched Gilles wrap his rags about his head, hiding his identity. "Aye. I think he regrets what he has done. Has he not betrayed his lord?"

"If he killed William, he did more than betray me." Gilles thumped his chest with a fist. "He sentenced himself to death."

She met his obsidian gaze. Sorrow filled her. "I will not be here to see it done."

Chapter Thirty

Gilles used his stick to forge a halting path through the bailey to where a few beggars awaited the handing out by Father Bernard of scraps from the manor kitchen. Less eager than the others, he took a cold leg of mutton. Most of the meat had been stripped by some man or woman who dined in his hall. As he gnawed at the bone, he watched for Trevalin. When he finally saw the man, he felt a chill run down his spine. Somehow, he had not really believed Emma. Yet Trevalin walked as if already dead. His footsteps dragged. His hair lay lank on his scalp. If Gilles did not know otherwise, he would think the man was suffering a wasting disease.

He hardened his mind against pity. If Trevalin had killed William, 'twas in a moment's passionate anger. But what he had done to Emma, nay that had taken calculation, the allowing of blame to fall on an innocent woman.

Ann Lawrence

Were not knights sworn to protect the weak? Trevalin had betrayed his vows in more ways than one.

Nicholas stood in the entrance to the stables. Out of the corner of his eye, Gilles spotted Beatrice, the object of Trevalin's a passion.

She ran to the stables, stopping there before his son. Without hearing a word, he knew she curried favor. She stood too close, smiling broadly, hands clasped behind her, rocking back and forth, thrusting her breasts for his son's attention. Nicholas shook his head twice, then shrugged and nodded.

A strangled sound drew Gilles's attention from the couple to Trevalin, who stood, hands fisted at his sides, but a few feet away. Beggars passed as though invisible, and most assuredly, Trevalin seemed not to notice those who scrambled next to him over the kitchen refuse. He muttered to himself. When Beatrice trotted toward him, he met her head-on, only a few feet from where Gilles crouched.

"What are you doing? His lordship may be young and comely, but 'tis said he much favors his wife."

Beatrice shrugged. "What's it to ye? 'E likes me. I offered to tend 'im at 'is bath tonight. 'E accepted."

"You bloody fool. What would he want of you in his bath save a quick ride between your thighs? 'Twill gain you naught but a bastard. Did you learn nothing from Sir William?"

"I learned ye can be rid o' a bastard easy enough if'n ye want to."

Trevalin grabbed her by the upper arm and hauled her close. "What are you saying?"

"I'm sayin' a woman needn't birth a babe lessin' she wants to." She snapped her fingers. " 'Twas gone like that!"

"Was it his?" Trevalin's voice trembled. "Or mine? Or don't you know?" His face had paled to milk white. "I'd have made you my wife."

"What would that git me?" She jerked from his hold and lifted her skirts, flashing her ankles and calves as she ran up the keep steps.

Gilles rose and, leaning heavily on his stick, made his way to the stables. His son stood in a stall, saddling his horse. No grooms were near. "Beatrice said you invited her attendance at your bath."

"By God's throat!" Nicholas gasped. "You scared the life from me." The horse swung around, his hooves dangerously near Nicholas's boots. He clouted the horse's rump with his palm.

"Well? Did you?" Gilles crouched in the entrance to the stable. He stared up at his son, who returned to tightening the horse's girth.

"What if I did? She is on my list of potential killers to question. 'Tis not only men who hate. We drew lots and Beatrice fell to me. She's a conniving wench, bent on bedding every man with a suitably full purse at his belt—or between his thighs."

"Drew lots?" He stood up, forgetting to disguise his height. Eye to eye, he held his son's gaze.

"Oh aye. Your wife insisted you would not find William's killer without our help, so we have made note of every lad and lass in Christendom who might wish William dead and then divided them into portions. Did you not get your share? She had charge of seeing to its delivery."

Gilles nodded. "Aye. She gave me a list."

Nicholas led the horse to the stable door. "I am off this minute to check the miller's tale in Lynn—as you directed. We've eliminated most of the other names on our list."

"And Beatrice?" Gilles spat out.

"Beatrice? She eludes me. I cannot determine when she left the keep—or if she did. I'll bathe her myself if 'twill gain the information we need."

"We?" Gilles gripped his stick so tightly, his knuckles ached at the effort.

"Roland, Sarah, Catherine, Emma."

"And will Catherine approve this bathing with Beatrice?"

Nicholas met Gilles's gaze. "Approve? Are you taking me to task for my behavior? Mayhap you should examine yours before criticizing mine."

Gilles let his son and the horse leave the stable without another word. He took a deep breath and closed his eyes. The familiar scent of horse and hay filled his head.

"Old man."

Gilles opened his eyes. Nicholas had returned. He stood framed in the stable entry.

"Catherine's land and coin, her brothers, made her a worthy mate, I believe you said when you proposed her as my wife. But I have learned to love her. Had she come in naught but a moth-eaten kirtle, I would have taken her. If you think Catherine would allow any other woman to attend my bath, you do not know her. Beatrice may say what she likes, doing is another matter."

"Emma and I think Trevalin saw William attack her that day, and mistook Emma for Beatrice. We think he might have killed William in a rage over the forcing."

Nicholas glanced over his shoulder. He came further into the stable shadows. "What would you have me do?"

"Watch him, especially around Emma. Set Catherine or Sarah to watch Beatrice. I want Emma protected at every moment. Whoever did this thing was willing to let her die."

"I will do as you wish." He touched his father's arm. "Your Emma asked if I would trade the cost of her board in Lincoln for a length of cloth each quarter. I believe she will leave here soon."

Gilles took a steadying breath. What was the point in triumphing if he savored his victory alone? A murmur of voices made them both look to the stable entry. Three men-at-arms were striding their way. Gilles gripped Nicholas's arm. "Protect her. She carries my child."

Any response from Nicholas was cut short as Gilles limped away, leaning heavily on his stick.

Emma sat on the feather bed and combed her hair. Angelique sat on a wolf pelt on the floor staring at Little Robbie. The boy crouched on his haunches, a frown furrowing his small brow.

"How can I 'muse her? She doesn't say nothing. Jest sucks her thumb like a babe."

Emma smiled at him. "She is a babe. 'Tis kind of you to come and amuse her, though."

"She's too young for dicing."

"I should think so!" Emma laughed heartily. "You must know some other games."

"Watch." Little Robbie snapped his fingers. At his fingertips appeared a silver coin.

Angelique pulled her thumb from her mouth. She soberly examined the coin when the boy handed it to her. As she brought it to her mouth, Little Robbie snatched it away. " 'Tis not food!"

"Where did you get the coin, Little Robbie?" Emma leaned down and held out her hand.

He hid it behind his back. " 'Tis mine. I dint steal it. The dead knight give it to me."

"Why?" Emma tried to keep her voice calm.

" 'Tis a secret. I promised."

Angelique tried to climb on Little Robbie's back. When he collapsed in a heap, Angelique squealed with delight. For a few moments, Emma watched the children play. Robbie would get on his knees. Angelique would try to mount him like a pony. Little Robbie would collapse. Their shrieks of joy brought tears to Emma's eyes. Robbie needed to play as much as Angelique. She imagined he'd not often had the opportunity.

"Now, Robbie, the knight is dead. You have no more need to keep his secret."

"Nay?" Little Robbie cocked his head. His cheeks had filled out a bit. The shadows around his eyes were fading.

"Nay." She pretended it was unimportant, picking up her spinning.

"He ast me to take a message."

"What was the message?" Her fingers fumbled the thread.

" 'Meet me at the mill pond,' " he said somberly, in a voice uncannily like William's. Then Robbie spun in place. Angelique imitated him and fell in a heap, hiccuping and dizzy.

"To whom did you take the message?" She held her breath.

"Her who's got the golden hair. Like yours. Bess."

"Beatrice?"

"Oh, aye. Her. Beatrice." He froze. "Should she be kissing me?" He sat very still as Angelique bussed him repeatedly on the cheek.

"I imagine 'tis my angel's way of thanking you for entertaining her."

Beatrice. Mayhap Trevalin had not killed William. Mayhap Beatrice had seen William at the mill and become mad with anger that he'd invited her and yet dallied with another.

Nicholas sat at Catherine's side by the hearth in the hall. He felt his cheeks heat. "I've been asked if I'd like an attendant at my bath this evening."

Catherine grinned over her embroidery. "May, is it? She stares at you whenever your back is turned."

Nicholas flushed even hotter. "Nay. Beatrice."

His wife's smile faded. She stabbed her needle into the linen. "Her. She would bathe a toad if she thought he'd take her away from here."

"Have I your permission to allow her attendance? We still do not know her whereabouts on the day William died."

"And how will a back-scrubbing gain you that information?"

He shrugged. "Mayhap you could come upon us. You could threaten to have her sent to Normandy—to a pig farm—should she not reveal her whereabouts that day."

She chuckled. "I think a pig farm suits her admirably, but if she killed Sir William, she will not be easily daunted by such threats."

"I was jesting." He touched her hand. "But an indignant wife, who chooses her words well, might still entice a slip of the tongue."

She linked her fingers with his. "As long as nothing else is enticed in the doing."

Beatrice simpered about Nicholas. He gritted his teeth. She supervised the bucket boys, then began to help him remove his clothing. "Yer a fine lookin' man, my lord."

"Why, thank you, Beatrice. When the . . . bath is done,

mayhap we could find another amusement to whittle away the long hours of the evening."

Her eyes grew round. "My lord. What are ye suggestin'?"

He endured the skim of her fingers along his chest as she removed his tunic. "A game? Chess?"

"I fear I've not played that game." She stood by the tub, a cloth held hopefully in her hand, her eyes just south of his chest.

He pulled off his linen undershirt and said a silent prayer Catherine would arrive before Beatrice attacked. "You said you'd attended others at their bath."

"Oh, aye. Lord Gilles." Her face colored and her eyes evaded his. A lie, he decided. Her gaze returned to his. "And, of course, Sir William."

"Ah. My father's bastard. You were quite privileged to serve both father and son." He stalled. "Fold this."

She dropped the washing cloth and hastened to do his bidding. "I were ofttimes called upon to serve Sir William. He were the finest of the knights. He offered to take me away with him." She sniffed.

"Did he?" Catherine spoke from the doorway. Her arms were crossed over her chest. "And did he offer marriage? Or did he just need a whore for his bath?"

"My lady!" Beatrice bent over the shirt, folding it carefully. "His lordship bid me tend this shirt—"

"His lordship has a squire." Catherine strode to stand before Beatrice. His wife was a hand shorter, but her manner made Beatrice shrink back. "I believe you have made an unfortunate choice here. I am in charge of the females on this manor." She rounded on Nicholas. "And you were warned that if you got another servant with child, you'd find a shrew for a wife in your bed. I want her gone. Send her to my brother in the Holy Land. He can sell her—"

"My lady!" Beatrice fell to her knees. "Please, I beg of ye. I'm a virgin. His lordship never touched me!"

Nicholas smiled sweetly at his wife. The Holy Land, by God. Much better than a pig farm! "I'm sorry, Beatrice, but we cannot lie. God will surely strike us dead." He hung his head. "We were touching—"

"Nay!" Beatrice burst into tears.

"The Holy Land. Tomorrow, my lord," Catherine said, shaking her finger at her husband. "Send Trevalin to do the deed. He'll see we get a fair price for her."

Nicholas hauled Beatrice to her feet. She tore out of his grip as if he'd burned her. "I swear, my lady. As God is my witness. We never touched. Never."

With a flick of her hand, Catherine dismissed Beatrice's words. She sat at the table and drew one of Gilles's parchments toward her. She unrolled it. "Here, my lord. This looks like a good place for her." She tapped the diagram of Gilles's stable addition. "Right here. An Arab prince might like her milk-white skin."

"Mayhap that's a trifle harsh for just touching," Nicholas mused.

Beatrice stared round-eyed at the parchment, tears running down her face. She wrung her hands. "I swear, my lady, I swear, we never did nothin' to dishonor ye."

"My lord?" Catherine cocked her head to the side.

She gave him a look that sent a small shiver down his spine. Thank God he was acting. He thought Catherine quite capable of arranging Beatrice's sale to perdition if she wished it. "Let us think of another way to punish her," he said. "A lashing?" He watched the color drain from Beatrice's flushed cheeks. "Aye. A lashing. How many strokes?"

Catherine rolled the parchment. "Mayhap none if Beatrice will tell us some gossip."

"G-g-gossip?" Beatrice stopped wringing her hands and stared.

"Aye. Who is loyal? Who is not? Who would cheat his lordship of his due?"

"The cooper—he clips coins. The reeve—he looks the other way if a wife mills her own flour." Beatrice spewed a stream of petty crimes against the manor.

Nicholas nodded his encouragement. When she took a breath he slipped in his question. "Where were you the day Sir William died?"

"Here, my lord. I swear it. All day." Her pale cheeks flushed anew.

"Come now," Nicholas prompted. "Surely you know some gossip about our most famous crime. How many lashes, my lady?" He lifted his brow in question.

"I swear it, my lord. Sir William sent me a message he'd come 'ome from Selsey, to see me, like. We was to meet at my father's mill. 'Twas our usual place, but . . ." She hung her head. Tears ran down her cheeks to spot her bodice.

"But?" Catherine arched a brow and tapped her palm with the rolled parchment. Beatrice watched the tantalizing movement, her head bobbing with each tap.

"But, I were angry wiv 'im. 'E dint ev'n say good-bye when 'e left for Selsey. L-l-looked right through me, like. I w-wanted to make 'im wait fer it. I dint go." She wiped her face with the back of her hand and looked frantically from Nicholas to Catherine. "I swear it, my lord, my lady. I dint go. I hid so's 'e couldn't find me. If I'd a gone, 'e might not be dead!" The first true sorrow etched her face. "I were mad wiv grief fer 'im. I loved Sir William, my lord." She wailed the last, burying her face in her hands.

Catherine stood up. "I suppose we can give her another chance, can we not, my lord? Mayhap she could ask Father Bernard for a penance for enticing you."

"Aye, my lady. We shall give her another chance. No lashes this time. But, Beatrice, you must promise not to tempt me again."

"Nay, my lord. Never. Never again."

Nicholas swept out his hand to the door. "Begone."

Catherine rolled her eyes as Beatrice dashed for the door. When it closed softly behind her, she turned to her husband. "Well, I suppose 'tis possible she might have wanted to make him wait; her words held the ring of truth."

Nicholas nodded. "I suppose. But from what we've heard, no woman made Sir William wait for anything."

"Could Trevalin have overheard Little Robbie deliver his message? He might have been seized with a momentary anger and rushed off to confront William. It would explain the stoning. A sudden anger, a weapon at hand. And passion—it is as responsible for the ills of the world as it is for the good." She touched his shoulder gently.

Chapter Thirty-one

"We have no way to prove it. We have only a boy's message as evidence, 'tis not enough." Gilles sighed.

Emma clasped her arms about her knees. This meeting, in the hour before dawn, was so different from the last. They had taken their places, each as far from the pallet as the room allowed. He stood; she sat on the dirt floor, back against the door.

"We can neither prove nor disprove that Beatrice hid from William," Emma said.

"What woman would hide from William?"

"We are not all fools to be held in thrall by a pretty face!" Emma tried to hold her temper. "It seems William's ill treatment came back at him tenfold if she is telling the truth. You reap what you sow."

"Is there no one who remembers seeing her about?"

She shrugged. "I feel it in my bones that it is Trevalin.

Ann Lawrence

He suffers. His betrayal is etched on his face. We must make him confess."

"How will we accomplish that?" Gilles propped his hands on his stick and rested his chin atop them. "We have no bait with which to set a snare."

"If it is justice you want, Gilles, then kill him," she whispered. "Send him to stand before God and take his punishment. Offer to fight him fairly, if you must, sword against sword, but end it."

She raised her eyes to his. How she loved him. How she ached inside that he was not tempted to give up his search. But now, when they had some hope they knew William's killer, he would never be dissuaded from his goal—or at least not by her.

"Trevalin could go to his death denying his guilt. I would be forever condemned to life as an outcast, or I shall be discovered and hanged again."

"Then we should no longer meet. I will take no more chances that you may be discovered through me. What if I caused your capture?"

It was as if she had not spoken. "The only end to this is Trevalin's confession—before witnesses." Gilles straightened up and stamped the stick on the ground with the force of his anger. "And let us face the truth here. He is half my age. What hope have I of defeating him? He is more than ably skilled—he is one of the best. I taught him myself."

"Half your age," she spat. "God save us!" She rose and dusted off her skirts. "I am going. I could not bear it should you be caught! Hanged again. I nearly died of the pain of it. Think of our child, if not of me!"

He did not speak.

She closed her eyes to hold the tears back. "You have made your choice. See this to its conclusion without me."

"Emma." He tried to take her hand, but she tucked it into the folds of her skirt. "We are so close to—"

"Death. Someone's—Trevalin's, yours . . . I cannot bear it. No one in Lincoln would know us, should we go there. I could weave, you could . . . " Her words drifted to silence. She saw on his face the futility of arguing. "Nay. I see that is not your way. In truth, you are no longer bored. For you, there is an exhilaration to the hunt, is there not?"

He had no answer for her.

When she was gone, he leaned on the door and stared at the pallet. The stones she'd placed between the blankets the last time they'd made love were icy cold tonight. Why could she not see that with the right approach, Trevalin might reveal himself? Then they could raise their children in peace at Hawkwatch, instead of hiding from life in Lincoln. And he wanted that peace.

If he closed his eyes, he could almost feel her skin against his, her warm breath on his throat. His eyes burned. She was right. Men did care for little save bed and blood. And why did he feel as if he'd had something precious at the tip of his fingers, only to have it slip away?

Emma carried only one word with her up the hill to the castle's postern gate, which she used to come and go in the dark of night. *Bait.* What bait might entice Trevalin? Love. If he'd killed William for love, he'd come to Beatrice's call, would he not?

But Beatrice could not be asked to stand as a lure to bring about the confession. "I shall be Beatrice," she said. Her words echoed through the stone passage that led from Hawkwatch's underground storage rooms. "I shall weave a trap for Trevalin, with myself as bait. And mayhap in snaring Trevalin, I can snare Gilles's heart once more."

Emma wanted no interference from Beatrice in her scheme, and so she sought the serving woman after the midday meal. She'd heard of what had transpired between Nicholas, Catherine, and Beatrice two days before. "I am sending you to Lynn, Beatrice. There is an inn, the Swan, by the water's edge, and you are to stay there the night."

"Whatever for . . . my lady?" Beatrice looked her up and down.

"Your insolence is staggering. I believe you have recently avoided a lashing—and worse—and yet your tongue is foolish."

Beatrice's face paled. "I meant no harm, my lady," she finished in a rush, bobbing a deep curtsey.

"That is far better. Now, many are still in need of clothing, especially the children, and our looms are not adequate to the task. You are to take two of the men and see to the purchase of the necessary cloth. It is important you tell no one where you are going, as there are those who would be most jealous of your task." She turned to go, then spoke over her shoulder as if in afterthought. "Oh, Beatrice, whilst there, as a small reward for your trouble, you may see a seamstress and purchase a new gown for yourself."

Emma watched with satisfaction as Beatrice rode out with two men at her side. She dashed to the chest that held the serving woman's belongings. Glancing about, she drew out a gown she knew Beatrice wore to scrub the floors. She wrapped up her hair in one of Beatrice's head-coverings, frowning at its grimy state. Head down, she wandered about the bailey, staying near to buildings and shadows, looking for Trevalin.

"Fetch his lordship a pitcher of wine, girl," Sarah called.

For a moment, Emma did not realize it was to her Sarah directed the order. She kept her face averted as she did as bid.

The gown gaped a bit at the breast, and strained at the waist, but when Emma slipped into Gilles's chamber, Nicholas barely glanced at her. "Put the wine on the table."

"Aye, my lord." She set it down, sidled close to him, and placed a hand on his shoulder. "What yer doing, my lord?"

He leapt to his feet as if burned. "Are you mad?" His eyes opened wide. "Emma! I thought you were Beatrice."

"Then 'tis time to see if we can lure Trevalin to the priest's confessional with the same ruse."

Nicholas smiled at her. "I can see the bent of your thoughts, but what's your plan?" he asked, inviting her to sit.

For the first time, Emma sat at ease with Gilles's son. "Gilles has put it about that Sir William's shade walks the village. I want you to be that ghost. When Beatrice makes a midnight tryst with Trevalin, he will find her with William. Mayhap he will react in the same way this time as he did the last—by attacking. Only Roland will be lying in wait to assist you."

" 'Tis foolishness! You endanger yourself and, I might add, my father's babe. I forbid it!" He poured a cup of wine and drank it down in one gulp.

She pounded her fist to the table. "I want my child to have a father. What's the good of being married to him if he is dead? I want to live as man and wife with him."

Ann Lawrence

"I think it a fine plan," Catherine said from the door, and entered with Roland. "I was just about to order a lashing when you spoke, Emma, and I realized you were not Beatrice."

" 'Tis uncanny, the resemblance, my lady," Roland said, taking Emma's hand.

"Then help me. I've sent Beatrice away and the moon will be full tonight. We can offer Trevalin a midnight pageant of sorts." Emma spoke in a rush before any more objections could be raised. "Nicholas will garb himself in William's clothing. He's the only man who is like unto him in size and bulk. If he wears mail with the coif on his head, who will not think him the shade of that knight?"

"We must tell Gilles of our plan," Roland said.

"Nay," Nicholas said. "He would not allow it."

"For once we agree," Emma said to him. "For we would endanger all he holds dear. You, me, his child."

Sarah slipped into the room with Angelique in her arms. When she saw Emma she gasped. "Emma! What are you doing in those clothes?" She looked about at their faces. "I sense a plot. What are you planning? I'll not be left out."

Roland sighed, then gave Sarah the rough outline of their plan.

She pursed her lips and considered the ceiling. "You will only need a similar mantle to the one William wore that day," she said. "It is the illusion of the thing you want."

Catherine agreed. "With the armor beneath, of course. I can concoct a mixture that will look like blood and gore and spread it over his features—"

"Please," Emma begged, her stomach protesting. "Say no more of it. Just do it. Tonight."

* * *

Gilles felt at home in the night. He needed to guard his face less, could lift his head and not fear so greatly that he would be recognized. The layers of clothing he wore to protect him from the cold flapped about his legs as he headed for the castle.

All day he had examined his motives, wandering about, half listening to gossip, half reliving the precious times with Emma.

She was right. He had been enjoying the hunt. It gave him a sense of usefulness, as the summing of accounts could never do. But Emma was also right that he might be giving up some greater good. As he had looked about him during the day, he saw families—fathers, mothers, children—going about their hard lives, and yet, they seemed at peace with one another and themselves.

As lord he could see to righting some of the problems in his village—the noisome alleys, the disputes over allotments.

But if he had not loved a hunt, would he have agreed to Catherine and Roland's plan for a false hanging in the first place? He faced the muddy waters of his motives.

Emma had forced him to examine his heart. Only a need for justice held him at Hawkwatch. Or was it vengeance as Emma suggested? And vengeance was a cold bed partner. The loss of Emma raised an ache in his heart that could not be assuaged. If she had already gone to Lincoln, he would follow her there. If she had not yet left, he would take her. Suddenly, he no longer cared if his name was cleared. He cared only that he had Emma and the children. He wanted to end his days with her by his side.

With a frown, he noted the drawbridge had not been raised, then shrugged. 'Twas no longer his manor. He was soon to be but a common man from Lincoln. If his son wished the gates open at night, 'twas his business.

Ann Lawrence

In the inner bailey, he resumed more of his beggarly aspect, moving with halting steps among the few folk who had not yet sought their beds. He crouched by the stable and watched the armory, looking for Little Robbie, who might carry a message to Emma.

No one stirred. He plucked up a twig and began to draw it over the ground, tracing impatient patterns.

A gasp made him toss the stick aside and rise. Sarah stood near his shoulder. She gripped his arm. "What are you doing here?" she hissed.

Gilles could not conceal a grin. "Am I so easily known?"

Sarah glanced about. "Nay, but I've seen you draw like that a thousand times. How many others will remember you did so?"

With a shrug, Gilles went down on his haunches again. "I was waiting for Little Robbie to carry a message to Emma, but now that you are here, you may serve as well."

She edged deeper into the stable's shadows when the moon burst through a bank of clouds and bathed her in light as bright as day. "A message?"

Gilles peered up at her. "Aye. Tell her to come here."

"Why?" She twisted her hands in her skirts. "I mean, she is most likely sleeping. Why bother her?"

"I must see her."

"Can it not wait until the morn?"

"What is wrong?" Gilles rose, a crawling sensation in his belly. "You are being evasive. Why?"

"No reason. Emma needs her sleep."

Gilles searched her face. "I command you, as the man who is still your lord, to bring her to me. Now."

The moonlight fled, plunging them into darkness. The

378

wind rose, whistling about the bailey. "I cannot. She is not here."

The sensation in his middle flared into flame. Emma was gone. He was too late. His need to find William's killer had driven her away. "Did she go to Lincoln?" He would seek her there, prove his love for her.

"Lincoln?" Sarah said. "Oh, aye. Lincoln."

Immediately, Gilles knew she was lying. Would Emma have proposed Lincoln and then gone elsewhere? And why? To be done with him and all the heartache he'd caused her? "I know you are lying. If she didn't go to Lincoln, then where is she? I must know. I cannot live without her."

Sarah stepped back. "Please, I cannot tell you."

He followed her into the shadows. "Aye. You will. I command it."

But Sarah was no longer looking at him. Her gaze shifted past him, in the direction of the armory. He turned to see what was more important than his need for Emma.

Mark Trevalin stood in deep conversation with Little Robbie, hands clasped behind his back. Whatever the boy said produced an immediate result. Trevalin broke into a run. He dashed past where Gilles and Sarah stood and into the stable.

Little Robbie also ran, straight for them.

"Nay," Sarah cried, hands up, palms out. "Later, boy. Not now!"

The boy's teeth gleamed in the meager moonlight. "I's delivered the message. Jest as ye wanted. Where's my penny?" Robbie held out a grubby hand to her.

"Later, boy. Later."

"Ye said a penny, and a penny I'm wanting."

Gilles looked from the boy's determined face to

Sarah's. "I'll give ye tuppence to tell me the message ye delivered just now," he said.

"Nay!" Sarah grabbed the boy by the arm and pushed him away.

"Sixpence," Gilles whispered. Little Robbie jerked from Sarah's grip.

" 'Meet me at the millpond. Beatrice,' " the boy said in a singsong voice. " 'Tis all I said. He were proper happy wiv it."

Suddenly, Gilles knew where Emma was, knew why she was not on the road to Lincoln. "Damn you all!" he swore at Sarah.

Trevalin appeared at the stable doors with his horse. He mounted and rode toward the inner gate, which was just being closed. He harangued the keeper for a moment until it was swung wide for him.

"Pay him, Sarah. Now." Gilles ran into the stables. He noted the missing horses. Nicholas's and Roland's. With shaking hands he slipped a bridle over a fast mare's head.

With a practiced vault, he leapt onto the horse's broad back, his stick in his hand. When a pair of grooms came hurrying down a ladder to see who dared steal a horse from the Hawkwatch stable, Gilles brandished the stick like a sword, fending off one man who lunged for the reins.

Sarah burst into the stable.

"Stay where you are or I'll have your thumbs!" she cried, pointing a finger at the grooms. They cowered back at the threat. This woman they knew—and obeyed.

"Don't go," Sarah begged, reaching for Gilles's hand.

Gilles dug his heels into the horse's flanks and sent the mount racing from the stable.

In a thunder of hooves, he flew over the cobbles. The keeper was just swinging the gate closed again. With a hoarse warning, Gilles made straight for him. The man shouted and leapt aside. In a moment, Gilles was through the narrow opening, into the lower bailey, across the drawbridge, and careening down the beaten roadbed.

The wind snatched at his rags. Moonlight painted a wash of white on surfaces, plunged shadows into black.

Sarah's entreaty had told him all he needed to know. For whatever reason, Emma was luring Trevalin to the mill. He remembered his words to her. They had no bait to snare Trevalin. His blood ran cold. Emma had found bait. Herself.

As he neared the grove of trees that sheltered the millpond, he slowed, bringing his horse to a walk. He dismounted and tethered the horse. With cautious steps to avoid the crackle of brush underfoot, he crept to the edge of the copse. A lone horse drank from the waters of the millpond.

He glanced about. Trevalin stood but yards away on the bank of the millpond, opposite where William had bled out his life. The mill loomed dark and silent behind him. Gilles gripped his stick, wanting to smash something in an impotent rage that he had had no part in the planning of whatever might occur here tonight.

The clouds parted. He gasped. Emma stood on the bank atop a discarded millstone. She was as still as a statue, head bowed. Her pose was reverential, almost goddesslike. The moon gleamed across her white headcovering. He could not see her face.

Gilles held his breath; Trevalin had moved. The man walked slowly toward her, stumbling several times along the perimeter of the pond. Moonlight glinted off the hilt of his sword.

Sword! Gilles would wager Trevalin had not brought a

sword to the mill when he'd killed William. A lover needs no weapon.

Trevalin had not come to this meeting as a lover.

Gilles lifted his stick and almost called a warning to Emma, but a moan rent the air. An unearthly ululation of agony. The hair on his nape rose.

"William," she called from across the pond. "William, my love. Come to me." Her words were breathy, not loud, and yet they carried to where Gilles stood in the trees.

Come to me. How the words tore at him. He wanted no other man to hear those words from her lips.

Although he knew it was a role she played, hearing her call out to William as one calls a lover nearly undid him.

"Beatrice!" Trevalin shouted. He halted, hands outstretched, not fifty feet from Emma on the reed-choked bank.

Gilles crept forward. He could not defend her hidden in the tangle of brush among the trees. Just as he stepped from the copse, a figure glided from behind the mill toward Emma. Spangles of silver glittered on the mail coif on the figure's head. His mantle, a luminescent blue in the moonlight, lifted and swirled about his powerful body. When he turned to face Trevalin, Gilles swallowed hard. The figure had no face.

Trevalin cried out. He stumbled to where Emma stood, but she ignored him. "Come to me. Love me once again," she called in her soft voice, and lifted her arms to the faceless horror.

The words pierced Gilles to the marrow. Trevalin shrieked an unholy cry.

The specter opened his arms to Emma.

Nicholas.

"Beatrice!" Trevalin called. But instead of going to her

as Gilles expected, Trevalin ran at the ghastly apparition, drawing his sword, slashing as he moved.

Gilles charged after him. As the blade descended on his son, Gilles swung his stick.

The sword hewed the wood in half, but deflected the blow. Trevalin whirled away from the ghost. He panted open-mouthed, eyes so wide the whites gleamed.

Gilles stood empty-handed before him. Trevalin swung his blade in an arc.

Gilles leapt to the side. The blade sliced his shoulder, ripping through the rags like a knife through butter.

"Nay," Gilles cried as Nicholas charged toward Trevalin. His son froze in his tracks. " 'Tis my battle," he gasped, sidestepping again from Trevalin's thrust.

Slowly, Trevalin moved forward. Stalking. His face twisted into a feral sneer. "Beatrice," he ordered. "Get behind me."

Gilles mirrored him, hands outstretched, defenseless.

"Gilles. My sword," a voice said behind him. Roland. Metal slapped his palm. The hilt felt wonderful, the weight of the blade a blessing. Old instincts rose.

Trevalin closed on him with a shout. Their blades met in a clash of metal on metal. Trevalin was shorter, heavier, but younger. In only a few moments, Gilles's body was covered in sweat. His rags hampered the free movement of his arm. His shoulder ached. His arm felt heavy and hot with blood.

He parried more than attacked. The moon hid, plunging the land into blackness, shadows melding water and sky.

Trevalin backed him toward the pond. Gilles played a defensive game, dodging, slipping away each time Trevalin's sword came dangerously close. Then he saw his chance. He danced left, turning slightly, shifting

Trevalin's position. If only he could hold him but a few moments more. The moon burst from behind a cloud. Emma stood there in a shaft of light, the ghost of a faceless William beside her.

"Beatrice plays you for a fool," Gilles shouted. He took a blow on his sword, the blades sliding on each other until they were engaged nearly hand to hand. Gilles jerked away. "Beatrice plays you for a fool," he taunted, just out of reach.

Trevalin howled, his eyes darting to where Emma stood in a wash of moonlight. When his gaze shifted, Gilles lunged forward, smashing his blade down in a sweeping motion. Trevalin's sword flew from his hand, skidding on the frozen, packed earth. Gilles spun and kicked Trevalin in the leg. With a moan he fell to his back.

In an instant, Gilles stood over him, blade pressed to his throat. "Come, Beatrice," Gilles called. "Choose a lover from among us. Will it be the living or the dead? Will it be William or Trevalin? Or mayhap you would prefer me—yet another dead man."

Trevalin snarled beneath the sword point. "Kill me. Be done with it."

"In good time." Gilles twisted the blade. Blood ran from the nick in Trevalin's throat. "But first I wish to know whom the fair Beatrice wishes as a lover."

Emma seemed to float toward them. "William." She whispered the name.

Beneath Gilles's blade, Trevalin fell still. His sneer twisted into a weeping mask. He arched his back and howled at the moon.

"William," she said again.

"You bitch," Trevalin screamed. "You mock me. I defended you. I saved you from rape!"

Gilles held him pinned to the earth with the blade. The temptation to slit Trevalin's throat, a temptation almost impossible to resist, came over him. Then Emma lifted her eyes from the pathetic man at Gilles's feet and locked her gaze on his as if she'd read his thoughts. She stared at him, eyes luminous. All her hopes were in her gaze.

She spoke to Trevalin, but watched Gilles. "I am Emma, not Beatrice. William was not raping Beatrice that day; he attacked me."

"Nay," Trevalin choked out. " 'Twas you. You. He tried to force you. I killed him for you. I smashed in his bloody face! I killed the raping bastard!" He began to weep.

Gilles lifted his blade. But Trevalin made no more move to rise. He lay back, palms outstretched to the heavens. Emma knelt by his head. She touched his forehead. "I am Emma," she said. "Beatrice is not here."

She looked up at Gilles. "He was the one who sent me to the royal court. He asked only what suited his purpose. He shifted the blame to save himself. God have mercy on his soul."

Roland hooked his hand beneath Trevalin's arm and jerked him to his feet.

With a snarling oath, Trevalin tore from Roland's grasp. A savage shriek of anger filled the air as he snatched Emma to his chest. He groped in his boot and drew a knife. "Back off." His blade gleamed in the moonlight, the point pressed to her stomach. "I'll gut her here if you come any closer. Drop the sword!"

The agony of seeing her in Trevalin's arms made Gilles spread his arms wide. But he held onto the sword.

Trevalin slit Emma's gown near the waist. She cried with pain. Gilles dropped the sword with a clang to the hard earth. Trevalin picked it up and flung it into the pond. He picked up his own and sheathed it, gripping Emma about the neck with the arm that held the knife.

Emma's cry had maddened Gilles, but he could not move. The blade now hovered at her breast.

To his left, Gilles felt rather than saw his son, a face-less horror, move in Trevalin's direction. "Hold," he rasped out. "Hold."

Trevalin dragged Emma to where his horse stood at the edge of the pond, reins dangling. Blade to her belly, Trevalin ordered her to mount. In moments, he'd swung up in the saddle behind her and was gone.

Chapter Thirty-two

Gilles swore. He sheathed the longest portion of his shattered stick down the back of his rags and ran into the copse of trees. He grabbed his horse's reins, tangling them a moment in his agitation, then leapt onto the mare's back.

Using only instinct and the uncanny connection he had to Emma, he rode blindly after them.

Once out of the pines, the land gave way to marsh. He could barely see, as the wind tore at his tattered clothing.

They rode the ancient paths, ones from Roman times, through the marshes, to the bay. To the sea.

Then he saw them, in the distance, a dark patch against a rising mist.

Why did she not take her chances and fall off? The babe. She would not endanger the babe.

A sweat born of fear broke on his skin, his shoulder burned, warm blood matted his rags.

Trevalin rode his horse at reckless speed through the marshes. Gilles followed. He drove his horse mercilessly along the narrow paths through the wetlands, parallel to the beaches of Hawkwatch Bay. They appeared and disappeared in the swirling mists. A light flickered at the water's edge.

The light became a fire; a small group of men clustered about it. Help. Then all thoughts of aid from that direction flew from Gilles's mind. Trevalin had veered away. Not toward solid land and help—toward the sands and the concealing fog.

"Jesu," Gilles cried.

The tides had turned. Low waves foamed across his horse's path. "Trevalin! You fool."

With a whispered prayer, Gilles kicked his mount's flanks and charged after them.

Gilles saw Trevalin glance over his shoulder and urge the horse to a faster pace. The horse stumbled, went down on a foreleg, screamed, and threw them into the water.

In a bound, Gilles leapt from his horse. Trevalin's beast floundered to his feet and shot from his master's grasp to race from danger. Emma rose, water streaming over her body. Gilles felt the icy water, knew she would die of the cold ere he could save her. She stumbled toward him, hands outstretched. Trevalin jerked her after him. They disappeared in a wall of fog.

When Gilles took a step, his foot sank in the glutinous suck of shifting sands. He whipped his stick from his back and probed the surface. The distance was lengthening between them. The water and mist intensified their every sound, though, and Gilles followed the thrashing noises, the grunts of Trevalin's efforts to drag a reluctant Emma through the surf.

Gilles swore and moved as quickly as he could, testing the surface. If he fell, if he was trapped, Emma was dead.

With a gust of wind, the mists swirled open, like a curtain parting. Trevalin's pace had slowed, hampered by Emma, who dragged her feet and flailed her arms.

"Trevalin! You're mad!" Gilles cried. "You'll drown."

"Get back," Trevalin shrieked. "Get back. I'll kill her." He jerked Emma against his body and Gilles saw the knife against Emma's throat.

With hands out to the side, Gilles halted. His feet felt numb.

"Let her go, Trevalin. Let her go, I beg you. I will not stop you. Flee if you want!"

Trevalin shook his head like a slumbering wolf wakened from a winter nap, and hauled Emma a few more feet away. Emma screamed. She went down in a hole, twisting in Trevalin's arms.

Gilles charged toward them, all thoughts of his own safety forgotten as Emma struggled in nature's grip. Trevalin pulled on her for a moment, then dropped her arm, backed away, and began to run in a shambling gait toward the far shore and Lincolnshire.

Gilles swerved toward Emma.

"Nay. Leave me! Catch him," she cried. "Don't let him get away." She dragged at her skirts.

Trevalin turned at her words. Waves foamed about his calves. A wall of mist rolled toward them. "You sorry bitch. I killed William to save you and you betray me!"

Gilles ignored Emma's entreaties and sloshed through the low waves to her. He grasped her arms and pulled.

"I can free myself. Go." She pointed at Trevalin.

"He doesn't matter. Only you matter," he gasped. "Sweet God, without you there is nothing."

Trevalin cut parallel to the coast and widened the dis-

Ann Lawrence

tance between them. In moments, his retreating figure was lost in the fog.

Gilles hauled at Emma's arms. She slipped from his grasp. With an oath, he cast off his rags. He tore the belt from about his waist and threw it around her. He cinched the buckle beneath her arms and twisted his hands in the loop. He pulled with all his strength.

"Leave me, Gilles. I'll free myself. You must stop him. He can prove your innocence."

He ignored her entreaties. She had no idea how close to death she was. *They both were.* Her skirts were thick with sand and water, weighing them down. He held the belt with one hand and knotted his hand in the rent in her gown where Trevalin had stabbed her. He tore the cloth apart, freeing her.

With a cry, she stumbled clear of the sinkhole that had nearly claimed her life. Gilles no longer felt his hands and feet. To be sure, he did not drop her, he kept his eyes on the belt and the grip he had on it. When she was able to gain her feet, he wrapped his arms about her and they stumbled toward the shore.

Three men coalesced from the mist enshrouding the land. They moved cautiously toward Gilles and Emma, weaving left and right in the shallow water as the surface beneath their feet proved unstable.

"Take her," Gilles gasped, near the limit of his strength, as one man ran ahead of the others. "She will die of the cold." The man, his long tunic tucked up at his waist, hooked his fist in the belt beneath Emma's arms and hoisted her before him.

The fog shifted. Smoke and flames were visible on the shore. Safety. So close. Too far. Gilles sank to his knees. His body shuddered with cold. Mist swirled to claim him.

390

Chapter Thirty-three

Gilles woke in his bedchamber, the sun striping the floor by his bed. He groaned and sat up. His shoulder ached beneath a mound of bandages.

His bedchamber.

His heart in his throat, he threw off the blankets. Where was Emma? He closed his eyes. His memory provided only the image of her in a stranger's arms, disappearing into the mist.

With shaking hands, he dragged on the clothing laid out carefully across his coffer: fine linen, the tunic he'd been married—and buried—in.

"Gilles!"

He turned to the door. Emma ran across the room and threw herself into his arms. "Thank God, my love," he whispered between hard kisses. "I thought you lost." He set her at arm's length and inspected her. "Your wound?"

Ann Lawrence

"Nothing compared to yours," she said, encircling his waist and hugging him close.

He ran his fingers along her cheek and tipped up her chin. "How I love you," he said against her lips, marveling that she was well and in his arms. He pulled her hard against his body. For a brief moment, she melted against him, her kisses as ardent as his. Then she leaned back.

"We are not alone," she said, smiling up at him.

Gilles turned, but kept her tightly within his embrace.

Roland strode across the chamber, followed by three strangers.

Roland went down on his knee before Gilles.

"What are you doing?" Gilles asked, touching Roland's shoulder.

"Begging your forgiveness. I let Trevalin get away from me. I let him take your lady. I should be stripped of my rank, lashed at—"

"Enough! Emma is here and quite well. Now rise." Gilles could not keep a touch of humor from his voice. "Truly, she is in better shape than I." He gently touched her waist where Trevalin had stabbed her. He felt the bandages beneath her gown and frowned.

She covered his hand. "I am quite well. A scratch only. Now, these men have news for you. We have been waiting for you to awake."

Roland presented the men, pilgrims who had camped on the shore of Hawkwatch Bay, their journey to see the abbey relics interrupted by the rising fog.

One man, the eldest, stepped forward and bowed. "My lord, we must bear the news that the man who entered the water with you and this fine lady has been found, drowned, his body washed ashore this morn."

392

"I must thank you for saving my lady wife. She is everything to me."

"Are you not curious as to why you are here and not in some beggarly bed in the village?" Nicholas d'Argent asked from the doorway. He came to stand at the pilgrims' side.

"I did wonder, but then thoughts of Emma drove it from my mind," Gilles said, and pulled her close to his side.

"It seems these good men saw you ride into the surf and followed, sure you would need aid. They heard every word Trevalin said—you know how sound travels on water. When we have broken our fast, we are off to the Duke of Norfolk."

"We understand the poor soul killed a valued knight and saw this fine lady, and then you blamed for it," one of the pilgrims said. "It is our duty to present the truth. He was taunting you with his triumph. Surely, God is seeing to his punishment now."

"Aye," Gilles said softly.

They stood in somber silence for a moment; then Gilles thanked the pilgrims again for rescuing Emma and bringing him to shore.

As the party departed, one man turned back. "We wanted to return this to you." He held out the belt Gilles had used to save Emma. "I suppose 'tis ruined; the colors have run," he said, and left.

Emma held the belt. "Nay, 'tis not ruined." She looked up at Gilles. "The designs are no longer linked, they are blended, no longer separated one from another, as we are no longer apart. It seems right, somehow." She looped the belt about Gilles's waist and buckled it. She stroked her fingers along the fine linen and silk threads. He covered her hands.

393

Nicholas cleared his throat. "There will be opportunity enough for that later. Now it is time you took your proper place."

Gilles looked at his son. "A few months ago, I considered myself at the end of my life, this manor a responsibility to be avoided. No longer. Now I feel as if I've all the time on God's green earth to live. I shall spend every moment of it trying to be what I was not—a proper father. A better husband."

Color flooded Nicholas's cheeks. "Think not that you are the only one who needs to examine his behavior. I fear I owe Emma and you an apology. She is your perfect mate. Two more stubborn people I have never met!" He grinned.

Gilles embraced his son. "Come. I will need you by my side." He took Emma's hand and led her from his bedchamber. Together with Nicholas, they took the stairs to the hall, crowded with what seemed to be every person of the manor.

Gilles approached the raised platform before the great stone hearth with a sense of being home.

"Gilles!"

Silence rolled through the hall as all turned to the flaxen-haired tot who stood with arms upraised to the tall man who stood with her mother.

No one spoke.

He went down on one knee. His voice was gentle. "Angelique."

Tears pricked at the edges of Emma's vision.

Angelique sidled closer to the man who knelt very still before her. Her thumb slipped into her mouth. She studied him from his close-cropped hair to his black eyes. She reached out and touched his chin with the tip of one tiny finger.

"No beard," she said in a whisper.

"No beard," Gilles repeated.

Her little finger traced the line of his jaw. "Gilles," she said more loudly.

"Aye, my child. I have been to heaven and am now returned." He scooped her up, then tucked her into the crook of his uninjured arm. He extended his hand to Emma. She smiled and linked her fingers with his.

Holding her hand, his son at his side, Gilles stepped up onto the dais and took his place, once more lord of the keep.

Golden Man
Evelyn Rogers

Steven Marshall is the kind of guy who makes a woman think of satin sheets and steamy nights, of wild fantasies involving hot tubs and whipped cream—and then brass bands, waving flags, and Fourth of July parades. All-American terrific, that's what he is; tall and bronzed, with hair the color of the sun, thick-lashed blue eyes, and a killer grin slanted against a square jaw—a true Golden Man. He is even single. Unfortunately, he is also the President of the United States. So when average citizen Ginny Baxter finds herself his date for a diplomatic reception, she doesn't know if she is the luckiest woman in the country, or the victim of a practical joke. Either way, she is in for the ride of her life . . . and the man of her dreams.

___52295-0 $5.99 US/$6.99 CAN

A Case Of Nerves
Angie Kay

Standing on the moors of Scotland, Alec Lachlan could have stepped right off of the battlefield of 1746 Culloden. Decked out in full Scottish regalia, Alec looks like every woman's dream, but is one woman's fantasy. Kate MacGillvray doesn't expect to be swept off her feet by the strangely familiar green-eyed Scot. But she is a sucker for a man in a kilt; after all, her heroes have always been Highlanders. Wrapped in Alec's strong arms, Kate knows she has met him before—centuries before. And she isn't about to argue if Fate decides to give them a second chance at a love that Bonnie Prince Charlie and a civil war interrupted over two centuries earlier.

___52312-4 $5.50 US/$6.50 CAN

Dorchester Publishing Co., Inc.
P.O. Box 6640
Wayne, PA 19087-8640

Please add $1.75 for shipping and handling for the first book and $.50 for each book thereafter. NY, NYC, and PA residents, please add appropriate sales tax. No cash, stamps, or C.O.D.s. All orders shipped within 6 weeks via postal service book rate. Canadian orders require $2.00 extra postage and must be paid in U.S. dollars through a U.S. banking facility.

Name_____
Address_____
City_____ State_____ Zip_____
I have enclosed $_____ in payment for the checked book(s).
Payment <u>must</u> accompany all orders. ❑ Please send a free catalog.
    CHECK OUT OUR WEBSITE! www.dorchesterpub.com

BELOVED WARRIOR
JUDY DICANIO

Jennifer Giordano isn't looking for a hero, just a boarder to help make ends meet. But Dar is larger-than-life in every respect, and as her gaze travels from his broad chest to his muscular arms, time stops, literally. Jennifer knows this hulking hunk with a magic mantle, crystal dagger, and pet dragon will never be the ideal housemate. But as the Norseman with the disarming smile turns her house into a battlefield, Jennifer feels a more fiery struggle begin. Gazing into his twinkling blue eyes, she knows she can surrender to whatever the powerful warrior wishes, for she's already won the greatest prize of all: his love.

___52325-6 $5.50 US/$6.50 CAN

Dorchester Publishing Co., Inc.
P.O. Box 6640
Wayne, PA 19087-8640